Tiffanie Darke had an insider's view of the restaurant world when she was Food and Drink Editor on the *Daily Telegraph*. Now, aged twenty-seven, she is the Features Editor on the *Express*. *Marrow* is her first novel.

0771

669 6211

MARROW

TIFFANIE DARKE

POCKET
BOOKS

LONDON · SYDNEY · NEW YORK · TOKYO · SINGAPORE · TORONTO

First published in Great Britain by Pocket Books, 2000
An imprint of Simon & Schuster UK Ltd
A Viacom Company

1 3 5 7 9 10 8 6 4 2

Simon & Schuster UK Ltd
Africa House
64–78 Kingsway
London WC2B 6AH

Simon & Schuster Australia
Sydney

A CIP catalogue record for this book is available from the British Library

ISBN 0–671–03751–X

Typeset by Palimpsest Book Production Limited,
Polmont, Stirlingshire

Printed and bound in Great Britain by
Caledonian International Book Manufacturing Ltd.

An Angel on Horseback

1 native oyster, freshly removed from its bed
1 slice of dark pink, streaky bacon, more flesh than fat
Salt and freshly ground black pepper
A squeeze of lemon juice

1. First prise open the oyster: using a sharp, strong, knife, insert the point of the blade into the hinge of the shell. Slide along the hinge, slicing the muscle, and twist to force the shells apart.

2. Slide the oyster meat out from its shell (it should quiver, still alive), and drain. Wrap the soft, silver flesh in the bacon slice, so that it is completely smothered. Pierce to fasten in its place with a wooden stake – a cocktail stick serves well.

3. Season with salt and pepper, place under a heated grill just long enough to crisp the bacon until it has closed tight around the oyster, then remove from grill, squeeze over a little lemon juice (the oyster should still be alive, so you should still see a shudder). Serve.

1

The Eurostar pulled up underneath the blue arches of Waterloo Station. The smooth gliding motion that had brought the train all the way from Paris slowed to an eventual halt and, with the tiniest of jerks, the train announced its arrival in London. With a long hiss the electronic doors swished open. Genevieve gripped the handles of her holdall, took a deep breath and got up from her seat. Through the train window, everything was familiar yet strange – a foreign country with a thousand things done differently, but still a train station, still a city. She would cope. She had to.

Genevieve moved along the corridor then stepped onto the platform. Daylight was dwindling into twilight and the station was full of the noise of another language. She headed through the huge domed concourse for the sign marked 'Taxis', emerging onto a grimy street round the back of the station. As she waited in the queue she looked up at the filthy buildings of Waterloo, shimmering in the heat-haze at the end of the day, girdled by swathes of grey snaking highways.

'Notting Hill, please,' she told the cabbie as the taxi drew up in front of the sign. Squat and bored in his T-shirt and jeans, he chucked his cigarette out the window and nodded for Genevieve to get in.

'Right you are, love,' he replied, as she climbed in the back of the cab, hauling her bag behind her. The driver pulled out, then glanced at his passenger in the mirror, taking in her young face framed by the shock of platinum hair, her skin lightly tanned by a summer obviously considerably better than his. Still, the British summer seemed to have arrived finally. After a grey, wet August, September was hot and still; in the city the air hung heavily, making the atmosphere close, sticky and oppressive.

Looks sixteen going on twenty-six, he thought to himself, reminded of his own daughter whom he had only hours ago chastised for her return home at three in the morning. 'Going clubbing', indeed. She was only bloody fifteen years old yet she drank in pubs and got into nightclubs. Girls nowadays – there was no telling what age they might be. Still, this one was definitely French, he knew that much from her accent. And by the look of apprehension on her face, this was probably her first time in London.

The cabbie prided himself on his instinct for people: he could always tell who they were, what they were up to. A lifetime of picking up strangers had taught him what went on behind faces, what made them tick.

'Which end of Notting Hill do you want then, love? Holland Park or Bayswater?' he asked, to open the conversation.

Genevieve knew the answer: it was Holland Park, the side of Notting Hill where the serious money congregated, where there were no apartments, just houses, where the cars were all convertibles or four-wheel-drives, where there were no supermarkets, just delicatessens. She had read this in a gourmet magazine.

'Holland Park,' she replied with confidence.

'You visiting relatives over here then, love?'

'I beg your pardon?' stumbled Genevieve, straining to make out what the driver was saying above the motor of the taxi and a passing siren. 'I'm sorry, I did not hear.'

'You here to see family, then? Any friends?'

'Oh, no, not exactly. Well, one person, maybe.' Genevieve supplied her ready excuse, repeated endlessly to her aunt and friends. 'Actually I'm a student and I'm coming to practise my English. I want to find a job.'

'Oh, I see. This your first time in London, then?'

'Yes, it is.'

'Your English is very good.'

'Thank you, I studied it at university.'

Genevieve looked pointedly out of the window. It was traumatic enough decamping to this country without having to deal with English conversation from a cabbie. She tried to recognise the landmarks as she swept past them – she had had a picture book of London when she was a child. Trafalgar Square, Hyde Park Corner, Marble Arch. The street-lights were on now, bathing everywhere in a balmy orange glow. They were stopping and starting in the Saturday-night traffic along Bayswater Road, and she amused herself watching the wardens sweeping through Hyde Park, emptying it of its visitors, before they shut the gates for the night. Then suddenly the monstrous hotels that lined the north side of Bayswater Road and the park on the south gave way to a twinkling strip of bars, shops and restaurants.

'This is Notting Hill Gate, love. Whereabouts do you want?'

Genevieve hesitated. She had to drive past it – just to see it with her own eyes. 'Bay Avenue, please,' she said, steeling herself.

The taxi driver glanced back in the mirror again – he hoped she had the money for this. Still, going to Bay Avenue, she should have. He turned right off the Gate down Pembridge Villas, to weave his way west across to Holland Park: Notting Hill's richer sister.

Notting Hill was glistening. Genevieve had heard it was one of London's more affluent districts and tonight she could see that all the money, all the fun, all the glamour were out to play. The city was in its element on a hot late-summer's night and she was in no hurry to reach her destination; she didn't mind sitting in the traffic, although the cabbie quite clearly did, irritably mopping his brow with a blue hanky. Genevieve just sat back, wide-eyed and drinking in the scenes played out before her. It was now past nine o'clock and already the streets were packed, picking up the overflow from the bars. In Paris this was normally a dead time: people didn't start to go out until about half ten or eleven o'clock.

Everyone looked healthy, and they were wearing clothes that spoke the international language of loot: the clean lines and crisp material of homogeneous and expensive designers. Usually a trademark of money without imagination, Genevieve thought, but Notting Hill had its eccentricities, she noted. A carefully cultured bohemianism, a studied thespianism even, in the flash of a vintage skirt, the brandishing of a cigarette-holder, dreadlocks in a suit. As she settled back in the taxi to observe them, she saw how the revellers were swigging from bottles and glasses; already a few looked unsteady on their feet, their eyes beginning to glaze over, talking louder than they needed to. With the alcohol and the weather, the crowd seemed to be breaking into a collective sweat under the hot evening air.

Genevieve's taxi sat motionless in the middle of Portobello Road, beached like a whale in a line of other taxis and flash Jags, throbbing BMWs and new-series Audis. The vehicles of the Notting Hill rich, ferrying their residents off to pukka dinner parties, West End plays, or so-and-so's drinks 'do'. Not so very different from Paris then, she smiled to herself, suddenly encouraged by the recognition of a common humanity, feeling alone but brave, doing at last what she had waited so long to do.

'Sorry, love, seem to be stuck in a jam,' shouted the cabbie, knowing very well his route was not the quickest, nor the most direct. He glanced across at the meter, now showing a hefty sum, and decided to take the next left off the road.

Peppered between the pubs and bars, Genevieve couldn't help noticing how many restaurants there were. All, without fail as far as she could see, were packed, their glass fronts and terraced pavements proudly showing off their clientèle:

the well fed, all preening, pouring, munching, chattering and showing off. Even from the cab she imagined she could hear the restaurants tinkle and screech with gossip and cutlery, forks scraping against china preparing elaborate mouthfuls to be poked between quivering lips. This was a place where money could be given a proper showing, where extravagance never looked vulgar, where you were rarely richer than the person sitting next to you. The Manhattan of London, she had heard it called, the Champs Elysées of the city. A place for the exclusive. Genevieve was impressed. Seamus had come far.

The cab was now winding down some residential streets and then all of a sudden it popped out onto a majestic, stucco-fronted avenue. Here, it seemed, they had found the epicentre, the beating heart of the area. Even more chichi than anything that had preceded it, Genevieve noted there were no cafés on this street, no newsagents trying to sell wrinkling vegetables from the baskets that loaded their shop-fronts. Instead, a parade of boutiques, cake shops, expensive-looking coffee bars and lights strung up amongst the trees, winking as the leaves fluttered in a gentle breeze. And in the middle of the street, about halfway down, flanked by two more trees planted in their minimalist ceramic pots was a double-fronted space, the walls opening up to a pair of windows, from which bright yellow light poured onto the pavement, great glass apertures to the dining room within. And above the windows, emblazoned in huge green, Roman-style lettering was its name: MARROW.

'Please, just here! Stop please, for one moment,' Genevieve begged the cabbie. She felt a tremendous sense of awe and her stomach was fluttering in excitement and terror. She had imagined this place for so long, but now the immediate reality of it was overwhelming.

As the taxi pulled over on the opposite side of the street, Genevieve peered out, watching as other passers-by, too, were distracted by the windows, walking past more slowly to catch a glimpse of the theatre within. Through the tall sashed windows, framed in rich, yellow fabric, Genevieve could make out the linen-dressed tables: privileged circles of delight, around which ruddy men and immaculately coiffured women were sitting, their pleasure worn smugly upon their faces.

'You got a booking for that place, love?' tried the cabbie, when his passenger failed to initiate further instructions.

'No, no I haven't. I just wanted to see it,' she replied.

'You'll be lucky to get in, I can tell you. 'Parently there's a five-month waiting list. Not even that Cher could get a table last time she was in town.' Oh, so that's it, thought the cabbie. He had her number now. She was just another one of those celeb tourists, like them Japanese girls always wanting to go to the zebra crossing on Abbey Road.

'Really?'

'Yup, one of the most exclusive places in London, that is,' pronounced the cabbie, in the manner of one who ate there every day. 'So, you getting out here?' he asked, wondering if she'd come for the doorman's autograph.

No, not now, she thought. Genevieve took one last look at the place, at the yellow glow that flooded out of the windows, the elaborately patterned gold wallpaper. The room looked as if it had more valances, pelmets and drapes than a ballroom in the Palace of Versailles. Suddenly she felt very isolated, very fragile and alone. She felt far removed from this world. At the moment, anyway. Quickly she wanted to move out of sight from the restaurant. She reached down into her handbag for the piece of paper with the address on it, attempted to pronounce it, but found her voice had failed her. Instead she passed it through the glass partition to the driver.

'The Venus Hotel on Earls Court Road,' he read out, nodding his head. Bugger that, he thought privately. If that was her destination, he was unlikely to be getting a large tip.

Lobster Cappuccino

125ml lentil purée
125ml lobster stock
1 teaspoon truffle oil
1 teaspoon double cream
1 morsel of lobster claw, about 5 centimetres long

1. Pour the lobster stock into a saucepan and slowly bring to the boil. When the smooth, pinky liquid begins to bubble, stir in the lentil purée. Gently heat until the liquid starts to thicken. Do not let the mixture boil: if you peak the heat too early, then the mixture will not froth to a cappuccino consistency later. Remove from the heat and stir in the cream and truffle oil.

2. Sautée the lobster meat in a little olive oil for a couple of minutes on each side – it doesn't take long for the meat to turn from a dull grey to a light vein-streaked pink. When the claw has curled up into a tight, fleshy mound, remove from the frying pan and place in the bottom of a cappuccino cup.

3. Reheat the stock mixture, add a little ice-cold butter and whip into a frenzy with a hand-blender until the liquid is frothing bubbles that will spill over the top of the cup when you pour it in.

4. Fill the cup to the brim with the mixture, so the pink claw at the bottom is completely concealed, an angry little *amuse gueule* waiting to surprise.

2

The doorman stationed outside Marrow had clearly taken his posture cue from a Coldstream Guard on duty at Buckingham Palace. He had noticed the girl in the cab only by straining to peer down his nose whilst his chin remained high in the air. She was shockingly beautiful, an angelic face disfigured by its frown. Momentarily confused, he had thought at first that she was a customer and was about to move across the road and open her cab door for her, but she had made no move to get out. Instead, she had peered out of the cab window and up at the façade of the restaurant. People quite often stopped to peer. In the end the cab had driven off, but the girl's face stayed with him: the apprehension in her large, blue-grey eyes, her plump lips slightly parted, the skin on her face clear like the flesh of a nectarine, her head haloed by that extraordinary pale-gold hair.

After musing on her for a few minutes, the doorman was distracted by the arrival of a chauffeur-driven Bentley pulling up right in front of him. He moved across to the back door and, in one swift, studied movement, had opened it and was proffering his hand to help out the passengers within. A bejewelled and white-haired lady in a long evening gown emerged at the end of his arm, followed by an elderly gentleman.

'Lady Fawsley, good evening to your ladyship. Lord Fawsley,' he nodded. It was his job to know who all these people were. His boss insisted on it.

Lord and Lady Fawsley smiled graciously back, taking

it for granted that they should be identified. Their names were known – of course they were. Both, however, had an air of anticipation, of excitement about them, and they shuffled eagerly to the front door, which was now being held open by the doorman. Once inside, encompassed in the cool golden glow, the lady surrendered her shawl and they were immediately seated on two richly upholstered facing armchairs in the window. As they waited for the two crystal flutes of champagne that were already making their way across the floor towards them, the two appeared to blend in immediately with the scene; within seconds of arrival they had seamlessly become part of the show.

Behind them they could see through to the dining room: fourteen fussily laid tables, surrounded by the faces of those accustomed to pleasure, but for whom even this was a treat. An awed hush blanketed the restaurant, and the low-toned conversation admitted only the chinks of the sommelier's glasses, the giggle of one over-delighted client or the stifled mumblings of ecstasy as the small, delicate morsels of food made their way off the plates and into waiting mouths. For each diner was being subjected to the delicate and extraordinary art of one of the country's foremost culinary prodigies: the irascible, the sexy, the dedicated and the irresistible Seamus Bull.

At just twenty-nine years old, Seamus was lauded by press and punters alike, a darling of the chattering classes. 'Such an eccentric!' 'Such raw energy.' 'Without doubt a culinary genius.' 'Ooh . . . have you seen his *hands*?' Indeed, as the cab driver had said, there was a five-month waiting list for one of the tables in this restaurant. Such was the breadth of his fame that the rich and famous would queue to be part of the exclusive crowd who could say to one another: 'Have you eaten at Marrow? Oh, you must go, the desserts are to die for!'

Tonight was no exception, with waiters in white tie delivering their heavy French accents as well as plates of culinary perfection with consistent aplomb. Like a well-oiled machine, the succession of plates were produced then drawn away, produced then drawn away, to be carried, scraped clean, into the furnace of industry that was the kitchen below. The inferno where the great genius was at work.

'Four lobster cappuccinos. Here, now, in forty-five seconds. What do I want, Marcus?'

'Four Lob Caps coming up, Chef.'

'Didier, you are over-poaching the tails tonight. One more dry tail and I'll shove it up your arse! Not so nice shoved up your arse when they're dry and scratchy, eh? Marcus, get back on the bamix – you're a fool if you think that's frothy enough. Where is the fucking engineer for the air conditioning? This heat is ruining the food. Michael, phone Adèle upstairs and tell her to sort something out – *now!* Who is responsible for the sauce going out on that ravioli? Take it back – it's shit, nothing leaves my kitchen looking like that. Sous chef, if you don't learn how to make that coulis properly by tomorrow, you're out of here on your arse. D'you hear? Someone get that fucking phone. Where are my Caps? Thirty seconds gone . . . I'm not waiting much longer, Marcus – no, I *can't* speak to her now, take a fucking message. Where are the warmed cups? *Where the fuck are the warmed cups?* Whose job is it to clean the fucking cups?'

Seamus Bull's staff had developed a highly accurate way of measuring the level of his not-inconsiderable temper. The strong, square-lined jaw that held his powerfully handsome face aloft would jut out, his normally full lips would thin into strained whitish lines and his dark skin would drain dangerously of its colour. This was a face known well by those who worked for him, but one seen only rarely by the public. In repose, his was a rough, but mightily alluring countenance, one that commanded a masterful sexuality that was quite irresistible to women, money men, photographers and PR ladies alike. He had once, whilst quite drunk, told a female journalist who was all too eager to encourage him, that cooking was the only activity, bar making love, where one used all five senses. He had become famous for it and his reputation of sexual prowess was matched only by the number of beauties the press snapped on his arm.

But his face was also one that, especially recently, could all too easily twist into an angry snarl. Ironically, this only served to heighten the power of Bull's magnetism: it lent him an air of danger that left all those who met him quite weak at the knees. For there was something about this curious mixture of roughness and sensitivity that made women look at Seamus Bull twice. One shot from his dark smouldering eyes and a woman could so easily feel her clothes falling off her, imagine his strong, broad hands grasping her waist, his Celtic features bearing down on her, his taut muscles straining underneath his shirt as . . . oh, their imagination could take them so much further, but for the sake of public decency most would look away.

It was indeed rare that Bull flashed the full force of his temper outside of the kitchen. He couldn't afford to – he was too much of a celebrity to get away with it. But his suffering showed: his skin had once been tanned, it had that latent glow about it, but now it had been made tired by the interminable hours he had spent in steaming hot, subterranean, neon-lit spaces. When he was angry, the veins on either side of his forehead would pulse, straining against his smooth temples. At such moments his strong, battered face would take on a life of its own, and if the warnings had not been heeded by those in his immediate vicinity, they would be prey to the hurricane of verbal and physical abuse that inevitably ensued. And at six foot two, with the muscular build of a Roman gladiator, not many stood a chance in a showdown with Seamus Bull.

At this moment all eighteen staff, on parade in their regulation white coats and blue check trousers, were engaged in monitoring the transformation of his face. All simultaneously shrank back behind their metal counters, their paper-crowned heads lowered over their respective tasks of chopping and slicing, frying and poaching, rolling and beating, whisking and blasting, tasting and sprinkling with the ordered chaos of a swarm of bees.

In the far corner, bent over the double sinks of steaming soapy water, Michael Shaw, the unfortunate kitchen porter, flinched in his market-bought Nikes. At five foot ten, Michael knew he stood no chance against what was coming. Even though his wiry body was beginning to toughen into the muscle required for the kitchen, he knew that, as the lowest in the kitchen pecking order, there was nothing he could do but take what was coming. And today it was his turn to take the crap – *again*.

Twenty customers that evening had ordered Lobster Cappuccinos. Marie, one of the waitresses, had forgotten to bus the washing-up tray from the lift hatch into the kitchen, so he had only just received the dirty cups to wash, rinse, polish and warm again for their next appearance. Plus, there were simply never enough spare clean cups for the simple reason that Seamus kept hurling them across the room. They were such an easy, handy size for bowling at offensive objects, and stacked as they were just above the pass – the point in the kitchen where Seamus stood checking every dish that left for the restaurant floor – the suppliers could rarely keep up with demand.

All the remaining Cappuccino cups were currently in the sink. As he reached down into the scalding murky water to pull them out, Michael was aware of Chef's enormous hands descending onto the collar of his shirt, then, bracing himself, he felt the stiff fabric scrape against his skin as the hands twisted the material tight around his neck.

'You are a stupid little shit, aren't you, Shaw? Don't

you understand your fucking orders? I think I'd be better off with a Japanese washing machine than you.' Chef's voice had dropped dangerously low now, the shouting had become a deep, throaty growl. Shaking Michael's neck as if he were a small farmyard animal, Seamus pressed his bulk menacingly against the younger man's back and, leaning over his shoulder, spat directly into his ear.

'You have the simplest job in this kitchen and yet you still manage to fuck it up! I have no room in my team for fuck-ups like you. You wanna work here? You work here only if you are the best, and at the moment a woman could keep up better than you. You fuck up this chain one more time and you're out, do you hear?'

Seamus paused, as if something had just occurred to him, and bringing his mouth right down to Michael's ear again, he asked, 'Why did I bother hiring you in the first place, eh? Answer me that.'

Michael dared not answer the question although both knew why. Michael had one real talent: his cooking. It was the only thing he knew how to do well, the only thing that inspired him, the only thing at which he could succeed. Fresh out of catering school and desperate for a salary to keep him and his father, he had come begging for a job two months ago – and Seamus liked it when people begged. But any kitchen newcomer had to start at the bottom, and if that involved a seventeen-hour day in a steaming hell-hole, with your arms constantly submerged in scalding water, then you accepted that as your lot. Because it also meant a slim chance of working your way up to an apprenticeship tougher than a 1950s boot camp, and maybe even to earn the golden apple: a job as a *chef de partie* in the kitchens of Seamus Bull.

Unfortunately, Michael was not impressing Seamus with his washing-up skills, and the toll of the gruelling six-day weeks on a twenty-one year old who had so much more on his mind was beginning to show.

Seamus's patience was wearing thin. It was time for some discipline – keep this bunch under control, set an example. Still twisting the collar of Michael's shirt, with Seamus's body mass of pure toned muscle equalling roughly twice that of his victim, he had no trouble administering the punishment. In a deft movement, Seamus's thick hands tightened their grip on Michael's shirt and, with a snap of his meaty elbows, Seamus had thrust his neck and shoulders downwards. The next thing Michael knew was the burn of the boiling, greasy water over his face as Chef plunged his face and upper body down into the sink.

Pausing a few seconds, Seamus heaved him up again, allowing Michael to roar with agony at the detergent in his eyes. Then he plunged him down again, this time fully submerging his head, even as Michael's body twisted to be free of Seamus's grasp. Seamus looked down at the head squirming beneath him and took a vague, calming pleasure from the control. As if to exercise his pleasure he held on for another two, three seconds as Michael's writhing became desperate. Finally he pulled him up, the sploshing of the water failing to drown out the heaving, gasping Michael as he brought his hands to his searing eyes, and struggled to control his breathing, his pain – and his anger.

'Four Cappuccino mugs now, please, Shaw – *and don't fuck up the production in this kitchen again!*' Seamus shouted as he shook him off like a bad smell. 'Your saintly fucking looks don't get you anywhere in here, boy.'

Chef was rarely in a good mood. The power he exerted in the kitchen over his army of crack gastronomic troops had, during the last couple of years, perverted itself into a dictatorship. Whereas he had once been a fun, inspiring boss to work for, he was now becoming little more than a tyrant. Upstairs, the folk who lunched, dined, breakfasted then lunched again had no idea of the chaos and terror beneath their feet that produced their portions of gastronomic delight.

Tonight, however, Seamus was blowing up like a tropical thunderstorm. He had many genuine reasons to be angry: the heat had reached intolerable levels in the kitchen as the air conditioning had been out since half-past eleven that morning and the only vent in the kitchen was a six-inch square aperture in the top right-hand corner of the room. It was a restaurant rule to keep the back door locked: once Seamus's fame had been established it had proved too handy a location for paparazzi lenses. The fish supplier had let them down again with a sub-standard supply of red mullet, naturally provoking Seamus into firing them on the spot (the seventh successive fish supplier to meet such a fate in the last five months). Of course, no one had been able to organise a replacement for tomorrow – all rival companies had already been fired from the job or claimed they were stretched to capacity. And the twenty-five-year-old Armagnac that Seamus had been forced into drinking since about five o'clock that afternoon had done little to lighten his mood.

Still, all these were normal pressures in the day of a chef and ones Seamus could usually handle. What was really eating him was something entirely different. Now was a crucial time in the restaurant world, just a few weeks before the hugely influential Michelin guide published its annual list of honours, awarding the cream of the country's restaurants a star, then the *crème de la crème* two stars. Three stars went to the tiny few who, as far as the French editors were concerned, stuck closest to the concept that food was a divine fiction. Gastro-fantasy made into art was what they sought as they troughed tirelessly around the country.

Seamus, the proud possessor of two stars, and by now so acclaimed in the media for his Wonder Boy talent as well as his outspoken ambition, was convinced the time had come for the panel to award him that third and final star. Never mind that only two other establishments in the whole country had earned the right to display those three golden globes outside their restaurant doors. The first, even Seamus had to admit, deserved them: a pair of elderly French brothers in Wiltshire with their grand millhouse restaurant produced food of such excellence you could almost taste their forty years of experience and dedication; a history that had made them famous throughout the world as ambassadors of the gentle art of cooking.

And the second recipient? Why, Seamus's direct rival, the London chef and restaurateur, Emmanuel Coq. The original fast and furious food genius who had climbed the rungs of gastro-success at a previously unheard-of pace, Coq's ascent had been aided by his much publicised stand-offs with customers and his string of marriages to a procession of famous women. Many people attributed to Coq the country's rekindled love affair with food, a country for whom chips and ketchup was once the national dish. Just five years older than Seamus, and his one-time boss, Emmanuel regarded him as an irksome terrier snapping at the heels of his undoubted monarchy of the restaurant scene. Seamus, on the other hand, saw himself as the great deposer. Coq might be King of Gastro-London, but his establishments now numbered six in all, while Seamus concentrated his energies on just one. And with it, he hoped to snatch the crown.

Just recently, however – and this accounted for his present, foul mood – Seamus had heard through the restaurant grapevine that his longed-for third star was in danger. Christ, it would make little difference to his business, he knew. Most of the fashion victims and gullible morons who walked through his doors had more money than taste buds, and did so mainly to catch a glimpse of the huge celebrity that toiled behind the kitchen doors, or so they could tick off on their list of 'must-go' places the ultimate accolade of dinner at Marrow. But for Seamus the third star would mark the end of ten years of longing. What is more, if he earned it this year he would be the *youngest chef ever* in the history of Michelin to have those three stars stamped after his name. How he lusted after it, compromised for it, sacrificed for it, toiling hour after hour, day after day, month after month, year after year. And he had sworn he would not rest until he achieved it! Sometimes, in rare moments of clarity, he would step outside himself, watch the shouting, measure the stress, and wonder if it was all worth it. But he did not understand any other kind of ambition, any other sense of self-definition: this was who he wanted to be and this was how he had to do it. And with that realisation he would plunge himself back into the fray.

Recently, though, Seamus had come to fear that this year he might well be denied that final mark of high achievement. That bent little arse-eating faggot of a restaurant reviewer, whose bitchy turn of phrase and snide witticisms so enraptured the readers of his wretched newspaper column, had been in to dine at Marrow ten days ago. And if he chose to review it negatively, there would be no way Michelin could then honour him, Seamus Bull, in the light of such an influential opposing voice. No one could go against the opinion of the mighty Rufus Ransome, or Ruthless Rufus as he was known, not even Michelin. How had so much power come to rest on this one, podgy creature? It was anyone's guess, but whatever scurrilous explanations Seamus could come up with, the situation remained the same. Unless he had Rufus's seal of approval, he would never be awarded that star.

And Rufus's meal had not gone well.

To earn three stars, not only must the food be exquisite, but every little detail of the dining experience must be present and perfect: attentive but not intrusive service, cut glass and crystal on the table, the finest wines faultlessly administered to accompany each of the six courses. But alas, the Chablis he chose to start with was corked (a sommelier's worst nightmare), a small chipping of clam shell had been found in his seafood consommé, the turbot he had requested had not been available, the quails' eggs topping the salade niçoise had not been runny in the middle, the oxtail had been underdone (the sous-chef had been sacked the next day) and, horror of all horrors, he had been delivered the wrong dessert. Justine, the waitress, had ceremoniously joined the sous chef on the pavement outside the restaurant the next morning.

And where was Seamus during this débâcle? The one night in the whole of the twenty-seven months since Marrow had opened, he had been absent, unavailable to preside over and marshall his kitchen, which had quite lost its way when loosened from its master's all-consuming control. Seamus had not turned up for the evening session because he had been, as he had put it, 'having his brains fucked out' by a journalist who, even by his stretch of the imagination, had proved the most thought-defyingly dirty little beast of his entire sexual career.

Commissioned by one of the big, glamorous magazines to write a feature on Seamus as their 'Man of the Year', she had insisted on an intimate setting for her interview. And Seamus hadn't been one to deny her when, in the waiting area of his restaurant, over afternoon tea, his hand had strayed up her silk-stockinged leg, gracefully bumped over the fastenings of her suspenders and come to settle, even to Seamus's surprise, on a gaping pair of crotchless panties. Naturally the interview had to be continued elsewhere, and as six, seven, eight and nine o'clock came and went and her stamina remained unbending, as bottles of vintage Krug were emptied and flung onto the hotel floor, as caviar was generously scooped onto and then licked off each other's most intimate crevices, Seamus had allowed himself just one night away from his chains.

As a chef's luck would have it, that was the night Rufus Ransome had been in – booked, of course, under a pseudonym. The newspaper review was due to appear in tomorrow's Sunday paper. If it was bad, the star would be out of reach.

As eleven o'clock approached, Seamus's nerves were now officially unbearable for his staff. He had hurled a plate of langoustine linguine across the kitchen because the pasta had been 'too fucking soggy', and it had spun like a frisbee until it made contact with the side of Sarah the pastry chef's head. A great hulk of a girl, Sarah had so far proved thick-skinned enough to bear the mantle of sexual abuse that fell on her as Seamus's token female member of kitchen staff. Seamus didn't believe in employing women as, he frequently told ethical campaigners, 'They can only work three weeks in every month'. However, one such related comment had made its way onto the front page of three national newspapers, and to avoid being prosecuted under some Fairness At Work Act, Seamus had been forced to take on a woman. Sarah was that woman, and any hesitation she may have had at the time was now so completely beaten out of her, she seemed unable to leave. Her friends' only explanation for it was either she was so infatuated with Seamus she was blind to her own abuse, or that she had become so punch drunk she was now incapable of making a decision to go.

The plate had split open Sarah's ear, and the wound had required an absurdly large dressing to staunch the flow of blood. The bandage now resembled more of a turban than a plaster. The kitchen, like Sarah's physical state, was beginning to look like a battleground as opposed to any sort of artist's palette. The oven door had been kicked in and no longer shut properly, and eight kitchen whisks had taken a hammering. Not to mention the remains of the bottle of Armagnac Seamus was using in an altogether futile attempt to steady his nerves.

Finally, as the kitchen clock clicked to 22:45, Seamus stuffed his hand in his pocket, pulled out a fifty-pound note, ground it into the sore and chafed palm of Michael's hand and ordered him to get a taxi to Kings Cross to pick up an early edition of the *Sunday Tribune*. Michael took the money and fled the kitchen, sighing as he heard the words 'messenger' and 'shoot' resounding loudly in his ears.

Seamus took another pull on his bottle of Armagnac and was disconcerted to find that nothing came out. It had been full at five o'clock. He began to feel sick with nerves, and was finding it increasingly difficult to focus on the plates as they were presented to him before they left the kitchen. As Sarah held up a lovingly assembled tower of sugar-spun pastry, oven-dried strawberries and champagne sorbet, Seamus's arm crashed down on the whole lot, sending it spinning to the floor. Naturally he cuffed Sarah across her undamaged ear, but even he noticed the fault may well have been his this time. He needed sorting out.

'Potter, go and see that wop Salvatore now!' he roared, his nerves descending rapidly into hysteria, his big, tense body struggling to control itself. Paul Potter was Seamus's Head Chef and right-hand man. Salvatore, proprietor of the 'traditional' Italian bistro situated next door to Marrow, had an uneasy relationship with his neighbour, based on the fact that Salvatore actually owned the lease of Seamus's restaurant. He was the 'mystery backer' who had financed Seamus to leave Coq's restaurant two years ago and set up on his own.

By acting as a restaurant financier, Salvatore was able to mask the fact that he was supplying Seamus, assorted members of his staff and indeed half of London with copious piles of half-polluted white powder (as opposed to the more normal two-thirds polluted stuff). In fact, Salvatore owned half the street, which was the reason why Seamus and Salvatore's other tenants tolerated the suspicious clientèle of the trattoria that was clearly a front for Salvatore's more lucrative business. After all, they did enjoy well discounted rates.

Seamus knew everything about the comings and goings of

variousmoustachioed, Armani-clad'businessmen' traipsingin and out of the back of his establishment, and made sure Salvatore knew he knew. Salvatore loathed the brashness of Seamus and was constantly amazed that such a brutish, anarchic man could turn out such ordered, delicate dishes, but as long as Seamus kept his mouth shut about Salvatore's business, then personal differences need not come between them. Marrow did a wonderful job of overshadowing his own empty little trattoria, and considering the amount of powder passing through Salvatore's candle-in-a-chianti bottle eaterie, the odd gram supplied here and there to the upmarket place next door was cheap protection.

Two minutes later, preceded by Paul Potter, a greasy head poked round Marrow's back kitchen door, spotted Seamus, half darted, half limped golem-like across the floor, delivered a little plastic bag into the groping hand of the now swaying chef and darted out again, before it could receive the blind side-swipe Seamus tried to administer. The latter loathed Salvatore's runner boy Marco even more than he loathed Salvatore himself.

Still, Seamus focused on the little white bag with overwhelming relief, wiped his arm across one of the metal kitchen counters – successfully spraying over the floor six pounds of minutely chopped carrots that Pierre, sous chef number three had spent the last fifteen minutes preparing – tipped a healthy dollop of the bag's contents into their place, pulled out another fifty-pound note, rolled it up, shoved it up his nose and, aiming vaguely for the pile, snorted an impressive amount of it through the note.

Three seconds of oblivion. The fog that had infested his head cleared with a hammer blow, his eyes, half-closed and unfocused, shot open, dilated, red and glaring. His courage returned, his self-possession, his power. He was Seamus Bull and he was the best chef in the country, possibly in the world. This was his kitchen, here were his staff, upstairs were his customers. And by Christ, were they lucky to be receiving the products of his talents tonight!

He passed the rolled-up note across to sous chef number three, who saw his moment for recompense following the lost carrots – not to mention a way of keeping himself awake for the last four hours of his seventeen-hour shift – and hoovered up the escaped powder. Then when Seamus waved away the returned banknote Pierre swiftly pocketed it and pulled another bottle of Armagnac from under the kitchen unit. Ah, sous chef three, smiled Seamus, he knows how to look after his master. Pierre simpered a smarmy grin.

Then Seamus started barking. 'What kind of a state is this fucking kitchen in? Sous chef, clear those carrots. What has happened to the oven door? Sarah, we need a lemongrass mousse to go with this dessert order now, and what the fuck have you got that thing on your head for? You look like you're off to the mosque. Albert, that plate of petits fours is needed *now*, not next week! Nigel, bring me coulis for this mousse. Sarah, this choux pastry hasn't risen properly! Barratt, plate the petits fours now! Where's Shaw?'

There was an uncomfortable pause in which no one volunteered the information.

'Gone to get the paper, Chef,' replied Paul, the Head Chef, finally realising the task fell to him by virtue of his seniority.

'Ah, the paper, yes,' said Seamus, his eyes gleaming as they relished the challenge. 'Let's see what that shit-stroking little fucker has to say about my mighty Marrow, shall we?'

On cue, the back door to the kitchen opened again and in walked Michael, his face wearing a look of terrified apprehension. Normally his expression was impenetrable, a closed and shuttered defence to the world; one which would show no fear but equally no anger. But not now.

Now no one could envy Michael his task. He stepped into the spotlight and prepared for his grilling.

'Well? What's he got to say about us then?' demanded Seamus in the clipped tone of one dreading the response, but disguising the fear as irritation with its deliverer.

'I don't know, Chef,' swallowed Michael.

'What do you mean, you don't know? Are you trying to tell me you didn't read it in the cab on the way back?'

'No, Chef, I didn't,' replied Michael, truthfully.

Seamus didn't believe him, and if this was going to be a stitch-up review he needed someone else to share the humiliation. 'Well, in that case I think you should read it out now, aloud, to the assembled company. Let's all listen to Ruthless Bloody Rufus's Homage to Marrow.'

'Chef . . . I, um, think there's something else you should see.'

'What else could possibly be of more importance to me right now, hey Shaw?' Seamus refused to be shaken by Michael's fear. 'Let me see: Saddam Hussein has invaded France, has he? Going to upset my supply of truffles? Italy finally decided on civil war over the north's Parma ham prices? Tony Fucking Blair introducing a new tax on eating, is he? Come on then, Anna Ford, tell us the news!'

Michael looked around, desperately hoping that one of the others might step in and deflect some of the attention, but it was useless. Only he possessed the tremendous and awful knowledge. Knowledge that he had to share.

'Here's the review, Chef,' he said quickly, passing across the relevant supplement from the pile that is the *Tribune*, in the vain hope that it might distract him for just one more minute. But Seamus knew from the look on Michael's face that something big was up, something even worse than a Ruthless Rufus review.

'What else have you got there?' he asked.

Michael passed across a copy of *News of the Globe*. 'Oh Chef, I'm sorry,' he said genuinely. 'It's on page five.' The news-stand sellers had been sniggering at it when Michael had arrived to buy the *Tribune*, and turning up in his chef whites had insisted he share the joke.

Seamus took the paper Michael offered him. The orchestra of the kitchen had ceased, leaving a deafening silence as everyone watched their boss. Slowly he looked down at the paper, opening it at the fifth page. There, spread across two tabloid pages, was the headline: SEXY CHEF DOES INDEED HAVE PRIZE MARROW! and underneath was a picture of Seamus, stark bollock naked with only a black 'censored' stamp covering his modesty, clutching a £300 tin of Sevruga caviar, looking as if he was about to pour it over the exposed breasts of – you couldn't see the girl but Seamus knew who it was, all right. It was the crotchless feature-writer! Or rather, crotchless she had been, but a feature-writer she certainly had *not* been. From the looks of it, she was instead an undercover reporter in the pay of Britain's dirtiest and most widely read tabloid.

Claret Jelly

5 leaves of gelatine
1 bottle of fine first-growth claret
half wineglass of brandy, XO
1 small jar deli-bought redcurrant jelly
Juice and grated rind of 1 organic orange
55g caster sugar

1. Soften the gelatine leaves in a little water, then drain.

2. Pour all the ingredients into a saucepan, bar the gelatine, and simmer for 10 minutes. Remove from the heat and add the gelatine leaves. Stir well until the leaves are completely dissolved. Pour into a mould.

3. Chill until set, turn out to serve. Watch it quiver.

3

Whilst Saturday night was proceeding in Notting Hill in suitably cataclysmic style, across town in Soho, Rufus Ransome was scraping the last few forkfuls of Châteaubriand off his plate, up past the *millefeuille* that was his chin and plopping the contents through his open, puckered lips. Rufus was a large man; so large, in fact, there was many a joke made about whether one could trace his genetic ancestry back, not to the chimp but to the hippopotamus. With bulging blue, glassy eyes, a smooth greasy pate adorned with the odd strand of his remaining dark hair, stubbornly grown long to paste across the dome of his scalp, short stubby arms and legs, at a squat height of only five foot six, he weighed in at an impressive seventeen stones.

It was hard to distinguish his features as Rufus looked as if he had been blown up like a balloon: everything had been drowned in the sea of fat that enveloped his body. Special accommodation always had to be made for him at restaurant tables and, indeed, cunning restaurateurs, in the vague hope of a favourable review, had in the past taken into account his vast girth when designing their interiors. One was even known to have had a custom-designed table made in the vain attempt of securing at least a line of praise in a Rufus review.

At fifty-two years of age, Rufus had spent a considerable amount of time fattening the turkey that was his life. As a child he had always been fed the best. His father, St John – a famous gastronaut who would travel for days to arrive at a particular Toulouse/Lausanne/Munich/Palermo restaurant – had sought to educate his family entirely through the medium of food. A part-time Professor of Social Studies at Oxford, he had spent his life in the pursuit of pleasure, ably assisted by his timid Scottish wife Mary, daughter of the Laird of Larg, and his tubby young son Rufus.

Mary clung to Rufus, severely testing the bounds of the mother-son relationship with her mollycoddling and indulgence. Due to complications at his birth, Mary had been unable to have more children after Rufus, and had long since lost physical contact with her husband. St John, on the other hand, was stern with the boy, deplored physical contact, using his lectures on the social history of their daily nourishment and each morning's formal handshake at breakfast to cement the father-son respect. And of course his pride in his son swelled as the boy began to develop the most sensitive palate. By the age of thirteen, Rufus could tell his Burgundies from his clarets, identify seventy-six different spices and list beef-bone marrow on Melba toast as one of his favourite dishes.

St John had been left a great fortune by Rufus's grandfather, and so the family spent the long vacations and, in fact, much of the terms, on extended 'research projects' abroad. From Vienna to Mombasa, Jakarta to Saigon, Beijing to New York, St John had indulged his obsession with the pursuit of the finest international cuisine. All of which information was assiduously recorded during the long hours St John spent in his study. He was researching a book detailing the sociology of the human race through its food, but unfortunately Rufus's father died when he was sixty, with his work unpublished, although all the research was neatly documented.

When Rufus was fifteen and the family were spending the summer in a rented villa just outside Amalfi on the western coast of Italy, he realised he was gay. Encouraged by his mother to indulge his pubescence in the histrionics and melodrama of the romantic poets, Rufus had taken to scribbling the odd line himself. It was while engaged in that activity one evening, by the light of the setting sun, that he had the revelation. One moment he was watching local boys playing their evening football game, the next he glanced down at his pad to the lines he had scribbled:

> *Oh that I could my union make*
> *With the great fire of youth,*
> *Bursting forth in a golden shower of ecstasy*
> *Towards their soft, brown limbs,*
> *Contented and dirty,*
> *Breathing easier in the sap of my own kind.*

Rufus took in what he had written, looked up at the flexing thighs and quivering buttock cheeks of the tanned Italian bodies and was overcome with the most raging desire. He had to walk home with the notepad over the front of his shorts.

St John had affected not to notice 'the trouble with his son' over the years, but of course he knew perfectly well – he recognised all the signs. St John had been doing it with everyone at Oxford, male students and staff alike, ever since he had taken up the post thirty years ago, but he couldn't mention it in front of Mary, obviously.

Then, when he was seventeen, Rufus had his lucky break. Already sexually active, he found himself picked up one night by the editor of a national newspaper. Rufus milked the situation for all it was worth, and afterwards asked for a job. His career never looked back, and he was now one of the biggest legends in what used to be Fleet Street. Just as the killer theatre critics of New York can close down an entire Broadway show with a single review, so Rufus Ramsome could now wield the same power in the increasingly competitive and mushrooming merry-go-round that is the restaurant industry.

Discerning, uncompromising critics are never the most popular people about town, regarded by those who do the doing, as opposed to the eating and commenting, as irksome obstacles on the path to success. But the national dislike of Rufus ran rather more personally. Although popular within his own gay crowd, others who knew him found it hard to warm to his condescending manners, intense selfishness and his rather boring conviction that the snide little sideswipes he published every Sunday were proof of his literary emergence as a modern-day Oscar Wilde.

His approach to food was old school. There was only one truly great cuisine in the world, and that was French. All this mucking around with fusion food – using a calaloo and mandarin tapenade to dress a kangaroo terrine for God's sake, and other such New World balderdash – was showmanship and Rufus would not tolerate it. It was an insult to the great traditions of French cooking.

Ironically, the one sensation Rufus had lost touch with was the simple pleasure of satisfying his hunger: he hadn't gone hungry since 1968 when his mother had been delayed delivering his weekly food hamper whilst he was up at Cambridge. He had been forced to survive on the products of his college's kitchen, but his fine and sensitive palate had rejected their vile offerings. There were some foods Rufus just could not bring himself to eat. Baked beans was one, Marmite another. He was the founder member of the school which regarded the Big Mac as the Bubonic Plague, Coca Cola as twentieth-century arsenic, and squirty cream on prefab supermarket meringue nests as nothing less than the work of Lucifer Himself!

Tonight, of course, Rufus was to be found in a restaurant. More than thirty years later, he had not allowed a single Saturday to pass without such a 'treat', and indeed, any day with a 'y' in it was considered fair game for a restaurant excursion in Rufus's book. This particular Saturday it was

Le Gavroche, where he was enjoying another expense account meal of what was, he considered, some of the finest traditionalist French cooking in the UK. After all, he reasoned, if one was to keep the edge against one's competitors, one simply had to eat out all the time in order to try out all these ridiculous new fads. He therefore ensured at least one weekly visit to a good French restaurant to remind himself of the benchmark.

For tonight's little foray into the world of £150 dinners, Rufus was dressed in a scarlet silk cravat, a brushed cotton, bottle-green check Van Heusen shirt, and a bespoke (well, it wasn't as if he was going to be able to slip his vast hulk into anything off the peg!) Savile Row suit of the finest Harris tweed. Polished brown Oxford brogues, cashmere socks – a present from his dear, recently departed little boyfriend Pascal, even though he had bought them on Rufus's credit card, but what the hell, Rufus had lots of money and poor Pascal had hardly any at all – and underwear specially stitched at Big Man.

His dining companion tonight was his old friend Jasper Mendelson, a property magnate who had made his money when he noticed there was a market for extravagant bachelor homes and had spearheaded the revolution in the loft-dwelling lifestyle. He had also, coincidentally, just split from his own boyfriend, Sebastian. As a result the two 'old faggots', as Jasper cheerfully labelled them – to which Rufus's indignant riposte had been 'Speak for yourself' – were burying their sorrows beneath one of the finest à la carte menus in London. All of which, of course, was being washed down with the classiest selection of first-growth clarets, before they departed to Club Louche to cheer themselves up with some new young blood.

'Would sir care to see a dessert menu?' questioned a voice behind Rufus's shoulder, discreet, attentive, and, oh dear, really rather seductive. Rufus craned his neck round for a better look at the owner of the angelic voice behind him. The folds of fat on his neck shook as they swivelled round on the great corpulent mass of his body.

'Why, my dear, a dessert is a must. How else is one to justify the glass of '53 Chateau Yquem that I don't mind telling you I'm fully intent on having. Wouldn't you say, Jasper?'

'Quite so, quite so indeed, my dear chap. Dessert is the drama at the end of the meal, the epilogue to a fine performance. No meal is complete without it. Now tell me, young man, what do you recommend?'

'Well, sir, of course we are famous here for our crème caramels, which would go perfectly with a glass of Yquem. In fact, I think you'll find they complement each other very well.' The waiter finished his speech with a little bob of the head, like a bow after a fine performance, his speech delivered in the hushed tones of an actor who has repeated the same lines for the same performance too many times.

'What a fine suggestion!' cut in Rufus, irritated that Jasper had deflected the waiter's attention from himself. 'And for me, do you have a personal recommendation?'

'I would suggest exactly the same, sir.'

'Well then, I'll have it too.' And with that Rufus snapped shut the menu with a grin designed to show off his stubby teeth to best effect, swizzled his shiny pate away from the hapless waiter, and resumed his commiserations with Jasper.

If there was one overriding characteristic in Rufus Ransome, it was his cunning and deeply felt ambition. His life of boys and dinners appeared idyllic enough, but below the surface Rufus had a selfish, greedy desire for more recognition, more money, more acclaim, more respect. He could not rest until he was seen as the modern-day Escoffier, the fountain of all knowledge about the world of food, and a master commentator on its role as art. He knew he had his enemies, but hidden behind the armour of his paper and his pen, Rufus could really dish it out, without ever once having to take it himself.

And that, of course, was the problem. Rufus was just a commentator and never quite got over those pangs of jealousy he experienced when a chef was asked onto a TV chat show or a radio programme, rather than himself. Like most 'lifestyle' feature-writers, he experienced the angst of one on whom great judgement was bestowed, with very little qualification. An amusing raconteur he might be, he thought in his darkest moments, but a respected sage he wasn't. His enemies would be fewer, or at least foiled, if only he could have his professionalism confirmed. Which is where the book came in. It was Rufus's ambition to pick up his father's work where it had been left off and publish the great work on gastronomy's social implications. Damn hard work it was, writing a book.

Still, at least he had the respect of Emmanuel Coq, the most famous chef in this country, procured by a series of shockingly sycophantic reviews. Coq had never opened a restaurant without a written fanfare from Rufus, who idolised the man and all he did. Coq, meantime, cultivated a pedagogic relationship with Rufus, inviting him to the odd intimate dinner that had Rufus basking in the glow of favouritism. During these meals the two would discuss the up-and-coming lights of the gastronomic galaxy, pinpoint those about whom Coq was paranoid, bitch about them and thus ensure them appalling reviews from Rufus.

Bull, who used to work for Coq until he left to open his own place, was seen as the Judas. Coq had had plans for a prime spot in Knightsbridge for Bull to helm under Coq's name, but a month before the deal went through Bull betrayed him and got into bed with that money man, Salvatore. Sold for thirty pieces of silver, noted Coq bitterly. It was now Coq's sole mission to bring about his demise: the *News of the Globe* set-up had worked beautifully – how Rufus had clapped at his plan! – but more cannons were needed to sink the ship. Emmanuel, however, was prepared.

Rufus adored the shared subterfuge of Coq's plots, and anyway was particularly offended by the brutish bully-boy tactics of Bull. Coq, on the other hand, was refined, delicate of flesh, knowledgeable, condescending. Just like his father. A real man.

'Oh Rufus, I must say, that was such a treat! I never eat like this except when I am with you. I feel much more cheered now. Better able to cope with the agony of losing my Sebastian.' Jasper's latest conquest had moved out of his apartment after six months, this very morning. 'Allow me to propose a toast. Perhaps we need a glass of Pommery to see this right? Waiter!'

'Yes, sir?'

'Two glasses of Pommery right away.'

'Very good, sir.'

'Jasper, I do hope you're going to say something cheerful.' Rufus found it most annoying that he had to spend half his time listening to Jasper's emotional woes when his own were much more important.

'Of course, my dear chap. Amazing what a bit of French beef and crême caramel can do for the spirit. Ah, here we are, thank you very much. So: to pastures new!'

'Pastures new!' returned Rufus. 'Which reminds me. Time for Club Louche.'

'Time for Louche indeed, Rufus.'

French bread

425ml lukewarm water
1 teaspoon white sugar
2 level teaspoons dried yeast
700g strong white flour, warmed slightly
1 level tablespoon salt
10g butter

1. Whisk 150 ml of the water with the sugar and yeast and set aside to froth.

2. Sift the flour and salt into a bowl and rub in the butter. Pour the yeast into a well in the centre of the flour, then pour in the remaining water. Mix to a dough.

3. Knead on a flat surface until the dough is springy and elastic.

4. Cover the dough with a bowl and leave in a warm place for an hour and a half to prove.

5. Knock the air out, then knead for another five minutes. Twist the dough into a long, fat cylinder, then leave for another half hour.

6. Place on a buttered baking sheet and bake at 230°C or until the loaf sounds hollow when tapped. Leave to cool on a wire rack.

4

Over at the Venus Hotel on Earls Court Road, meanwhile, Genevieve Dupont was checking herself into one of the cheapest bed and breakfasts the city had to offer. Cheap because it was frequented by, and situated amongst, those for whom life was a struggle. Prostitutes and drug addicts, hit men and runaways, travellers and the homeless, winos and beggars, all, at one time or another, found themselves passing through the area of Earls Court. The only restaurants round here were cheap diners with all-day 'Full English' specials consisting of two lard-fried eggs, sunny side up, sausages made of God knows what, halved tomatoes grilled into submission by the hours they spent underneath a hot lamp, bacon that had congealed into hard, crispy lumps of fat, two rounds of toast and a mug of tea you could stand your spoon up in. A much more traditional approach to British food.

Genevieve threw her bag down on the narrow bed in the corner of the room. Earls Court was obviously not in the same league as Notting Hill. Indeed, when the taxi driver had dropped her at the hotel door – which had been half-lit by a purple neon sign flashing *Vacancies* – some shadow had crept out onto the pavement and tried to sell her something. She wasn't sure what the man had been saying, but she had been sure she didn't want whatever he was offering.

The old man behind the reception desk had shown her upstairs to one of his empty rooms. It wasn't much of a room at all – with grey walls, a crooked wash-basin, a lumpy bed and a precariously wired table lamp – but it was cheap and it was clean, which was what really counted, and it would do until she found something more permanent. She had been advised by the tourist information service that the hotel was *not* in a desirable area, but she had said that all she needed was somewhere cheap and fairly central.

So this was it, she was in London. She didn't usually like cities: she hadn't particularly got on with Paris where she had spent her university days, yearning for her village life, but Genevieve had an element of the stoic about her and didn't really mind the means as long as she reached the end. Which was, of course, why she was here.

She sat down on the bed and stared at the wall opposite. Her poor father. She hoped he didn't mind, or at least understood. Ever since he had died she had had this uncanny sense that he was watching her, was with her – and as she was doing something he had absolutely forbidden while he had been alive, it left her feeling nervous. The last few months of his illness had been terrible. He had made her promise not to return from Paris to nurse him, so as not to compromise her studies, although he knew he was dying. Genevieve had been relieved: she adored her father, but she had adored him as the man who loved her. Not as the rancorous, cancer-ridden old man who had so successfully exiled her from her own village.

She had been a good daughter, obedient. Her English mother, whom her father had met in an impossibly romantic scenario on a ferry bound for a holiday across the Channel, had died of uterine cancer when she was five, and at a very early age Genevieve had become aware that her Papa needed her to alleviate his sense of loss, to comfort him for the absence of the woman he had loved so much. It was true Genevieve was the apple of her papa's eye, but that eye had not twinkled so much after her mother's death. The whole of Genevieve's childhood had been spent trying to revive her father's sparkle.

They worked hard. Her Papa was a baker and *patissier* by trade, and the two of them ran a shop in the little village where they lived, a place named Grèves, just south of Versailles. Monsieur Dupont's loaves were known for miles around, and people would drive into the village sometimes twice in one day to buy them. The shop was always busy, and while her Papa worked the ovens at the back, Genevieve, as soon as she was old enough, sold the bread in the front of the shop.

As she grew up, more and more of the clear-skinned Anglo-Saxon beauty of her mother became evident in her face: the porcelain complexion that tanned a Mediterranean bronze during the summer months, the soft blue-grey eyes that had such a sad appeal to them, and the shock of her violently blonde hair. Hair so blonde it was almost white, so fine it was surrounded by a thin halo of wisps, so long she had to plait it into a long braid which hung down her back every morning, before setting off for the bakery to help her father.

By the age of twelve Genevieve had begun to develop what were now her full round breasts, and not long after her waist pinched in, her hips stepped out, and her legs grew long and shapely. By the age of fourteen, she had left the angelic body of her childhood behind and metamorphosed into a beautiful young woman.

Boys had not interested her for a long time, not until she was nearly sixteen. For the first few years of her womanhood, before her mind had caught up with the maturity of her body, she had been teased mercilessly at school and through the village as she walked home: the common reaction of pre-pubescent boys when faced with an undeniably beautiful, sexy girl. It had made her uncomfortable with the way she looked; she had hated her breasts and when she realised she had to go and buy a bra, she had deliberately bought it too small in the hope that her chest would bulge less. Her attempts were fruitless.

Her sexuality, however unawakened, was obvious to all who saw her, and her shyness with it had only served to add to its charm.

The candy-pink striped apron she used to put on over her school uniform every morning and evening before and after school, just tantalised with its hidden treasures. Each customer who strolled into the shop was greeted simultaneously by the angelic vision of Genevieve and the wall of heavily scented air that poured out of the shop's baking ovens and hung around her in clouds. She smelled so delicious that, at night, most of the young men of the village would dream you could eat her.

Grown men, who had come in for a single baguette, would fall under this double spell; transfixed by Genevieve, their hunger sharpened by the dulcet wafts that emanated from the kitchen and from the lines of little baked treats that were stacked under the glass counters of the shop, they would find themselves leaving with armfuls of pains aux raisins, petits fours, pains au chocolat and tartes aux pommes, all prettily wrapped by the delicate fingers of Genevieve, as she curled the pink ribbon round the boxes.

M. Dupont was of course pleased by the extra business, but at the same time he was uneasy about his daughter's beauty and the effect she had on male customers. He would, therefore, lecture her frequently on the cunning and manipulation of men, the evils of sex and the punishments God brought on those who transgressed. As sex was the last thing Genevieve thought about at the time, she ignored his fire and brimstone sermons, and never allowed his fears to enter her own head. Instead she would ask him about England and the English, the race that made up half her being but which was still a complete mystery to her.

Genevieve had fallen out with her father precisely seven months after that first day of May six years ago. She had never before looked at a boy, or been attracted by one – they were so stupid and juvenile, the village men – until, of course, that May. Months afterwards the fruits of her summer had begun to ripen and she eventually could not hide it from her papa. She had had no one to turn to. Left alone, sixteen years old, she had been forced to do what he had ordered, and had spent her Christmas in hospital. Never had she been so miserable, so confused, so ashamed. She had loathed her father for what he had made her do and the two had found it very hard to forgive each other.

She had so wanted to have the baby at the time, but he had refused to listen to her, and she supposed she understood now his reasons for a termination. With the father of the child absent, the humiliation in front of the rest of the village had made him unable to deal with his young daughter's sexuality.

But what had been worse had been his inability to deal with his daughter after the event. She was scarred, her insides had been quite literally ripped apart, she had been abandoned and she couldn't understand it. He had looked for the answer in the bottom of his bottle of pastis, and his only comfort to her had been to slump in his armchair, shouting about the English, the bloody English, and how they had ruined his life. Yes, she understood his reasons. But his decision had eventually killed him. Three years later he had developed stomach cancer, and his death was prolonged and painful. It had been a relief when, twelve months ago, she had finally been able to lay the embittered man to rest.

Had she helped kill him? Reason said not, but she had to find out what had happened, why she had been left alone. She had to resolve the questions in her life, the cause of the events that had destroyed her happiness.

Genevieve unzipped her bag and took out the diary resting on top of her neatly piled clothes. She hadn't written in it since he had died, it had been too painful. The diary went back ten years. There was a lot in it. She sighed and placed it on her bedside table, took out her wash bag and turned to the basin with the mottled mirror hanging above it. Her face was tired, she could see that. Her skin looked grey but that was rather more to do with the artificial lamp than anything else. She tied back her long blonde hair, brushed her teeth and splashed cold water on her face. When she washed her hands, the hot water from the immersion heater was scalding.

She turned back to her holdall and dug out the little framed picture of Papa holding her when she was a little girl. Dupont's eyes were shining. He had once told her that her mother had taken that picture, but she had no recollection of it. Genevieve felt a stab in her chest. Her father, the baker. She remembered the yeasty smell of him when she sat on his lap, his firm, dry lips when he kissed her forehead when he came to say goodnight. She remembered, later, Papa's anger and coldness. She leaned the picture frame beside her bedside lamp.

As she climbed into bed, she winced at the unaired scent of the sheets. She glanced across at the little silver photo frame.

'*Je vais faire ce qu'il faut faire, Papa, je te promets.* I will do what needs doing Father, I promise.'

Champagne Soup

1 bottle of pink champagne
1 stick of cinnamon
10 egg yolks
8 tablespoons caster sugar
2 tablespoons icing sugar

1. Heat the cinnamon in the champagne, not quite to boiling point so as not to lose the alcohol.

2. Whisk the egg yolks and sugar until thick and pale. Stir in the hot champagne.

4. Pour the mixture into ramekins placed in a roasting tin. Pour boiling water around the ramekins and bake for 40 minutes at 150°C.

5. Chill. Dust with icing sugar to serve.

5

Whilst Genevieve was lying awake in between the musty sheets of her Earls Court hotel, Club Louche was enjoying a particularly busy night, even for a Saturday. Amongst the torn leather and distressed wood panelling of the club's furnishing, the usual suspects were by now settled comfortably into their nightly rituals. Around the silver buckets of champagne that littered the low tables and the armies of overflowing ashtrays and half-empty glasses, the Beautiful People were gathered. They stood and sat, milled and perched, preened and leaned, flirting, gossiping, shrieking with delight at an unfortunate story about one of their own, pushing back their hair, teetering on their heels, smoothing their dresses, watching, being watched – loving being watched.

Only the privileged few drank in Club Louche. Only those given the sartorial nod from a pre-elected committee of style were granted membership to drink from the long, low bar that ran for a generous length of the room. The men, hunched comfortably into their accustomed positions on their stools, leered at the parade of beauties that swarmed around them. In one corner lounged a poet, whose frank, drug-obsessed raps coupled with his indignant, romantic pose had just earned him a lucrative deal with the record company boss who sat opposite him; in another two members of the latest girl band sensation were slowly getting smashed with a gaggle of hungry male admirers, each of whom was convinced that his combination of Paul Smith suit and smooth charm would earn him a place in the glorious pop beds of one or maybe even both of the starlets.

An outré actress, waving her rainbow Sobranie around, was treating the director of her one-woman show to a soliloquy on the loneliness of treading the boards, and an ageing rock star was seated at the end of the bar, his trips downstairs to the marble-topped toilets becoming increasingly frequent. The latest Supermodel had just made an entrance with several designers, her personal assistant, manicurist and booker in tow, causing the literary party that engulfed the entrance to pause as one at the breathtaking, room-sucking vacuum of her beauty. A Saturday night not yet reaching the epic expectations one would expect of the Club Louche, but certainly warming up, as – Ooops! – one of the girl band fell off her chair.

And in the middle of this throng, ringmistress of the circus of self-promoting, self-obsessed, self-regarding London, stood Marion Maltese, cracking her public relations whip. Slim, tall, dark Marion, with the fine-drawn swarthy features of true Italian beauty inherited from her mother, stood with the air of one who is supreme mistress of her circle. A founder member of the club, it had indeed been Marion's brilliant idea to offer the powerful and the influential the attractive package of free membership, a late licence, a dirty playground and a strict door policy. That was their deal: hers was that she successfully gathered all those who were important under one roof each night. The tentacles of Louche stretched from Westminster to the South Bank, Sandringham to the Royal Academy, Fleet Street to Inner Temple, top shelf to bottom shelf, and Louche now acted as her salon, wherein she conducted her business. Any deal, any idea, any transaction that took place under the roof of Louche inevitably had to involve Marion, and her public relations skills had lent her the reputation of something of a Svengali figure. However, as Marion well knew, this had more to do with her staying power, her glamour and her ability to be in the right place at the right time (namely Louche), than any professional gifts with which she might have been born.

Single, ferociously independent and looking ten years younger than she actually was (no one had any idea she had celebrated her forty-fifth birthday last month), Marion could spot a deal being made in any corner of Louche. One look from beneath her arched brows – that swept dramatically over the hollows of her scalding green eyes – and the deal-makers knew Marion needed to be cut in. 'You cannot do anything without PR' was the Maltese mantra all succumbed to, and none questioned. No make-up, just a tan, and a flash of deep crimson on her lips convinced even the most dubious punters they needed Marion on their side. From the slick tail of lush, dark hair gathered high on her head, her body snaked to the floor, one fluid curve of neck, shoulder, breast, waist, hip, leg – and more leg. Tonight, all this was smothered in a simple, thin black dress that covered everything, but masked nothing. It was around Marion that Louche danced to its tune, and around Louche that much of London, and indeed the country, revolved.

Seamus, by this time, was flying. With the Armagnac to calm his nerves, a bottle of Cristal to celebrate the publication of his sexual prowess, and the best part of a Margaux '62 to drown his sorrows at Rufus's astonishingly bitchy review which he had finally got round to reading, now under his belt, plus most of Salvatore's little bag to keep him standing – and shouting – Seamus was on a roll. After the initial tantrum in the kitchens of Marrow, he had left his last customers in the capable hands of his maitre d', Albert Bresson, and decided to continue his orgy uptown.

If Seamus knew how to work hard, then he certainly knew how to play hard, too. He was being ably assisted in this task by his butch right-hand man, Paul Potter, who had a neck so thick-set he could balance an entire haunch of venison on the back of it, and Nigel, Paul's silent, sturdy deputy. Both men had spent the last hour listening alternatively to Seamus's rants about the dirt that constitutes tabloid newspapers, and then unstinting praise for its nonetheless accurate standards of reporting. 'The stallion chef can stir my sauce anytime' was the *News of the Globe's* ultimate conclusion in its profile of 'London's most outrageous talent', who had 'the sexual energy of a fullgrown stag, and a member the size of – well, a very large vegetable'. The reporter could also exclusively reveal 'that Belfast-born Seamus Bull had named his famous posh London restaurant after his own prize-winning Marrow'.

Rounding Hyde Park corner now, the cab that carried Seamus, Paul and Nigel ploughed through the West End towards the central destination for all those who wanted their Saturday-night behaviour conducted in front of everyone else who mattered. The cab was cruising towards Club Louche like the ferry across the Styx. In the back, Paul was racking up three more white lines on the back of a mirror and passing them under the noses of the wild-eyed Nigel and the ranting Seamus.

Seamus was a little confused. Obviously the target of his tirade was the filthy, cheap, self-aggrandising press, but although the review in the broadsheet had been damning, the tabloid story had been far from uncomplimentary. On the contrary, in fact. And his figure did cut rather a fine dash in the picture – taken by a telephoto lens through the window of Claridges. Caught between dismay at being the victim of the oldest trick in the book, and triumph at such a glowing write-up of his sexual prowess, Seamus's flushed face, it would be fair to say, was partly derived from pride.

As he scooped up the line with a tremendous snort, pausing only to allow his eyes to glisten with water as he came back down to earth, he cried, 'Fucking bitch! I can't believe she did that! Still – ha! – at least she got the size of my cock right. Might have to get this cutting framed for my toilet wall! Still, her little revelation about the restaurant name isn't exactly going to go down well with Lord and Lady Fawsley.'

'Mick and Keith'll like it though,' chimed in Paul, as Nigel saw to the last of the powder.

But then Seamus's face flushed deeper as that other nasty business came to his mind. 'I tell you fucking what, though, if I so much as catch a glimpse of that camp little twat Rufus I'm gonna have a right fucking moment, I can tell you. Not responsible for my actions if he shows his face anywhere near me.'

As for the review, well, Rufus's turn of phrase had been crushing. He had 'reserved judgement on Marrow up until now', he wrote, never allowing his opinion of Seamus as a person to cloud his reaction to the food, but he had taken no prisoners with this review, using it as a personal crusade 'to stamp out the practice of over-inflated culinary egos'. He introduced the piece by declaring he had eaten at Marrow twelve months previously, when he had judged it worthy of its two stars, but said that it now appeared something disastrous had happened in the kitchen. Seamus began to repeat the review's more punishing phrases – phrases he had by now committed to memory.

'The interior is obviously far too concerned with ostentation and glamour; the décor simply serves to distract the diner from his atrocious imitation of fine food; the cooking displays a distinct lack of flair and invention, as if the chef is too scared to break his mould.'

'Scared! The bastard thinks I'm scared!' Seamus snorted. 'I'll show him! And as for: "The turbot was off, I was forced to eat brill in a batter that was so soggy I practically had to wring it out" and, "The sauce was so intense it completely obliterated the fish, which incidentally had the texture of a limp rubber balloon" . . .' By now he was spitting out these words, painfully aware that Rufus's woeful restaurant experience was going to be read nationwide tomorrow.

As the taxi turned into Soho, preparing to deliver its highly charged crew to the doors of Club Louche, London seemed to have an air of stillness about it, like the deathly calm that precedes the riot of a seasonal hurricane.

'You're having a fuck of a laugh if you think I'm paying that, mate. You take ten quid and be done with it.' Seamus was erupting from his minicab outside the club, and had already entangled himself in an argument with the cabbie, who was fed up with extending further credit to the obviously well-to-do owner of Marrow. Like many of the rich, Seamus found it hard to deal in the vulgarities of ready cash.

'But you already owe us over £300 from last month, and until that's paid my boss says I can't give you any credit. Sorry, guv'nor, but that's the way it is.'

'You deal with my secretary when you're talking about money, not me. And for that fucking cheek you can tell your boss that's the end of his contract with my restaurant.'

Seamus turned on his heel, his gofers shadowing him close behind, and flung open the doors to Club Louche.

As you enter Louche you first have to pass through a reception area which is always manned by two graceful but stern-looking beauties. Those who are not members are required to wait in reception until a member comes to collect them, causing much embarrassment to the sofa perchers who hang on the tails of the fast set. The other purpose of the reception is to forewarn the bar staff of any unsavoury elements approaching. Even before Seamus had got through the front door, Cassandra, the flaxen-haired beauty on the desk tonight, had watched the light skirmish with the taxi driver through the window, and was on the phone to alert the bar.

Seamus was another founder of the club. Brought in

originally for advice on the food, as his celebrity star rose with the media's revelations of what a naughty boy with pots of money and attitude might get up to, he gradually became one of its most notorious members. His renowned manic approach to getting wrecked of a Saturday night (Sunday was the only day Marrow didn't open), had more often than not culminated in him staggering into a taxi with a Louche beauty clutched under one arm and a bottle under the other, to the accompaniment of the flashing lightbulbs of the paparazzi. The odd bottle/pool cue/ice bucket that fell out of a Louche window also had to be explained. Indeed, these were the incidents for which he was best known, but they served only to heighten the public interest in catching a glimpse of him in his own establishment. Headlines such as *BULL SEES MYSTERY BLONDE*, *CHEF STORMS OUT AGAIN*, *PHOTOGRAPHER PANCAKED IN CHEF'S HIT AND RUN* and so on, kept the reservation list in his restaurant overflowing. No one, however, had ever kissed and told before; although the parade of women through Seamus's bachelor flat had been more or less unstinting for the last four years. None had yet succumbed to the lure of a tabloid cheque, least of all with a full-frontal nude photograph.

Cassandra was already alert to tomorrow's headlines, little imagining they had already been written.

'Good evening, Mr Bull. How lovely to see you.' She smiled diplomatically.

'Evening, Cassandra.' Seamus sniffed, wiping his nose with the back of his hand. He glowed at her, then said, 'You should know that tonight is the last night when everyone in the world doesn't know the size of my cock.'

'Indeed, Seamus?'

'Yes, Cassandra. Tell me, do you need to know the size of my cock?'

'Frankly, no Seamus.'

'Then it appears you are alone in your ignorance,' grinned Seamus manically, and with that he moved on, gofers in tow, to the bar.

As he entered the room, a ripple went out amongst the female company. Seamus Bull was without doubt one of the sexiest men in London – sexy because he was devastatingly handsome and had the body of a god, sexy because he knew how to do it; how to turn on the charm and talk to women, how to seduce with the eyes, the fingertips and champagne. But sexy most of all because he was dangerous. Seamus Bull was not stable, and Seamus Bull was available for one night only. This was what attracted women to him like bees to a honeypot. The man was a challenge.

'Seamus, I see you've brought your filthy habits, sorry, talents, to us once more,' murmured Marion as she offered her cheek up for a kiss.

Seamus obliged, taking in the physical, feline bomb that was Marion Maltese. 'Indeed, you filthy whore,' he whispered dirtily into her ear, 'but you know,' and here he applied the mock charm he knew she expected from him, 'you just say the word and I roll over.'

Seamus had known Marion for years, and had indeed slept with her fairly early on in their relationship, but had quickly decided, once he had got her clothes off and her naked body into his bed, that she had the sexual allure of a stick insect. Like many truly beautiful women, her prowess in bed did not match the promise of her charms. Of course he entirely respected her professionally for her skill as a manipulator of the London scene, a Mephistopheles, as he had heard her called, of the city's playgrounds. Marion, in turn, liked to propagate the myth that her sex-life was high octane and involved something like the occasional Bavarian Prince or jet-set tycoon in locations such as Mustique or St Moritz. Which was far from the reality.

'Paul, Nigel,' she nodded as she stepped back and observed the sweating, wild-eyed threesome.

'Right, I want that table which those cunts over there are sitting at, and I want two bottles of Cristal '82, and three Cohiba Number Fours. Tonight, Marion, I'm extremely upset.'

'Seamus, you know I can't ask people to move.'

'Of course you fucking well can. Everyone in here's already turned round to have a good gawp. I'm the star attraction, they'd do anything to talk to me.'

Marion opened her mouth to argue the point but knew from her years in the business that arguing with a man at the alcohol level Seamus was currently sustaining, was futile. Instead she asked, 'Do you know the people on that table? That's Henrietta Gross-Smythe, the society columnist from the *Sunday Tribune*, and her latest squeeze, Piers Limone, who is, I believe, in your business.'

'Oh yeah, the owner of those little theme cafes,' returned Seamus, referring to the three furiously glamorous Turkish restaurants that were currently swelling London's foodie circuit.

'Seamus, we're in there, mate. I fancy that bird every time I see her in the paper.' Clearly Nigel had already made up his mind on the wisdom of joining the couple, and wasting no time Marion led the group off towards Henrietta and Piers.

Thrilled that they should be chosen to be in such rough and ready celebrity company, and to the envy of many of the club's lesser members, Henrietta and Piers stood up to greet the approaching charge of chefs. Henrietta was not a diarist known for her intelligence, but had managed to build a roaringly successful column out of her charm, her social connections, her capacity for mild self-irony, but especially her ability to wear free Versace dresses. She had been going out with the restaurant tycoon Piers Limone for almost – shriek!

– nine weeks now, even though at thirty-six he was
nine years her senior. Piers was tall, dashing, handsome
and richly accessorised in Rolex, tie pin, orthodontically
enhanced teeth, 9-carat gold cufflinks, and Gucci loafers.
He was the kind of man who was always pictured at polo
matches, glass of golden bubbly in one hand, impressive-
looking aristo-babe in the other. He extended a tanned,
manicured hand towards Seamus: 'Seamus Bull, what an
absolute pleasure to meet you!'

'All right mate,' nodded Seamus, swamping Piers's
delicate digits with his own huge hand, before swiftly
withdrawing it and turning to Henrietta as she sat back
down in her chair.

'You work for that bastard newspaper, don't you?'

Seamus's direct challenge was delivered with such a
mischievous look in his eye, such an obvious sexual
leer, that Henrietta found herself quite unhinged. Like
most women, she suddenly found his rough features
really quite alluring. Next to the groomed, effeminate
figure of an upper-class businessman, the manly charm
and sex appeal of a working chef instantly drowned any
claims to Henrietta's affections Piers may have had over
Seamus.

'Yes, yes I do,' she stammered, unable to take her eyes
off Seamus's face, patently aware that as he towered over
her chair, her head was directly level with his crotch.
'Oh, I do hope the paper hasn't done anything to
offend you?'

'Well, yes, actually it fucking well has,' shouted Seamus,
lingering for a few more seconds over Henrietta before
settling himself in the chair between her and Piers, and
prepared to launch with renewed vigour into his theme.
His chair, conveniently (and not by accident) was the
highest at the end of the room and afforded the best
view of the bar. It thus served excellently as a podium
from which to launch into his tirade to best public

effect. Marion, who had neatly seated herself with the group everyone was looking at, laid a hand consolingly and territorially on Seamus's knee.

Seamus raised his voice a decibel or so and made sure his cursing was clearly enunciated so there could be no mistaking his meaning. He knew how to work this club, almost unconsciously: his very presence was enough to draw attention. The drinks materialised swiftly after a nod from Marion, and were now being delivered to the table in the form of two large silver buckets and a tray of flutes.

'That shit – and I'm sorry I can't excuse my language because the shit deserves it – of a restaurant reviewer,' and here Seamus spat out the words in disgust, 'has decided to take out his poncy little foibles on my restaurant. Frankly, I'm very fucked off that he should be so vindictive and petty about me and my staff's work, and if I so much as set eyes on him then I swear I'll bust his weaselly little head from his flabby little shoulders.'

'Ohmigod, what did he say?' trilled Henrietta, clearly delighted she was about to be privy to some pivotal morsel of earth-shattering gossip.

'Darling, do tell all,' shrieked Marion for the same reason.

By now Henrietta was practically jumping up and down in her chair, her smooth, massaged, fake-tanned legs stretching out beneath her faux-hippie Voyage dress – a look designed to suggest threadbare poverty, but which cost about £700 a go – her immaculately highlighted, curly blonde hair irksomely falling across her fairly plain, and therefore inoffensively attractive, face.

'Tell me, tell me, I loathe the little man too,' she squeaked, to the consternation of the coiffured Piers, who shifted uncomfortably in his chair. He certainly didn't want to be taking sides in this argument: Rufus had so far reviewed his own establishments reasonably well.

'You think he's a prat too?' smirked Seamus, spotting allies.

'Well, I wouldn't put it like that, but let's just say that he and I are not exactly bosom pals. He once propositioned my little brother in a restaurant toilet. Poor Jemmy cried for weeks afterwards. Even though he's twenty-four now, he still can't get a girlfriend he's so traumatised by it.'

Seamus clearly loved this idea and, suddenly inspired in the way only the really drunk can be, set forth on a 'brilliant idea' to 'compile a dossier of his worst crimes', which they should take to Seamus's newfound friends at the *News of the Globe* and sell for vast sums of money, propelling Rufus sweetly and surely down the river. Meantime, several more bottles had arrived, and the assembled party were now glugging down the £160 bottles of arguably the finest champagne money could buy.

'Christ, this is vintage Cristal, who the fuck ordered this?' cried Seamus in horror, catching a glimpse of the label as Paul filled up the glasses.

'You did, Seamus,' replied Nigel, making his usual useful contribution to the conversation.

'Make the next lot House,' he ordered Paul, as he grabbed the hand of Henrietta and took her off downstairs to the toilets, much to the consternation of Piers, who rather wished he was going too.

Returning to Chris, her informant behind the bar, Marion had gathered that Ruthless Rufus himself, no less, was on his way to Louche with a companion and had just phoned ahead to reserve a table. Potential disaster, was her first thought, until she had worked out how to spin the situation to her advantage by pretending to each she was on the other's side. Looking over to Seamus's table, she noticed that both he and Henrietta were still downstairs, presumably in the toilets. Piers remained, making what looked like very strained conversation with Paul and Nigel, who had their backs to the room.

That was the moment Rufus chose to make his entrance. He looked just like a fat duck, thought Marion as he waddled across the floor, his chins sticking out like a beak, his stubby little legs struggling to support the great mass of belly above them. Behind him an identical shape – Jasper Mendelson, the property tycoon – was waddling along in tandem. As Marion swiftly made her way towards them before they could be approached by anyone else, the two noticed her, beamed and, thrilled they should receive a personal welcome from the Queen of the court, said in unison, 'Marion, my dear, how wonderful to see you.' *Mmmwaah, mmwah.*

'Rufus, the pleasure is all mine – and Jasper, how are you?' *Mwah, mwah.*

'Simply wonderful, thank you. Celebrating my recent return to bachelorhood.'

'Oh, I am sorry to hear that,' Marion cooed as she angled the two gentlemen down to the other end of the room. 'Not taking it too harshly, I hope?'

'Well, my dear,' began Jasper, suddenly downcast and dramatic, drawing in a deep breath ready to go through all the gory details once again, but once was enough for Ruthless, who cut him short, snapping, 'No, in fact we are back in action tonight, Marion. Anyone interesting in?'

'Ah, you'll have to have a look for yourselves. In the meantime can I buy you two a drink?'

'Certainly. How wonderful of you – two Scotch on the rocks, please,' replied Rufus and then, never one to pass up the offer of something for free, added, 'And you couldn't secure a couple of Louche's fat Montecristos as well, could you, my dear?'

The table and chairs to which Marion had guided them were sunk into a recess at the back end of the room: the

perfect table for watching other people, as it was quite
hard to discern the faces of those sitting at it, lit, as it
was, from the lamps mounted on the wall behind. Still
Marion realised the situation was precarious, particularly
as Henrietta and Seamus then came bounding up the
stairs, the former giggling and flighty. The two fairly flew
back to their seats, Seamus shepherding Henrietta's bottom before him in between his forearms, whilst grinning
at Paul and Nigel from behind her shoulder. Another
easy conquest. It was fortuitous Seamus's attention was
elsewhere, for had he given a single backward glance he
would have spotted Ruthless behind a cloud of cigar
smoke as he puffed away on his newly lit Monty.

'Look, Jasper, it's that dreadful chef, Seamus Bull!'

'So it is, old chap. I say, is he really as terrible as they
all say he is?'

'Oh absolutely, the man's a brute. What's more, got
a damned inflated view of his cooking. No secret to
anyone he's after Emmanuel's spot as numero uno in
the cooking showroom. Had the most dreadful meal at
his restaurant last Saturday, absolutely dreadful.'

'Isn't that, uh, whatsit called, Marrow? Place you have
to book five months in advance?'

'Ha! I think I'd rather book my dentist five months in
advance. Oh, I say, look at that gorgeous little specimen
over there!'

'Where? Oh yes, I see. That's Dean Hocknall, isn't
it? He plays Sean in *Eastenders*,' chimed in Jasper, who
videoed all the soap operas every day and watched them
before going to bed each night.

'So it is! An actor, oh how perfectly marvellous,
Jasper. Look at his dear curly hair. Isn't he just the
sweetest thing?'

'You know, I've heard he's our type of boy.'

'You haven't? Oh, how thrilling! Let's get him over
here for champagne straight away.'

Henrietta and Seamus were by now engaged in 'deep' conversation, Seamus animating his rantings with great circular gestures of the arms and over-zealous vocal emphases. Marion was hanging about in between the two tables now, not wanting to be inveigled into any ensuing scene, and satisfied she had done all she could to ensure both parties thought her sympathies lay with them. She was, nevertheless, keeping a keen eye on the situation.

Paul and Nigel were bent low over a bottle of Jack Daniels involved in an intense discussion about Henrietta's cup size whilst Piers sat alone on the edge of his chair failing to join in either conversation. The low mutterings of those two thuggish-looking creatures opposite he couldn't even hear, whilst the rantings of Seamus, to which Henrietta was unable to contribute much due to Seamus's sudden preference for soliloquy over dialogue, were pretty much direct forms of abuse to one of the most influential people in his business.

Suddenly feeling particularly excluded, Piers thought he would take a stroll via the bar to the toilets. It was always somewhere to go. An engagement you could rely on, the toilet, in times of severe social distress. 'Excuse me,' nodded Piers to the assembled company, who all continued to ignore him as he got up stiffly, smoothed down his shirt and headed for the stairs.

Piers's patience with Henrietta was running out; she wasn't paying him any attention now Seamus was on the scene. Well, he wasn't going to be upstaged like that in public, especially not by such a foul-mouthed brute. Besides, wasn't that his polo chum, Dickie Ribbon, over there in the corner, with rather a tasty-looking filly? Indeed it was, but unfortunately for Piers, as he was making his way across the bar, he suddenly found himself pressed up against the two corpulent structures of Jasper

and Rufus who were en route to catch the attention of
Dean, the unsuspecting soap star.

'Piers! Hello, old chap,' began Rufus, attempting a
mwah mwah but put off by Limone's instant recoil.
'Haven't seen you in a while. How the devil are you?'
and pumped his hand instead. Never one to miss a
chance to chat up a rich restaurant associate, Rufus
had momentarily forgotten the diversion of Dean at the
bar and, smooth as a creamed vichyssoise, attempted to
engage Piers in conversation.

'What do you make of Emmanuel Coq's new place –
Mirage? Been there yet?'

'Er, actually yes,' hesitated Piers, suddenly terrified of
Seamus the human rage machine at his table. 'Just been
tonight, with Henrietta, as a matter of fact.'

'Ah, Henrietta, is she here? How is the dear girl?'
asked Rufus, craning his neck to see if he could catch
a glimpse of his co-columnist Henrietta Gross-Smythe.
'Such a fine writer she is,' he exclaimed, entirely safe in
the knowledge that this statement was completely untrue.
Fortunately, being such a squat little man, he wasn't too
well equipped to see further than Piers's right shoulder,
which was deliberately placed in his line of vision.

'Er, not here with me. I mean to my knowledge.
Elsewhere. With others.' Split up with her! Ah yes, that
was it, then he would be clearly dissociated from Bull,
should anything untoward happen. 'Well actually, we are
not together any more. You know, not since we, ah, we
finished our meal.'

Rufus looked at Piers quizzically, but then thought he
had never understood these camp chaps who still slept
with girls. By the time both realised any further attempt
at conversation would be futile, Jasper had managed to
reach the bar and was even now buying young Dean the
soap star the pint he had requested.

Piers excused himself – he really couldn't bear to

talk to this odious little man any longer, he would much rather be talking thoroughbreds with Dickie – and wriggled his way out of the crush at the bar. Rufus, meanwhile, had to shove and barge his way to the front of the bar to find Jasper and Dean. He arrived just as the two of them had decided a quick trip to the toilets was in order.

'Where on earth has Piers gone?' exclaimed Henrietta, as she finally noticed the empty seat beside her. Nigel and Paul broke off their discussion to shrug their shoulders and reappraise Henrietta's breasts, then responded quite cheerfully to Seamus when he suggested both provide him with a little male company downstairs. All three stood up and charged off across the bar, leaving Henrietta all on her own. Sighing, she realised that in the space of just half an hour she had managed to scare off not one, not two, not even three, but four men. No one seemed to want to talk to her, let alone go out with her. She had managed a couple of dates with Piers but it seemed he had done a runner now as well. Sadly, Henrietta didn't really enjoy this life but it seemed to be her job. Ever since Daddy had lost all his money to Lloyds, Mummy had made her go out and 'get either a job or a husband'. Failing miserably in the latter, she had managed to excel at the former due to the fact that going to parties was about all she had been good at, ever since she had been launched as a deb at seventeen. It always left her standing guard over two empty bottles of champagne and four abandoned jackets at the end of the evening, though.

No way was Jasper going to have Dean all to himself, and the three of them were now uncomfortably crammed into one tiny little toilet cubicle.

'Here you go, Dean,' encouraged Jasper as he manoeuvred his arm to pass Dean a silver straw. Dean leaned across Rufus's stomach, then stretched a little more until, with his feet now lifted off the

ground and his body balanced precariously on the
substantial girths of the two gentlemen, he found the
toilet ledge through the target of the straw and hoovered
up his line. His shriek of terror as Jasper, enraptured, had attempted to stroke his proffered arse, was
smothered by a sudden commotion outside as the
room filled with the shouting of Seamus, Paul and
Nigel.

'Well, if only she can get me an introduction at one
of his famous little soirées I can turn up and kick the
living shit out of him. Someone's got to do it,' boomed
Seamus's voice.

'Wouldn't it be more discreet to pay someone to
do it for you, boss?' reasoned Nigel in a rare moment
of clarity.

'No, absolutely not. I want that pleasure all for myself,'
came the reply.

For some reason an ice-cold shiver travelled up Rufus's
spine as he remembered the homage to causticity he had
filed for his restaurant column in tomorrow's paper.
Seamus couldn't have read it, could he?

'Oi, who the fuck's in the toilet? Hurry up in there!'
banged an agitated Paul as the door shuddered under
the barrage of his fist. Dean was looking stricken and
distinctly claustrophobic. All he wanted was to get out
of that cubicle now.

'All right, all right,' grumbled Jasper as he retrieved the
accessories of his habit off the top of the cistern. 'Just
coming.'

'No!' mouthed Rufus, bashing Jasper in warning on
the arm, having suddenly developed a heart-racingly
uncomfortable panic and a full glowing sweat. 'It's
Seamus Bull!' he hissed at Jasper.

'So?' enquired Jasper, obviously not in full possession
of the facts, but it was too late. Dean, panicking at his
coke tart behaviour, had unbolted the door, and was

catapulting himself from between the two juddering stomachs through the tiny gap ready for flight upstairs.

'Oi oi, nice little party here then,' sneered Seamus, catching a glimpse of the two further bodies behind the toilet door. 'Come on out of there, we haven't got all fucking night.'

Jasper was the first to appear round the corner, rather confused but desperately trying to maintain his dignity in the path of the fleeing Dean, as he straightened his tie and wiped his nose with the back of his hand. The three men stood menacingly in a row between him and the door, but parted like the Red Sea as he shuffled past.

Rufus stood petrified, crammed up behind the door, unable to stop Jasper, but terrified of the prospect of being left alone with Seamus and his henchmen. Screwing up his eyes, he decided the only thing he could do was run for it and hope to reach the safety of public life upstairs before anyone could catch him. As he bolted out the door, he ran smack into Nigel, rebounded off his chest and landed on his vast pillow of an arse on the floor.

'Well, look who it isn't,' drawled Seamus in amazement, a slow grin spreading across his face. 'It's little Ruthless Rufus Ransome, all a-tremble on the floor. Not so very ruthless now, are we? Feeling a little bit cowardly?' This last was said with a crescendoing tone of fury. Paul and Nigel also appeared enraptured that this good kicking material had just landed so coincidentally at their feet. Neither of them was too pleased with Rufus's salacious desire for bad-mouthing establishments: both of them had long experience of his comments on their cooking, and here at last, their quarry before them, their boss appeared to be considering doing something about it.

'What about it, eh, boss?' smirked Paul, his bloodlust rising.

'Very good of you to drop in on us tonight, on the eve of your publishing sensation, Rufie baby,' goaded Seamus. 'Oh yes, don't think I haven't seen it, maestro. So your duck was "forgettably minimal. Calling it bland would be doing it a favour", would it? Your lemon soufflé tasted "cancerous", did it? And the service was entirely "in the manner of a small army of Uriah Heeps: namely, ingratiating to the point of infuriating"?'

'Now look here,' stammered Rufus. 'That's just my job, you must understand—'

'Don't you tell me what I must and mustn't do!' thundered Seamus. 'And just for that I think it's time for what you've had coming to you.'

By now Rufus had got to his feet, but later he realised this had been a mistake. A few kicks in the stomach as he lay on the floor would have been infinitely preferable to what ensued. As he struggled to an upright position, he had turned his shining face up in supplication to the towering inferno of Seamus, but the sight of his blubbering chins and piggy little eyes had been too much for the Marrow chef to bear. In an almighty jerk, Seamus had careered his raging head towards Rufus's face, butted him – Clunk! – on the forehead, and knocked him out completely. He watched with glee as the fat man crumpled to the floor again in a pile of quivering jelly.

Unfortunately, however, Rufus had refused to come to. Lying piled up on the floor, it had taken four stretchermen a lot of panting and bother to get him into the back of the ambulance. It wasn't in fact until the following day that Rufus woke up. As the low buzz around him gradually thinned out into the sound of individual voices, Rufus found himself in a clean, white gown pinioned under the crisp linen sheets of a bed in St Thomas's Hospital.

The Bacon Buttie

2 slices of cheap white bread
3 greasy rashers of fried bacon
Butter
Tomato ketchup
Brown sauce

1. Butter the slices of bread, or if you prefer, drizzle over the bacon fat from the frying pan instead.

2. Lay the rashers on one of the slices of bread, then cover in ketchup and brown sauce to taste. Press the second slice on top firmly.

3. Serve immediately, accompanied by a large, chipped mug of strong tea with plenty of sugar.

6

Sunday was an exhausting day for Genevieve. She woke up to the sound of shouting in a foreign language outside her door and in a bed that felt strange and uncomfortable. For the first two or three seconds of waking, she thought she was back in her flat in the Quartier Latin underneath her duvet, and wondered about the noise, the dirty grey bedroom wall opposite with the crooked wash-basin and copper pipes plumbing it to the floor, the scratchy feel of the bedsheets. Then, finally, she remembered. She was in London.

She got up, negotiated the shower at the end of the corridor when the shouting had gone away, dressed, and wandered out into Earls Court Road looking for breakfast. At the nearest place she found, a greasy spoon opposite the Tube station, with Formica tables and congealing bacon under a hot lamp, she had a stroke of luck. As she walked through the door, a gnarled woman with nicotine skin and a voice like a shrieking peacock, whom Genevieve identified as the owner by the dirty pink pinny pulled round her extraordinarily large girth, was in the process of firing a girl of a similar age to herself. Judging by the protestations of the screaming woman, it appeared the girl was late, and as she walked out of the door throwing her filthy apron behind her, Genevieve picked it up, handed it to the woman and asked for the job.

Mave, who was indeed the owner of the Happy Egg diner, looked her up and down suspiciously, so Genevieve quickly explained that she had worked in a cake shop most of her life, could serve, talk to customers, operate tills and most of all was reliable and would turn up at work on time every day. Mave was a bit confused by Genevieve's accent at first, but this *was* Earls Court after all, and she was pretty sure the girl was honest: she had that look about her. Mave prided herself on the fact that she could always tell these things. So she had grunted at Genevieve's pitch, told her her wage was £4 an hour, she would pay her in cash at the end of every week, no questions asked, and today was only a trial.

Genevieve couldn't believe her luck. She needed to find a job to survive in London, but had never thought she would find one this quickly. Her Papa had left her no money: all his spare funds had gone on her education. All she had to her name now was a few thousand francs in her account, and some property: the shop and their old home – hardly places she cherished any longer.

All of that first day she kept her head down, did exactly what Mave told her, didn't drop or break a single item of crockery and only needed the till explaining once. By five o'clock Mave had told her she could come back the next day, starting at half-past six. Genevieve had an income.

It had been a tiring day, but although it was two or three years since Genevieve had worked in her father's patisserie, she was more mentally exhausted than anything. She had to concentrate so hard when people spoke to her in order to understand what they were saying, but she seemed to get by very well, and felt pleased with herself. She *could* cope, she *could* do this on her own. She only needed to ask Mave what 'the full English' meant. And 'Nice pair of tits, darlin',' both of which she had encountered more than a few times.

What had struck her so far as most strange about the English was their extraordinary eating habits. They ate sliced packaged bread instead of fresh; drowned everything with vats of vile tinned baked beans, and smothered the lot in tomato ketchup and some revolting-looking brown sauce. Everything served in the caff was accompanied by flat, glistening chips which Genevieve had to fish out of a bucket of bubbling oil. She had never seen (or smelt) anything like it. And everything had to be washed down with cups of tea and milk – she had heard of the English fascination with it, but was stupefied by the quantity she had seen drunk in one day. She personally found it revolting, and had stuck to the lesser of two evils – Mave's instant coffee.

The owner had registered Genevieve's astonishment when she caught sight of her boss wrapping her salivating jowls around what seemed to be the caff's best seller – the bacon buttie. Mave's mood had thawed sufficiently towards Genevieve to try and explain its attraction. She even sent her on her way at the end of her shift with one wrapped up in a paper bag. Genevieve had attempted to eat it whilst sitting on her bed in her hotel room, but had found the taste and texture very strange. Not wholly unpleasant though, she would grant Mave that.

That night, she had fallen asleep by nine o'clock, and was awake half a minute before her alarm went off at six o'clock the next morning. Years of experience had taught Genevieve that she only needed twenty minutes to get herself up in the mornings, and with the caff only just round the corner she was already waiting outside the door when Mave arrived at half-past. The owner grunted at Genevieve, let her in and asked her to start the breakfast service while she settled down with a cup of tea, a Rothmans SuperKing and the *Daily Star*.

Customers started arriving by half-past seven and Genevieve was pretty much responsible for the service all morning. Finally, at twelve o'clock, she was granted a reprieve when Mave dispatched her down the road to Kwiksave to buy more white pepper for the table shakers. Genevieve had wondered what it might be in the shakers.

The English called the white stuff pepper? Where she came from it was black or green or pink, but never white, and it came in corns and you ground it freshly yourself.

Her route took her past the newspaper-seller who was just setting up his pitch for the day. Like most men, he couldn't help but notice Genevieve strolling along the pavement in the sunshine, and he gave her a broad grin and a 'Mornin' darlin' as she walked past. Genevieve smiled back at him: she was beginning to feel almost comfortable in this city now, and was proud of herself for getting a job and being able to do it. Mave didn't ask her any difficult questions, nor did the landlord of the Venus, and no one seemed to mind what she did. She felt completely free and in control of her life, and in the morning sunshine not even Earls Court Road looked too bad. She was beginning to feel ready to sort out what she was going to do next.

On the way back from the supermarket, clutching a large bag of pepper to her chest, the newspaper-seller nodded to her again and, pointing to her pinny, asked her if she was working in Mave's caff. Genevieve stopped and replied politely that she was, and it was while the seller was trying to think of something else to say to delay the curvaceous vision of pink and blonde before him that Genevieve noticed the poster pinned to the front of his stand. *MARROW CHEF LANDS HIMSELF IN PICKLE.*

Shock pulsed through her body, and without hearing what the man was now saying she looked over to the pile of newspapers he had recently untied on his counter and saw that the front page of one was dominated by an enormous picture of Seamus, being escorted by what looked like policemen.

Genevieve picked up a copy and read the caption beneath the picture: *Chef Seamus Bull was last night taken in for questioning concerning a fracas with the* Sunday Tribune *columnist Rufus Ransome who sustained head injuries during a skirmish in Club Louche late on Saturday night. He is now recovering in hospital. Full story page 3.*

Recovering herself as best she could, Genevieve asked how much for the paper, gave the man some money out of Mave's change, took the paper and ripped open the front page as she hurried down the road back to the caff. She suddenly felt very exposed, as if a dirty secret was out and everybody knew it was her.

Inside were pictures of both Seamus and Rufus Ransome, one of some building known as Club Louche and another of Marrow, the place she had seen on Saturday night. Above them ran the headline THE KNIVES ARE OUT BETWEEN CHEF AND CRITIC. She read the story quickly, hungry for information on this man she hadn't seen in six years. She was dismayed by his appearance: he looked older, less fit than before, and his face was beginning to look haggard, even in the smiling press shot.

It appeared from the story that Seamus was being sued by some restaurant critic for physical assault, following '*a particularly vindictive review. This is just the latest in a long line of incidents that have marked the so-far illustrious career of fiery chef Seamus Bull,*' ran the story, '*which cynics assume he has masterminded to publicise his restaurant. But there is the feeling now with this last, Bull may have taken matters too far.*'

Genevieve was shocked. Seamus in a fight? Suddenly she needed to find him, see him for herself, find out who he was now. This wasn't the Seamus she knew, but then the Seamus she thought she knew wouldn't have walked out of her life six years ago, leaving her in the mess he did and never once contacting her. What had happened to him? Suddenly her fear fell away, and she was overtaken by an intense curiosity, a raging desire to face this man now, tell him what had happened to her, describe the chain of events he had set in motion in her life, challenge him, make him take responsibility for it.

But even as she thought of what he had done, of what a monster he had proved he could be, she was overwhelmed with the same desire for him she had experienced all those years ago. He had once marked her escape to freedom, but now it felt as though he had made her life his prisoner, and she could not shake him off. He had taken her childhood from her, taken her father too, for the abortion had destroyed him as surely as it had destroyed the child within her. And the moment when she sloughed off the cloak of naivety and innocence she had carried around until then, the moment she had discovered herself – had become aware of who *she*, Genevieve, really was – that was the moment Seamus had walked into her life. When he walked out he had taken it all away.

Cœur à la Crème

2 heart-shaped moulds
150g cream cheese
1 egg yolk
2 tablespoons sugar
Grated rind 1 orange
1 teaspoon vanilla extract
Pinch salt
200ml double cream
Fresh berries

1. Beat the cream cheese until very light and fluffy. Then beat in the egg yolk, sugar, orange rind, vanilla and salt. Whip the cream until it holds its shape, then fold into the cheese mixture.

2. Cut squares of cheesecloth to come about 10 centimetres out of each mould when used as a lining. Moisten with cold water, wring out, then carefully line each dish.

3. Fill the cheesecloth-lined moulds with the cheese mixture, then fold over the ends of the cheesecloth to cover the cheese. Place the moulds upside down on a cake rack overnight in a fridge to drain.

4. To serve, unmould this wonderfully cheesy dish onto a plate and dress with fresh berries.

7

Seamus took in a sharp breath of the morning air, and squinted against the sun. At twenty-two, he was slimmer, his face fresher, not so ground down by years of troglodyte dwelling. His skin was tanned from the fairer weather, but his forehead still creased into the frown lines which he had had since childhood. He had arrived here, in the middle of this strange countryside, four months ago, and was only just beginning to feel at home in its foreignness. He wasn't used to these green fields. He had grown up in towns, mostly in the grim, disciplined prisons they called Children's Homes and had then moved straight to London as soon as he had qualified from catering college three years ago. He had never been to France either; he had only once had a holiday in his life – in Hampshire, at the home of some rich man who took in under-privileged kids for a week as their summer treat. Seamus had hated that, seeing all the things other people had and he didn't. It was like having your nose rubbed in how shitty your own life was.

As for Ireland, where everyone insisted he was from, he had been moved to a home in England from Belfast at the age of twelve and had never gone back. He wouldn't know what the Blarney Stone was if it came and hit him in the face. He had also had to learn pretty quickly to drop any trace of an Irish accent when he arrived in England.

He didn't understand the language people spoke here in France either: the other chefs gabbled away in their slang, and with his pidgin French, comprised mostly of gastronomic terms, he couldn't keep up. No one talked to him – he was the stranger, an anomaly they didn't understand, and to start off with that had been fine with Seamus. The last thing he wanted was to explain himself to these people. He had spent much of his time alone since he had arrived, working or drinking a glass of red wine at the Café des Amis. He felt himself an observer, watching, waiting till he returned to his own country. He was pleased with what he was learning about food, and particularly pleased with the way that he saw it being appreciated. He liked the way people lived their lives here. They set store by family and community, and food was used as a celebration of that. It was one of the reasons Seamus felt so alien: this was something that had not, so far, been part of his life experience.

Grèves was calming after the rush and noise of London. The medieval houses that hung down over the cobbled streets were small and pretty, compared with the imposing grey architecture of Piccadilly. And everywhere was green, open space: the village was surrounded by miles of land, punctuated by valleys and rivers, the fields parcelled up into hundreds of square little vineyards.

He was working for Guy Chevrot, the legendary French chef, in the kitchens of his famous restaurant Les Feuilles du Temps. He had transferred under the recommendation of his previous boss, Albert Winkelmann at the Ritz Hotel in London, after he had begged and pleaded to be given a chance to learn about the real cuisine of France. By now, Seamus was a commis chef, one below a sous chef, four below Head Chef. He had been working in kitchens for three years, and had graduated from the mass-production banqueting halls of tinned roasts into the caverns of artistry that lie beneath the world's top restaurants. Sure, he had had to go back to the bottom, but washing up at the Ritz was better than 140 covers of gammon steaks with a pineapple garnish. Three more months of this and he would be ready to return to London as a sous chef. Already

Chevrot, who was pleased with his progress, was talking about recommending him to his cousin's country-house hotel in Northumberland. Summer in France, then back to England as the leaves began to turn. His life was beginning at last.

Genevieve swung through the door of her father's bakery and patisserie, the finest in Grèves. It was still early as she put the denim jacket she was carrying onto the stand behind the counter, tied the pink apron over the curves of her lithe body and reached up to secure a strand of hair falling over her face. Hurrying, she darted across to the hatch where she collected a pile of loaves her father Henri was passing through.

'Bonjour, Papa,' she called through the hatch as he scowled at her through a stream of complaints. She was late. She bent her head down and kept quiet until he had finished, then turned to deposit the loaves.

Silence ensued. It was hard, very hard for Genevieve to get from her father anything approaching the love she knew he held for her, unless it was after midnight and she was bringing him the last glass of anis. Then he would mumble diminutives into her hair as she sat on the floor at his feet, her one dose of affection. Sometimes he would cry at how much she looked like her mother. Then she would tell him it was time for him to go to bed, would help him to clamber out of his armchair and along the corridor to his bedroom. Every night she would come back and clear his glass, wash out his ashtray, and slip his Gauloises and lighter into his jacket pocket ready for four o'clock the next morning when he would leave the apartment for the patisserie.

Last night she hadn't been able to sleep, thinking about the future. How long was she going to have to do this? She was sixteen now and wanted a life beyond the dull village they lived in – beyond the boys who hung around on street corners and called her a whore because of her body. Beyond the distress of a father in eternal mourning for her lost mother.

She had no close friends, for she spent all her free time working in her father's patisserie – despite the tut-tutting of various women of the village who thought it unnatural to keep a girl so locked up. The fact was that the older and prettier his daughter got, the more important Henri Dupont considered it to keep her where he could see her. But what was there in Genevieve's life beyond working either side of her school day and cooking, caring, and cleaning for her Papa? All the girls her age hated her because of her looks, all the boys were too immature, or too silly for her to be interested in them. Her father had few friends apart from his cronies at the Café des Amis, and they were hardly people with whom Genevieve wanted to spend much time. She needed something else in her life.

Seamus lived above the restaurant more or less in a broom cupboard and had his board and lodging for free, along with a little pocket money, in exchange for the apprenticeship. Every night after service had finished and the last customers had left, the staff would sit round one of the tables upstairs, Chevrot would open a bottle of brandy – how good it was would depend on how well the evening had gone – and the chefs would stay and drink till three or four in the morning. Seamus would accept his glass of brandy but his brain would soon tire with the effort of translation. He understood more now than when he had first arrived, but no one made any concessions to speak slowly for him. He was always the first to bed.

This morning, he had woken unusually early, and arrived in the kitchen downstairs to find the night chef swearing at the bread oven. It had, apparently, broken, and the 2 a.m. batch of bread that was meant to have been baked for today's customers lay unrisen on its baking trays. From the man's gesticulations, Seamus gathered that he was to go into town and buy some from the patisserie. Fine by him. Seamus knew where it was; he had once had to rush out mid-service at lunchtime to replenish their stocks when – again – the bread oven had broken down. Guy Chevrot was just too much of a tight-fisted Frenchman to replace it. Anyway, he would enjoy the walk. And so in his chef's white jacket and his blue check trousers, he set off on the mile-long walk to the village.

The morning light shone through the patisserie windows, the dark wood of the walls and ceiling yielding sluggishly to the bright rays lancing through the dust-ridden air. The polished glass counters shot back the rays in reflection, masking the lines of delicate pastries parading like soldiers beneath them. Behind the counter a wall of woven baskets were filling up with baguettes, demi-baguettes, pain rustique, pain de campagne and the special loaf of bread that Henri baked and that was known for miles around. The heavy odour of dark, polished wood mixed sweetly with the scent of sugared almonds, croissants and rising pains aux chocolat. Genevieve was busy collecting the loaves and filling up the baskets, before the seven o'clock opening time.

As he approached it now, squinting against the sun washing up the High Street, Seamus could already smell the sweet perfume of the pastries in the morning air. He had a strange feeling in his stomach: as if something was about to happen. He breathed in deeply, intoxicating himself on the smell, and reached out to seize the brass handle of the shop door. He pulled, it resisted. He looked at his watch: it wasn't quite seven. He'd have to wait. He turned and looked around, as if he might see another patisserie, then, turning back, he cupped his hand round his face to peer through the door.

As he did so, the door was flung open and standing in its place was a figure. Seamus couldn't take it all in at once.

The smell hit him like a wall, the shock of pink candy on her long apron, her bright, bright white hair, her eyes, her slender neck, her chin. He stood, as if transfixed by her face while she reeled from the shock of finding someone right outside the door. The two stared at each other. Their stomachs rolled over.

'I'm sorry,' he blurted out, forgetting his French after half an hour's thinking in English. He didn't know what he was apologising for: for frightening her or for staring. She was staring back.

'You are English?' she asked.

'Yes, yes, I am.'

Genevieve paused, looking at him again with amazement. 'Oh. Hello.' The beauty broke into a smile that dazzled Seamus's whole insides. Her soft pink lips parted to reveal her milky white teeth, and a dimple on either side of her mouth.

'Hello,' he replied, hardly noticing what he was saying.

Genevieve had never seen anyone quite like this man before. He was different from other people round here, older, interesting. And she was very conscious of how big he was. His strong arms wrestled with the seams of his white jacket, his shoulders were wide and his face seemed so dark. He was held in a spell that Genevieve had noticed before in men when they first laid eyes on her. With Seamus it served momentarily to quell his usually rough features.

'Hello,' he said again, after a few seconds.

He was English and his accent and voice thrilled her. It was from far away and a different place: she wanted more of it. Embarrassed by her feelings which, frankly, were all over the place, she smiled at him nervously. Both stood there, holding each other's gaze, languishing in the hypnotic moment.

It was only when Henri shouted for Genevieve, and she jumped and turned, that the trance was broken. She ran into the shop, feeling suddenly guilty for some reason. Seamus paused, then followed her. Genevieve had run back behind the counter and was now speaking through the hatch to a gruff, old man's voice. She reappeared with a tray full of croissants, which she tipped into a wicker basket.

'Excuse me, my English is not good. Er, you want to buy somesing?' she asked, trying to act nonchalantly. In the exchange with her father Genevieve had had time to recover her thoughts, and to mask her confusion in activity. The man meanwhile stood awkwardly, waiting for her attention.

'Yes, yes please. For the restaurant.'

'For the restaurant?'

'Yes, um Les Feuilles du Temps,' confirmed Seamus, pointing vaguely in the direction he had come from.

'*Ah, mais oui, maintenant j'ai compris. Vous avez besoin du pain pour le déjeuner?*'

'Oui, les petits pains. Cent, s'il vous plait.'

'Sans? Without?' replied Genevieve, perplexed.

'A hundred?' tried Seamus.

'*Mais bien sûr,*' she realised, and smiled again – from shyness. He blushed, she blushed, then went back to the hatch to speak to the gruff voice. She was called into the bakery and, not looking at Seamus, she disappeared through swing doors, reappearing a minute later with two great sackfuls of bread rolls.

Now she could not even look up at him; her cheeks burned brightly and her hands were shaking. Her knees felt as if they were about to give way.

Seamus was delighted. He had never seen such exquisite beauty, such young and naive behaviour. The girl was blushing, she couldn't look at him. He took the sacks and his eyes fixed on her face.

'*Merci, mademoiselle,*' he said, then, unable to resist, added in English, instinctively in a lower tone, aware there was someone working in the kitchens behind, 'What time do you finish work here?'

Finally, Genevieve had to look at him. She didn't understand what he had said; she needed to see his face. It was a strong face, capable, full of another world.

Seeing she didn't understand, Seamus said it again slowly, with actions, pointing at his watch, her and the door.

Genevieve didn't know why he was asking the question. *'Aujourd'hui?'*

'Yes, yes, today,' said Seamus gently. Smitten.

'At seven. I finish at seven,' Genevieve murmured back, her blonde hair framing her flushing face.

Seamus smiled at her, his eyes full of amazement, his happiness infectious: she caught the mood too, and her face dimpled into a smile back.

'À ce soir, alors,' he said, picked up the bags of rolls, seized the door and walked up the street as if he was walking on the moon. He noticed nothing, all he could see was her.

Genevieve stood alert, her body twitching in responses she didn't know she had. Her stomach vaulted as she realised she would see this man again, tonight – he must come back! She rushed to the window and watched him disappearing up the street.

Both knew something had happened between them, something physically explosive. Seamus had had women, but none he liked, none who held his attention even, let alone cared for. None had impressed him so much as this charming, gauche young girl – and her beauty! It took his breath away to recall it, and for the first time in longer than he could remember, he felt himself grinning. His concentration was over for the rest of the day.

How on earth was he going to find an excuse to slip away to meet her at seven? He couldn't – he knew it was impossible. That was when the kitchen was at its busiest, with the prep for dinner. As the day wore on, Seamus went through a hundred excuses in his head. He was ill? That wouldn't work, Chevrot wouldn't take that as an excuse not to work. He had to make a phone call? But not one long enough to get him to the village and back. He could send a note. But then he would have to explain to one of the monkey waiters at the restaurant that he wanted a note to go to the goddess in the patisserie. Not really an option. He could go and get more bread – but the ovens would probably be fixed by now and already baking the dinner rolls.

There was nothing he could do to get away. Except walk out. He could just not be there – take out a bag of rubbish and not come back. Seamus couldn't believe he was even contemplating it. He was working so hard to impress Chevrot and had been for months, he couldn't let it go now. But he had to see her again! It would have to be tomorrow morning. There was nothing for it: he would have to sabotage the ovens tonight after everyone had left, and be sent to fetch more bread in the morning. He only hoped she worked there every day. Tomorrow was a Friday. How would he last till then?

Genevieve lingered outside the shop. It was a quarter past seven, her father had shooed her off home to go and make his dinner twenty minutes ago. Genevieve couldn't believe the Englishman wasn't there. She looked up and down the street for the fiftieth time, walked over to the other side and looked again. Then she walked round the back of the shop to the delivery van entrance and waited there. Had she mistaken what had happened between them this morning? In a few minutes her father would be out wanting to know what she was doing. It was now twenty-five past seven. He wasn't coming.

Genevieve felt sick. She had been convinced all day he would arrive. He hadn't. She had got it all wrong. Her throat bloating and strangling her, her eyes pricking with tears, she turned the corner of the road and ran home, blinded by the salt water of her humiliation. She had waited all day through school and her evening shift to see him again, just to glimpse him. She thought he would come and he hadn't.

Back home she got her papa a plate of cheese and ham, a jar of gherkins and a bottle of beer and left it for him on the kitchen table. Then she locked herself in her room, climbed into bed, shut her eyes tight and tried to forget this new emotional hammer-blow to her life.

Stoically, as she had done for weeks after her mother died, after the bad times with her father, after his drinking binges, she got up the next morning, splashed cold water on her face and shut out the thoughts that had been haunting her all night. She forced herself to forget the way her body had felt in the shop yesterday morning, the way it had felt every time she had thought about him yesterday and through the night. Enough was enough. It was fine dreaming, but at the moment she had to do what had been determined for her. She would be going to college in September for two years, then she would have a chance. Her father had told her he wanted the best for her, and he would send her to a university. It was why she was working: saving on staff wages meant Henri had been able to build a little trust fund for his Genevieve. Everything was planned.

She had no right to be silly, she told herself, to invest this man with the responsibility of any part of her life. So why couldn't she shake off his memory? Why had he struck such a chord? As she rounded the corner for the shop, she balled her fists. She must be firm with herself.

And there he was, standing outside the shop, leaning against the window, hands in his pockets. She stopped and stared. He saw her and grinned, dumbstruck again, and her heart leaped into action in her chest. Immediately she thought of her Papa inside and urgently beckoned him away from the shop window.

Seamus followed her as she backed around the corner of the street, and turned to find her quite suddenly there, in front of him. They were close, really close. There was a pulse in Genevieve's brown neck and he could see the beginning of her bosom in the deep V of her white blouse. He looked into her face, turned up to his, and mesmerised, without a thought going through his head, he brought his hand up to her cheek.

His touch sent a shockwave through her. He was so close she could smell him, sense his strength; his presence was overwhelming. She was tall, but the top of her head barely grazed his shoulders. She put her hand up to his, and he caught it, turned it over and stared disbelievingly at her long graceful fingers. He had something to say. He knew it by heart, he had learned it in French last night with his dictionary so he wouldn't get it wrong.

'*Demain, demain,*' he stuttered. He was amazed by how unsettled her presence made him: no one – guardian, teacher, boss, foster parent let alone a woman – had ever disturbed him like this. '*A sept heures, ici, pour le tout jour. Je ne travaille pas demain. Je veux te voir.* Please, please meet me here.'

'*Demain, je dois travailler toute la journée,*' Genevieve gabbled, her thoughts racing. Everything she had been steeling herself into thinking was gone. She was hopelessly vulnerable: she had no control over the way she was feeling.

Seamus's face fell. 'Till seven?'

'*Oui, jusqu'à dix-neuf heures. Non,*' she contradicted herself. She would tell her Papa she was going to visit her aunt in the afternoon, to ask for help with her maths. Henri sometimes let her have the afternoon off as business slowed, and in any case they had an extra person in on a Saturday. Usually the assistant just stayed for the morning but perhaps . . . Genevieve would wing it.

'*À midi, ici,*' she told him, suddenly making up her mind.

'*Midi?*' That meant midday, didn't it?

'*Oui,*' smiled Genevieve, nodding her head. Grasping his

wrist and turning over his strong arm, she pointed at the twelve on his watch face.

'Twelve o'clock,' smiled Seamus, his heart leaping. 'Here tomorrow. OK.'

And that was the beginning of their summer. The beginning of three months of subterfuge, of meeting at night and in school breaks, and stolen moments at weekends. Chevrot gave his staff Saturdays and Sundays off: age had dulled his ambition, and he insisted only on a five-day week now, lunch and dinner. Although previously this had left Seamus bereft and alone, now suddenly his time was filled with the pursuit of Genevieve.

The pair would run off into the fields together, touching each other's bodies, struggling to make themselves understood, him in his pidgin French, her in her textbook English. Together, they taught each other how to communicate. They would swim in rivers, climb the hills and sit, she between his legs, snuggled against his comforting body as they looked out over their world. He would touch her, gently, terrified of breaking her or being rough with her, his hands shaking all the time with his controlled desire. He was so transfixed by her, so mesmerised by her beauty he dare not do anything else. He knew she was a virgin and he couldn't bear to force anything if she was not ready.

He knew she wanted him though. Genevieve had never before felt drawn to anybody, the way she felt drawn to Seamus. With just one touch he made her body react so violently; and as for her mind – she had never guessed it could think like this. But everything felt totally natural and fluid, and in any case she was powerless to stop it. She had never encountered sex before and all she knew about it were the terrible things the nuns at her school threatened and the smutty inanities the other girls boasted of in the toilets. She wanted this man more than anything else.

It happened three weeks after they first met. It was a Sunday: the day free for both of them, and Genevieve, using her aunt as an excuse again, had got away after Mass. Henri had retired quite happily to the Café des Amis. Seamus had caught her in a hug as she rounded the corner to their meeting point behind the cathedral, and kissed her delighted lips again and again. Already they were so comfortable with each other all their inhibitions had disappeared.

They had run off through the woods and down the hill to the other side of the valley. Genevieve had promised to show him 'Le Lac Bleu', the blue pool in a clearing in the woods, about half an hour's walk away. It wasn't a big pool, maybe fifty metres across, and it was blue from the local clay, soft, creamy grey clay that squidged between their toes. They had taken off their socks and shoes and as the day was hot, gloriously hot, Seamus had removed his jeans and T-shirt too. He stood in his white shorts, his lithe body perfectly silhouetted against the glare of the sun.

It was now midday; the birds and cicadas were too hot to sing, and the wood was bathed in silence. They approached the pool underneath a big weeping willow that hung over the bank. Genevieve, in a short, floral dress that the sun shone straight through when she was running out in front of him, laughed as she lifted up the fronds of the tree and disappeared behind them. When she turned round she saw he had followed her. Suddenly, in the cool shade of the tree, she was acutely aware of his toned, muscular legs and she found herself drifting towards him; she caught his hand and, kneeling down in the soft clay, kissed both of his thighs, holding their quivering strength in her soft palms. Her hands travelled down to his calves, feeling his hairs prickle with her touch, and came to rest on the back of his knees. She leaned into his legs, her breasts grazing his knees, her cheek resting against his upper thigh. She felt incredibly close to this person she knew so little about. She kissed his thighs again, overwhelmed by her affection for him, and again her hands ran up the backs of his legs.

She turned her face up to him, but all she could see was the growing mound in his shorts. Seamus's face had glazed over, his eyes flickered open and caught hers, and as he looked deep into her, he felt himself sink to his knees directly in front of her. Placing his hand gently on the nape of her neck, he pulled her head forward towards his until their lips were touching. Her tongue slipped out and felt the wetness of his mouth, while Seamus's other hand shifted up the side of her cotton-clad skin, and rested on the edge of her breast.

Suddenly, urgently, Genevieve wanted him to touch her, to feel her breasts, take control of her, to take over. She felt something inside her waking up, a new sensation of desire that was overpowering the movements of her body. She melted against his flesh, which was hard and taut and strong. Seamus moved his hands down over her back to her buttocks and pulled her into him, forcing her to feel the long hardness straining from his shorts. He lifted her dress over her head in one fluid movement, and kept her eyes held to his. Deliberately he didn't look, sensitive to her virginal nakedness, and first he touched: he brought his hands up to her breasts and closed his eyes in ecstasy as he felt the silky hardness of her button nipples. Her breasts filled the palms of his large hands and felt soft, creamy and alert.

By now, Genevieve had lost the power of conscious action. All she could feel was a wetness between her legs and an urgent dull ache she had to obey. She brought her hands down to his shorts, and discovered the shape, the size and the quivering hardness of his cock. She caressed it, stroking it gently, following her instincts. Encouraged by the soft moans he was now making in her ear, without really knowing what she was doing, she pulled the waistband of his shorts down over his groin and buttocks, keeping her face turned up to his in adoration. Their knees were sinking into the mud now, and as Seamus pulled off his shorts he lay Genevieve down on her back in the soft clay, catching, for the first time, the sight of her milky breasts standing upright in perfect mounds.

He caught his breath. Her body was so beautiful, so perfectly proportioned. This was his first sight of real beauty. All the ugliness he had grown up with melted away, and he felt as if he had been let loose, suddenly given a rare chance to be a different person, to have a different sort of life. He was glimpsing something new.

Reaching out, he traced the shape of her breasts delicately with his fingers, feeling her shake beneath his touch. Now she pulled him down to her urgently, and forced her tongue into his mouth, desperate to be closer to him, in him. Seamus groaned, helpless, and plunged his tongue back into her mouth. The note of urgency ran through both their bodies, and grappling with each other now, they clung together in the soft clay.

Seamus writhed against her body and, twining her knicker elastic in his hand, he yanked down the last barrier between them. His hand floated up between her soft, wet thighs, gently stroking them as he traced his hand nearer and nearer the top of her legs, until it rested on the sweet, pulsing flesh of her clitoris. There he let it rest, letting her take in the shock of his touch.

Genevieve was arching her spine; her head was thrown back, her eyes shut and her mouth had fallen open. Straining to his slow caresses now, her body melted beneath his touch, half-excited with its discovery of this new feeling, half-tremulous at its power.

Seamus closed his eyes in concentration; the discovery of this girl sent desire raging through his body. He tried to blank his mind, and closed his eyes, but no sooner had he done that than he had to open them again to check it was not a wild fantasy. Gripping onto the edge of explosion, he suddenly felt her hand reach down to his cock. Her touch was nearly too much for him.

He pulled away and with his last vestiges of self-control, he looked into her eyes and asked her quickly, 'Do you want this? Genevieve, *tu veux?*' They both knew what he meant and she begged him to continue, overpowered by her own desire.

Now it was too much for Seamus. Desire took over and he moved his knees up between her legs. He was sliding, unable to get a grip in the clay, and felt at the end of his cock the soft wetness of her flesh. The two of them were slipping in the mud and Seamus couldn't remember if he had pushed or fallen, but suddenly he was inside her. Genevieve cried out, half in agony, half in ecstasy, and Seamus closed his eyes in an effort not to come right then. Genevieve was gasping for breath but suddenly her clay-covered hands were all over his back and buttocks as she pushed him further inside her – God, she wanted more, she wanted him in deeper. The pain was ecstatic, and as she thrusted against him, he rolled her over and pushed her up so she was sitting on top of him. With handfuls of clay he smothered her breasts and swirled his hands down over her belly and then up her back into her soft blonde hair.

On top Genevieve was in control. She could draw him in as deep as she wanted and she loved it. Her hair hung around her shoulders and chest in great sticky clumps as she rode up and down. Her face was flushed, her eyelids half-closed. She was riding him now, each elevation easier and more slippery as she seemed to be getting better and better at it, then suddenly she noticed that Seamus's eyes were shut, his mouth was open, and as he cried, 'No, Genevieve, no,' he erupted inside her in great waves of overwhelming passion.

Omelette

2 eggs
Salt and freshly ground black pepper
A good knob of butter

1. First crack the eggs: as we all know, you can't make an omelette without breaking the eggs.

2. Don't whisk the eggs too vigorously. Instead just break up the yolks into the whites with a fork. Season.

3. Melt the butter in a pan and swirl it around until it coats the pan completely.

4. When the butter starts to froth, pour a little back into the egg mixture and stir in. Then pour the mixture into the pan and using a wooden spoon draw in the edges of the omelette towards the centre, allowing the pools of liquid egg on the surface to run back to the sides of the pan.

5. When the omelette is almost set, flip it out onto a plate so it doubles back on itself.

8

'Who's that? Shaw, is that you?'

'Yes. Who's calling?'

'Who do you think it is, you fool. Listen, are Paul or Nigel there?'

'No, no one's here, Chef. I open on a Monday morning.'

'Fuck! Just my luck. Well, you'll have to do then. Now listen carefully because I've only got one phone call and you can't fuck this up. Not like you usually do. Are you listening, Michael?'

'Yes, Chef.'

'Right. Now I'm in the West End Central police station and I need you to get me out. I'm being charged at the magistrates court this morning, and you have to find me someone to turn up there and post the fucking bail. Do you hear? Marylebone Magistrates Court at 10 a.m. Bail will be a five-figure sum. Five figures – got that?'

'Chef, but Chef, who do I call? I don't know anyone with that kind of money!'

'Michael, don't you fuck this up for me. Call Marion – yes, that's it, call Marion Maltese straight away and tell her the situation, and whatever you do, make sure she sorts it out—'

Bip, bip, bip, bip, bip . . .

'That's it – I haven't got any more time. Call Marion, her number is in the address book—'

Michael stared at the receiver in disbelief. He had no idea quite so much was expected of a kitchen porter. Making

the tea, washing the floor, pretty much constant physical
and verbal abuse, sixteen-hour days six days a week, ritual
humiliation, beatings – fair enough. But posting the boss
out of jail? He was left with little choice though: if he
didn't get Seamus out of jail he could kiss goodbye to
his job. He ran his hand through his hair and frowned.
Was all this hard work and punishment really worth it? He
wanted to be a great chef, and he wanted to learn from the
best, but the life Seamus lived and the kitchen he ran were
verging on the absurd. Michael needed advice, he needed it
badly, but the only person who could give it to him was his
dad – he had worked in restaurants all his life, and would
soon tell him if this was normal or not. You didn't get
much response off a ventilator though.

Ring Marion Maltese, that's what he had to do. He had
seen her a few times before, since whenever she came
into the restaurant she made a big show of visiting the
kitchens – something that annoyed Seamus intensely. She
was one of those women Michael knew he would never
understand, and neither did he want to. She would throw
open the kitchen door, wander in as if she owned the
place, a picture of perfect glamour and beauty, her lithe
and fragrant body an astonishment amongst the sweating
hulks of the chefs. Her entrance was always dramatic,
and totally disrupted the thick air of male competition
and ego that flew about the room. Awed and expectant
faces of customers she had brought down with her would
appear behind Marion's shoulder as she tossed a few
flirtatious remarks to Seamus, threw in a deep, husky
laugh then disappeared back upstairs. But there was an
air of insincerity about her that Michael had detected
immediately. He suspected it wasn't Seamus she liked at
all, but his job and his status instead. However, Marion
was the only person Michael had seen Seamus allow into
the kitchen besides staff, so either Seamus didn't realise
this himself, or if he did, then he ignored it.

So Michael guessed this was payback time for Seamus. If Marion was his friend then she would help him out. He looked at his watch – 6:30 a.m. However sweet-natured she might be when she visited the kitchen, Michael knew she wasn't exactly going to appreciate the timing of this call. Nothing for it, though. He ran upstairs to the bar of the restaurant, dug out the Marrow address book, and flipped through the pages to M. There were three numbers for Marion: two landlines and a mobile.

Michael hesitated: he was not very good on the phone, nor was he much good at talking to women. They looked at him strangely, but he had yet to realise this was because they were admiring him rather than finding him wanting. Michael was completely unaware of the attractions of his own body – it was never anything he had ever paid any attention to, other than with the girls from the estate. But they didn't count because they did it with everybody. The thought of talking to this imperious, glamorous woman at half-past six in the morning and asking her to post bail for more money than Michael had ever seen in his life was a fairly challenging prospect. Especially as the kind of people who ate in this restaurant were a world away from his experience. They certainly didn't live on a council estate in Kilburn, take the Number 28 bus twice a day and spend their Sundays staring at a plastic lung. They lived in Knightsbridge duplexes or Holland Park mansions, travelled by chauffeur-driven limousine and spent their Sundays at health farms, probably. But Michael had no choice: taking a deep breath, he picked up the phone and dialled the first number.

'Hello, you have reached the offices of Marvellous PR. I'm afraid there is no one here to take your call at present, so please leave your message after the tone.'

Michael replaced the handset. The second number then.

'Hi, you're through to Marion. Leave a message and I'll call you back.'

Michael hated talking to answer-machines, and as he opened his mouth to speak he realised he had no idea what he was going to say, particularly as Marion didn't have a clue who he was. He hesitated for a few seconds, then put the phone down. He must try the final number. Michael tapped out the digits on the keypad, praying there would be a reply. The line patched through and began to ring.

'Janetta?' screeched a female voice.

'Er – no. This is Michael, actually.'

There was a pause of a few seconds before the voice on the other end demanded: 'Michael who?'

'Michael Shaw from Marrow, the restaurant. Is that Marion?'

'Marrow the restaurant?'

'Yes.'

'Well, what the fuck are you doing ringing me at this time in the morning?'

'Um, Seamus has asked me to.'

'Why? What's happened?'

'Seamus has been arrested and he asked me to phone you to help.'

'Jesus Christ! So who are you again?'

'I'm Seamus's kitchen porter.'

'Is this a joke?' Her voice turned nasty.

'No, no it's not,' insisted Michael. 'Honestly. Seamus needs someone to go to Marylebone Magistrates Court this morning and post bail for him so he asked me to phone you. He's in court at ten o'clock. He said bail would be five figures.'

'He said *what*?'

'He said you would help him. I'm sorry, I'm just passing on the message.'

'Seamus gets his kitchen boy to phone me at six-thirty in the morning, who in turn expects me to get down to some dirty little courthouse and bail that idiot out for a ridiculously large sum of money?!'

'Um, yes.'

'Jesus Christ. Excuse me while I just get over this. I'll call you back in five minutes.'

Marion was astonished. She had been expecting a call from her lover who had mysteriously disappeared half-way through the night, and instead here was some slave from Seamus Bull's kitchen asking her for upwards of £10,000. Had Seamus gone completely mad? Clearly. Still, she assumed this had something to do with Saturday night at Louche. Marion's brain rapidly clicked into gear, despite the early hour. If she was to sort this little mess out then Seamus would owe her. *Really* owe her. And of course, she could bill him for it when she was good and ready . . . She got back on the phone.

'Martin?'

'Er, no, it's Michael.'

'Whatever. I'll deal with it. Your boss will be back with you by lunchtime.'

'Marion, my saviour. What can I say?'

Marion held open the door of her chauffeur-driven Jaguar for a drawn and ruffled-looking Seamus as he bounded down the steps of the courthouse. Leaning back against the sleek navy-blue body of the car, mini-skirted, sunglasses on, Prada bag tucked under her arm, Marion simply smirked. Seamus was relieved and grateful, yes, but he knew that smirk. He wasn't getting this treatment out of friendship. He understood that.

'Get in quickly, before the press realise they are on the wrong side of the building.' Marion had successfully managed to persuade the courthouse's porter to let Seamus out at the side entrance. She didn't want the world knowing her part in this. Yet. At least not until she had got Seamus to agree to it.

'Marion, I can't thank you enough,' he told her now. 'You have no idea what a fucking terrible night I have just had.' By the look of him, Marion could probably guess. His skin looked dirty, his eyes were bloodshot and he stank of stale booze, disinfectant and all manner of unpleasant fragrances Marion sensibly chose not to identify. Still, she couldn't help noticing that even in this state the man looked incredibly alluring – he might just as well have got off his horse, removed his stetson and blown the smoke off the end of his pistol. Seamus leaned over and planted a grateful kiss on Marion's cheek. She wrinkled her elegant nose and unapologetically fished a bottle of Chanel No. 19 from her handbag and sprayed it onto his chest.

'God, darling, do excuse me but I can't get in the car with you reeking like that.'

Seamus winced, but kept silent, grateful to be free and now just needing his shower, his bed and as many painkillers as he could lay his hands on. 'Tell me the worst,' he croaked. 'The review – I've lost the star, haven't I?'

'St Thomas's Hospital please, Driver,' ordered Marion, ignoring him.

'Hospital?' exclaimed Seamus. 'I don't smell that bad, for fuck's sake.'

'Well, darling, I have a plan.'

'You surprise me,' he replied sarcastically, and braced himself for her next words.

'This is the deal: I get the charges against you dropped, then you and I go into business together and build the biggest and the best food emporium in the country. Opposite Mirage.'

'Yeah right. What do you mean opposite Mirage?' Marion knew she had Seamus's interest now.

'Yes. I have been doing some work on your behalf this morning and am now in possession of a number of facts I think you should be aware of. First fact: you are *not* going to get your third star this year, although Coq will keep all of his. Second fact: one of the most powerful food journalists in the country hates your guts! Even more so now than he ever did, and whatever restaurant you build, and wherever you build it, he will slate it. You will never, as long as Rufus Ransome writes and lives, be the owner of three stars. What is more, the aforesaid critic is currently lying in state in the private wing of St Thomas's Hospital with a bump on his head the size of a grapefruit and only one thing on his tiny little bruised mind. Which is to sue your sorry arse into a Third-World-sized debt. Third fact: the *News of the Globe* was a set-up – for which Emmanuel Coq and Rufus Ransome are responsible.'

'You what?!'

'Coq wanted to ensure you were not cooking when Ruthless went in to do his review. Your weak spot was not too difficult to identify.'

'You fucking what?!' Seamus's pallor intensified and, despite his fatigue, he felt ire rising up inside him. 'Coq paid the journalist to seduce me?'

'Yup, and Ruthless knew about it.'

'The fucking lowlife—'

'Seamus, it's far too early in the morning for me to listen to your stream of abuse. The final fact is that we are now on our way to St Thomas's Hospital so that you can apologise to Ruthless, personally, face to face. Now, I have arranged for an army of press men to be there to witness your apology, so for God's sake smarten yourself up a bit.'

Caviar Tart

1 pastry case
8 hardboiled eggs, shelled
150g unsalted butter
½ teaspoon grated lemon rind
5 spring onions, chopped finely
300ml thick sour cream
1 pot finest Iranian beluga caviar

1. Whizz the eggs, butter, onions and lemon rind together until the mixture goes glug. Season to taste.

2. Spread the mixture over the bottom of a pastry case and 3 centimetres up the sides. Leave to chill for 40 minutes in the fridge.

3. Spread the sour cream over the crust and leave to chill for 1 hour.

4. Spoon the beluga thickly and generously over the cream. Serve in slices with a glass of champagne.

9

While Seamus was making his escape from the courthouse, Michael was staring into a murky brown liquid bubbling inside one of Marrow's steaming cauldrons. Underneath his chef whites he itched: the air conditioning was still not fixed and the thin film of sweat that coated his body was chafing against the starched cotton of his work clothes. The bones in the pot rose to the seething surface every now and then, offering a flash of brilliant white against the dark liquid in which they danced. A glimpse of orange would also occasionally emerge as a sliced carrot was buoyed up to the surface, or the white-veined skin of an onion slice that would shyly peek an alabaster cheek.

He checked that the muslin-wrapped julienne of herbs was still holding together – God forbid Seamus should find a stray thyme leaf in his precious stock. He had brought the huge saucepan to the boil over three hours ago; by now, the stock was developing the full, rich flavour his boss demanded. Soon it would be time to heave the scalding metal tub off its gas ring and drain the liquid into another container to cool. Twice already in the past six months Michael had managed to tip some of the boiling liquid over himself; the red blisters on his hands refused to dry out and heal when, day in and day out, they were subjected to the heat and moist conditions of his steaming prison.

He poked a long metal spoon into the pan, pushing the veal bones to the bottom, stirring the julienne around in the liquid. Then he scooped a tiny amount of the veal essence out in the curve of the spoon and, blowing the steam away, raised the ladle to his lips. His nostrils were overpowered by the pungent, meaty smell, and he allowed the reduction to coat his lips and tongue, smacking them together in the way Seamus had taught him. His mouth reacted to the fleshy flavour, but he knew he could squeeze more from the bones, reduce the liquid further, strengthen even more the stock that was the base of all Bull's great creations.

'Shaw – that stock ready yet?' demanded Paul, temporarily in charge in Bull's absence.

'Another half an hour and it'll be perfect.'

'Not fucking good enough, Vermin. What time were you in this morning to put it on? Not fucking early enough obviously; we have lunch service beginning in half an hour and we need more stock now. Stay and clean the ovens again tonight. And every night until you learn about timing in this kitchen!'

Paul was grinning, enjoying the jeering he was allowed to employ as temporary boss, and for good measure he swiped Michael over the head with a twisted tea towel. The corner caught Michael in the eye, causing him severe pain, but he refused to cry out. He ducked away and turned his head so Paul wouldn't see the water running from his eye down his cheek. Inside his blood boiled, but Michael held himself in check. Paul was even more of a bully than Seamus; as a natural coward he was completely inadequate until given the decoration of leadership. Then he would release his cruel side, but Michael was damned if he was going to let him get any satisfaction from it.

'I'm sorry, Chef, but tonight I have to leave early. I did tell Mr Bull last week. You see, I have an appointment with my father's doctors at the hospital. I can't change it – they won't see me on Sunday. They say I have to come tonight.'

'And who's going to do the service for dinner then?'

'Well, Mr Bull said he was going to try and find a replacement.'

'And did he?'

'I don't know.'

'Well, if he didn't, then you can't go, can you?'

Michael paused, wondering how best to tackle Paul. Certainly he couldn't argue with him; he couldn't let it look like his authority was being undermined.

'No, Chef,' he said finally.

'End of story then,' crowed Paul, warming to his newly acquired managerial skills.

Michael hoped Seamus would show up later – he really needed this time off and Seamus had understood that. The doctors were worried about his father's progress on the ventilator and were concerned that his coma was irreversible. They were also worried that, should he ever recover, he would be severely brain-damaged. Michael wanted his dad back desperately: he was all he had. But the doctors, after eighteen months of round-the-clock care, were beginning to suggest that perhaps Michael ought to consider an alternative solution. They insisted he meet them tonight. He had to go.

'Oi – get the fucking phone will you,' shouted Paul as his massive jowls wrapped themselves around a large ham roll. Michael was now halfway through heaving the stockpot off the stove and it was only with a huge effort that he was able to return it and stop the phone ringing before it rang off of its own accord.

'Kitchens,' he gasped.

'Erm, hello. I – please may I speak with Seamus Bull?' The girl's voice was soft, hesitant. Clipped, with some sort of European accent, it was also impossibly sexy, despite its quivering tone. Michael's whole body shook in reaction. It was a voice like he had never heard before.

It took him a moment to gather himself, before replying: 'No, I'm afraid Seamus isn't here at the moment. Can I take a message for you?'

'Please, what time will he be there?' The voice was still

timid, trying to remain calm, but Michael could hear the panic in it.

'I'm sorry, I don't know. He's usually here now, it's just that . . . well, he has some other business. I hope he will be in this evening.'

'What time, please?'

'Well, he should be here by half six, seven o'clock.'

'OK, thank you, bye bye.' And the line went dead.

'There you are, you see – that weren't too bad, were it? I told you he wouldn't be there, and now you know when he will be there so you can go and surprise him. Perfect, innit?'

Mave was delighted – she hadn't had so much fun in years. Little French Orphan Annie walks in off the streets, looking like a cream bun all wrapped up in pink string – and she's only the ex-girlfriend of London's biggest chef! There had to be something in it for Mave somewhere. Just so long as she kept the girl on her side, it could be her fifteen minutes of fame. And it was something to tell the girls later down the Crown and Goose. Gassin' Mary would be well put out by Mave's luck. Always claiming her Bill had every pop star and member of the Royal Family in the back of his cab – well, this time Mave had Seamus Bull's ex-girlfriend working for her in her café – so you can just stick that up your jumper, Mary.

Genevieve stared at her boss doubtfully. She had been forced to admit the connection when Mave had spotted the shock in her face and the discrepancy in change from the white pepper. She clearly never missed a trick. Why had she felt the need to buy a paper all of a sudden? she had demanded, and as not even a crack member of the CIA would be likely to withstand questioning from Mave, Genevieve only lasted two minutes before cracking.

She hadn't told her the whole story, of course – just that she hadn't seen him in a few years and was thinking of looking him up, but that had been enough for Mave. She had Genevieve on the phone, with her on the extension in the office, quicker than she could roll a bacon sarnie. Genevieve had guessed Seamus probably wouldn't be there – he could still be in prison for all she knew – but she had to admit she was burning to make contact in some way.

What she was going to do now though, she had no idea. But she could tell Mave did. Curiously though, she was feeling stronger by the minute. It seemed Seamus's world was not so perfect, not so self-assured, and spotting his weaknesses made her feel bolder, better equipped to deal with him when the time came. She had so much to ask him, to throw at him, and yet at the same time she had this uncontrollable urge to be back in his arms again, to let him transport her to a different place, as he had done before, to smother her with his attention, treat her as she wanted to be treated – no, she knew it wouldn't be like that. She wouldn't fall for him again, she told herself.

'Driver, pull over here on the right, will you?' The chauffeur drew up against the kerb just beyond the Ritz Hotel. *Caviar House* read the sign on the shop window above the reflected sleek curves of the Jaguar. Superimposed over the racks of caviar, bottles of obscure Polish vodka and the delicately engraved silver and crystal implements for the disposal of said items, were the two figures in the back of the car. One was Marion – erect, alert, leaning forward – the other was slumped, dishevelled, his head buried in his hands. Seamus. He was tired, very tired. He needed to sleep, he needed to wash and he needed clean clothes. He was also irritated, but too tired to get angry. He didn't like it when someone else was in charge. Even when it was Marion.

'Right, Sweetie, now you pop in there and buy Rufus a suitable Get Well Soon present.'

Seamus slowly turned his face towards Marion. It wore

an expression of pure disbelief. But she was not fooling about.

'I'm serious, Seamus. If we are going to make this plan work you will have to eat the odd mouthful of shit, but I promise you, you'll have the last laugh.'

Seamus was not following Marion, and his sense of irritation was increasing. 'Marion, I'm not doing anything until you tell me what your grand plan is,' he snapped. 'I'm knackered, I'm dirty, I stink, I've just spent twelve hours in a police cell with only a kiddie fiddler and a bastard hangover for company, and right now I'm meant to be in my restaurant prepping the lunch service, not farting around with you in the back of a motor parked outside the Ritz with you ordering me to go and buy my sworn enemy a pot of beluga. Excuse me if my instinct is to tell you to fuck off.'

'Excuse *me* if I remind you that you are in no position to tell me to fuck off when I have just posted a £10,000 fee for your early release from jail, Seamus. Now I'm about to make your fortune, starting with the £10,000 I borrowed on your behalf. And it all begins with you walking into that caviar shop, buying the biggest tin of beluga in stock, one of those little mother-of-pearl spoons they do to eat it with, and presenting it to Rufus – *graciously* – in front of the national press. You are going to apologise for any offence caused, say something along the lines of "moment of madness", and offer to pay for his treatment. Then you are going to announce your contrition: how Rufus was right, how Marrow is not working in its present incarnation, and how you are, in tribute, going to be temporarily closing it down.'

Marion paused for breath, and to think, briefly. 'No, don't say temporarily just yet,' she went on. Seamus was speechless. 'Just say you are going to close it down. Then you will pose – smiling – for a picture with Rufus, crouching at his bedside, proffering your caviar – label to the camera, obviously. And you will be looking very humble. Say something about jail teaching you a lesson. Rufus will then be forced to drop his charges against you so he does not appear peevish – he will think he has won anyway – then a week later we will call a press conference and announce we have bought the lease for the site opposite Mirage. Then, like a phoenix from the flames, the new Marrow will be born. Bigger, better, more commercial, more marketable – and it will wipe out Mirage completely. *Now* do you get my drift?'

Seamus stared at Marion. If he didn't know her better, he would think her a lunatic. He had never heard anything like it. 'Brilliant,' he said sarcastically, 'but where exactly are we going to get the money for this site?'

'Well, I shall own twenty-five per cent – the bank have agreed to lend me the money against the collateral of Marvellous PR, and there is the divorce settlement from my last husband I have yet to invest. Fifty per cent will be owned by Salvatore, with whom I had a very pleasant conversation this morning. He is, as you can imagine, desperate now to get you off his street due to the fact that you are exciting far too much of the wrong sort of attention. He is finding it particularly irksome trying to conduct his business discreetly when the country's press is parked outside his door. The last twenty-five per cent will, of course, come from you.'

'But I don't have any capital.'

'Then you'd better find some, otherwise you will find yourself employed by me and Salvatore on a chef's wage. Frankly, darling,' and here Marion changed her tone, dropping her voice down an octave, softening her glaring green eyes, and leaning across to place one of her carefully manicured talons on Seamus's knee, 'you haven't got any choice. If you don't apologise to Rufus he will sue you, and even if you defeat him you will spend the next six months in court fighting the case. By which time Salvatore will have terminated your contract on Marrow and you will find yourself without a restaurant and without any money. And without a PR. Now be a good boy and go into Caviar House, buy the best bloody fish eggs you can find and hurry along with me to the hospital. When we get there do not open your mouth – just follow me and say and do only what I tell you.'

Seamus let out a low groan, and returned his head to his hands. She was right. His back was against the wall. Slowly he reached for the handle, opened the door, heaved himself out of the car, and staggered into the shop. As Marion watched his figure rippling in the morning sunlight, reluctant, yet ha! resigned, she sat back in the seat, and allowed her own body to relax for the first time that day. Her ruby lips broadened into a smirk, and she allowed herself a smug flicker of self-satisfaction as she reached into her handbag for her packet of Cartier. Her fortunes too were about to take a new turn. If this venture came off she would never have to work in PR again. Her long fingers flipped the lid of her silver lighter, spun the flint, and conjured a tall yellow flame from her fist.

Rufus heaved himself up on the mountain of pillows provided to support his substantial frame. Instinctively he reached one pudgy hand to the swollen purple lump on the right-hand side of his forehead, and winced in pain.

'Damn that uncouth brute,' he cursed for the two-thousandth time that day, but with little feeling. No, Rufus was not really mad. In fact, although he could never admit it, he was secretly delighted. A copy of today's *Standard* lay open on his lap, and he stared once again at his picture on page three, next to Bull's. Really, it was the most remarkable media coverage for such a trifling little event, but coverage Rufus wholly welcomed. He had never been page three news before, but Bull's attempt to knock his head off had granted him celebrity access. Suddenly he was a star, and how marvellous it was! At that moment there was a knock on the door.

'Come,' croaked Ruthless, in his best dying tones.

'Rufus, how wonderful to see you!' Into the room strode Emmanuel Coq, elegant in his Boateng suit and Gucci loafers, his thinning dark hair swept back immaculately from his gaunt Roman face. 'What a dreadful thing to have happened. I have come to offer my condolences,' he said, proffering a small silver tin in Rufus's direction.

'Oh, my goodness,' spluttered Rufus, quite overcome with the thrill of having the country's – some might even say the world's – premier chef visit him personally in his hospital bed. Flushing profusely, he accepted the gift, and read aloud off the tin. '"Iranian Imperial Caviar" – my, what a treat, Emmanuel. You really shouldn't have. I say—'

'Please, don't,' interrupted Coq. 'It was the least I could do for you after everything you have been through. Honestly, what can I say? Such unbelievably barbaric behaviour from that brute. How are you feeling?'

'Oh well, you know, I mustn't grumble, but the doctors are convinced my concussion is still lingering, and I've even had to have a brain scan. The results were very worrying, but Sister says she should be able to discharge me soon. As for this ghastly swelling,' and again Rufus heaved a flabby paw up to his brow, 'God alone knows when I can be seen in public again. It does so ache, and clogs up the sinuses appallingly. I suffer from the most dreadful headaches in the afternoon, I can't tell you. I do hope it is not permanent, otherwise Bull will be paying very dearly, that much I *can* tell you.'

'On that point,' broke in Coq, keen to halt the litany of self-pity, 'I wanted to speak to you actually, Rufus. Tell me,' he asked, drawing up a chair and suddenly looking very grave, 'is it true you are pressing charges against Bull?'

'Indeed, my dear chap, quite true. Don't you think it is

the only thing one can do? I mean, for pity's sake, I haven't even had a darned apology out of him yet.'

'Well, how interesting. And I assume your paper will be financing the court case?'

'Um, well, I hadn't quite thought that far ahead . . .'

'Because you *have* thought of the implications of such a public scandal?'

'What do you mean?'

'Well, we both know that Bull is nothing but an uncouth yob,' and here Coq leaned across conspiratorially towards Rufus, 'someone who would never understand a gentleman's code, if you know what I mean. He would stop at nothing – *nothing* – you can be sure, to wriggle out of such a mess.' Here Coq paused, and stared into Rufus's face to see if he had caught his drift. Rufus stared expectantly back, not too sure what it was Coq was driving at. Coq began again.

'Let us say that there are certain . . . how can I put this? . . . *practices*, that Bull knows about and could probably mention in court, or to the media, that may, should it come to it, perhaps be used against us in a way we might find it difficult to ignore.'

But Rufus's face remained as blank as a ball of puff pastry. Coq drew in an irritated breath and persisted. 'A certain "freelance journalist" employed to massage the load on his shoulders . . .'

'Oh!' Suddenly Rufus found Damascus. 'Yes, yes indeed, I catch your meaning. But surely . . .'

'Well, who's to say, Rufus? Of course it doesn't stop there, you know what I'm saying. Certain hospitality that you have enjoyed at my expense – freely given from the bottom of my heart, from one friend to another, of course – but from the lips of Bull it could suddenly become, dare I say it, a charge of,' and here Coq paused for effect, and looking Rufus right in the eye pronounced the word, '*bribery*?'

The accusation hung between them like an unexploded cluster bomb. Coq allowed the pause to continue just long enough before he swept the foul word away.

'Now, it would never do to have someone like Bull up in the dock, allowed free rein to spout what he liked about our gentle art, would it, old friend?'

Suddenly, Rufus's headache had returned. He looked over at Coq, who was leaning into him, urgently, in the bedside chair, his face tight. Rufus knew Coq had a point. He had never thought it before, but all those press trips to France, those cases of wine at Christmas, the hampers on his birthday, the hospitality in uncles'/cousins'/friends' hotels, not to mention all those free meals – even the set-up with the supposed journalist. With a good lawyer Bull could bring the house down on the cosy relationship people like Rufus enjoyed with people like Coq.

'Yes, yes, well, I do see what you mean,' said Rufus, his head buzzing with confusion as he wrapped his brain around the implications of what Coq was saying.

'Good, that's settled then. I do hope you feel better soon, Rufus, and should you decide to drop the charges, you know I will be delighted to host a recuperation feast for yourself and a few friends once you are out of this Godforsaken antiseptic pit.' And with that Coq wrinkled his nose, stood up, shook Rufus firmly by the hand, and turned for the door. Just as Marion, Bull, a photographer and an excited-looking journalist clutching a notepad and pencil came bursting through it.

'Emmanuel!' shrieked Marion, momentarily thrown off-balance – but only momentarily. 'How wonderful to see you. Here to offer your sympathy, no doubt?'

'Yes indeed, and just on my way out, actually. I see you've brought quite a party with you, so I shall leave you to it,' he smirked, and weaving past the hack and the snapper, negotiated the deflated hulk of Seamus, last in the door. Seamus, on seeing his rival, stood up squarely to greet him.

'Coq.'

'Bull.' The two men nodded to each other, then Bull stood aside to allow Coq to pass, closing the door behind him.

By now Rufus was quite stunned, not to mention petrified by the towering presence of the man who had so recently committed such heinous injury to his person. In the tiny room on the private ward there was only enough space for one or two visitors, but now Rufus's room contained four extra bodies, one of whom – Seamus – was loitering in a manner which seemed to take up as much room as possible, thought Rufus. But he had never received so much high-level attention in his life – he was proud and yet shaking like a leaf.

The photographer was barely in before he was snapping away at him, and this served to concentrate Rufus's energies. His vanity eventually got the better of him, and aware of his rather unflattering pose he managed to splutter: 'Put that damned thing away! What the hell is going on here? Don't take any more pictures of me!' Then, his agitation at seeing the perpetrator of his lump again becoming difficult to control, he screamed, 'And what are *you* doing here, Bull? Get out now! I'll not have you anywhere near me. Nurse!' he cried, adopting a most pitiful pose.

Seamus was trying hard to stifle a laugh at the ridiculous sight of Rufus thrashing around like a walrus on his sea of pillows, but was saved by Marion stepping directly between the two of them.

'Rufus, please, calm down. Seamus has merely come to apologise. He knows he did the most dreadful thing on Saturday night, and pleads drunkenness and insanity. He will never lay a finger on you again, of that I absolutely assure you. I am, by the way, now acting on behalf of Seamus, so you have nothing to fear as you know I have your best interests at heart. Now Seamus, come here, make your apology.' Then, mouthing sotto voce across the room,

Marion beckoned again to the photographer. 'Get this shot in. Rufus, smile!'

A blinding flash caught a startled Rufus reaching out to grab the bucket of beluga that Seamus was passing across the room to him as reluctantly as possible, trying to maintain as much distance as he could between himself and the repulsive fat man.

'Wonderful, well done!' beamed Marion. 'Now, Rufus, I do hope there are no hard feelings. You know it was just a mistake, and Seamus is so dreadfully sorry, aren't you, darling?'

She glared at Seamus and nodded for him to respond. Gritting his teeth, Seamus drew himself up to his full height, looked down at the snivelling lump cowering beneath him, and doing his best to drive the sarcasm out of his voice, said, 'Rufus, I am very sorry I hurt you. It was an accident, and I would like you to accept my apology.' In the far corner of the room the journalist was scribbling frantically as the photographer blinded the entire party yet again with another flash.

'Now Rufus,' interrupted Marion again before Seamus could lose his calm. 'We also want you to know that we have taken on board the very wise words of your review,' Rufus's eyes darted nervously between Marion and Seamus, expecting either one of them to pounce at any minute, 'and we have decided to act upon them. Haven't we, Seamus?'

'Oh yes, Marion, we have,' glowered Seamus, a smirk forming on his face as he began to enjoy the deception. Marion paused for effect and waited till she had Rufus's full attention, then, with all the pomp and ceremony she could muster, and a backward glance to the journalist to check he was getting it all, she announced: 'Rufus – Seamus Bull is closing Marrow down.'

The perfect food combinations

Some marriages are made in heaven

Duck and Orange
Strawberries and Cream
Tomatoes and Basil
Bangers and Mash
Foie Gras and Sauternes
Caviar and Vodka
Coffee and Chocolate
Lamb and Rosemary
Bacon and Eggs
Pork and Apple
Marmite and Toast

10

Genevieve sat on the edge of her bed. Once again she found herself alone. She was used to just her own thoughts for company, though; even at college in Paris, although she knew plenty of people and was popular enough, she didn't have anyone she could really talk to. Now she felt utterly useless. After all the effort it had taken to get to this city — now it seemed she couldn't follow through the objective. She resented being bullied by Mave but knew that she was secretly waiting for someone or something else to take control. Why?

She had to admit to herself it was because she wasn't sure she was doing the right thing. Six years had passed since she last saw Seamus, and *mon Dieu*, how much she had changed in that time! He must have changed too. He wasn't a boy any more, he was a man — she could see that from the photo in the paper. Of course she had followed his progress — the Parisian gastronomic journals she had got her hands on had written fulsomely of his talent and his ground-breaking restaurant.

Seamus Bull wasn't an employee bullied around in a kitchen any more, he was what he had always said he wanted to be: his own boss, with his own business. But he was also in the public eye these days, behaving badly, a real liability. From what she had seen of him so far, she was less and less inclined to confront him.

This behaviour — assaulting someone, getting arrested — was all too similar to the way he had treated her once he had left France. This was the side of the man she hadn't understood, and she had come here to find out which was the real Seamus. Should she root him out after all? Did she want to confront him, or did she not care; was it just an excuse for someone to rescue her from her miserable life? Did she need someone else to rescue her? Why couldn't she do it on her own?

These questions were difficult to answer, but something told her that the passion the two of them had shared that summer didn't come twice. There was no doubt that what had passed between them had been exceptional, and had shown her a dimension to life she had never known existed. She needed to see him again to find out if that feeling was locked in the past, irrecoverable, or whether it could be revived, and acted upon. Her life could not progress until she knew the answer to this. Genevieve laughed sadly. She could deal with abortion, death, cancer, mind-numbing work, poverty, and rejection: but she couldn't confront this one man.

She shifted uncomfortably on the thin, creaky bed and lay down facing the stained grey wall, her thoughts tangled and spinning. She smiled to herself as she realised she was even thinking in English now: she remembered Seamus telling her once, as they walked along a flower-strewn country lane together in the evening sun, that the night before he had dreamed of her, and that in his dream they had spoken in French. He was so excited because he said he had been speaking it fluently. She had marvelled at the joy he got out of that achievement, but she understood it now: she was getting a kick out of being able to work at Mave's caff, and developing her own life here.

No, she decided finally. She could not deny the huge underlying urge to see Seamus one more time. Her motive was partly sexual, but she also had questions she wanted answered. She also realised she was simply curious. She wanted to see how six years had changed a man she had loved – maybe still loved. Was he still sexually attractive? She had met no one to match his magnetism before or since. And how had he allowed his success to turn him into this monster who now featured on the front page of newspapers?

Genevieve vowed she would go to Marrow that very same night. Mave was right – she should just front him out and get it over with as quickly as possible. The longer she left it, sitting here stewing in her horrid hotel room, the more difficult it would become. The man on the phone had said Seamus would be there by seven. That's when she would go. Just turn up at the restaurant, walk in the door, say hello and see what happened. She had nothing to lose and everything to prove: she was alone in this world and she had to take responsibility for no one's actions apart from her own now. And if it all went pear-shaped then she would go home: but at least she would know once and for all. She would know who he was and how he was.

Genevieve looked at her watch. Five o'clock. Mave had let her go early, on condition that she told her everything in a blow-by-blow account at work the next day. She had been practically dribbling with anticipation. Genevieve picked up her washbag, let out a sigh, and set off for the shower to get ready to go out.

It was still a hot evening, and she had plenty of time, so she thought she would walk. Setting off up Earls Court Road she was soon amongst the grander dwellings of Kensington, then, checking her *A to Z*, she made her way up Kensington Church Street to Notting Hill Gate. London was sluggish in the heat but the people were cheerful tonight, smiling at her as she walked past. The traffic on the Gate was deafening when she arrived – it was the rush hour and convoys of buses were clogging up the lanes. She took the subway to the other side and set off down Pembridge Villas. The houses here were even more ridiculously huge: ornate and impossibly grand, but so beautifully white in the evening sun, framed by the blossoming trees that lined each side of the street.

Suddenly Genevieve felt hot: the walk had made her perspire, and she cursed herself for not getting a bus. Damp patches were beginning to form on her white T-shirt, and she rustled her long, cotton skirt about her legs to make a draught and cool herself. She reached into her handbag for a tissue. It was at that point the butterflies set in. The anticipation of the confrontation suddenly hit her in the stomach and she began to tremble with nerves. What if he didn't recognise her? Well, at least then she would know it hadn't meant the same to him. She stopped walking and leaned against one of the garden walls, taking deep breaths. Clenching and unclenching her fists, she forced herself onward.

The staff at Marrow sat round one of the tables, stunned. Two weeks' free wages and a possible job at the end of it, Seamus had promised them. Paul had peered at Seamus doubtfully. He knew all this was coming from Marion, and he didn't like it. He couldn't understand what she was playing at. What's more, he suspected his boss didn't like it either, but was unable to admit it.

'I know it's a shock but it's time for us to move on from this. We will never get that third star now – not because we're not good enough, but because of the prejudices of a certain man, and I think we all know who I am talking about. There's no use us working our butts off six days a week for little return if we're not going to get the rewards we deserve. It's time, boys, that we were paid some real money.'

Seamus paused, took a slug of his Armagnac and resumed. 'I can't tell you what the plan is yet because it's all still meant to be completely secret, and none of you must breathe a word to anyone. Suffice to say it will be bigger and better and there will be good jobs there for each and every one of you, should you want them.'

The staff were quiet, regarding their boss with affection. So what if he was the biggest bully in the world? He also managed to inspire incredible loyalty amongst the people who worked for him because they knew he was motivated by passion – a passion for his food, and a passion for excellence. His ambition motivated all those around him, and they all believed in everything he said and did. He was the boss, and he was the best.

Paul and Nigel, however, who knew Seamus personally and had watched the disintegration of his social exploits from mild fray to carnage over the recent months, thought differently.

'Paul, will you cancel all the orders with the suppliers tonight? We're not going to open here ever again. Pay them what you need to. Michael, will you sort out the kitchen? Chuck all the perishable foods away and freeze everything you can. Freeze all that stock you made up this morning as well: those veal bones cost a fortune. Nigel, will you deal with the maintenance? Cancel the cleaners, we don't need them any more, and cancel the rubbish collection as well. Adèle, you'll have to leave some sort of message on the answerphone saying we're closed, but not a hint that we may be opening again. And I'm afraid you'll have to phone all the tables reserved for tonight and the next three months and inform them what has happened. Sarah, you can help her with that. Be as polite as you can – no use pissing off the clientèle more than we have to. The situation is delicate, as you can imagine, but I'll tell you all as soon as I have something definite to report.

'In the meantime, take two weeks' holiday – on me – and let's meet back here a fortnight today. And before I go, I just want to say thank you to all of you for everything you have poured into this restaurant.' Here, with uncharacteristic emotion, Seamus glanced down at the floor and only just regained control of his voice, 'Yes, we have not got our third star but we still deserve it and we will have to compensate for it in other ways. You are a great team and although I know I'm not the easiest of bosses, I value you all individually and collectively. Thanks.' And with that Seamus got up and walked down to the other end of the restaurant, his hands on his hips, staring out of the window.

The staff meanwhile, once Seamus was out of sight, let out a collective gasp of disbelief. This was the moment when they were most impressed with their master. Not when he was shouting at them, or banging them over the head with a saucepan, but when they were basking in the glow of favouritism. Under the rare and strained affections of such a difficult boss, his staff became emotional. Adèle was forced to reach for a handkerchief, and the waiters were looking distinctly uncomfortable.

Eventually they moved, acting on their instructions. Together they picked up the chairs and placed them upside down on the tables. The sommeliers went to their trolleys and started cleaning their implements, wrapping them up and packing them carefully away. Paul went downstairs to the kitchens and began phoning the suppliers. 'Just as well,' he grumbled quietly to himself. 'We've actually sacked every fish supplier in London by now.'

Watching his staff shut down the restaurant suddenly seemed incredibly depressing, and Seamus couldn't bear it. Clapping his hands together he announced: 'Drinks on me in the Ladbroke Arms,' referring to the pub at the bottom of the road that had become something of a staffroom for them all. 'I'll see you there when you've finished.' And with that he walked out of the front door without a backward glance.

The staff visibly relaxed when he left the restaurant, and they all began talking at once. Some conjectured that this was the end of the line for Seamus Bull, for although there was no doubt about his talent, his behaviour had definitely deteriorated in the last six months, most agreed. But none were tempted – yet – to return those phone calls begging them to take jobs in other restaurants all over the city. An ex-staff member from Marrow was a valuable commodity. Despite their fixed set of ideas about how a job should be done, they were always fired by Seamus's enthusiasm for food and were blessed with the experience of watching and learning from a great chef. It was, without doubt, a lucrative training, depending on how long you could hang on under Bull's violent tutelage: how long you could last before his temper cracked you. Albert Bresson, the maitre d', seemed convinced this was the end of the road for him: he had been looking to retire anyway and he conceded that, while working for Seamus had been one of the most challenging periods of his career, it had also taken about ten years off his life expectancy. Sarah was stunned, terrified by this new freedom. She felt like a fairground goldfish who can't swim out of the plastic bag into its bowl.

Everyone, however, was curious about this new place. Where was it? What could it be? Didier said gloomily that if it was a money-spinner then it was most likely a national chain of Marrow pizza and pasta bars, with ice cream scooped from a plastic tub and pre-prepared toppings to sprinkle on top. Michael, although devastated that this looked like it could be the end of his dream apprenticeship, was privately relieved that he was now going to be free to meet with the doctors at the hospital. He'd expected to have to fake an illness or worse just to bunk off, and that would have cost him his job anyway. At least this way he had two weeks' pay in hand before he had to get something else. There was no way Seamus would take Michael with him to the new place, he thought resignedly. The boss hated him – that much was obvious, because he wasn't like Paul or Nigel or the rest of the tough boys who worked in Seamus's kitchen, and because he refused to subscribe to the boot camp mentality. He fell in with it, but he knew that Seamus knew he rejected it in his head.

Needless to say, everyone had now gone off to the pub, leaving him to clear away and lock up. He was just giving the floor a final sweep when he heard the delivery bell go at the top of the stairs. It was seven o'clock – no one delivered at this hour and, anyway, Nigel had cancelled all the orders. He knew Adèle had cancelled all the tables tonight; only some of the ones for lunch tomorrow had been uncontactable. He leaned his broom against the kitchen wall and climbed the stairs.

The person standing outside the door was definitely not a delivery man. Most emphatically not. Michael stood staring at Genevieve for what seemed like a full minute while she rang the bell again and made signals that he should let her in. Her clothes were loose but the proportions of her body were plain enough, topped by the most exquisite face. Michael thought he had died and gone to heaven, until interrupted by another ring, when he finally made it as far as the door and opened it up. By now the woman's face was looking confused, especially when she peered past him and saw all the chairs up on the table.

'Hello. I'm sorry to disturb you, but are you closed?'

Michael immediately recognised the voice from the phone that morning. This was the body that went with the voice. Amazing. The girl looked decidedly puzzled – as well she might.

'Yeah, we are, I'm afraid. I spoke to you on the phone this morning, I think – you were looking for Mr Bull?'

'Yes,' said the girl, obviously relieved something was understood between them. Michael and the staff were quite used to Seamus's women turning up at the restaurant, in various states of satisfaction – either very, because they had what Seamus called an FFG (Freshly Fucked Grin) plastered over their faces, or three weeks after the event when they would appear not very satisfied at all, as Seamus would have since declined to get in touch with them. Could this woman be one of them?

She was not Seamus's usual type. They were usually dolled up head to toe in some slinky designer number and turned up at the door with one leg bent, the other tucked behind them, balancing coquettishly on their heels. This girl looked like she had a much more important mission. And she was foreign, which was strange. Also, she wasn't treating Michael with the disdain most of them did, looking down their noses snootily at the hired help. He knew they did it because they were desperately trying to maintain an element of cool when it was obvious they were only here for Seamus's body, but still it was rather unpleasant to be on the receiving end of it.

Normally Michael couldn't even look them in the eye – it was so excruciatingly embarrassing when he was the one sent up to say Seamus wasn't in when he quite clearly was, because he was famous for always cooking in his own kitchen. However, this girl had such an open and candid look about her he couldn't help but meet her gaze. Quite often he found it hard to look anyone in the eye, and he wore on his face a shuttered expression, as protection against the outside world. But he felt instantly at ease with Genevieve. She wasn't like the customers who came here, and she wasn't like the other women Seamus knew – people such as Marion, who were alien to Michael.

'Well, I'm very sorry but since I spoke to you something extraordinary has happened this afternoon. Mr Bull has announced he is closing down the restaurant, as of today – and he is not coming here any more.'

Genevieve's face crumpled. 'No!' she cried, unable to accept that she might have lost her last chance of tracking Seamus down. Had all her efforts been in vain? Michael was moved by her distress – it was plain she was genuinely upset – so he asked her in for a cup of tea. Genevieve looked up at him, surprised, then all of a sudden amused.

Tea! The English answer to everything. But it was welcome, and after the drama of such an anti-climax, she gratefully accepted the invitation and followed him inside.

Michael had an hour before he needed to be at the hospital. It seemed pointless trekking all the way home only to take a bus again, so he was perfectly happy to hang out with this girl for a while. Anyway, he was pleased for an excuse not to go down the Ladbroke Arms – he never felt very comfortable drinking with the rest of the staff when they still treated him as the kitchen slave. But then he thought he ought to tell this girl where Seamus was; she looked desperate to find him.

'You know, you may find Seamus in the pub at the bottom of the road. He has taken everyone there because of the restaurant,' he told her, but then quickly added: 'But to be honest, I don't advise you to go. He is buying everyone drinks and it could be a little – boisterous.' Michael was thinking of her: he had seen Seamus humiliate girls in public before. But he was also surprised to find he was quite keen to spend some time with her.

'Oh really?' responded Genevieve. Funnily enough, now she was inside Marrow, she didn't want to leave. She was happy for the moment to be in civilised company and regain her composure before she set out to find Seamus again.

'I'll show you where it is after the tea, if you like,' offered Michael.

'Oh, thank you,' replied Genevieve as he disappeared down the stairs to boil some water. She looked around at the restaurant's grand walls and paintings, fingered one of the wine glasses on the side, and traced her hand over the wood of the bar. It was an amazing place: just like some of the flashiest restaurants she had seen in Paris.

'Why has it closed down?' she asked Michael when he returned.

'We had a bad review and now it looks like the third Michelin star Chef wants – you know that's the most you can get – is not going to be given to us. So he's shut the restaurant.'

Genevieve smiled. How like Seamus that was! But she was amazed he had even two stars – he was only twenty-nine, and in France three stars went to very old and experienced chefs who had been cooking traditionally for years. 'Two is pretty good,' she commented.

'Yes, I know – but not for the boss,' replied Michael, setting down a mug in front of her. It seemed strange to be sitting in the front window of Marrow with one of Seamus's women. He looked into her face and she smiled at him, as if she knew very well what he was talking about. She thought it funny he called Seamus 'the boss'. He smiled back, relaxing for the first time that day, letting her beauty wash over him. It seemed to be cleansing him of all his worries, like an answered prayer.

The boy had a sweet face, kindly, and that was something she had not seen since she arrived in London. Genevieve felt remarkably relaxed in his company.

'My detective skills tell me you may be French,' teased Michael, as he offered her the sugar.

'Yes, but my mother was English – so I'm only half-French.'

'And do you live here?'

'Not exactly. Actually I'm visiting and it's my first time in England.'

'Oh!' exclaimed Michael. 'Welcome then! What do you think of it so far?'

'I am working in a little café on Earls Court Road, and my language is getting better all the time,' she told him, and Michael nodded encouragingly. 'But London is a big city and I don't know if I like cities very much. I think I prefer the countryside, where I come from.'

Genevieve was astonished to find this was the most she had ever admitted to anyone about herself since she had arrived. Actually, aside from Mave and the odd customer, this young man was the only person with whom she had actually had a proper conversation. It seemed strange talking about herself, but natural too.

'I know what you mean,' he was saying easily. 'They're very noisy and busy, and they smell, too.'

'Yes, of traffic fumes and dust and dirt and sweat. Ugh. And the people. They are all so busy too.'

'Stressed is the word,' corrected Michael. 'No time for anyone but themselves.'

'Oh, I thought that was just the English.'

Michael looked up at her and saw she was smiling, and laughed with her. He decided it might be an appropriate moment to ask her what he was suddenly very curious to know. 'So where did you meet Seamus then?'

Tricky question, thought Genevieve. She replied vaguely, without looking at Michael's face: 'I met him before, when he was in France.'

'My goodness, that was a long time ago,' replied Michael.

'Yes, yes, I suppose it was. Six years ago in total.'

Six years, thought Michael. 'And you haven't seen him since?' he asked.

'No, I haven't,' replied Genevieve, noting the look of worry on his face.

'He is a big man in London now, you know.'

'Yes, I saw the paper,' nodded Genevieve. She knew something about him since he had left her, but not enough. 'What happened?'

Michael had to bite his lip. As much as he wanted to warn this girl, tell her about how the legend of Seamus Bull was deteriorating because of drink and drug abuse, how the media were only just catching up with him, how the one monument to his talent left standing had just been closed down, how he feared for his boss's sanity even – he couldn't.

'Maybe you had better ask him that,' he said honestly, and Genevieve understood his loyalty.

'So now where do *you* go? Your restaurant too, you work here?' she asked, gesturing to the empty room.

'Yes, I do. I'm not sure. The boss has given us two weeks' paid leave so I'll be all right for a while. My father's in hospital at the moment so at least that means there'll be more time to visit him.'

'Oh, I'm sorry about your papa,' said Genevieve. It was the first bit of genuine sympathy Michael had heard uttered about his dad – and he loved it that she called him Papa.

'What's wrong with him?' she went on gently.

Michael didn't want to say. He never did. He wanted to say he had had a small operation and would be coming home soon, that there was nothing to worry about. But he couldn't. Genevieve noted with alarm his hesitation, and saw the pain flicker across his face. She recognised it.

'You know, my father was very ill for a long time. I can understand. It's horrid,' she said in a low voice.

Michael nodded weakly. There was a pause and he seemed still to be thinking about it, so she continued: 'It dominates everything. You don't feel you have anything left for yourself any more – no reason really to . . . well, do other things.'

Michael looked at her strangely. She did understand. Genevieve was pleased to see what she was saying was true for him too. She hadn't spoken about this to anyone before. It felt as if she was purging herself: just saying it, putting it into words was instantly giving her some perspective.

'My father, he died, and when he was gone it was like a house with no roof. You know, when the roof over your head which protects you, and comforts you, and makes you safe and is part of you, it's not there any more. Suddenly the wind and the rain and everything can come in. It's very scary.'

The two looked at each other, the words hanging between them. Her father had died – the word chilled Michael. He couldn't talk about this, but she was talking for him, she was voicing his feelings – in a foreign accent, but in a way he had not been able to.

'Thank you,' he said.

Genevieve smiled.

'Actually, you know, I've got to go quite soon. I could show you the pub where Seamus is, if you like.'

'Is he there with many people?'

'Only the entire staff of the restaurant!'

'Maybe it would be better if you gave him a message instead. Would you mind?' asked Genevieve, suddenly not ready to face her ex-lover and his cohorts.

Michael noticed that she was looking nervous again. Setting his cup down, he leaned across to her and said kindly, 'Funny – he makes me feel like that too.'

For the first time in a long time, Genevieve laughed.

Microwave Meal for One

1 packet
1 microwave

1. Remove sleeve from packet.

2. Pierce film lid several times.

3. Place in a microwave category B for 4 and a half minutes, or category D for 4 minutes.

5. Leave to stand for one minute.

11

Seamus sat alone on his bed. It had been a big week: events had passed more quickly than he could register them, but their mark on his memory was not helped by the obligatory bingeing session that followed each of them. It had been deliberate: carried along on a PR storm of Marion's making, the press had been hounding him all week and he had been forced to take refuge in Louche. The closure of Marrow had even made the last item on the evening news on Tuesday night, and Marion had been delighted: so much so that she had invited him out for dinner 'on Marvellous', but he had not been in the mood. She didn't seem to realise that Marrow was his baby. Gone.

The trouble was he knew deep down Marion was right: such a small venture as Marrow was never going to be the number one restaurant because, in the big game, in the circus of success and failure, it was not about talent but manipulation and marketing. And Seamus had never really bothered with that. The Establishment would therefore never let him win. They were out to destroy him just because he was talented and didn't play the game by their rules – so he had to surprise them first before they did him in. The new Marrow was still a secret, although there were rumours flying about town.

He kicked off his boots and lay back on his bed. He didn't live in this place – he just slept here, and scarcely that. He was usually either working or out drinking. So far this week just drinking. He hadn't wanted to go to bed sober, but knew he couldn't keep on like this. Marion was bandying sums of millions of pounds around – where the fuck did she think he was going to get that kind of money?

Seamus rolled over on the bed onto his front and put his head in his hands. His mind raced and he knew he wouldn't be sleeping for hours yet. He glanced over at his bedside table but he didn't have any drugs left. Probably a good thing, he mused. He noticed he had been taking them less for fun these days, and more because they were there. They undeniably helped. A near-empty bottle of Jack Daniels sat on the floor. He reached for it and emptied it into his mouth. The liquid scorched down his throat, the momentary physical sensation transporting him from his problems. If only there was someone he could talk to. One person he could share this with, who understood the reasons for his ambition. His hunger, he suspected in his darker moments, grew out of little but a lack of alternative desire. He had no love for anything but his restaurant and his own goddamn cooking talent. His ambition had starved his emotions to death.

Suddenly he needed to feel the heat of another body, the closeness of someone next to him, to feel a togetherness he couldn't get from anything except sex. Who could he call? One of several women, he thought ruefully. None of whom gave a fuck about him apart from the fact that he gave them a good time in bed and they got the kudos of bedding a celebrity. He reached for his mobile phone and scrolled down the address book. A blonde waitress, a red-headed PR girl, a mousey publishing assistant, a spiky hotel manageress, a foxy young journalist. He didn't know what any of them were like as people but he could tell you the dimensions of each and every one's bust and arse. He glanced at the clock by his bed. Half-past eleven. It would have to be someone working late so he did not appear too rude. He smirked at his crassness. The hotel manageress might be working. He called the hotel – yes, she was on shift.

'Lucille? It's Seamus here.'

'Well, hello there. I haven't heard from you in a while.'

'Well, here I am, honey. I wondered if you were doing anything after your shift?'

'Seamus!' admonished Lucille, playfully. 'Is this one of your disastrously timed booty calls?'

'Yeah, darling, it is. Not too bad timing, I hope?'

The spiky hotel manageress recalled the last night they had spent together, over a month ago, and knew that despite the time – and her husband – wild horses wouldn't keep her away from a repeat performance.

'No, Seamus, it's not too bad. Actually my husband's away.'

He'd forgotten she had a husband. 'So, are you doing anything later?'

'Well . . . nothing too pressing, shall we say?'

'Would you like to come over?'

'To your place?'

'Yes.'

'Mmmm. If you make it worth my while.'

'Of course I will.'

Lucille bit her lip as she twisted the phone cord round her finger. She was thinking some more about their last night together, and the unexpected anticipation of another was making her very hot. She closed her eyes and opened her mouth. 'See you in half an hour,' she breathed, then put the phone back on its hook.

Seamus smiled: he loved the liberated late thirties woman. Knew when a shag was just a shag and was enough out of touch with regular sex to be grateful for a jump when it came along. Good, energetic, body-pleasing sex. Something he bet she never got from her husband and certainly better than any form of self-gratification.

He woke up with a start, shocked to find his arms around her. Normally he turned over before he went to sleep, firmly presenting his back to his bed partner. He never slept like this. He moved his arms quickly, and woke her in the process.

'Mmmm, Seamus, what are you doing?' she mumbled, groping for his crotch in her sleep. Panicking, he swung away, lifting his legs onto the floor, and rubbed his face with his hands. He looked over at the blonde mop sticking out from under the duvet. He wanted her gone. He didn't want her seeing him or being with him now. She had served her purpose last night but he wasn't about to spend daylight hours with her.

'I have to go to work now.'

She turned over and looked him in the eye. 'I thought you had given all that up?' The look told him everything he needed to know about what a shit he was. He didn't respond.

'So you want me to go. Mind if I have a shower first?' she asked sarcastically.

Seamus looked away, ashamed, and mumbled, 'No, of course not. I'll get you a towel.' He pulled on his shorts, found a laundered towel, laid it on the end of the bed, then hid in the kitchen until she had gone. Back to work then.

Work now had a CLOSED sign hanging in its window. Seamus had so far avoided returning to Marrow, knowing how upsetting it would be to see the place empty, unused, only two Michelin stars in the window. It felt strange, he thought as he let himself in the door, with nothing to do in the middle of a weekday. Normally he would have been slaving down in the kitchens for several hours by now – as it was he was only just opening the shop. It was the first time he had been back here since he had declared the place closed. He hadn't been able to face it before. A restaurant without people – it was like a Kosovan village after the Serbs had been in, thought Seamus, never one to see his personal tragedies in perspective.

He walked in the door, through the reception area

and stood in the middle of the empty tables. Silence. It looked like a graveyard, he thought gloomily, the chairs upturned on top of the tables like tombstones in memory of customers who once came here.

Seamus smoothed his hand nostalgically over one of the crisp linen table cloths. The enormity of the task ahead was daunting: he had to start all over again, from the beginning. First he had to think about staff for this venture. The new place was going to be huge and it would be difficult finding enough good people, those who worked like him, to his standards and accepted his discipline. Decent staff were a nightmare to find in London. Due to the explosion in restaurants in the last few years, a young chef could now have his own place by the time he'd had only a few years' experience in the kitchen. There were few hungry, eager young chefs around any more – after all, who wanted to work sixteen-hour days six days a week to learn a trade when you could now buy anything you wanted in a deli, from a supplier or over the counter? All the knowledge you needed to open a restaurant was a recipe for fish cakes and an ability to serve them up with wasabi sauce and enoki noodles. Or anything else that sounded exotic or fashionable – and that you could buy in a tin.

All this would be discussed tomorrow. It was the first backers' meeting for the new Marrow, at lunchtime in the Pig and Trough. The Pig and Trough was the obvious place for it: far enough outside of London to be away from prying ears and media snappers, it was run by an eccentric young German, whose respect within the industry was enormous. He was a chef's chef: often spending days perfecting a single terrine, and charging the earth for it. Only someone who could appreciate the intensity of flavour and the diligence that went into achieving it would be prepared to pay what the German asked for it. Any innnocent punter who should wander in off the street looking for a pint of Fosters and a ploughman's would have a fit. '£16.95 for a plate of pâté? You must be joking!' At which point the German would appear, his face red and fuming, his carrot-top hair sticking up like a blazing inferno from the top of his head, and chase the poor unfortunate punter out of the door.

Consequently, the Pig and Trough had few customers, but the ones it did have were highly appreciative. The place had become legendary as the seduction scene for backers to woo away young talent from their current masters, and persuade them into newer, more lucrative ventures – half of which went down the drain in six months when enoki noodles fell out of fashion.

The thought of the forthcoming venture made Seamus sick with nerves. Somehow he had to come up with £1 million for his share in the business – by tomorrow. Needless to say, not even the most macho banks were going to lend that kind of money into an industry as capricious as his own. He needed capital, and that was one thing he didn't have. He had the flat, bought with his share of profits after the first eighteen months of Marrow, but that wasn't enough. He hadn't even taken a salary during the first year of Marrow's life, living only off what Salvatore gave him.

Salvatore, as majority shareholder, had been as keen as Seamus for the place to succeed and the two, although they never saw eye to eye on a single issue, and as much as each thought the other a lunatic, had learned to hold a deep-rooted mutual respect. Salvatore respected the fact that Seamus did something amazingly creative and was driven by a genius he himself didn't possess. Seamus saw in Salvatore the most successful businessman in his field, with the ability to hold on to the power that went with it. They wouldn't have been Seamus's methods, for sure, but you had to admire his professionalism, and his dedication. Seamus had never once seen Salvatore relaxed. He was always working.

Suddenly the phone began to ring, piercing the stagnant air of the restaurant. Startled, Seamus whipped round to where the noise was coming from and stared at it for a few seconds. Someone ringing up to book a table. But there was no table. There was no restaurant, there was no food, no drink, no cooking, no nothing. No more Marrow. Seamus clenched his fists and felt angry – very angry. He swore at the phone, distraught with grief that his baby no longer breathed and kicked.

'Haven't you heard that Marrow is closed by now? It's been announced on the national fucking news, for Chrissake. No More Bookings, OK?' he shouted uselessly at it, as the answer-machine picked up the call. *'Hello, this is Marrow. Unfortunately the restaurant is now closed and we will not be taking any further bookings,'* came the clipped tones of Adelè's automated voice.

'Seamus, are you there? It's Michael, I've been leaving messages for days. Someone came to see you, I have a message for you. Please ring me if you get this – I'm on 0181 485 7743.'

Seamus stared at the phone in amazement. What the fuck was that all about? Michael the kitchen porter? Michael, the Kid Who Could Cook?

Michael had arrived at Marrow's kitchen door just over six months ago, with a raging desire to prove his determination, his worth as a chef and above all with an uncompromising desire to learn the trade properly and to succeed as a classically-trained chef. Seamus recognised the hunger in his eyes. But for Michael, Seamus knew, this need to succeed was motivated by very different reasons from his own. Michael was doing it for his father: although the man was clearly dying, Michael wanted to prove himself, make him proud, in this world or the next.

Seamus admired the ambition, recognised the strength. Since he had arrived, Seamus had consciously been putting him through his paces, making life tough for him in as many ways as he knew how – and he knew how. He wanted to break him, see how much he could bear, and Michael had become the kitchen victim, the butt of everyone's jokes and boots. Amazingly, he still kept going.

Seamus continued in the manner of one conducting an experiment, morally justifying the torture by insisting it was to be the making of the man. By the time Michael had finished working in his kitchen, nothing in life would stand in his way. And he would be a great cook.

Michael's touch with food was the other quality Seamus recognised: an instinct and respect for good produce, and an understanding of taste and pleasure that Seamus rarely saw. No one else in the kitchen – or in London as far as Seamus could see – had that raw talent. Except perhaps Coq, he had to admit grudgingly. He had it. Seamus was glad Michael had come to him though. Now he could really teach him how to cook – his way. He wouldn't want someone like Michael falling into Coq's hands.

So what was the boy doing phoning him? He'd written in the staff contracts that they weren't allowed to take another job while they were in his pay, so that couldn't be it. Nor could he be ringing to resign. He had a message from someone? Who, for God's sake? He played the answer-machine tape back and noted the number, then dialled it.

'Hello?'

'Michael – it's Seamus.'

Michael paused on the other end of the line. Seamus had never referred to himself by his first name before, and he didn't know what to call him now they were out of the boundaries of the kitchen. He couldn't call him Chef.

'Hi,' he replied, successfully avoiding calling him anything at all. 'I've been trying to reach you. I have a message for you from a girl.'

From a girl. Great, thought Seamus. And he was hoping it might be something important.

'Which one?' he sighed, bored to death with the answer

before Michael had even supplied it. The trouble was, much to his chagrin, Michael had forgotten what she was called. So taken by her beauty had he been when she had handed him her phone number, the unfamiliar name had gone in one ear and out the other.

'She was French,' he tried, anxious to sort this problem out once and for all. He felt responsible for the girl as they had got on so well and she had seemed so upset, so nervous when she had come to the restaurant, and he had spent so long trying to track Seamus down.

'French? Are you sure it wasn't just a French name, like Lucille?'

'No, no it wasn't Lucille,' replied Michael. 'It began with a G.'

'G? Sorry, mate, don't know any French birds beginning with G.'

Michael was racking his brains now. He knew the importance of this message and he couldn't believe he had blanked her name. 'She was young, had really blonde hair . . . she was very pretty.' Michael really wanted to make Seamus remember, before he got bored and put the phone down; he owed it to the girl. But Seamus had already lost interest.

'Look, cheers for taking the message, Michael, but it really doesn't matter. You gonna come back in for the staff meeting next week? I want you there. You're good, you know that. I need you for other things.'

Michael was shocked. These words had never passed Seamus's lips before. 'Genevieve!' he shouted in triumph.

Seamus froze.

'Genevieve! That was her name, Chef! . . . Chef?'

There was a silence from the end of the phone, then a deadly serious voice asked him: 'Where did you see Genevieve, Michael? Where did you see her?'

Michael was astonished by the tone; there was an edge to it, an urgency. 'She came to the restaurant.'

'My God, when?'

'The day we closed. I had to lock up, the others went to the pub, she turned up. I didn't give her your phone number because you told us not to—'

'Fuck what I told you, Michael! What happened?'

Michael did not react to Seamus's treatment, and carried on unfazed. 'She gave me her number and said if you wanted to call her to do so, but if you weren't interested, to leave her alone.'

'Fucking hell, how long ago was this?'

'Last Monday, five days ago. I have actually been trying to get hold of—' Michael tried to explain, but Seamus wasn't listening.

'Quick, give me the fucking number now!'

Michael was annoyed that Seamus had managed to find another reason to be pissed off with him, and he tried again to justify why he was, in fact, only doing his boss a favour.

'Chef, I have been trying to reach you at the restaurant, but no one was picking up messages, and I didn't have your home number—'

'Just give me her fucking number!' screamed Seamus.

Chocolate Cake

175g butter
175g caster sugar
100g chocolate, melted
225g self-raising flour
2 eggs, beaten
60ml milk

1. Cream the butter and sugar together until pale and fluffy.

2. Beat in the eggs one at a time, adding a little flour with each addition. Gradually fold in the remaining flour.

3. Mix in the chocolate and the milk.

4. Spoon into a 20cm round cake tin, greased, and bake at 180°C for 40 minutes.

5. Allow to cool on a wire rack.

6. Slice in half, spread with clotted cream inside and on top and decorate with fresh English strawberries.

12

Seamus dialled the number immediately, then hung up. Genevieve: her name was like a bolt from nowhere, jolting him back to a time very different to this. He had been so much younger, and more innocent. Alone in a strange land he had met this girl. She was so extraordinary it was almost as if she was from another world, not just another country, and she had captivated him. Her skin, her hair, her sweet, sweet smell – it was all pouring back into Seamus's mind now. That summer had been bliss. In that summer he had come of age. She had touched him deeply, but his return had been so quick and brutal, before he knew it, he was plunged back into the grey days of winter and endless kitchen work, and that summer had seemed like a fairy story. He could not believe it had been real, so he didn't let himself think about it at all.

Presuming this was the same Genevieve – and how many more could there be answering exactly the same description from Michael – why had she come? Why now? What was she doing here? What was he going to say to her? He had to admit the thought of her made him excited, particularly as the more intimate moments of their affair drifted cloudily into his mind, and there had been no doubting their physical compatibility. He remembered also her sweet and utter devotion, and his for her: their feelings for each other had been more pure and close and sincere than any he had ever had from anyone. Ever.

So why was all this happening now? Although not a naturally superstitious man, Seamus couldn't help remarking on the coincidence of the crisis in his professional life and this epiphany in his emotional life. The return of the one woman for whom he had ever felt anything at exactly the moment when he most doubted himself was an extraordinary coincidence.

He dialled again. Who was to say she had not gone back to France already, having waited five days for him to call? Who was to say it wasn't her, but some misunderstanding; Michael had got the name wrong or something. The anticipation of speaking to her was intense, but more than her voice, what he really wanted, he realised, was to see her, see her in all her delicious resplendent beauty. He just had to find out where she was and go to her, he thought, shock and desire wiping out any logic.

'What?!' screamed a voice down the other end as Mave snatched up the phone.

'Hello?' asked Seamus, hesitating to see if he had got the right number.

'Look – what do you want?' came the impatient reply. Clearly someone was in a terrible temper.

'I'm trying to find a girl named Genevieve. I was given this number. Do you know her?'

'There's a girl of that name what works here.'

Seamus's stomach fluttered, despite himself. 'May I speak to her, please,' he asked patiently, trying to ignore the rudeness of the speaker.

'No, you can't. She's not here.'

'In that case,' he began again slowly, through gritted teeth, 'when will she be back?'

'In arf an hour. When she's 'ad her tea break.'

'Oh thank you, thank you.' Now Seamus was ecstatic; Genevieve was within reach. 'And can you tell me where you are, please?' he begged, desperate not to lose his temper with the singularly unhelpful crone on the other end of the line.

'This is the Happy Egg Diner on Earls Court Road.'

'Fantastic, thank you. Which end of the road is that?'

'We're right opposite the Tube station, but if you're coming to see her I don't want you distracting her. She's working till six and she can't stop and chat, you know—'

But Seamus had hung up.

'Well, I never! The cheeky sod.' Mave was not used to being hung up on, and her mouth opened and closed like a goldfish as she struggled to find words for someone with an even worse telephone manner than her own. But she was too busy with her *Daily Star* to dwell on the meaning of the phone call for long.

Genevieve swung back down the street carrying the wrapped box under her arm. She had been up to Chelsea to a cake shop to buy Mave a treat, for after the last week she knew she owed her a lot. Despite their apparent differences, the two now got on really well. Mave amused the French girl with her litany of grumbling and complaints about anything and everything – from the latest antics of the Royals which she eagerly hoovered up from her daily paper, to the filthy habits of the customers who ate in her establishment. Genevieve was a godsend for her – the first casual foreigner she had taken on this summer who actually knew how to do the work – and did it. Mave hardly needed to lift a finger any more.

After the initial excitement of her employee perhaps being connected to someone famous, she was quite content to comfort Genevieve with her own personal stories of one-night stands in Paris with Humphrey Bogart and Tyrone Power. The girl seemed amused to hear them and would sit through them time and again without yawning, which Mave appreciated. She had, she told Genevieve, once been a great beauty in her youth, just like her. But she had been spurned and used too, the results being that she was now wedded to her job, which was much more reliable and financially rewarding than any man could be – she would tell Genevieve that for free.

'Blokes – they're ruddy useless, love! Learn that young and you'll save yourself a lot of heartache as you get older. You mark my words.'

Genevieve had become grateful for Mave's daily lectures; they had insulated her from disappointment and she was beginning to think that what she suspected was true: her trip over here was just a fruitless search to find herself, not Seamus. Of course he wouldn't remember her – or want to remember after so long. How did she know it had meant as much to him as it had to her? He was her first lover, for God's sake. 'They say you never get over your first,' sighed Mave, then she chuckled bawdily. 'Although I can't say I remember mine at all!' Anyway, even if it *had* meant something to him then, well, he was a different person now.

'You see, Jenny,' said Mave, who couldn't quite get her tongue round Genevieve's foreign name, and so had settled on its nearest English equivalent, 'these men are in love one moment, gone the next. Fall like a ton of bricks, then months later they're bored and move on, by which time we've just about got around to falling for them. Sod's law, they call it, sweetheart. Sod's law. It's all true, you know. Men *are* from Mars, women are from Venus. That chap had it absolutely right.' Mave would then pause, look over to Genevieve and say, 'Mind you, if he clapped eyes on you now, he'd probably think differently about starting again. Shouldn't think it'd take much.'

Mave had come to terms with her own mountain range of cellulite and saggy bodily parts years ago. Beauty in another woman was merely an affirmation of her sex as the fairer – just as long as she wasn't showing it off, mind. Jealousy didn't come into it. On the contrary she found Genevieve rather ornamental, and it was quite obvious they were gaining a few more regulars now than before she had arrived, which was very useful.

'Hi, Mave!' Genevieve called as she burst through the door. 'My God, it is still so hot out there! I'm sweating, I can tell you.'

'Well, you'd better wash quick smartish, there's a customer over there waiting for his chips and beans fifteen minutes now.'

Genevieve grinned. She no longer took these comments to heart; it was just Mave's natural conversation.

'Guess what?' she told the older woman excitedly. 'I bought us something special. How do you say? A treat. It's from me to you, to say thank you for everything. I feel a lot happier now.'

For once Mave was speechless, and turning round from the tea urn she had just begun to polish with a dirty J-cloth, she took in the spectacle of Genevieve in her white shirt and pink skirt holding the ribboned package towards her.

'Well, bless me! For me? Well I never, what have you got there, lassie?' Mave moved towards her to look in the box, and Genevieve flipped the lid open to reveal the most sumptuous concoction of carefully crafted chocolate, strawberries and cream.

'My!' gasped Mave, who knew a thing of calorific beauty when she saw it. 'What you gone and spent your wages on that for? You get precious little as it is!'

But Genevieve could see Mave was touched, and that made it worthwhile. She moved the cake out of the way of the ash trajectory of Mave's Rothman, and set it on top of the counter as she reached for a knife and two plates.

'I think we should eat it now. As it's so hot, it will melt. This is a cake like my father used to make in France.'

Then all of a sudden the café, which up to that point had been filled with the streaming sunlight, darkened. Both women turned to see what had caused the sudden eclipse and stared at the enormous silhouette standing on the other side of the door, blocking out the sun. Genevieve's heart skipped a beat. The figure looked familiar but it took her a couple of seconds to recognise him. It couldn't be? But before she had time to think, the door was flung open and the figure was inside.

Genevieve took a sharp intake of breath. My God, it *was* him.

Seamus's eyes had to grow accustomed to the dim light inside but he knew it was her. He could smell her first. There she was, in all her incongruity, still surrounded by pink ribbon, cake, an apron, but her face – older, maturer, wiser, perhaps – was still unbelievably lovely. She was levelly returning his stare with a look that was so direct he remembered exactly why he had grown close to this woman. And a woman she was now, without doubt. Instantly everything that was good and worthwhile in Seamus's life distilled itself into that one figure. In a second he was back in the French countryside, young, healthy, optimistic, and all of a sudden he was reminded again of the true happiness he had once known. His heart leaped in a way it hadn't done in years. He stared at her, grappling to regain control over his feelings.

'Genevieve,' he managed, in a voice that resounded with relief more than anything else.

She stood there, absolutely motionless with shock, quite unprepared. Her mouth dropped half open, her hand remained poised with the carving knife to slice into the cake. He was so different; he looked exactly the same but different – she could tell the years had worn him. His face was rougher, his neck thicker-set, his body bigger if anything – but it hit her like a wall; he was still the most magnetic and attractive man she had ever seen.

Yet at exactly the same moment, the litany of pain that this man had caused by his departure hit her too. In a lethal combination she hated him yet she was drawn to him – this arrogant, easy figure lounging in front of her as if nothing had ever gone wrong between them, nothing had ever happened of note to stall their mutual attraction. Genevieve felt rage inside her, but she was quite unable to express it, frozen as she was by the shock of his presence. And, to her utter frustration, she experienced again the huge sexual pull he exerted over her. Parts of her trembled at it, as the white screen of her mind tried to sort the images that flashed up before her. She had to react in some way, but she was too confused for her body to know how.

Then all of a sudden a strange thing happened. After so many years of waiting and imagining, after so much tension and expectation, after so many scenarios played out in her mind, Genevieve felt an enormous giggle rising inside her, swelling up, growing bigger and bigger, rising out of her stomach, up her throat, until suddenly she exploded, dropping the knife right in the middle of the cream cake, clapping her hand to her mouth and bending over double as she desperately tried to control herself.

'Seamus, Seamus, I'm so sorry . . .' she tried in between her spasms, but speech just wasn't working. She tried to compose herself and think of something to say, but the whole thing suddenly seemed so ridiculous. 'You killed my papa! Slice of cake? I had to have an abortion! Cup of tea? You spoiled me for ever! How about a bacon sarnie?' With these sentences running round and round her brain, all Genevieve could do was bend over her cream cake and grasp at her stomach while Mave looked on, speechless for the second time that day.

But not for long. Realising that neither party in front of her was able to move the drama on, she took it upon herself to kick on the proceedings. 'Seamus Bull, I take it?' she rasped.

'Yes, that's right,' replied Seamus without taking his eyes off Genevieve, half-curious, half-delighted at her giggling fit. But mostly, just taken with the sight of her. Nothing

had held his attention in quite the same way before
or since.

'You took your time, didn't you?'

'I beg your pardon?' Seamus turned to face Mave,
recognising from her voice that she was the same harridan
from the phone.

'I said you took your time. This girl was going half insane
waiting for you to show up. You celebrity types, I don't
know, think you rule the world. Well, there's little people
out there too, you know!'

Seamus was quite taken aback by Mave's assault, as well
as secretly delighted to hear that Genevieve had been going
'half insane' waiting for him. But Genevieve, who sensed
Mave's tongue might just be about to run away with her and
reveal more than she wanted her to, miraculously gained
control of herself.

'Seamus, hello,' she said awkwardly. 'It's been so long,
I'm sorry, I just—'

'That's OK,' he said, putting an end to her confusion.
The two stood feet away from each other but the air
between them was as tense as a pulled rubber band. The
café was completely silent as the customers stared at the
extraordinary scene playing out before them.

Seamus bent towards her and as he did so she could feel
the heat from his body. Leaning over the cake, he reached
down into the box and retrieved the blade from its sticky
folds. Turning it carefully in his hand so the blunt side,
which also had no cream on it, pointed towards her, he
offered it back. No gesture could have been more gallant at
that point. Her insides melted and she looked down at the
knife as if it were some kind of peace offering, an altruistic
gesture designed to show her things could be different. She
struggled not to let her inner turmoil show in her face.

The closeness between them was unbearable now, he
could almost feel her breath on his face. Genevieve continued to look at the knife – and his hand, my God, his

strong, enormous hand – then, turning her face up to his, looking him directly in the eye, she drowned herself in his gaze. She reached across the space that separated them, and slowly grasped the knife-handle. She began to pull and for a split second Seamus resisted, willing a connection, before releasing it into her grasp.

Genevieve turned the corner of her mouth up, then said slowly: 'Thank you,' her words invading the hot, still space between them. He smiled at her and she felt years of anger drop away.

'I'm sorry, I know this is all a bit sudden for me to turn up here unannounced', began Seamus, retreating into formalities.

'Well, you hung up before I could ask you your name,' interjected Mave, clearly insisting her cameo role in the show not go unnoticed.

'But I only just got your message, and I was afraid you might have gone,' Seamus continued, ignoring Mave. He hadn't spoken with such gentleness in years.

'Oh,' replied Genevieve, making time as she tried to work out what to say and do.

'Is this where you work?'

'Yes, I started this week. I came over to find a job to practise my English.' Genevieve blushed at the half lie, but her voice was strong and self-possessed enough for Seamus not to notice and instead he took her at her word and nodded.

'Can I see you sometime when you are not working?' he asked, aware of Mave's hawk eyes and bat ears. He needed to talk to Genevieve in private, away from other people.

'Yes, of course. I only work during the day.'

'Then how about tonight?' jumped in Seamus, eager not to let Genevieve go in case he was imagining all this, desperate to drag her back into his life. Genevieve hesitated. It was useless pretending she had anything better to do, but tonight was too soon; she needed to work out what she was going to say first.

'I can't, I'm sorry. Perhaps tomorrow?'

'Yes, of course. Tomorrow is fine. Why don't you . . .' Seamus thought quickly, What? Where? Dinner? A drink? His flat? Ugh, no – not that place he hated. Where could he take her that he liked? His mind was blank – he couldn't think of anywhere, apart from Marrow. 'Why don't you come to my restaurant?' he said, quite struck with the idea. 'It's closed now, so it will be completely private, and we can be alone.'

Unbelievable, thought Genevieve. He hasn't even realised what he has just said. He's just assumed – correctly, of course. Alone with Seamus? Half of her was already undressing him, the other half was possessed with rage at him.

'I'll cook for you,' he cajoled, his face broadening into a smile, his eyebrows perking up. It was the first time he'd had any inclination to cook in weeks. But suddenly that was what he wanted to do for her.

Genevieve found it impossible not to respond. 'OK, that would be nice.'

Now it was her turn to smile, in silent acknowledgement that his charm was most definitely working on her again. Seamus hadn't remembered that smile for a while. He was shocked at how potent, how contagious it was. How it transformed her face from one of beauty into near divinity. Seeing it again was like being reunited with a very dear and very old friend.

'You know where it is, don't you?' asked Seamus, knowing Genevieve had been there to find him.

She blushed. 'Yes, yes I do.'

'About eight then?'

'OK, eight o'clock, I'll see you there.'

On hearing that, Seamus's face broke into a smile that melted both of the female hearts in its presence and,

physically unable to get any closer to Genevieve in case
he took her in his arms and ravished her right there, he
turned on his heel and left the café. As he rounded the
corner, his head buzzing with adrenaline and long-forgotten
endorphines, he had only one overriding emotion, and
punching the air, he shouted, 'Yes, yes, yes!'

Genevieve, on the other hand, made straight for a
chair. She was shaking from the shock and tension of
the encounter and her knees had gone weak. Mave picked
up her J-cloth, shook her head and said to herself and all
those who had been following her train of thought through
the last few days, 'Nope, didn't think it would take much.
Just one look, that's all, and already he's cooking Madam
a fancy dinner in his fancy restaurant.'

And so, rather than let any situation get the better of
her, Mave resumed her ranting at its usual consistency and
volume. 'There's a turn-up for the books, eh Jenny, isn't it
now? I must say, you were right: he is quite impressive in the
flesh,' she commented, glancing slyly across at Genevieve
who had gone very pale. 'I can see why you fell for him
all those years ago. But he's a man now, mind, young lady.
You be careful. All very well inviting you for a fancy dinner
in his posh restaurant – what a show-off, I ask you – but
he's human like everyone else. Same intentions as any man.
You just watch yourself, love.'

Genevieve was terrified. Tomorrow she was going to be
alone with Seamus. What was she going to do? How did
she feel now? Did she want to tell him half the stuff that
had gone on? Did she care about him any more? Her heart,
at that moment racing at twice its normal rate, told her she
obviously did.

'And that's another thing,' Mave grumbled on. 'You
don't want him getting his wicked way with you straight
off.' Actually, thought Genevieve, smiling into her hand,
the prospect was rather delicious. 'You've got to remember
to keep a bit back for yourself. Play your cards close to

your chest, young lady, and then you'll always have one over on him.'

Genevieve didn't look up at Mave. *'Mais oui,* Mave, of course.'

Pigs' Ears

Not all offal is regarded as wholly pleasant by modern-day sensibilities, but it is enjoying a resurgence in the public's perception of food fashion. Brains, cheeks, trotters and tongue are all quite often found on restaurant menus. Even a whole head has been known to adorn a dinner-table in recent times, if not as often as in ancient. But rarely are ears.

Not all animals' ears are good to eat, but those of the calf and pig have been judged so, their texture – managing to combine both gelatinous and crunchy – a particular favourite in the East. Other countries also celebrate them: Brazil includes them in its national dish, the *feijoada*, a sort of pig and bean stew, and Germany is particularly proud of its *Erbensuppe mit Schweinsohren*, a split pea soup with pig's ear.

The ears must be boiled, baked and basted for a long time to soften the cartilaginous meat, and then can be served on their own.

13

Beep, beep, beeeeeeeeepppppp!!!!!!!!

'For God's sake, Marion, shut the fuck up!' yelled Seamus, his head out of the window as Marion sat on the horn of her convertible Porsche Boxster, below.

'Well, get a bloody move on, will you?' she screamed back. 'We've got to meet Salvatore in the fucking country-side in an hour!'

'OK, OK, I'm coming. You could always try the doorbell, you know – most people do,' grumbled Seamus, retreating inside his flat. Five minutes later he was leaping into the passenger seat of Marion's brand new red sports car.

'Christ, bit small this, isn't it?' he said, deliberately making a show of trying to squeeze his legs in.

'All the better to cut you up with, sunshine,' growled Marion from behind a severe strip of black glass, monogrammed with the gold letters GV, which succeeded in covering half her face. 'What took you so bloody long? I thought you were a morning bird?'

'I am,' said Seamus, but left it at that. By no means was he going to tell her he had been getting things ready for tonight, for his seduction feast extraordinaire. He wasn't going to pollute the thought of Genevieve by discussing her with Marion. No way.

'So, feeling excited, Little Miss Power Trip?' teased Seamus, leaning across to Marion and giving her mini-skirted thigh a squeeze.

'Fuck off, Seamus,' she replied as she put her foot down on the accelerator and swung her baby out into the road.

'New car for the occasion, I see.'

'Unfortunately it's just on loan. I managed to persuade Porsche to take Marvellous on for six months last night – hence the motor. Anyway I can't stand being driven around – much prefer to do the driving myself. Don't you love my style?'

'Always, darling, always,' he replied playfully, and the two of them laughed as they roared off through Holland Park towards 'the countryside'.

Despite the insults, Marion was glad Seamus was in a better mood today. She had been convinced he was going to foul up the meeting with Salvatore, whose support wasn't in fact quite in the bag yet, due to his doubts over Seamus's 'temperament' as he called it. Not to mention his irritation that his sweet deal with the Notting Hill Marrow had ended, and he needed to find a new cover for his restaurant.

As they stopped at the traffic-lights Marion flipped open the dashboard to reveal two white lines chalked up on a mirror.

'Get that down you, boy – we've got business to do and I want you on top form.'

Seamus never said no, and managed both before the lights turned green.

Salvatore slid off the cream leather banquette and out of the back of his chauffeur-driven Mercedes. As ever, he was accompanied by two suited security men in dark glasses who talked to each other through earpieces but never uttered a single sociable word to present company. They never acknowledged or spoke to you unless they first had Salvatore's nod.

While the chauffeur closed the door behind them, the three simultaneously straightened their ties and set off crunching across the gravel towards the door of the quaint little stone pub. The sun was still beating down remorselessly outside, but inside it was cold and dark, and almost empty, save for a hirsute, craggy old man standing sentinel behind the bar and a large Irish wolfhound lying panting on the stone floor. At the entrance of the mafioso and his two henchmen, the dog's hackles went up and he began to growl threateningly, until his master behind the bar warned him off. He followed the men everywhere with his gaze instead.

Salvatore nodded to the landlord and asked for three sparkling mineral waters. The three men stood in silence at the bar, observed by the ancient tender. A clock ticked slowly, its pendulum emitting a low, dull thud that echoed through the room. There was no sound from the kitchen.

'Salvatore, darling! I'm so sorry we're late, bloody traffic. How are you?' Marion burst into the pub and strode straight across to the bar, her spike heels clicking noisily over the stone floor. She bent down to air kiss either side of Salvatore's puffy, serious face.

'Marion,' he acknowledged, not making the least attempt to air kiss back. 'Seamus,' he nodded to the nonchalant figure now leaning up against the bar beside him.

'Afternoon. Pint of bitter, please. Salvatore.' Seamus reached across and the two men shook hands.

'Well, here we are, isn't this exciting?' chirrupped Marion nervously. 'Now, have you discovered which one is our table yet? Ah yes, hello, I booked a table for three. Under the name Marrow,' and here she turned to the men and gave an exaggerated wink. Then, unpeeling the black bar from across her eyes, she laughed, 'Ah, that's better. I can see you all now.'

'You can have whichever table you like, madam,' replied the landlord steadily, gesturing to the emptiness of the pub. Imperceptibly, Salvatore nodded towards one in the far right-hand corner, and immediately his two suits walked over to check it out.

'Marion, what are you having?' asked Seamus, realising she was the only one without a drink.

'Oooh, glass of bubbly, don't you think? What have you got?' she asked the barman, and as he bent down and struggled to read the labels on the bottles stacked up in the fridge, Seamus and Salvatore followed the suits over to the table.

'So Seamus,' began Salvatore, once they were settled, 'I hear you have another leetle business proposition?'

Seamus knew Salvatore too well by now to arse around with all the small talk, and he was not the kind of man to be intimidated by Salvatore's scary mafioso tactics either.

'Well,' began Seamus, who was perhaps a better business negotiator than Marion gave him credit for, 'the way I see it, Salvatore, you have an awful lot of cash you need to, shall we say, "place" somewhere. And you and I both know that the circulation of that cash is efficiently carried out by a restaurant business. Now, as I have decided to re-invent myself and my restaurant on a much grander scale, the way I see it is you get to deposit larger sums of cash, so ensuring your business runs quicker and more efficiently. Wouldn't you say that makes sense?'

'Yes, Seamus,' grinned Salvatore, greasing a thick palm across his black, shiny pate. 'I would.'

'So are you interested?'

Salvatore raised his eyebrows in that 'Persuade me' kind of way, at which point Marion appeared juggling glasses and an ice bucket.

'Here we go, boys. I ordered a bottle in anticipation of a toast. Piper Heidsieck OK? Apparently that funny little German chap won't have anything else.'

'That funny little German chap you refer to is one of the most enigmatic culinary mavericks in this country,' responded Seamus, stung, eager to protect the judgement of one of his own – especially one who posed no threat to him.

'Funny, I thought that was you, Seamus,' she responded quick as a flash. 'Champagne, anyone?'

'One moment,' dismissed Seamus as he continued to address Salvatore, much to Marion's growing irritation. 'Now, as you know, my restaurant business is already established and successful in its own right, so the risk factor of achieving success in the first six months – which we know is crucial – is greatly reduced.'

Marion, who did not like being elbowed aside in business discussions, was not going to let Seamus cast her into the role of the beauty of the operation only. Especially after all the preparation she had done, when clearly all Seamus had done was roll out of bed.

'Of course, Seamus, but we are talking about a major re-invention here. This place is going to be so large-scale it will make the Marrow of Notting Hill look like a takeaway bar. But with the right marketing,' and here she wagged her finger for emphasis and looked Salvatore straight in the eye, 'we can make it the only place to eat in London.

'Firstly we have a prime location: Knightsbridge. Entirely central, suitably upmarket, and an area already known as a honeypot for people who want to spend money. And of course an area with an already established culinary reputation: right opposite being Emmanuel Coq's new flagship restaurant, Mirage. However, what we have in mind is on a much grander scale. Look at these plans, Salvatore,' and here Marion reached into her leather briefcase to produce some neatly rolled architect's scrolls. 'I had these drawn up by Archie Peaks, the famous architect.'

At this point she checked Salvatore's face to see if he had registered just how exclusive Archie was, and what a coup it was to have him on board. Seamus did a double-take; he didn't know anything about this! Archie Peaks was seriously hot property, and was usually far too busy designing airports and nuclear power stations to worry about piddly little restaurants. But she had him.

'This is how he envisages the space working,' she said as she unrolled great swathes of drawings across the table.

'On the ground floor, as you can see, we have an open-plan, walk-in café area, very continental, where people can drop in for glamorous coffee and cigarette appointments. Of course we'll break the world record in what we'll be charging for a cappuccino, but it will be the privilege of drinking it in these surroundings which will count. On the floor in front here is an exhibition area where we will be inviting all the up-and-coming Brit artists to exhibit their new work, thus instantly attracting the art buyers who, as we know, have plenty of money,'

'And very little sense,' interrupted Seamus, who had met a man the other day who had paid £10,000 for a congealed fried egg sitting on a crooked table.

Marion ignored him and continued: 'Next to the café is a top-class patisserie: the largest set of dedicated baking ovens in Central London, and facilities to deliver. Bye bye, Patisserie Valerie. I tell you; any cake worth its calorie content will have to come from Marrow, once these little ovens are up and running.

'Up a level is a huge supermarket, covering the entire floor. Now this is the real draw: this food, although staggeringly expensive, is also the best you will find anywhere in the city. Chefs have to go to Billingsgate market in the morning to buy their fish fresh, Smithfield to fight for the best cuts of meat, then all the way out to New Covent Garden Market for fruit and veg. Our special fleet of Marrow sourcers will undertake that task every morning on the general public's behalf and bring it all back here for sale under one central roof.'

Marion jabbed at the drawing with her manicured fingernail for emphasis. She was on a roll now, she knew she had both men completely in her thrall and was beginning to enjoy herself. She was more than a little proud of what she had pulled off. It was, after all, going to make her her fortune.

'Added to that,' she continued, 'we will have a team

of crack chefs on the spot who will be freshly making up deli-style products to order – a Thai marinated tuna steak, say, or a Russian salad – whatever you fancy. We will also have food counsellors whose job it is to guide you through the supermarket, tell you where everything is, what you should buy to go with what, advise you on the latest cooking trends – you know, stuff like how it has to be galangal in the stir fry now as ginger is so yesterday – that sort of thing. And of course they'll tell you how you should cook it all. Attached to this leg of the business will be a catering firm, should you feel too tired to cook the food once you have bought it – or, of course, if you need to cater for those all-important dinner parties that the chattering classes so love to indulge in.

'Now the third floor,' she continued, 'will be the cheaper bistro version of the flagship Marrow on the fourth floor. With 1000 covers,' and here it was all Seamus could do not to spit the swig of beer he had just taken all over the table, 'we will be providing Seamus Bull-style food for cheaper prices – OK, only slightly cheaper – but at twice the speed and with double the efficiency. Just imagine the turnover!' She paused for effect, deliberately not looking at Seamus, who she could tell was choking over the very idea of a 1000-cover brasserie. Salvatore, however, was now looking very interested.

'The top floor I regard as being particularly to your taste, Salvatore. It will be a private dining room, and rather like its own self-contained penthouse, will have a private reception room, bar and dining area. For parties from five to fifty people it is available for hire, with absolute discretion and privacy, and it will be personally catered for by Seamus himself. And it will be ludicrously expensive and terribly destinational, and therefore a magnet for all those who can afford it. There, what do you think?'

Marion had come to the end of her pitch, and judging by the smug grin on her face, she knew it had been good. Seamus was simply flabbergasted. He had never seen anything so ambitious in his entire life.

Salvatore remained silent and perused the drawings. But his skin had begun to glow, and Marion took this as a good sign. Due to the nature of his business, he understood greed, ambition and the need for glamour. This project involved all three, on a scale hitherto not seen before. And it now had three of the best people in the business behind it – Marion doing the marketing, Seamus doing the cooking, Archie Peaks doing the design. From the plans it looked sumptuous.

'So,' said Salvatore after an interminable two minutes of silence, during which he had been scrutinising the plans and Seamus and Marion had hardly dared breathe for fear of disturbing him, 'tell me: how can it fail?'

Seamus was ready for this. 'It can't fail. There are four necessities in life – fucking, sleeping, eating and shitting, and everyone has to indulge in all four. There will never be a shortage of people who want to eat. We will simply provide the best food and the best place to eat it in. This is a city – millions of people live here, millions more fly in and out. For them in particular this kind of affair is obligatory. Londoners and their hunger are not going anywhere. And anytime anyone who doesn't live in the city pays it a visit – Marrow will be the only place to eat.'

Salvatore nodded. 'And do you have planning permission yet for such a large operation right in the middle of Central London?'

'The building itself doesn't actually need much doing to it externally,' explained Marion, who had gleaned all this from Archie. 'Really all the changes are internal, and Knightsbridge is already recognised as a commercial area. But,' she hesitated, 'I do believe that if there were to be any problems, and you were to come on board, the chairman of the committee is a personal friend of yours, Salvatore?'

'Client, not friend, Marion. I don't have friends. Clients are much more useful in matters of bribery.'

'Quite, so I can't really see that being a problem,' answered Marion.

'So what did you say the breakdown in expenditure would be?' Salvatore asked Seamus. Like all Italians he was a firm stickler for macho law: women could talk interior design and soft furnishings till their lipstick wore off, just as long as they left the money to the men. Of course Seamus had no idea, but he wasn't going to let on, and opening his mouth to spout forth some claptrap about percentages and wait and see, Marion jumped in with, 'We need two million from you to convert the interior, which the builders promise they can do in two to three months, then Seamus and I will each put up £1 million – this will pay for the marketing, the PR, the start-up costs and any legal problems we might encounter. I have a budget here for you,' and again bending over her briefcase Marion whipped out a bound report and deposited it on the table.

The lady had certainly been busy, thought Seamus, impressed, keeping very quiet about his share of the money. Salvatore also looked impressed; he wasn't used to figures coming out of ladies' mouths – he found it rather sexy.

'And how will you sustain the turnover? Because it will have to be massive for a place like this,' gestured Salvatore with a swipe of his arm over the plans.

Marion smirked before delivering her favourite line: 'There's nothing good PR can't do.'

Salvatore studied her carefully, then in an almost visible process of decision-making, he picked up the bottle from the ice bucket and asked: 'Champagne, anyone?'

All three investors, as those who are in the possession of a powerful secret are wont to do, smirked at each other. Salvatore was in – it was written in his face, and Marrow, mark two, was now full speed ahead.

*   *   *

The rest of the pub was beginning to fill up. A few business lunches, the odd local, but everyone there had to be seriously into their food to stomach the contents of Thomas Grüber's cooking. You couldn't order – you got what you were given, couldn't be allergic to anything, couldn't leave anything uneaten, and vegetarians were definitely not tolerated. Any complaint and you were out: a policy most chefs envied, hence their veneration for the establishment. And a policy most ordinary people – like Marion – found entirely absurd. In fact, she did not enjoy eating food full stop, preferring instead to deposit it down the toilet immediately after swallowing it. But she recognised it as a fashionable commodity and therefore would never admit to her predisposition for a liquid-and-pill only diet. So when the starter was placed before them, Marion felt distinctly queasy. When she was told what it was, she nearly vomited right there and then.

'Pigs' ears can be delicious,' encouraged Seamus, noting Marion's distress with amusement.

'I'm sorry but I've never quite got this thing about offal,' was all Marion could reply, but she was aware that the eyes of Salvatore and Seamus were on her, and the dish was recognised as a challenge. If she wanted to play restaurants with the big boys, then she had to eat the damn pigs' ears. She tried to focus on the plate, on the dried-up, wizened bits of browny pink flesh which stared up at her, but knew it was useless. She groped for her handbag.

'Mmm, they certainly smell delicious,' she attempted feebly, breathing through her mouth, as underneath the tablecloth she manoeuvred her clutch bag onto her lap.

Seamus was by now chewing his, and had a look of critical concentration on his face. Salvatore was inspecting his, rather as a carpenter might inspect a piece of wood. He passed it across to one of his henchmen to test. The henchman did not look pleased. Marion took advantage of the situation to drop one of the ears directly into her handbag. She then made a great show of chewing and saying how lovely she thought it was. The men looked at her astonished. They never would have credited it.

It was at that precise moment that Marion's bacon, as it were, was saved. For who should walk through the door, fat man in tow, but none other than Emmanuel Coq, out with Rufus for the Get Well lunch, promised to him in hospital.

Rather like two large tigers in a cage, there was only room for one ego in that room, and the moment Coq entered, both men were instantly aware of the other's presence. Seamus immediately looked up from his plate, smelling a rival, and spotted Coq across the other side of the room, just as Coq's eye was immediately drawn to Bull's. Salvatore and Marion saw the change in Seamus's body language and followed his gaze to the wiry man at the door, shadowed by the squat silhouette of Rufus. Both sat up, waiting to see what would happen.

Seamus fixed Coq with his steely glare, but Coq turned directly to Seamus to fix *him* with a cold eye. Then, galvanised by apparent anger, Coq stormed right over to their table.

'A little bird tells me a rumour. The site opposite Mirage is up for sale, and there are interested parties I would not approve of.' Coq challenged Bull directly, ignoring everyone else on the table.

Seamus glanced at Marion, who looked terrified – confrontation was one thing she was not good at. She was talented at being nice to people, but she wasn't a lion-tamer, and she didn't like it one bit when events spun out of her control. However, this was just the sort of situation Salvatore thrived on. He nodded at Seamus and Seamus knew this meant he was in, the deal could go public, and he had his, and his guards', full backing to face Coq down.

'Your little bird sings a pretty tune then, doesn't he,

Emmanuel?' countered Seamus, relishing the situation – one in which he knew he had the upper hand.

'On the contrary, Bull, he does not. For you, of all people, to open a site – even a sandwich bar – anywhere near one of my establishments I take to be deliberate provocation, and I would fight tooth and nail to stop you!' Emmanuel snarled, momentarily deprived of his smooth, continental cool. His mouth was set into a thin, pursed line and through his lips you could see small white flashes of his pointed teeth.

'Oh really?' replied Seamus casually. 'My goodness, I'm terrified,' he continued, his tone heavy with sarcasm, his smirk showing how much he was enjoying the moment.

'Don't dismiss me, Bull.' Little flecks of saliva were beginning to appear at the corners of Coq's mouth now. 'I can still cause you a lot of harm.'

'Game's up, I'm afraid old Coq. Time for some young blood to move in on your patch.' Seamus was beginning to really enjoy himself.

Now Rufus had had time to waddle over, he appeared at Coq's elbow, and gathered there was indeed truth behind the rumours. Apart from anything else, the combination of these three people sitting around a table covered in architect's plans meant it hardly took a genius to make a conclusion.

'Marion, I'm surprised at you!' he exclaimed in his shrill tone. 'I thought you kept better company!'

Now she had been directly challenged, Marion realised she had to play from her sticky wicket. 'You know I'm friends with everyone, darling,' she attempted feebly, thinking of all the establishments on her client list that depended on the fat man's favourable reviews.

'So is it true, Seamus? Are you re-opening Marrow?' Rufus asked.

'I'm considering it,' he replied affably.

'And have you applied for the site opposite Mirage?'

'I may have done.'

'Then you are a liar and a cheat as well as a brute and a bully!' flounced Rufus, now clearly agitated. 'You told me you were closing it down,' he whined. Rufus was put out because he had incorrectly surmised, with a little help from Marion, that Bull's closure of Marrow signalled his resignation from the restaurant world altogether. Such was the sensation value of this news, plus the obvious ego-flattering aspect that it had been triggered by one of his own reviews, that Rufus had devoted the entirety of his next weekly column to the subject. He was going to look a fool now when it became apparent that far from quitting, Bull was not only back with a vengeance, but back so soon.

Meanwhile Coq and Bull had been staring each other out and Salvatore's two henchmen were beginning to look a little jumpy. Marion, now realising she had absolutely no control over events and not wishing to contemplate the possible outcome of a bar-room brawl, took matters into her own hands. Seizing the plans and stuffing them back into her briefcase, she announced: 'Right, Monsieur Coq, as you have been so aggressive in your manner towards us here, I fear we shall have to retire somewhere with a more civilised clientèle. Any information you wish to know will be divulged at a press conference at the Hyde Park Hotel at nine-thirty tomorrow morning. We will see you there.'

All would have been well had Marion not then leapt up, forgetting her clutch bag was still perilously balanced and open on her lap. As she moved, she fired the bag out from under the table, sending the contents – lipstick, a large pot of pills, a silver mirror, a plastic bag of white powder, her purse and one dried pig's ear, skidding across the floor.

Thomas Grüber, who had, like the rest of the pub, been watching the interchange, fascinated, looked down at his feet to discover one of his precious, dried Italian sow ears nestling between the sole of his shoe and the floor. Marion, mortified and flushing a deep crimson, scrabbled around on the floor in an attempt to retrieve all incriminating objects, and flanked by Salvatore and his gofers on one side, and Bull, whose hypnotic staring competition with Coq was continuing, on the other, made hastily for the exit. As she passed the lanky chef on her way out, he stopped her with his arm.

'Madam, your ear,' he challenged her, pointing to the floor and clearly indicating she should retrieve the offending item and appreciate it in the way he had intended. With a look of disgust, Marion could take the humiliation no more, and defying the lore of the chef, replied instead: 'Sir, your customers!' and stalked out.

'You mark my words,' Salvatore muttered to her when they were safely in the car park and the henchmen had finally been able to remove Seamus from Coq's proximity. 'His temperament will be our undoing.'

Asparagus with Hollandaise Sauce

90g butter cut into cubes
3 tablespoons white wine
8 white peppercorns
2 egg yolks
Salt and pepper

1. Put the wine and peppercorns together in a pan, bring to the boil and reduce by two thirds. Remove the peppercorns and leave the wine until lukewarm.

2. Beat in the egg yolks until they have the consistency of thin cream.

3. Place over a gentle heat and add the butter a cube at a time, beating continuously with a balloon whisk.

4. Meanwhile place the asparagus spears stalk side down in a pan with a few inches of boiling water. Cover and steam for five minutes, depending on the thickness of the spears.

5. Continue beating until the sauce is light and smooth; thick but still pourable. Season with salt and pepper.

6. Drain the asparagus and serve with the sauce drizzled over.

14

Genevieve handed over the money to the taxi driver, then took a deep breath as she turned to face the restaurant. The taxi pulled away, revealing the large green sign in front of her: MARROW. She was excited now as well as nervous, for tonight she would get some answers, answers from the man who had altered the course of her life.

But how different she was now from when she had first visited this restaurant; her mind then had been full of fear and trepidation. She felt empowered now – by her experience of finding and coping with work in a foreign city, and by doing it on her own. She felt empowered too by the old wives' wisdom of Mave – one more used to the knocks of life than she was – and jubilant after five days of mistakenly assuming Seamus didn't care about her. She was much more confident after meeting Michael, as well, because he had restored her faith in the good nature of men, and particularly of British men. Yes, she told herself, she could be strong tonight. She had sufficient protection now to expose herself to him in a battle of intentions. She would make him answer, she told herself, and she would make him pay.

Seamus was calmer now after the events of lunch-time. Suddenly his career seemed unimportant beside cooking again – and of course, beside Genevieve. Even her name sent a thrill through him. Two of his most intimate passions, cooking food with the most noble of intentions, and a woman, about whom he cared more than any other, were both coming together tonight.

He unloaded the produce out of his bag. That morning, he had got Michael to trail round all the best Marrow suppliers in London and he had done well: Seamus had everything he needed. He lifted out the artichokes: they were bright green, at the peak of their season; two fat, round globes tightly wrapped, their succulent bracts waiting to be peeled apart, leaf by perfect leaf. He rinsed them under the powerful stream from the tap, sliced off their stalks and placed them, bulb down, in a pan of boiling water. Next he pulled out a bright yellow lemon from the bag, brought it up to his nose to check the smell, nodded his approval, then sliced it open and squeezed one half into the artichokes' water. He smiled: they were going to be utterly delicious.

Seamus knew this evening was not going to be straightforward. There had been reproach in Genevieve's look when he had found her in the café, and he didn't blame her. He had never got in touch with her after he had left Grèves, even though he had promised to do so. He delved in his memory for the events that had followed the happiest time of his life: all he could remember was that when he had returned from France, sent home in disgrace once her father had discovered their affair, his summer with her had no longer seemed real.

Once Guy Chevrot had been informed of Seamus's reasons for departure he had withdrawn the offer of recommending him to his cousin's Michelin restaurant in Northumberland, and Seamus had ended up working in some grim, Gothic country-house hotel in the Yorkshire dales. There, he once again had had to learn to work alongside another group of people whom he didn't know. There was a standing joke in the trade that chefs didn't have families – they only had kitchens. This was because they spent so much time working, often far away from home, that there was never any time left for anybody else – your colleagues became your family. But not for Seamus, who had learned through his childhood, bumped from one foster family to another, that you kept yourself to yourself – forming lasting relationships just left you vulnerable.

That winter had been gruesome, and the only way he had been able to bear it was by wiping Genevieve from his memory. He had been allowed a short period of happiness, but no more, and he had had to pay for it. He never imagined he would see her again. Never imagined that summer of fantasy would return and he might get a second chance.

He unwrapped two thick steaks, cut tenderly from the fillet, blood red and shining under the kitchen light. The fresh, bleeding flesh felt like silk in his hands. Now that he had seen her again, his attraction to her was as intense as ever. Perhaps more so, for they were both more mature, more experienced people. Before, she had been a schoolgirl, a virgin, and he had been so much younger, had achieved nothing by then. He ground salt and pepper over the slabs of meat, then set them aside on a plate.

He had to seduce her all over again, he knew that. He pulled out another brown paper bag: this time it contained a bunch of late summer asparagus. He had been worried that the spears would be too tough by this time of year, but his seller in New Covent Garden always knew the best places to pick from. And this time he had excelled himself: the stalks were as thin and tender, the spears as fleshy and bulbous as Seamus could have wished. He grinned with pure delight – excellent produce. Out came another bag, brimming with succulent green leaves for a salad; in another the reds, blues and purples of late summer berries glistened like jewels. He would have to do very little cooking with produce as perfect as this, which was a relief to Seamus, as it had been a while since he had actually cooked himself, rather than co-ordinated a team of chefs around him. Really, he thought, this was all you needed for fantastic food: honest raw materials, simply handled.

He would blow Genevieve away through her taste buds. Food was his way of expressing himself, and he had so much to tell her.

Genevieve peered in through the restaurant window, but she could see no one. The place was as dark and empty as a morgue. She was early, she knew that, but that had been deliberate. She had wanted to catch him off-guard. She smiled as she realised she was beginning to take on the military tactics of Mave.

Then she noticed that round to one side of the restaurant was an iron staircase leading down to what looked like the basement. A door was open, and she could hear the clattering of pans coming from behind it. She tiptoed down the stairs, and peered inside.

Seamus had his back to her, and was bending over one of the steel counters in the kitchen. He was wearing a white T-shirt and a pair of jeans, and underneath the soft cotton she could see the muscles of his back flex as he picked up something heavy. She thought of that day by the lake so many years ago, when he had been wearing similar clothes, and she felt a quiver of delight and anticipation run through her body. No! She must not let these feelings cloud her thoughts. She closed her eyes and forced herself to remember everything she wanted to talk to him about. By the time she opened them again she had successfully summoned a litany of accusations.

More detached now, she watched him pick up something green in his hands, it looked like asparagus. He was fingering the stems for delicacy, holding them in a way that denoted reverence as well as criticism. She watched from the door as he sorted through the produce quickly but with infinite care, discarding anything not up to his exacting standards, setting aside what he deemed fit. Then he took a knife – she saw the blade flash as it caught the evening sunlight streaming in through the door – and deftly started to slice it through the stalks. Genevieve couldn't help but be transfixed by the sight of him: his hands, his shoulders, his arms, and the way his body moved in response to the food around him. A curious mixture of brutishness and artistry, sensitivity and insensitivity, power and delicacy.

Suddenly, dealing with the struggle being played out inside her head and body, she felt herself paralysed. She could not move, she could not speak.

Seamus stopped what he was doing. The air in the room had thickened. He knew she was there now. Slowly, he turned his head and saw her, standing in the doorway. He balked. Even in his memory he could never quite capture the beauty of her. Framed by the doorway, she looked like an apparition, the ghost of his summer past. Except, he noted the message in her eyes: they were boring into him with a steeliness he did not recognise, hurling a volley of challenges at him. He did not look away; he did not look at any other part of her. He met the intensity of her stare and returned her gaze directly, countering her hostility with a look that was soft and lingering, trying to absorb her anger with the constancy of his gaze, as if he might suck it out of her once and for all. He smiled at her in as friendly and casual way as he could manage; the vegetable knife in his hand still poised in mid-air.

'Hello, Genevieve,' he said calmly. 'Why don't you come in?'

She paused; just long enough for him to know it was her decision to walk into his kitchen, rather than his invitation. She walked cautiously over to where he was standing, each step taken as warily as a cat when stalking its prey.

'You found it OK?'

She nodded. She still could not speak, struggling as she was between rage and desire; she could not trust herself to do or say anything until the latter had been defeated. He gestured to a work surface beside him.

'I'm sorry, the food is not quite ready yet. Will you wait a minute?'

Unable to resist the onslaught of Seamus's charm any longer, Genevieve was grateful for an excuse to look away and let her eyes fall on the surface in front of him. She said the first thing that came into her head. 'You English eat your asparagus late.' Her tone was caught between accusation and surprise.

'Trust me, these will be delicious,' he said, and he scooped them up and stood them, stalks down, in a pan on the hob behind him. As he turned away she watched his shoulders swivel and, unable to help herself, found her gaze dropping down to his perfect torso.

While his back was turned she used the opportunity to hop up onto the work surface: this would make her head level with his, help to create the illusion that they were physically equally matched. But when he turned back they found themselves alarmingly close, face to face with barely six inches between them. Both flinched at the other's proximity. The atmosphere between them crackled.

Seamus walked hastily over to a fridge on the other side of the room, and drew out a bottle of white wine. He walked back to the pan, his face shrouded in serious concentration, and placed the bottle on the side next to a decanter of red. He let the spears fall completely into the water now, and stood over them, waiting for the moment when he judged them tender.

For Genevieve, the silence was uncomfortable, although Seamus seemed relaxed. She felt hopelessly at his mercy – he was controlling the situation; she had to do something to turn it round so it was on her own terms. But she had so much in her head she urgently needed to say to him, anything else she could think of to say seemed unbearably trivial. The longer she left it, the worse it got. She had to say something and she could only say what was in her head. Without thinking, she blurted out: 'So, Seamus, are you going to tell me why you never answered my letters?' The question flew like a missile, through the air.

Seamus winced. He paused, registering the spoken assault, then turned back to her, his fingers grasping one of the spears, and looked her straight in the eye.

'Genevieve, I never got your letters. I was sent to work in another place.' Then, without missing a beat: 'And now I will prove to you I know what I am doing with English asparagus.' As she opened her mouth to reply, he posted the swollen tip of the asparagus spear in between her lips.

The green flesh fell apart on her tongue, blocking the words that had risen in her throat, the sweet, earthy flavour flooding her mouth, her nose and her throat. To her dismay, Genevieve felt the exquisite flavour and texture dampening her anger, distracting her mind. His hand was still poised near her mouth, and her eye alighted on it. His fingers were long and graceful, and even though they were blistered and callused, Genevieve remembered how sensitive and artful they could be. All she could think was how close they were to her face, how easy it would be for him to unfurl one of his fingers and stroke her cheek. Then she prayed he would not; she would not be able to bear it.

When Seamus saw the spear had had the desired effect, he turned back to his hob, and whisked something in a pan that was sitting over a low heat at the back. 'Good?' he asked her over his shoulder, praying he had won the first battle.

Genevieve recovered herself. 'Not bad,' she replied.

Now he was twisting a corkscrew into the bottle of white wine, and as he pulled it out she watched his arms strain against the sleeves of his T-shirt. She looked quickly away. He poured the wine into two glasses he had plucked from the shelf above him. Watching him, she tried again.

'You can have no idea of what you brought into my life . . .' Almost before she had started her sentence she was overwhelmed by the most powerful aroma: Seamus was holding the wine inches from her face. The glass balloon into which he had poured it was wafting up intoxicating clouds of peach and apricot.

'A Le Montrachet '78. A divine wine for you,' Seamus said, offering her the glass and gently mimicking her accent. 'Try eet – eet's fantastique.'

Genevieve knew this wine, but only by reputation. Her father used to tell her about his cousin who worked on the vineyard, and of course, it was one of the greatest French wines. Of all the Burgundies, the Le Montrachet was supposed to have more scent, a brighter colour, a longer flavour and more succulence – everything about it was meant to be intensified. And 1978 had been one of the greatest years this century for white Burgundy.

Seamus could see she was impressed. Hypnotised by the smell, Genevieve grasped the stem of the glass, then brought its rim up right underneath her nose and inhaled deeply. The heady, heady smell of summer, she thought. She tipped the glass into her mouth and let her tongue take the first of the sensations. They welled in an explosion of fruit around her mouth.

Seamus watched her register the smell and the taste, excited that she was so pleasured by it, triumphant that it was having the desired effect. 'Beautiful, isn't it?' he asked gently.

Slowly she looked up at him. The touch of the liquid on her lips, the coating of its exquisite flavour on her tongue, the headiness of its perfume – it had all weakened her. He mustn't see it, she thought.

'Yes,' she attempted nonchalantly. 'It's French. The best wine always is.'

He smiled at her. 'My sommelier would agree with you.'

He lifted the glass from her hand, gently brushing her fingers against his own as he did so. She jumped at his touch. Still looking at her, standing closer in front

of her than before, he lifted the glass to his own lips.
The fragrance voluntarily closed his eyes, and he lifted
the glass, inhaled and sipped. His face gave away his
pleasure. When he looked at her again it seemed her
eyes had glazed over watching his. Now, without letting
his eyes leave her face, he reached down with his free hand
and found hers, determinedly limp, and lifted it up to the
stem of the glass.

'Genevieve,' he said, relishing every syllable of her name.
'Try it again.' He wrapped her fingers around the stem of
the glass, briefly clasping her fingers in his, then released
her and stepped back. Almost losing his own control, he
turned back to the hob.

Genevieve breathed, trying to calm herself, using the
pause as his back was turned to muster her strength,
and banish the heat between her legs, the trembling that
wracked every part of her body. But every breath she drew
in was distilled through the heady aroma of the Burgundy
and it loosened her brain and intoxicated her mind until
she felt her head beginning to spin. She tried to concentrate
instead on the pan he was standing over. Inside was a light,
foaming yellow sauce. Her eyes closed again as she inhaled
the scent from the wine she was unable to put down. She
took another sip. It was too good a wine to leave in the
glass: something Seamus had counted on. He glanced over
at the decanter which held a Lafite Rothschild '61.

Seamus was now beating the sauce with a metal whisk
and she could not help but notice the tendons in his
forearms straining against his skin.

'Seamus,' she began again, summoning all the images
into her mind that would defend her from this passion.
She was almost desperate this time, pleading with him
to recognise that what she really wanted him to do was
address the terrible things that had been left unsaid. 'You
have to talk to me about what happened . . .'

Seamus was merciless. While she was speaking, he had

dipped the top of his little finger into the foaming mixture, and before she could finish what she was saying, he had brought his finger up close to her rosebud mouth. 'Try,' he spoke over her and, embarrassingly, hypnotised by the sheer magnetism of his presence, she had taken his foam-soaked finger in her mouth, caressing the tip with her lips as she released it. The sauce spilled into her mouth, a warm, buttery flow of bubbles that popped then melted on the tip of her tongue. Her eyes closed as her body surrendered to the sensation, and she ran her tongue back over her lips to gather more of the rich, frothing flavour. It escaped over her tongue and disappeared down the back of her throat.

He was watching her, intently.

'It's like the choux pastry my father used to make. So — light, so . . . full of air.'

'Perfect,' whispered Seamus.

Genevieve felt as if she was on two planes: on one she wanted to crush Seamus, on the other she was melting in front of him; she was not in control of either.

He was moving across the kitchen now, and reached up onto a shelf where he grasped two warmed plates. He brought them back to the counter where she was sitting, and she thought she heard one of the plates tremble as he set it down. He arranged the spears, then picking up the saucepan, drizzled over the yellow sauce. On the side of each plate he placed a sprig of chervil.

'That's the herb of my home!' exclaimed Genevieve, nostalgia triggering something deep inside her, not knowing what was going to come out until she had said it. 'It used to grow on the roadsides in Grèves, sprouting all through the summer. You could smell it as you walked along.'

'I remember,' said Seamus, pointedly. For him too the smell brought back so many hot and balmy evenings they had spent together that summer. He recalled the two of them walking along, the chervil fragrance invading their nostrils, his arm gently around her waist and the touch of her soft thigh on his hand as he caught her dress up between his fingers.

He turned towards her but this time he could not trust himself to look at her face. Instead he fixed his gaze on her lap. Her skirt had risen up above her knee, exposing a little of the flesh of her thigh. Oh, how he wanted to trace the line of her leg up her inner thigh, to ... but not yet.

'Let's eat, I've laid a table down here,' he said abruptly.

Across the other side of the kitchen Genevieve noticed a small table, draped in white linen, with cutlery and glasses laid out. Then, quite unexpectedly, as she braced herself to jump off the counter, she felt his large hands spread underneath her arms, and in one quick, easy motion, Seamus had lifted her off the counter and onto the floor. Breathless, he pulled her slightly towards him before he let go. The adrenaline coursed through her body.

'Mademoiselle, dinner is served. Please take your seat,' he said gesturing to the table. She walked over. He lit the candle in the middle. She pulled out her chair. He turned off the kitchen lights. Outside dusk was falling, and as they sat down opposite each other, their faces lit by the glow of the naked flame, his legs were so close to hers underneath the table she could feel their heat. But they weren't quite touching.

Now they faced each other, the table drawn like a battlefield, laden on his side with hope and optimism, the promise of his salvation even; on hers with all the restraint and defiance she could muster to control the pulse now pounding through every part of her body. Their eyes focused on each other. Genevieve's lips had fallen slightly apart, her heart was beating madly now.

His arms reached across the table. She thought he would take her hand; instead, he picked up her glass and lifted it to her.

'Genevieve,' he began, struggling to say something honest, something from within his very bones, 'I can't tell you what an overwhelming surprise it is to see you again. You are more beautiful and more sexy than ever.'

Seamus was rejoicing in the unfamiliar sensation of happiness, revelling in living, in the sweet pains that were swamping his brain and his body. He remembered them from six years before. Right at this moment, the girl before him was everything his life needed, he knew that. She, and what she could represent, suddenly seemed to replace all the notoriety and the ambition that made up his present life – and his future hopes.

She took the glass from his hand. He picked up a spear and dipped its bulbous, succulent tip into the foaming sauce and, resting his elbow on the table, offered it to Genevieve. She leaned forward, and although she had intended to take the asparagus from his hand with hers, instead found herself taking the spear in her mouth, breaking it off just before the stalk. A flicker of what looked like agony passed across his face. As the green flesh broke up, and the sauce spread like a creamy film over her tongue and the insides of her cheeks, she felt the last of her defences crumbling.

Now he picked up his fork, and while his eyes never once left her face he pierced one of the spears and repeated the sensation in his own mouth. The two slowly reached for their glasses of Burgundy and simultaneously brought the thin rims to their lips. Replacing the glasses, they moved in closer, and suddenly his knee had caught hers under the table. A stab of hot energy ran down through Genevieve's stomach and flamed between her legs. Her pupils flinched, and Seamus noticed. He reached across the table for her hand, but somewhere in Genevieve's mind an alarm went off and she snatched it away.

'Seamus!' she cried out, in an attempt to bring them to their senses. His name cut through the air like a carving knife. Startled, he stared at her. 'Please. Talk to me. Tell me, why did you never . . . ?' Genevieve couldn't finish the question, but both knew what it was. She needed to know the answer: Seamus didn't have one for her.

He stood up quickly from the table, picked up their plates and went back to the metal counter. Genevieve sighed and slumped back in her chair in despair. He returned with two more plates, bearing the artichokes.

Genevieve was glad of something to do with her hands, to stop them flying up to his face, tracing the line of his jaw, parting his lips, scratching out an answer from his silent features. Obsessively, she began to peel off the petals, ripping them from the stalk, watching the bulb become smaller in her hand, as the leaves fell away, bringing the heart closer.

Seamus drew in a deep breath. He knew he could not ignore her any longer. 'Genevieve . . .'

He was going to say something now, thank God. She stopped peeling off the petals quite so viciously.

'You come and find me six years later, and I'm not quite the boy I was then.' He paused, searching himself for the truth, driven by the desire to be worthy of this beauty in front of him. 'I think I was confused. I didn't understand . . .'

Seamus was struggling. He tried again. 'I don't think I believed anything that happened to me was any good. We all make mistakes, Genevieve; losing you was certainly one of mine. And here you are in all your beautiful glory sitting opposite me across this table, and I wonder myself what happened.'

The petals were still falling away; Genevieve's eyes were still fixed on the artichoke, waiting for its soft centre to reveal itself, its little heart of pale green flesh to yield itself up from the pointed leaves around it.

'If you had any idea of the effect you have on me you would never doubt for one moment the way I feel about you. About your skin, your face, your perfect body. Even your hands that are so busy with that artichoke.'

And suddenly he grasped her wrist as it pulled off the final petal. She gasped and looked up at him, and saw the desire open and naked on his face. He guided her hand, limp in his, up to her mouth which she opened on reflex and she bit into the soft flesh of the multi-layered heart. It disintegrated in her mouth: the taste was sublime. She moaned in reaction to her pleasure and it broke him. In one movement he was out of his chair, kneeling at her feet, his hands over her bare calves. Her hands flew to his hair. She leaned down and brought her mouth to his and the first touch of their lips against each other sent their heads spinning back to a time long ago, a delicious time they were conjuring up now in his restaurant kitchen. Pressing their lips together urgently, they savoured the sweetest thing either had ever tasted, then began to explore it with their tongues, pushing ever deeper in a thirst for more.

Genevieve felt herself being lifted out of her chair, cradled in his strong arms and pressed against the reassuring warm hardness of his chest. Their lips never left each other. Then, vaguely, she felt Seamus turn round and lay her down across one of the cold metal kitchen counters, its sensation a thrilling contrast to the heat that was pouring from her body. Now his palms were shaping the curves of her breasts, waist and hips, his broad splayed hands encompassing the width of her sides delicately but urgently, as if he were holding her body together. She brought her hands up to his chest and traced the outlines of his torso, but was not satisfied until she had touched him. Pulling his shirt urgently out from his waistband she brought her arms up underneath his T-shirt – his soft skin shocking to the touch. He felt the silky flesh of her forearms brushing against his chest. Skin on skin.

He broke his mouth away, looked deep into her opening eyes, glazed and drunk with desire, and ripped off his

T-shirt. His chest was as strong and defined and captivating as it had ever been, and Genevieve began to plant butterfly kisses over its width, gathering his nipples in her mouth, pulling luxuriously on them. She felt him tug at her own T-shirt, and she threw her arms up in the air in surrender as he pulled it over her head. Grappling with the cotton straps of her bra, he released her breasts and they swung against his chest, her hard nipples brushing against his skin. Both shuddered in pleasure.

Pulling her away from him he drank in her appearance, quite amazed by how perfect her body appeared to him. Her skin had a golden glow; her nipples were a dark chocolate brown. Unable to resist any more, he brought his hands up to trace the perfect mounds of her breasts, their smooth skin caressing the inside of his chafed, workman's palms. He bent down and took one perfect nipple, erect and hard, into the soft wetness of his mouth.

As his teeth gently squeezed her, she found herself already fighting off her climax. She reached for his belt. Fumbling, she undid the clasp, then pushed the straining buttons of his fly through their holes. His cock sprang out, and as she pulled down his trousers, she felt his hands underneath her skirt, skimming her inner thighs, caressing the cloth of her panties, feeling the wetness and heat from between her legs. He grasped the waistband of her panties, and she lifted herself so he could pull them down over her thighs, and off over her feet.

Without any hesitation, both of them teetering on the brink of climax, he pulled her across the counter towards him, bringing her legs either side of his hips, his cock level with her, desperate to explore her. She pulled herself further to the edge, until she felt the tip of his cock nestle against her and, unable to control herself, not caring any more, slowly she pulled his massive length into her, inch by inch.

Both were stultified by pleasure, frozen by the force

of the sensation, not wanting to move in case it pushed them over the edge. Feeling her soft heat enveloping him, Seamus screwed up his eyes in an effort to control himself, but Genevieve was moaning, and the sound of her was too much for him to bear. He pulled back, then pushed into her, and as he did so he felt her shudder inside. It was too quick – he pulled out of her again, but the moment he did so he wanted to be back inside her.

Obeying some deep desire inside herself, and wanting to give him more before she came, Genevieve turned herself over, so she lay with her stomach on the counter, her buttocks turned up to him. Grasping her hips, he guided himself slowly into her. The pressure was exquisite. As her sweet cunt clasped his cock in the spasms of her orgasm, he felt himself released inside her. They came all over each other, their muscles pulsating for what seemed like minutes. Overwhelmed by love and affection for her, Seamus gathered her up, and pulled her into him.

Eventually, when he had recovered his breath, he pulled her gently off him, and whispered into her ear: 'My beautiful Genevieve, I am now going to take you to the most sumptuous bed in London where I am going to make love to you properly: slowly, as you deserve.'

Limp against him, racked by her juddering orgasm, she could only nod weakly in his arms.

The two thick steaks still lay bleeding in the corner, the Lafite Rothschild left to degenerate in the decanter.

How to open a bottle of Champagne

1. Firstly, you will need to chill the champagne to the required temperature. 6 to 10 degrees centigrade is recommended. Generally this involves chilling a normal-sized bottle in a fridge for a good few hours beforehand, but longer will be needed for magnums, jeroboams and Nebuchadnezzars.

2. Tear off the foil. Then, placing the thumb on the top of the cork, untwist the wire cage.

3. Holding the bottle at an angle facing away from you, grasp the cork in one hand and twist the base of the bottle with the other. Let the pressure in the bottle do the work for you.

4. Pour at a 45-degree angle into flute glasses – these preserve the bubbles better than saucer-shaped ones.

5. Quaff.

15

Whilst Seamus was doing his best to make amends for lost acquaintances, Marion was doing her best to sustain current ones. Down at Club Louche, word was already out that Marion and Seamus had teamed up on a joint venture, and although no one knew exactly what it was, the combination of the two personalities made it sound extraordinarily exciting.

Exultant from her performance at lunchtime, if a little humiliated over her exit – but she had glossed over that so many times now she wasn't sure if it had actually happened or she had just imagined it – Marion was allowing herself a little celebration. Well, not so little. After being entertained by Salvatore for a few hours with some of his finest produce and the odd bottle of Krug, it had seemed a shame to call it a night when he had clicked his fingers, summoned his car and shaken hands with her, 'his sexy leetle beezness partner'. So she had gone on to Louche.

And by that stage Marion was itching to tell someone the whole grand plan from start to finish. To discuss in minuscule detail the largest opening party London would ever witness, to show off the array of services such as others had only dreamed of, to vent her wildest fantasies for the penthouse parties and to crow over a PR operation that was going to keep Marvellous busy for months – just as well, she thought stoically: taking on Marrow was going to drive all of her other restaurant clients elsewhere. Needless to say, word was already out that something was going on. Rufus had been forced to admit his mistake to

his editor, who had told the newsroom, who had been
sent out scouting and had therefore told everyone, that
Marion and Seamus had been having lunch together over
some architectural plans. The pair were up to something,
for sure, but no one knew what, where, when, how
and – more importantly – on what scale this venture
might be.

Marion looked around to see whose ear she could
whisper her new big secret into – expunging from her
mind her other encounter with an ear that day – and
spotted, as ever, Henrietta Gross-Smythe over by the bar.
Right, thought Marion, if I tell her then it'll be all over
town by the end of the night. Perfect.

'Darling, how are you?' *Mwah, mwah.*

'Oh Marion, I'm so well, how are you?' *Mwah, mwah.*
'You look pleased with yourself: had a good day?'

'Like you wouldn't believe, honey.'

'Oh, do tell! I must say I'd heard a little rumour something was afoot. Sounds as if it might be tremendously
exciting. Oh sorry, I forgot, let me introduce my walker for
tonight.' Leaning over, Henrietta whispered conspiratorially
into Marion's ear, 'I understand one is not allowed to say
boyfriend any more, and he certainly isn't my partner 'cos
all we've done is snog – once.' Then turning to her 'walker'
she announced: 'Marion, meet Henry Hampson. He works
in television.'

Henry turned out to be the rather dapper man leaning
against the bar to Henrietta's right, and with his tanned
skin, slicked back blond hair and foppish public-schoolboy
looks, he just about carried off the cravat and jacket
he was wearing. Just, noted Marion. Turning her gaze
upon him, and slowly undressing him with her gaze as
it lingered from head to toe over his body, she then
fixed him with her most provocative look and offered
him her hand.

'How nice to meet you, Henry.'

'And you,' he returned, now completely in her snare. Henrietta yawned. This usually happened when she introduced Marion to her menfriends. However, she noticed that tonight Marion's performance was a little less polished than usual, her speech even slightly slurred. Also, she noted Marion was unusually carrying a glass of fizz in her hand. She was a stickler for sobriety at Louche, and had often lectured Henrietta about it, saying, 'You've no idea what you miss when you're pissed.'

'Celebrating, are we?' Henrietta asked.

Marion, who was not in the least bit interested in Henry really, but knew that a contact in television was a contact in television, graciously signed off her eye-contact with him with a nod, and seizing Henrietta by the elbow, she whisked her away.

'Oh, I've got the most amazing bit of news to tell you!' she giggled, jigging down the stairs, Henrietta struggling to keep up, both women negotiating the descent as quickly as their stilettoes would allow.

'What, Marion? Where are you taking me!' Henrietta shrieked, knowing full well she was off for a noseful.

'Come to the Ladies and I'll tell all.'

After they had finished in the toilets and were touching up their make-up in the mirror, Marion asked, 'So, tell me darling. Before I start with me, I want to hear all about *you*. Got a new man, I see. So what's the score with Henry, then?'

'He's my Piers replacement. Frightfully boring, but rather sweet.'

'Hear no evil, see no evil, date no evil, darling. Makes for an easy life.'

'If a totally dull one. I'm bored, Marion, I need some excitement!'

'But, darling, what could they possibly do to make your life more exciting? You fly to New York three times a week as it is.'

'Oh, I don't know. Someone to fuck me differently or something, I guess.'

Marion, who up until this point had regarded Henrietta as something of a conservative when it came to matters of the duvet, raised her eyebrows and gave her an approving nod. 'Absolutely, darling. One should learn a different position every month, is what my mother used to tell me.'

'Crikey,' said Henrietta. 'I only know three!'

'Oh sweetie, all you have to do is ask,' drawled Marion, this time giving Henrietta the benefit of her come-to-bed eyes. Henrietta looked rather startled by the come on, and Marion decided that she was probably not inclined her way – yet. To lighten the situation, she told her, wagging her Chanel lipstick in Henrietta's face: 'Just remember, a woman's favourite position is CEO: Chief Executive Officer.' Henrietta was delighted with this and made a mental note of it for her next column.

By the time the women had both partaken of Salvatore's finest and reappeared in the bar, Henry was usefully talking to someone else.

'Now come here, Henrietta,' said Marion, marching her over to a table on the other side of the bar. 'I need your undivided attention for this. Firstly you must understand it's a big secret, so I don't want you telling anyone, OK? At least not until it's announced tomorrow morning. Right?'

'Of course – you know how discreet I am.'

'Yes, exactly.'

'Marion!' Henrietta tried to sound offended.

'Now listen, it's about this project Seamus Bull and I are setting up together. I can tell you, sweetie, it's going to be huge.'

'So what is it?' asked the younger woman excitedly, glad to be the first to know, and already glancing round the bar to see who she would tell.

'Well, it's not exactly a restaurant, and it's not exactly a club, and it's not exactly a bar, or a market – it's all of them all together, in the most enormous four-floor Knightsbridge food frenzy!' And from there Marion went on to detail the exact aspects of the project – with a large amount of poetic licence of course, to the increasingly open-mouthed Henrietta.

'I want to walk in and you know what I want to smell? I want to smell sizzling steak and Chanel No.5! I want to see cocaine and cod everywhere; I want to be blinded by the clouds of cigar smoke – oh, I *love* the smell of Montecristo A in the evening! I want to see women in tailored waists sitting down to six-course meals, men looking nervous when the sommelier hands the wine list to the woman, people-watchers craning their necks from their tables to see who is sitting where, cigarette girls dancing about and having their bottoms pinched by drunk City boys. That's what a restaurant is all about, my darling. I've known it for years, I've just never been able to do it – until now.'

'My God, Marion, you're a genius. It's going to be huge!'

'Of course it is, cherub, and you must be there.'

'You can count on it: I'll put it in my column on Sunday.'

'*Every* Sunday!'

'Er, yes OK, every Sunday then.'

'You see, it's about "just-affordable glamour". I know to you and me that sounds like an oxymoron, Henrietta.'

'An oxy what?'

'A contradiction in terms, my darling, but it is one that will keep the masses coming. That brasserie upstairs is going to have to turn round thousands of customers a night, and for that we are going to have to widen the net. Not everyone can be truly glamorous – let's face it, not everyone can afford it, darling. But this will give everyone a chance, for one night only, to run with the rich and famous. To eat the food of Seamus Bull, to dine within the illustrious portals of Marrow. They will be coming up in their coachloads from Essex and Kent and wherever else it is they hide out, to indulge in the illusion that they are part of the scene, that they are one of Seamus Bull's favoured customers.'

'I see,' said Henrietta, who believed she had encountered these masses several times before. Garage openings and inaugural supermarket foundations in the Home Counties were her speciality, that was what she got paid to promote, and Henrietta had frequently rubbed shoulders with such 'coachloads'. She was somewhat unconvinced by Marion's conviction they could be glamorous for a day. But she couldn't halt Marion in the middle of her verbal Cresta run and besides, she didn't like being negative.

'One thing's for sure: it's going to make you and Seamus a lot of money,' she said generously.

'A lot of money!' screeched Marion in return.

'And what are you going to do with your fortune when you have it, darling?'

'I'm going to buy an island in the Bahamas, build a great big marble palace and run a harem for the rest of my life. I shall live on a diet of sun, sea and sex and I shall never have to work again.'

'How marvellous!'

'Darling, feel free to visit whenever you like,' countered Marion, letting her knee accidentally brush against Henrietta's as she uncrossed her endless legs. Henrietta blushed and decided to change the subject.

'So let me get this straight: you persuaded Seamus to do this by getting Rufus to drop the charges?'

'Quite.'

'And how exactly did you get him to do that?'

'PR, darling. It's the answer to everything. Talk of the devil, there he is. I expect he's got something to say to me, and oh look, no surprises, Emmanuel Coq's over there too. I swear, the two of them are joined at the hip. And with Rufus's hips, who could tell?'

Rufus was looking and feeling distinctly disgruntled, despite his 'exquisite' lunch, and was complaining to Coq that the encounter with 'That Brute' had caused him severe indigestion. His real problem, though, was that something big was about to go down in the food world and he wasn't a part of it. For the first time he had the slightly uneasy feeling he might have backed the wrong horse. He ordered a large bowl of pitted olives and a double G and T.

'Good God, there's Marion again. She's got a cheek showing up here,' he spluttered, conveniently forgetting this was actually Marion's club and that not every establishment in London was at his beck and call. But he was dying to hear more about 'the project', and suggested to Emmanuel they go and do some digging. Perhaps they could even try to warn her off, he suggested. Coq, who was busy thinking, and had been since lunch-time, couldn't agree more.

'Good plan, Rufus. To wage a successful war, one must have good intelligence.'

'Best go on a sortie then,' Rufus replied. He was mildly surprised by how seriously Coq was taking this: it lent the project added gravitas, that was for sure. And if Coq was worried, that worried Rufus more.

'Now Marion,' started Rufus, having waddled the length of the bar, 'do you, you poor sweet girl, have any idea what you are getting yourself mixed up in here? You are consorting with a drugs baron and a psychotic maniac who is under the mistaken illusion that he can cook, and you are trying to open a restaurant with them?'

Rufus left the question open-ended in the hope Marion would enlarge on the restaurant's description. He needn't have worried.

'More than just a restaurant, Rufus.'

'It's practically a theme park!' squealed Henrietta, who loved knowing things other people didn't, and in particular showing off about it, unfortunately thus ensuring that her special knowledge was quickly widely shared.

'Really?' asked Rufus.

'Sounds dreadful,' said Coq, as he planted himself on the bench next to Rufus and irritably threw one leg over the other.

'You'll come to a sticky end you know, Marion,' tutted Rufus again, the great cowls of flesh enveloping his face and neck quivering as he shook his head.

'No,' threw in Emmanuel. 'It will be worse than that. You will lose everything.'

Marion, who had never managed to work her charm on Coq, did not mind affirming him as the enemy now, and threw him a Drop Dead Immediately look. It bounced off Coq like rain off an oil-slick.

'You know, there are those who bite off more than they can chew, who think too big, who put style over substance, and you know they inevitably end up in a nasty mess,' drawled Coq.

'Is that so?' Marion countered. 'Well, I have always rated style over substance, particularly when it's on a grand scale. You know what we women always say: size does matter!'

At which point Henrietta was unable to control herself any longer and collapsed in giggles into Marion's lap.

'Do excuse us please,' said Marion, standing up and hauling Henrietta with her. 'This girl has gossip to spread.'

'I can't believe you said that!' squealed Henrietta, still trying to recover herself. 'Particularly when it's a well-known fact,' and here Marion joined in unison: *'that Emmanuel Coq doesn't have a cock!'*

This particular urban myth had started when Coq had divorced his second model. She had used the 'fact' in court as her defence against adultery when Coq had caught her in bed with his maitre d'. The case had since gone down in judicial history as the first time a judge had publicly asked the plaintiff to get his cock out. Legend had it that the model had, more or less, been telling the truth. Coq was left fuming and scarlet on the bench.

Marion and Henrietta returned to the Ladies, a flurry of heels, swinging hair and shrieking, leaving the fat man and the thin man, as Marion had taken to calling them, to gnash their teeth and dream up plans for sabotage.

'Oh, what a fantastic double-act those two make,' screamed Henrietta. 'This new Marrow is going to be the most fun London has had in ages, you know!'

'I do know,' replied Marion. 'But that Coq has got a nasty bite. I can see I'm going to have to watch him. Maybe it was a little tactless securing the site opposite his, but I did it because I knew it would be the final inducement to Seamus. If a reincarnated Marrow could be seen as a personal snub to his sworn enemy, I knew he'd sign up without a doubt.'

'And has he?'

'Can't wait for it to open – all there remains for him to do is write the cheque.'

'Mmm, the most important part.'

'Oh, don't worry about that. Seamus has got pots of money. You know how successful Marrow has been.'

'Seamus told me posh restaurants don't make loads of money.'

'No, but the endorsements he does do. He must have it – or if not he can get it. For Christ's sake, it's the only thing I'm asking him to sort out. I'm doing everything else myself.'

'Gosh, he's going to be huge on the scene if this comes off.'

'It can't *not* come off, Henrietta,' snapped Marion, who was fed up with everyone's incredulity. She'd show them.

'And you say he is single?'

Marion paused, mid-lipstick sweep. Brilliant! Why the hell hadn't she thought of it before? Then casually continued the swipe. 'And terribly lonely, you know.'

'Poor thing.'

'Yes, I know. He really needs a partner right now. There's a chap with passion and excitement. My God, if someone was looking for something a bit different then they need look no further.'

'Oh, really?'

'Yes, Henrietta,' said Marion, looking her full in the face now.

Henrietta blushed again, then sighed: 'Oh, but he couldn't possibly be interested in me.'

'What utter rubbish! Don't you remember last time he was all over you? Piers couldn't get you away from him! I'd say he was rather keen, knowing him as I do.'

'Would you?' wondered Henrietta, intrigued. Maybe he was exactly what she needed. Enough of this posh stuff: she should try a bit of rough.

'Can you imagine what an awesomely powerful couple you would make?' Marion conjectured aloud. 'You with all your amazing connections and thousands of friends, Seamus with his reputation and his talents, his fame and, of course, his money-spinning business. That would certainly keep you on Concorde, darling. There would be no stopping the two of you! You would rule the city!' Marion had to steady herself against the sink in her excitement.

'More champagne!' she cried. She was having the time of her life.

Meanwhile Rufus and Coq were plotting. Although Coq seemed convinced a super-huge Marrow couldn't come off, he nevertheless appeared unduly worried just in case it did. He needed a plan.

Rufus, on the other hand, was trying to reassure Coq that one killer review would send the whole place up in smoke 'just like the last Marrow. Ha, ha!'

Coq rolled his eyes. 'Silly fat fool. You are deluded about your own power, Rufus! Don't you see: the people going to this place won't be the readers of your column. It's

the common man! They don't care what you think —
they have no taste. Christ, Bull will probably be serving them steak hâché à la McDonald's, or Kentucky
fried goujons. And they'll love it because it will come
on a monogrammed plate with a sprig of chervil on
the side. It's going to be *so* vulgar! And what's worse,
it's going to completely ruin the view from my restaurant.'

'You could always move,' tried Rufus unhelpfully.

'Never!' came the reply. 'It mustn't be allowed to open,
we must stop it now.' Coq continued to think. Rufus didn't
dare move or speak for fear of breaking his concentration.
Emmanuel was a scary man when upset. Which was, Rufus
seemed to remember, the reason why he had decided to
venerate him in the first place.

'Staff — he'll never find the staff,' Coq said suddenly.
'He'll need hundreds for a place like that. Good staff
without jobs do not exist in London. He'll have to poach
them.'

'In that case we'll just jolly well poach them back!'
spluttered Rufus. 'In fact, I've got a brilliant idea: why
don't we begin with his present staff? Let's offer them
twice the money for jobs at Mirage.'

'I have already invited them to join me at Mirage. I may
get some that way, but the rest . . . it's not enough on
its own.'

'OK then,' tried Rufus again. 'What if there was an
archaeological burial ground beneath the site? Then they
would have to abandon the building and open it as an
exhibition instead!'

'Good, but not that good as the site's already there,
you nincompoop. They don't even have to build — just
restructure internally. That's the beauty of it. There must
be something we can do. Rufus, I'm going back to my
kitchen to think. You do the same and we'll both come
up with some plans by the morning. Anything to stop Bull

opening an infernal supermarket opposite my restaurant!'
Coq wailed. 'I simply can't bear it!'

'Don't worry, Emmanuel, we'll find a way!' spluttered
Rufus, although he'd never felt more lacking in ideas. He
never was good at thinking on an empty stomach.

Wake up

One cup of black tea with lemon
Half a grapefruit
One glass of freshly squeezed orange juice
One pot of freshly made coffee
Sugar

1. Start with the tea. Best taken whilst still in bed.

2. Pad to kitchen. Prepare juice and fruit. Take at table, with newspaper.

3. Shower, change. Enjoy the coffee. Sugar optional.

16

One broad shard of white sunlight penetrated the room from underneath the black blind, lancing the air like a warrior for daylight. Two of the windows were completely blacked out, but the dark blind on the third had not quite been pulled down to the sill. The huge bed in the centre of the room, draped in folds of black silk, was illuminated by the beam of light on its right side, but the figure that lay motionless in the centre was impervious to the rays. Blindfolded, she lay like a corpse, her arms and legs spread-eagled, her alabaster body completely naked on top of the black sheets.

The silence was broken by the shrill ringing of the telephone. The figure stirred, reluctantly, and the arm reached out across the sheet to the marble side table and picked up the phone.

'What?' the body mumbled.

'Marion? It's Fuzz here. This is your wake-up call. You're holding a press conference in the Hyde Park Hotel in thirty minutes.'

Fuzz was Marion's right-hand woman at Marvellous. She knew after she had spoken to the somewhat celebratory Marion at ten o'clock last night that she was going to need the wake-up call today. Behind every successful woman is another woman, Marion would chant at her, every time she rattled off a list of orders.

The figure sat bolt upright in bed, airline mask still on, and emitted a low wail.

'I've sent your car to pick you up in fifteen minutes. Have you got everything you need?'

The figure wailed again, dropped the phone, and scrabbled with its mask. Underneath it was not a pretty sight.

'Fuck!' began Marion, urgently looking round. 'Fuck, fuck, fuck, fuck, fuck, fuck!' she continued, each *fuck* getting louder and more desperate until she found her handbag, unloaded it of its pills, poured out a handful, then grabbing a large glass of clear liquid from the bedside table, attempted to swallow them down. With a scream, the liquid and the pills reappeared in a projectile fountain over the bed.

'Fucking vodka!' she shrieked, and scrabbling for more pills, headed for the bathroom.

She had ten minutes, but Marion was practised in the art of speed dressing: she had been doing it all her life. Grabbing a long black Ghost dress and cardigan, her large black sun visors and a tube of Clarins on the way, Marion emerged, nine and half minutes later, prepared. Walking into her vast shoe mountain she chanted, 'Choo or Blahnik, Choo or Blahnik?' before deciding it was a Choo day. Then she grabbed a bag from a rack of nearly fifty, emptied the contents of her previous night's clutch bag into the new one, changed the battery on her mobile phone, and stepped out onto her doorstep just as the chauffeur was reaching to ring the bell.

'Morning, madam. Hyde Park Hotel?'

'Hell would be preferable,' replied Marion, then remembered, as she smelt her own vodka breath, that she had forgotten to brush her teeth. 'Fuck – my teeth!' Turning to re-enter the house, she changed her mind. 'No, no time.' Reaching into her bag she scrabbled about until she found her breath freshener, and sprayed the entire contents of it into her mouth for what, thought the chauffeur, seemed like a remarkably long time for anyone to hold their breath. That done, she dived into the back seat of the car. Her head, immaculate now from the outside, was little more than a building site within. Marion spent the car journey in repertory karmic meditation – her only remedy for a hangover.

Slowly, languidly, Genevieve stretched out her leg from under the cotton covers. Her soft golden flesh was encircled around the toned, muscular body of Seamus, their limbs twisted up together with the white sheets. Her blonde hair spilled over the vast expanse of his chest, and both, in their sleep, wore a look of utter contentment and satisfaction on their faces. The night had been long and luxurious. Genevieve had never been taken to a hotel before – at least not a five-star one, and beside them an empty bottle of Tattinger lay drunkenly against the side of its ice bucket, testament to the decadence that had recently taken place.

Seamus stirred too now, and wrapping his arm around her soft chest, in the depths of his unconsciousness he registered the soft round bulbs of her nipples, and his cock began to rise.

'Mmmmm,' he sang into her ear, as he turned her over, spooning her small voluptuous body against his. Genevieve's eyelids flickered, and focusing on the large masculine hand that held hers tight, she smiled again as she began to remember the night before.

'Mmmmm,' she sang in return, and closing her eyes again, nestled against the mounting hardness pressing into the small of her back.

Then somewhere a mobile phone began to ring. Both smiles on both faces collapsed as consciousness and the cool reality of day took over. Seamus reached out to find the phone, scrabbling in the clothes that lay discarded around the bed.

'Seamus? It's Marion. Our press conference starts in ten minutes. Hyde Park Hotel. I have a car waiting outside your flat, now answer the doorbell and get in it.'

'I'm not in my flat.'

'Well, where the fuck are you?'

'In the Lanesborough Hotel.'

'Right – that's just round the corner – you can fucking well walk. Ten minutes, Seamus.' And she hung up.

'Oh my God,' he groaned into Genevieve's ear. 'Work.'

Genevieve lay frozen, her returning consciousness gripping her in horrific morning regret of The Night Before.

'What time is it?' she asked him, hiding her face so he wouldn't know her mind.

'Time for work. I have to go, baby, I'm so sorry. You stay here and enjoy your morning.'

'I have to work too,' she replied, but waited for him to get up and go before she made a move.

Michael clicked the kettle button on and sighed deeply. Through the dirty, stained kitchen window he looked out across the Kilburn estate. All around him, high-rise towers sprang up from their concrete base, each window a testament to the poor damned souls living behind them, he thought. The heat was making everything on the estate smell: the marauders who had been through the rubbish bins had spilled their contents all over the kids' playground – really clever to have the bins next to the playground, thought Michael – but then it didn't really matter because the only kids who played there were the teenagers doing smack. Sanitary towels dressed the roundabout, broken bottles the swing. Rotting food detritus formed a thin carpet over the floor and dirty needles scattered the ground at the bottom of the slide. Michael turned away from the view, disgusted. He knew he had to get out of this place. But only when everything was resolved.

In the cramped kitchen, high up above the playground, the kettle clicked, waking Michael from his reverie. He reached for a mug and a tea bag. If his dad was still around he'd make a pot. But he wasn't. He poured the water into a single mug, and bent down to open the fridge door. It smelled of rotten food too: damn, thought Michael, the electricity must have gone off in the night again. He held his nose to the lip of the milk carton and wrinkled it in disgust. Black tea then.

Picking up an old periodical, he tried to fan himself. The windows in the front room wouldn't open in case people tried to throw themselves or each other out of them: only the tiny apertures in his bedroom and the kitchen would let through any air. But there was no breeze. He walked back past his dad's room into his own: the room was barely big enough for his bed, single as it was, and he had to hang his clothes from a rail he had fixed from the ceiling. His two changes of chef's whites hung listlessly from the rail. Washed, ironed, pressed and useless. He hated not having anything to do. He missed the restaurant kitchens, missed the cooking – or the little of it Seamus let him do. He couldn't wait to get back to work. Lying on his bed, the small square of glass in the corner of his room allowed him a window on the world. Looking up, all he could see through it was the sky. It was a deep, deep blue. Michael thought again about Dr Roberts's words, words he couldn't banish from his head even if he had wanted to: the doctor's grave, serious tones haunted Michael's every waking and sleeping moment.

'He is not the person he used to be, Michael. Even if, miracle of miracles, we manage to raise him from his coma – and I won't deny it's happened before – the amount of oxygen his brain was starved of at the time of the accident and the state he has been in for the last nine months lead me to believe, based on my medical experience, that he will be severely mentally disabled.'

Michael had blanched at this at the time, and he blanched again now, thinking of it.

'We need to make a decision about what we are going to do.' The words spun round in his head in a flurry of confusion till Michael could stand it no more and he turned on his radio to stop the doctor's voice invading his brain.

'*Thiiiiiiiings can only get beeeeeetter, can only get . . .*' blared the radio, and Michael snorted in disgust.

The problem was, he still had hope. You heard so much about miracle cures: paraplegics who learned to walk again, stroke victims who made full recoveries, coma patients who came round – and were fine. He couldn't deny his father that hope. It was the least he deserved. The doctors couldn't deny it either. Though they had said his chance was one in 10,000. One in 10,000! Well, what if he was that one?

'Remember that anthem?' crooned the DJ. 'Ah, those were the days, eh? But what was the year?'

He looked at the radio with contempt. The clock clicked its fading red digital numbers to 09:39. He had been awake since five that morning. He considered trying to get his old job back, working in one of the West End's fashionable bars, or even trying for another chef's apprenticeship, but he wanted to give the Bull training a go, and didn't wish to do anything that would jeopardise that. He desperately needed something to distract him, something to stop him thinking about this awful decision: one that would leave him wracked with guilt if he went one way, and tortured with uncertainty if he went the other. Work removed that pain, even if it was hellish and tremendously demanding. Anyway, somehow it made him feel less guilty if he was suffering too. Less guilty that he had not seen the car coming.

The shock memory that flashed into his brain horrified him again, and he flung back the covers and stalked into the bathroom. Bathroom was a rather generous description of the stand-up dribble that masqueraded as a shower and a cracked, yellowing washbasin. He had called the council about it every day for the last two months, and still no one had been round to mend it. He had been desperate to move from this flat for years, but his dad had always dug his heels in, saying it was his home and he wouldn't be happy anywhere else. Ever since his accident at work – he had slipped on a wet floor and damaged his back – his dad had been reliant on Michael for lifting or stretching. He had urged Michael to move on, but both knew his dad wouldn't survive without him.

He stepped into the plastic cubicle and turned the tap on. Nothing, just a gurgling. He waited. More gurgling. Still nothing.

'I don't believe it,' he said, unable to comprehend how everything could go wrong at once. The kids had obviously been playing with the pipes again downstairs and he would have to try and get hold of the council to get them reconnected. No shower was a horrific thought in this weather.

The radio was now screeching out: ' . . . *and I miss you, like the desert missed the rain . . .*'

'One of my favourites, but can you remember from when?' asked the DJ.

Michael had had enough of this and he flicked the radio switch off. It was too early to go to the park and find a game of football – no one would be there. The silence in the flat was deafening. Into the living room then: the telly. He switched it on: *Tom and Jerry*. That was better. He settled down to watch it in the sole threadbare armchair. Jerry was now being bandaged up, put in an ambulance and taken to hospital. Michael seized the remote and flicked the channels. His father's one great luxury, that Michael had paid for, was satellite TV, and he had been loath to cut it off since he was in hospital. After all, he had been convinced he was coming home soon.

He began to surf through all the desperate channels: German porn, the picture fuzzed out so all you could hear was the ridiculous Teutonic groaning, some cardboard Spanish soap opera, kids' TV, more kids' TV, a bouncing dwarf reading the weather, a model sashaying down a catwalk in just a hat and skirt, a volley ball match, Marion – *Marion?* There, on the Sky news channel was Marion Maltese, sitting up behind a desk talking to a sea of reporters and taking questions. Michael jerked awake. Marion! What was she doing there?

'So, will the new Marrow be much bigger than the old?' someone asked.

Marrow? Suddenly Michael was fully alert, his miserable reverie forgotten.

'Oh, yes,' enthused Marion, her face half-hidden behind the most enormous pair of sunglasses Michael had ever seen. 'It's going to have four floors and a projected turnover of over 10,000 customers a day.'

'Jesus Christ!' said Michael aloud. He rarely swore, and never in front of his father, but he had been picking up bad habits in the Marrow kitchens. She was talking about Marrow! This must be Seamus's new thing. 10,000 customers a day? What on earth was his boss thinking of? You couldn't produce good food for those sorts of numbers. And where did Marion come into it? he wondered. Seamus always said he couldn't stand her. But then Seamus always said that about everyone.

'And what is Seamus Bull's statement on this?' came another question. At this point Marion turned round to the immaculately suited blonde standing behind her and accepted a piece of paper as the blonde spoke hurriedly in her ear. Then turning back to the crowd, Marion formally read out: 'Seamus Bull is naturally delighted to take his personal project onto such a high commercial plane and promises the excellence and quality of cooking that so far has been denied to too many people by the space constrictions of his current restaurant. He intends to make excellent cuisine easily available to everyone.'

The reporters seemed unconvinced.

'Has this got anything to do with the disastrous review

Marrow got in one of the Sunday papers recently?' came
another question from the floor.

'What review?' smiled Marion sweetly.

The assembled throng giggled.

'What does Emmanuel Coq say about you opening
such a huge place right opposite his new restaurant?'
came another.

'Oh, I'm sure he doesn't mind at all. After all, what
can a four-floor food emporium possibly do to limit his
business?' More laughter from the floor.

Michael could hardly believe it. Seamus was really going
for it. A four-floor food emporium opposite Mirage? It was
incredible. Highly ambitious – about as ambitious as it got,
in fact. He really was going to need a lot of staff then.

'And when can we expect to hear from Mr Bull on the
matter?'

'Well,' replied Marion slowly, turning round to consult
with the blonde behind her, who was fiddling with the
earpiece of a mobile phone, 'he is going to be here
himself very soon. He was, as you can imagine, out
celebrating last night, and consequently is a little late for
this appointment.'

Again more laughter, but Marion knew this was what the
press wanted to hear. They had their image of Seamus as
the hell-raising bad boy, and as long as they didn't go too
far with it, it gave Seamus the extra column inches they
needed. All coverage was good coverage at the moment,
Marion told herself. She just had to keep the interest up
till the opening. But where the hell was Seamus?

'Morning everyone,' came a voice from the back of the
room. 'Beautiful day, isn't it?'

Right on cue the man himself appeared, striding purposefully up the centre of the room. He looked fantastic
– his face was wreathed in the most enormous grin, his
body carried with it the freshness of someone who had
just stepped out of the shower, his hair still slightly damp,

shining under the television lights. But today, more than ever, Seamus Bull positively exuded strength and power. There was an awed hush, then, prompted by Marion's plants in the crowd, a slow handclap started a crescendoing applause that had developed into a full-blown cheer with whoops and whistles by the time Seamus had taken his seat on the podium. It was nothing short of a rock star's welcome. Seamus had to stop himself waving as he strutted up the steps.

'So, ladies and gents of the press – and television too, I see, I hear you have been told about my exciting new plans. I tell you, by the time Marrow is finished, this country will never have seen anything like it.' Seamus was on top of the world. This was the biggest and happiest day of his life: everything seemed to be back on course. 'I believe it will seriously improve everybody's quality of life and teach us to eat in a way that is healthy and delicious. You won't even have to go there to benefit, as everything you need for breakfast, lunch or dinner, catered or uncatered, can be delivered within a fifteen-mile radius. By this time next year, if you're not eating Marrow food, it'll be because you're out of the country.'

Michael was impressed. Seamus certainly had his old hypnotic aura about him again – clearly everyone believed every word he said. Michael hadn't seen that confidence and control in Seamus for a while, but here he was, back on his very best form. The time off had obviously done him good. Michael saw Seamus had the whole room in his thrall, and the camera was hypnotised by him. His dramatic entrance had made fantastic television and Seamus could probably say or do anything now and it would be lauded as the word of God.

'I have worked very hard, for a number of years, to get my cooking to a standard of excellence that I alone demand.' Seamus paused for dramatic effect. 'And you know,' he began again conspiratorially, in a slightly lower tone of voice so everyone in the room had to lean closer to catch it, 'it's only now I feel I've reached that level. But reached it I have, and I do assure you, oh yes I do assure you: I am good and ready to move on to something bigger, something better, something enormous and life-changing not only for those who work there but those who go there. And the new Marrow is It.'

Marion whispered something in his ear. Michael rather fancied it was, 'Steady on'. Honestly, what a load of rubbish. He had to hand it to Seamus though – he was certainly impressive.

'I promise to maintain the standards and quality of the previous Marrow faithfully, and I guarantee that anyone who eats any of my food or that of my own personally hand-picked and hand-trained chefs will not be able to tell the difference from the food I cooked in the previous Marrow of Notting Hill.'

A pause as the audience frantically scribbled in their notebooks.

'Any questions?' asked Seamus, who was quite used to dealing with the media by now. Usually it was a shove or a punch if they got in his way late at night, but he was shrewd enough to know they could help him too and it paid to give them what they wanted now.

'But Seamus, didn't you want to get three Michelin stars first?' came a brave voice from the middle of the room. 'The guide refused to award you the third star again this year. Do you think that is fair?'

Seamus fixed the reporter with a glare. 'Perhaps I and the Michelin inspectors judge our food by different standards,' he replied coldly.

Perhaps you drink too much and do too many drugs, thought Michael. You lose control in your kitchen when it could be avoided. Your palate isn't what it used to be. You've forgotten what you were doing there in the first place.

'Any further questions?' interrupted Marion quickly before Seamus lost his cool – always a danger.

'Yes. When can we expect the opening?'

'Work begins there this morning,' replied Marion cheerfully, 'and we hope to have the opening well before Christmas. Anything else? No, good. OK, we'll finish it there then, folks. Press releases will be handed to you on your way out, and any further information can be directed through the offices of Marvellous PR ...' The picture flicked back to the studio where the bouffant newsreader turned her face to the camera.

'Well, there we have the breaking news for London, with live pictures direct from the Hyde Park Hotel. Seamus Bull has closed down his famous restaurant in the city's Notting Hill, only to replace it with plans for a gigantic new emporium in Knightsbridge. Sure to get the capital's appetite going,' grinned the newscaster in her usual anodyne fashion. 'And now for the other headlines for today. Tony Blair has announced that the government will be forced to put up the rate of income tax before the next election ...'

Michael switched the television off and mused over what he had just witnessed. It didn't sound like Seamus's style, a huge cafeteria-style eating palace, although he was not surprised to hear it was being erected opposite Coq's place. That sounded more like the Seamus he knew. It had to be good news as far as a job was concerned, he thought, but no way would Seamus be cooking any more. In those sorts of places the Head Chef sat in an office, Michael thought ruefully. Well, he supposed he'd know more after the next staff meeting.

Seeing Seamus reminded him of that beautiful girl. The image he had of her at the door of Marrow was so clear: lit up like an angel by the sunshine behind her, the few stray blonde hairs wisping around her face had formed a fuzzy halo in the sunlight. He wanted to talk to her some more:

he wanted to know more about her. She had been so open with him, so refreshingly honest and candid. Somehow he felt she would know just what to do about his dad. When he had first seen her, her physical appearance had been so overwhelming he had half expected her not to speak. He would have been content just to gaze at her.

When she had begun talking he had become mesmerised by her lips, pink and full, then gradually he had turned his attention to the rest of her face, clear and open, and then it had struck him: her words. Her voice had been timid at first, until she had felt comfortable with him, and then it had been deep and sure. She spoke with the knowledge of personal grief. She knew what he was suffering, that much had been clear. He liked her. She had moved him.

Living on a council estate and spending all his waking hours in an underground kitchen meant Michael did not get to meet people like that very often. Once again Michael knew he had to change things, this life was not what he wanted for himself. His only new acquaintances over the last months had been the doctors and nurses at the hospital, he thought with horror. And at once the images came crashing back. His father on the bed, the awful, droning, relentless hiss of the ventilator, his father's pale, deadly, inanimate face.

He considered going to find the girl to ask her to help him: she had said she was working in a café on Earls Court Road. It wouldn't be too hard. But he had to dismiss the idea. This girl was a friend of his boss's. He suspected the errands Seamus had sent him on yesterday, quite out of the blue, might have had something to do with her, but he couldn't know for sure. What right did he have to pry? He didn't even know what their relationship was.

Stay well away, he told himself. But he'd do anything to escape the stifling oppression of this flat. Anything to get out of the misery of this estate and the lonely commute to the hospital and back. He had taken to playing football every day in the local park, sometimes twice a day, just as an excuse to break the monotony, to escape his thoughts about his father. No, he thought, he would wait till the staff meeting later that week, find out from Seamus if he had found her, and what she was to him. If he had cast her off like all the rest of his women, then maybe Seamus wouldn't mind if Michael went to find her. After all, he just wanted to talk to her. He would explain it, he thought. Seamus would understand.

But first the council and the water. Michael steeled himself, and reached for the phone.

Couscous

The staple grain of North Africa, couscous is a form of semolina, made from durum wheat rolled into pellets.

Traditionally it is cooked in a *couscoussière*, a covered earthenware pot with holes in the base which fits onto another pot in which a stew is cooked. The couscous cooks in the steam.

When ready it should be light, fluffy and full of air. It is served with the stew.

17

'And what time do you call this?' Mave was standing outside the caff's front door, hand on hips, Rothman shoved in the corner of her mouth. Genevieve was hurtling across the road from the Tube station as quickly as the traffic would let her.

'I'm sorry, so sorry – I promise it won't happen again,' she apologised breathlessly, as she eventually made it to the safety of the pavement. Genevieve was genuinely sorry to have let Mave down – this job was important to her, and Mave knew that, but it did nothing to lessen the sharpness of the cafe owner's tongue.

'I should think so too, young lady. I dunno – I suppose you're just the gullible little fool I took you for in the first place.' Mave was standing fearsomely in front of the door, blocking the entrance. Genevieve prayed this didn't mean she was sacked.

'One scent of a man and you mess everything up for yourself. I could sack you right now. That's what happened to the other girl who was late, wasn't it, eh? So why should I keep you on? Give me one good reason.'

'Because I promise that as long as I work for you I will never be late again,' tried Genevieve, looking down imploringly. Mave, although she was peeved Genevieve was late, was far too interested in what had happened to her the night before to sack her – at least until she had satisfied her with the full details.

'Well I tell you, my girl, if you are, you'll be straight out on your ear, no question. All right? Do you realise what I've had to do so far this morning? The work of two, that's what. I've swept, I've cleaned, I've cooked, I've taken the money. I haven't even sat down for a cup of tea yet and it's half-past ten! You get to work right away, my girl. And you can start with making my breakfast.'

Although Mave was itching to hear what had happened, she wasn't going to ask Genevieve just yet, not till she had made a pretence of calming down first. That girl was really going to have to work for her wages today. Couldn't have that sort of behaviour setting the tone for the rest of their working relationship. You had to sit on these young girls right from the start, in Mave's experience. Mave couldn't help guessing at the reason for her tardiness, but she'd have to get it out of her bit by bit when the rush of customers calmed down. Widowed over ten years ago, this was the sort of action Mave didn't get to see any more – which was a relief as far as she was concerned, as the thought of having to take her support stockings off in front of anyone else these days was mortifying. But she still liked to hear about it, though. Especially when it involved somebody famous. (Genevieve noticed with horror that Mave had already stuck a hand-written notice up on the door saying *Patronised by Seamus Bull*.) After the tea service, Mave thought. She'd get it all out of her then. It was the least Genevieve could do to make up for being late. Oh yes, she thought, she'd get every last detail from her. That would keep the girls amused at Bingo tonight.

Genevieve, for her part, was quite relieved Mave appeared to have taken a vow of obstreperous silence for the moment: it allowed her more time to think about what she had done and what she was going to do. She knew Mave would have last night out of her sooner or later, but in the meantime she had to complete the chores Mave set on her like a plague.

Finally, after the teatime rush, Mave sat her down at one of the tables, lit up a Super King, and demanded to hear the worst. Genevieve kept cool, and went into as much detail as she could without giving her true feelings away. She knew Mave was desperate to hear it, but she didn't mind sharing it with her – besides, she sort of wanted to say it out aloud to see how it sounded. Had it been real? Had it been as good as it felt, or was it just sordid? Did all those things really happen? And more importantly, *should* they have happened? And if they should, why was Genevieve weighed down by an appalling sense of guilt – and fear at seeing Seamus again.

However, Genevieve imparted none of this to Mave. She told her only what had happened. She told her about seeing him in the kitchen, about the asparagus and the sauce, about how it had tasted, about the wine he had chosen, about the way he had moved around his kitchen, the way he had made the food, the way his fingers could judge ripeness with a single touch, the way he had become irresistible to her, the way he had coaxed her, cajoled her, and then how it had all exploded right there in the kitchen on top of the work surface.

'He's a raunchy one, that Seamus Bull!' screeched Mave, delighted she had some real juice for later. 'But no great French Resistance, I see?' she jibed, intrigued by the way Genevieve couldn't meet her eye.

'No, not exactly,' replied her employee uncomfortably.

Then she told her about the hotel, about how he had said he wanted to spoil her, how he felt everything he had achieved so far had really been done for her so they could have a life together, how he had never meant to desert her.

'But the point is,' and here Genevieve raised her eyes to Mave for the first time, and said in a manner that sounded as if she was trying to convince herself, 'by that time it felt so right and it felt so natural, I couldn't not do it.' She paused, trying to figure it out in her own head. 'You see, there was this strange thing, Mave, that it felt OK because it was no different from anything I had done before.'

'That don't make it right, Jenny.'

'No, maybe not,' the other sighed, trying to understand the way she felt.

'So what d'he say? "Sorry, I didn't mean it?"'

'Something like that. It turns out he was sent away, by my father. My father went to see his boss and made him send Seamus back to England.'

'And he didn't write to tell you?'

'He said he tried.'

'And your letters that he didn't answer?'

'They were sent to his old restaurant and he wasn't working there any more. He said he didn't get any. He was given a placement in a different hotel, his English boss had been pissed off with him because he had upset his cousin's friend. He said that was when he got truly ambitious. When he realised you couldn't compromise, you won some things and you lost others, and all you could do was build for yourself. He says this whole restaurant thing, he thinks it was all a replacement for me, only it never made him as happy.'

'A likely story,' said Mave, raising her eyebrows in disbelief and drawing deeply on her fag.

'So you think it's not true?' challenged Genevieve, slightly miffed that her boss wouldn't let Seamus's fantasy run its course. Mave fixed her with her gimlet eye.

'Well, what do you think?'

Genevieve sighed. 'I don't know. I just don't know. What I do know is I wanted him.'

'And now?'

'I still want him, and all the reasons that I fell in love with him in the first place are still there. But I don't know what else is there. He's still the man who left me, and still a man who can get himself arrested. But if what he says is true – and none of it is his fault – then everything is perfect.'

'Huh, that's pretty unlikely,' snorted Mave cheerfully. Sucking the last dregs of her tea noisily out of her cup, she warned, 'You just go carefully, young lady, you hear me? Men are born liars and they'll wriggle out of anything. They can get themselves out of any situation they like but it's only because us women are soft and we let them. Far too soft on them, we are.'

Mave stubbed out her umpteenth fag. 'I tell you I don't like it, I don't like it one bit,' she went on. 'You know there are bad stories that go around about that man, and maybe that's all they are – stories. But what if even some of them are true? Will the same thing happen again? Does he really care about you?'

Mave had clearly taken on the custodial role with Genevieve since the beginning of their relationship. Ever since Mave had forced her to confess to the Seamus Bull affair, and she had encouraged the reunion, Mave had felt slightly responsible. But exciting as it was to have your waitress dating the town's leading celebrity, she couldn't help worrying for her. Still, Jenny wasn't a timid little thing. She might give that impression, thought Mave, but what she liked about her was her front. Coming over to a foreign country, getting a job, facing down the man. Behind her sugar and iced bun image there was a tough 'un determined to get what she wanted.

'Problem with you French is you're all so bloody romantic,' she continued. 'You need a good dose of English cynicism, you do. A good harsh spoonful of reality.'

'I think I've got it, haven't I?' asked Genevieve, smiling at her.

'Ha! You won't listen to a word I say,' Mave replied as she heaved herself up out of her chair, picked up her teacup and started for the kitchen. 'I can tell you it's not all lovemaking on top of tables and asparagus tips at dawn. Oh no.' By now Mave had reached the kitchen and was about to disappear behind the multi-coloured fringe of plastic tails when something else occurred to her. A question she knew she had to ask 'for the girls'. Turning round, she asked bluntly: 'So is it true he's got a whatsit the size of a marrow?'

Genevieve blushed scarlet.

'I'll take that as a yes,' wheezed Mave, trying not to drop her teacup with laughter.

Seamus came to pick Genevieve up from her B&B at eight o'clock. He had made her promise she would be there for him before he had left that morning, and wouldn't leave her until she had agreed. Genevieve regretted it deeply now: she needed more time to think before she decided what to do next, or what she wanted. Mave's words were ringing in her ears and she knew she was in deep water. Too much had already happened between the two of them for this to be a light-hearted affair.

She showered the day's smoke, grease, fumes and detergents off her, and shampooed her hair. Grabbing her towel she ran back to her room and looked in vain in her wardrobe for something to wear. She was surprised at herself: she realised she wanted to look sexy. Seamus had reawakened something in her. She noticed she didn't have anything in the remotest bit alluring: just loose T-shirts, long skirts and jeans. She had compiled this wardrobe deliberately. She had been so uninterested in other men – and so preoccupied with keeping them away from her, that she had never considered dressing up to show herself off. There had only ever been one other since Seamus. She had slept with him mostly because her aunt in the village had warned her that she 'had to get back on the horse'. Only this time, the aunt had shaken a packet of pills at her. In fact she had left it two years, until she had arrived at university, before she attempted to 'ride' again.

His name was Jean-Luc. He had been sweet enough but no great earth-shaker. They had gone out for about eighteen months in all but mostly because Genevieve felt too apathetic to end it, dreading any confrontation with him. He was studying history, she was doing languages and they had bonded over their books in the library. He was a boy, thought Genevieve, but a nice boy. She regarded him as an intimate friend – a kid brother, even. He had wanted to marry her, but she knew she didn't love him. At least not in the way she had loved Seamus.

She pulled out a knee-length floral skirt and a white T-shirt that was slightly smaller than the rest and had a V-neck that showed off a little of her cleavage. She pulled it over her head and, looking in the mottled mirror that hung above the basin in her room, she noticed it traced the curve of her breasts and waist quite closely. She traced the line down her side with her finger. It felt good to be back in touch with her body again: it had been a long time but, she smiled, it had definitely been worth the wait.

Downstairs she heard a sudden commotion and recognised Seamus's voice – but not the sweet, caressing tone of last night. This time he was shouting, and the sound shocked Genevieve. It was ugly. Sensing something was wrong, she ran out of her room and down the stairs. By the time she got to the bottom Seamus had fallen silent, and was standing leaning against the reception desk looking furious.

'What's the matter?'

At the sound of her voice his head snapped up to look at her.

'Genevieve!' Seamus looked stricken. 'What the hell are you doing staying in a place like this?' He strode over towards her and cupped her face in his hands.

The man behind the reception desk was not happy and seemed to be pretending he wasn't there. He was clearly glad of the desk between them. Initially, when Bull had first walked through the door, he had been rather chuffed with his visit from the town's leading chef, but not any more.

'What do you mean?' asked Genevieve, confused.

'It's disgusting! This place is practically a brothel. For Christ's sake, there's a bloke selling crack outside!'

'What is this crack?'

'Better you don't know. This is not the sort of place for someone like you,' he said with a tenderness that seemed quite incongruous from the man who had been shouting earlier. But Genevieve was hurt now, insulted by his reaction to where she lived.

'Oh yes?' she replied. 'And who is someone like me?' She looked at him defiantly. Seamus realised he had over-stepped the mark.

'Look, it's just – it's just not a nice area, OK? Things happen round here, round places like this. Take it from me – this is my city and I know these things.'

'It's been fine so far. Anyway, it's all I can afford.'

'There are much nicer places than this you can stay. Go and get your bags, Genevieve, we're leaving. How much does she owe?'

Seamus turned round to direct this last to the landlord. He, being a wise old bird, had sized up the situation immediately, and said: 'Well, she has booked in to the end of the month, and I'm afraid the cancellation fee is eighty per cent, which means, let's see . . .' and he began tapping his fingers quickly over a calculator.

'Just tell me how much she owes, man!' Seamus was half shouting, still furious that Genevieve was in this dread-ful place.

'Wait, Seamus. What are you doing? Where am I going to go?'

'You can come and live with me,' he replied, reaching for his wallet.

Genevieve was dumbstruck. 'What?!'

'I said come and live with me.' He looked up at her. Her face was defiant but confused. He tried another tack.

'Look, babe, it's stupid you staying here when you could just as easily be living with me. My place is not flash but it's a damned sight better than this. You'll be more comfortable and it won't cost you a penny. Besides, it could do with a woman's touch.'

Genevieve's face remained implacable, especially at the last comment, although Seamus seemed oblivious. She couldn't believe he was trying to bulldoze her like this. Unbelievably, he was already getting out his credit card.

'Seamus,' she said quietly. 'No.'

He paused and looked at her. Her face was unreadable, but Seamus was a man who usually got what he wanted. He persisted. Walking over to the staircase, he placed his hand on her arm.

'I just want to try and make things up to you, OK?' he said tenderly. 'Forgive me if I come on a bit strong, but please, at least let me try to make your – and my – life better now that I have a second chance. I can make things nicer for us. Let me, please.' Seamus looked as if he really meant this, and Genevieve responded better to this approach, secretly flattered he was already thinking of them together, thrilled he wanted to try and improve things. Her face broke into a sympathetic expression again, but she refused to be bullied.

'OK,' she said, eventually. 'But not like this.'

'That's going to be three hundred and twenty pounds please,' said the receptionist, eager to get the money in the bank.

'I'm not leaving,' Genevieve called over to him. 'Let me go and get my handbag,' she said to Seamus, 'and we will go and talk. We need to, but we can't here.'

Seamus nodded, but he was fuming inside. She was defying him – he couldn't believe it. He wouldn't have it – no one defied him any more. And anyway, he reasoned to himself as a plan hatched in his head, his actions would be the best for her in the long term. And suddenly the thought of having her in his flat was far too enticing for him. The moment her back had disappeared round the top of the staircase, he walked back to the reception, leaned over and pressed his face right up to that of the sweating landlord's. Handing over his credit card, he said through gritted teeth: 'You take that money off this card, and tomorrow morning, when she comes down those stairs, you tell her she can't stay here any more. Do you hear me?'

'Yes,' quivered the man, understanding Seamus perfectly and snatching the card and running it through his swipe machine as quickly as possible.

'I don't care what excuse you use, you just make sure she leaves tomorrow. Understand?' And to seal the deal, he pulled a crumpled £20 note out of his pocket and slipped it over the desk. The man pocketed it swiftly, passed him his receipt to sign, and was whistling into his filing cabinet by the time Genevieve had reappeared.

Saying nothing, Seamus took her by the hand and led her out onto the street without a backward glance.

'Seamus, it's not that bad, you know. I've been fine there so far.'

The yellow light of a taxi appeared round the corner, and Seamus stuck out his arm to hail it. It stopped and he opened the door for her. Genevieve stood her ground, looking into his face.

'Get in, please. Let me at least show you where you could be living.' His face was white, Genevieve noticed. She saw he was absolutely furious. She got in and turned to face the window. Seamus looked out of his window on the other side.

After several minutes of strained silence, Genevieve eventually asked, 'So where are you taking me?' Seamus had been using the time to regain control of his temper. It had risen up inside him like bile when he had arrived at that fleapit. How long had she been living like this? Why wouldn't she let him do anything about it? But he could not show her any more of his anger than he had already, and he wrestled to get a grip on himself, to calm his temper down. When he felt like this he was used to shouting and screaming, but he couldn't with Genevieve, he realised. He wasn't in his kitchen now. Things were different with her, and he had to fight his instincts to open his mouth and let all the foul temper fly out of it.

'Paddington,' he replied, tight-lipped, forcing his emotions down.

'Is that where you live?'

'Yes, it is,' he replied, and finally looked across at her and her beautiful face. 'I'm sorry – you know I didn't want to cause a scene earlier.'

'Seamus, a lot has happened to both of us in the last years, and we are not the people we used to be. I am not a child any more, I am a woman. I can look after myself.' I was forced to grow up rather abruptly, she thought, but decided she could not go into that with him right now. She needed to see more of him first. Genevieve smiled. It was quite endearing, she supposed, that he was so protective. Nice even, that he wanted to look after her. But he had to learn she was capable of looking after herself now. She picked up the hand that was resting on his lap, obeying her instincts to settle the situation. She stroked the thumb gently, then looked into his face. 'Thank you for inviting me to stay,' she said, noticing the calming effect she was having on him. 'It's sweet of you and I do appreciate it.'

Seamus enclosed her small hands in his and, in a moment of intimacy, reached across and pressed his lips on hers. Inside their chests, both their hearts began to thunp.

The taxi drew up outside an impressive crescent of terraced Regency mansion houses.

'Right you are then, guv'nor,' tried the taxi driver when his passengers continued to ignore their location and carried on kissing each other instead.

'Oh right, thanks, mate,' broke off Seamus, and opened the door. As he reached for his wallet, he suddenly panicked:

had he changed the sheets since the spiky hotel manageress had been? Shit! He reckoned he hadn't.

He let her in the front door of the flat, then moved through the room quickly, picking up clothes and towels. In the bedroom he ripped off the sheets and threw them into the laundry basket, then frantically scanned the room for anything that might incriminate him.

Genevieve waited uneasily in the living room. It was a beautiful flat: the large floor-to-ceiling windows flooded the living room with light, and the high ceilings and cornicing gave it a grand, glamorous atmosphere. The furniture – what there was of it – looked soft and comfortable. A huge white sofa faced a television in the corner, and over by the windows a wrought-iron table was surrounded by six high-backed chairs. The floor was a polished, light wood, and at the far end of the room the space opened out into a functional stainless steel kitchen, separated off from the room by a breakfast bar. But there were no pictures on the walls, no books, no music, no photos. The place looked like a show flat. A Philippe Starck fruit bowl of lemons even stood on one of the kitchen counters, just like in estate-agent catalogues. He must have bought the place exactly as it was now, thought Genevieve. It gave no clues to his life.

Seamus finally reappeared from the bedroom. 'You know what I'm going to do now?' he said, noting her unease and taking control of the situation. He definitely liked the idea of having her here, he decided. 'I am going to go outside, leaving you for just two minutes,' and here he guided her across to the window and pointed to the busy street below, 'and you see that little supermarket down there? There's a very nice Arab man who runs it and sells the most amazing selection of nuts and dried fruit and spices. I am going to buy some of those and some of his excellent couscous; I am going to bribe him into selling me the most succulent chicken breasts he has in his shop, and I am going to make us a Moroccan feast.'

Genevieve smiled again, excited by his picture of the evening, touched by his enthusiasm and reversal of spirits. He, on the other hand, was hungry for more of that smile, and wrapping his arm round the curve of her back, he turned her into him.

'Then I am going to . . .' and here Seamus bent his head towards hers and whispered the rest of his promise into her ear. Whatever it was, it made Genevieve flush all over her body, from her cheeks all the way down to her sweet, soft and suddenly damp vagina. All thoughts of discussing the past flew from her head.

Summer Pickle

10 limes
100g caster sugar
1kg of mixed: cucumber, de-seeded, peeled and chopped,
red onions chopped, green beans, blanched and chopped
1 fresh red chilli, de-seeded and chopped

A fiery spice paste of, for example, tamarind, ginger,
cumin, cardamom, star anise, cinnamon and nutmeg,
ground together and bound with vegetable oil

1. Squeeze the juice from the limes into a bowl. Add the sugar and stir until dissolved.

2. Stir in three generous tablespoonfuls of spice paste – and the chilli.

3. Stir in and coat the vegetables.

4. Pack into a jar and leave to fester.

18

Genevieve slipped out of the B&B earlier than usual the next morning. Determined Mave should not find a single cause for fault with her work, she had insisted on going back to the hotel last night, despite Seamus's pleas that she stay at his flat, that her job didn't matter. He seriously underestimated her if he thought that: she might be falling for him again but she was going to have a safety net this time. And her job and her own place were that net; as long as she had them she wouldn't be reliant on him, practically speaking. Emotionally, however, she wasn't sure how much longer she would be able – or would want to – maintain her distance. That, she thought, still smiling from the night before, was arriving more quickly than she could have imagined.

Ever since she had first seen him again, in Mave's caff, there had been no mistaking the presence of the old chemistry. In the face of their passion, they were both pretty helpless. But Genevieve didn't think there was too much wrong with that, as long as she kept her independence. And besides, she relished the freedom of having her own job, her own income, her own place to live. She had never had this before: until now everything she had done had been at the behest of her father – even university. He was the one who had been keen she go and get a degree. The abortion hadn't been her decision either. Looking back she realised nothing ever had been – until now.

As she rounded the corner, she heard a voice shouting rudely behind her: 'Oi, miss! Come back!'

She turned to see the galloping hulk of the landlord in his dirty vest and trousers pursuing her down the street. She stopped and waited for him to catch up.

'Now look 'ere, miss, you can't stay in my hotel any longer,' he wheezed.

'I'm sorry?' she asked, confused.

'You've got to leave the Venus, love.'

'What? I don't understand! Why?'

The landlord paused a second, struggling for a decent excuse, until he realised he didn't have to give one.

'Because I am the landlord and I say so,' he told her rudely.

Genevieve was crushed. Just when she thought she had some measure of control, it was being taken away from her.

'But why?' she asked, her mortification clearly visible. Not even the landlord could be totally immune to her charms, and he decided he had to say something.

'That man last night,' he attempted, still gasping for breath. 'Nasty piece of work – won't have that sort in my establishment. You've got to go. Just pay me to the end of the week. I'll let you off the rest.'

Genevieve was dumbstruck. She was being thrown out of her room like some criminal. And all because of Seamus's behaviour. The landlord couldn't do this to her.

'Please, no. I'm sorry about that – he was rude but he won't come again, I promise. I'll tell him not to. No one will come. It will just be me. I will bring no more trouble,' she implored, but it was useless. The landlord had already turned his back and was walking away from her.

'You can check out tonight,' was his only concession, thrown back over his shoulder, without even turning his head.

The moment she arrived at the café, Genevieve tearfully told Mave what had happened.

'The bloody cheek of it!' Mave exclaimed. 'I tell you I

know that character – Dodgy Harry, we call him. He's no good; you just can't trust him. You're better off out of there, my girl. You want to go to that place down the road my brother runs. May be a little bit more pricey, but he won't treat you like that. Terrible! Still, I can well believe it from Harry. Here, I'll give my brother a ring, see if he's got a spare room. He'll sort you out.'

Genevieve thanked Mave but the episode had blown her off-kilter, and she felt indignant that it was Seamus's behaviour which had derailed her life yet again. If she had needed any further proof of Seamus's impact on her life, then this was it. OK, so the Venus Hotel wasn't a very nice place, but she had been living there for a while now and she was used to it.

As it turned out, Mave's brother couldn't help her: term had started and his place was already packed full of foreign students. But he had a friend in West Kensington, and it sounded like there might be a chance of a room there. Genevieve slipped off in her break to go and have a look. It turned out to be a very similar establishment to the Venus and, situated off the North End Road, seemed to be home to a similarly cosmopolitan selection of residents. It was still near enough to Mave's to make it worthwhile though, and if anything her room was nicer – it was on the top floor and had a huge sash window looking out over the rear of the building. The only problem was the rent: it was going to cost her an extra £40 a week which, on the salary Mave was paying her, was quite a lot.

Genevieve had hoped to be able to support herself in England, but if the worst came to the worst she knew she could borrow from a bank against the property her father had left her. She had no idea what they were worth, but she couldn't imagine their tiny home and a baker's shop in a village in rural France were worth much. Genevieve had told the solicitors that she wanted to sell the baking business and had also instructed them to put the house on the market

– after all, she hadn't lived there since she moved to Paris for her degree course. She could not imagine any time in her life when she would want to go back and run the shop, or to live in that village again. Even if she missed her home, and her aunt, there were too many sad memories in Grèves for her ever to want to return. In fact, both properties were due to go up for auction at the end of the month.

Seamus, meanwhile, was waiting for Genevieve's call. He was convinced that after seeing his flat she would cease her stubborn insistence on living in such a grotty hotel room, when she could be sharing a home with him. But by the afternoon when she still hadn't contacted him, he phoned the landlord, suspecting that he had taken his money but not kicked Genevieve out as agreed. However the landlord confirmed that he had asked her to leave and told Seamus she was moving out that night.

Seamus was suddenly struck by paranoia: did this mean she was returning to France? What if she had found out he had paid the landlord to chuck her out? Guilt, of course, did little to ease his anxiety and in the end he decided he had better ring Genevieve at work. Unfortunately, Mave got to the phone first, and she had a few choice words for him on the subject of his behaviour. Eventually, Genevieve had to wrest the receiver from her.

'Seamus, it's me. I have been asked to leave my hotel.'

'Yes, that much I gather, but whatever for?' he feigned, with mock surprise.

'The landlord didn't like you shouting yesterday.'

'You what?'

'It's true.'

'He's chucked you out because of me?'

'Yes, he said that,' replied Genevieve patiently. Seamus cursed the landlord for not coming up with a better excuse. He should have told him what to say, damn it.

'That's terrible. What a bastard! You must come and live

with me immediately, at least till you find somewhere else. I'll come right over and pick you up. I told you that place was dodgy.'

'No, the place is fine. They just didn't like you.' She was determined Seamus was going to understand this was his fault – again.

'Sweetheart, I'm sorry, let me come and collect you.'

'No, Seamus, it's OK, I've found somewhere else. Mave's brother's friend has a hostel in West Kensington. I'm moving in tonight.'

Seamus was crushed. Genevieve didn't want to move in with him. He had had her chucked out of her hotel unnecessarily. He couldn't decide if he felt more upset because his plan hadn't worked, or because he had behaved like such a heel. He learned from the incident, however, and was careful to treat her differently from that moment on. She was a very determined lady now, and was proving a lot harder to manipulate than he first imagined. None of his other women had ever been this difficult – but then he had never cared about any of his other women. Seamus relished the challenge. He would need to persuade her: force wouldn't work.

As he set about launching the new Marrow, and builders and suppliers and staffing problems all began to exert their pressure, he appreciated the time he spent with Genevieve all the more. She brought normality and peace into his life. Instead of going to Louche every night as he used to do, they would go out for dinner, to the cinema or just stay in. Quite apart from the fact that every time he saw her his heart quite literally leapt inside him, he was learning to feel again, and he could not wish for a sweeter or more receptive teacher. He no longer desired the numbness alcohol and cocaine gave him – instead he drank because he enjoyed the taste rather than because he needed it for a crutch. Instead of swigging from a bottle of Armagnac, he would let Genevieve, who knew a surprising amount about wine, choose a single bottle for them to share. It amazed him to discover he enjoyed it more.

When he had spent all day running round restaurants recruiting staff, sourcing suppliers, ordering equipment and supervising the refurbishment of the building, the idea of spending the evening in bed with Genevieve was all he could wish for. There was a hell of a lot to do at Marrow – more, he and Marion discovered, with each day that passed, and between the two of them they had their work cut out. So it was a joy to know that at the end of it all he had Genevieve waiting for him. No one was telling him how wonderful his cooking was any more, but Genevieve's smile when she saw him was all he needed to know about being appreciated. Their passion for each other if anything became stronger, and, as the weeks passed, he began to feel that, with her at least, he might finally be getting close to what he was looking for. Her straightforwardness, directness and sense of self-possession were inspiring to him. The more time he spent with her, the more convinced he became that he needed her permanently in his life.

But engineering their perfect union was more difficult than he had imagined. Genevieve, it seemed, was set in her ways. He desperately wanted her to give up her job and move in with him. She could help out at Marrow if she wanted something to do – he knew she would be invaluable to them. But Genevieve was adamant she wanted to continue working at Mave's. He couldn't understand it – she worked hard for peanuts in one of the grottiest eating establishments in London. It was embarrassing for Seamus and it was certainly intensely frustrating. But he knew better than to lose his temper in front of her again, and he was careful that she never saw the darker side of him.

For her part, Genevieve was amazed. She had never expected this man could make her feel happy again, even though she had secretly dreamed and hoped he might.

But here she was, in London, in love. It was because of this secret dream, one she had nurtured since that first summer, that she was so willing to accept his explanations for everything that he had failed to do. Besides, it was obvious he genuinely cared for her, particularly in the way he talked about their future together. With every day that passed he seemed to become more and more sure that they were destined to be together. Certainly he was difficult but, she reasoned, his motives were always pure, and anyway it made him more of a challenge, more exciting to be with. He had made a fuss in the hotel because he was worried for her; he didn't ask her about her past because he knew it hurt her to talk about it. She shouldn't blame everything that had happened on him, she told herself; she had, after all, been entirely complicit in everything they had done together, and she certainly couldn't ask him to take responsibility for her father's behaviour.

Surely what really mattered was now. Genevieve had come to England looking for answers, but she had found so much more. So far she had not seen him repeat the behaviour she had witnessed in the Venus, and more and more she found him to be the man she knew he could be and had hoped he still was: tender, affectionate, warm and devoted. She saw no evidence of the tantrum-throwing, carousing bully that his reputation (relayed to her via Mave) would have everyone believe. On the contrary, he was quite the gentleman with her.

And her job: she loved working at the café, particularly as Mave was fast becoming her friend, and it was improving her English no end. She had Seamus, but she still had control of her own destiny. The more she saw him, the more important it was, she reasoned, she keep something back for herself. Life had taught her that much at least. And if that meant her job and her own place, then Seamus would just have to accept it.

'Very wise, my girl,' Mave had advised, who would have

been annoyed to see the back of the best worker she had
ever had.

But Seamus was not so insensitive that he could not see
Genevieve was holding something back. He knew it was
to do with their time in France – he guessed she had
not quite forgiven him for deserting her yet, but he was
hoping it would blow over as long as he could prove himself
worthy this time around. Whatever it was, he wasn't about
to tackle it head on. Equally, Genevieve guessed that despite
his euphoria at finding her again, she didn't make everything
perfect for him. She sensed an unease in him about his new
venture. She shared his pleasure that he finally had a way to
realise his ambitions, and was thrilled to have found him at
such an exciting time, but he didn't seem really convinced
about it. Aloud he assured her Marrow was going to be
the biggest and best food project London – no, the world
– had ever witnessed, which made Genevieve smile, but
every now and then she would catch a flash of anxiety, or
was it fear? pass over his face. He talked incessantly of his
new restaurant, but something wasn't right and he wouldn't
let her know what it was. Maybe he didn't know himself.

She couldn't help wondering what this Marrow meant
for her, if their relationship was to last. She liked London,
but every day something would remind her it was not her
home, whether it was the way people treated each other,
or the endless jokes she had to take about frogs, or even
the struggle to find a decent cup of café au lait. Still, they
didn't discuss these things because they were too busy being
in love and they didn't dare spoil it.

It was a couple of weeks later that Genevieve bumped
into Michael again. Seamus had been pleased to take him
on at the new Marrow, and Michael was relieved – even if
his status as whipping boy seemed to have changed little.
Genevieve had never visited the new Marrow; had never
seen Seamus at work. If she had she would have seen
that just because he was not in a kitchen it didn't mean

he didn't behave like a tyrant. If anything, the pressure of the impending launch was greater than sixteen hours of non-stop service: no one, after all, had ever attempted to set up something on this scale before, and with Salvatore wisely keeping a low profile, the bulk of the work fell to Marion and Seamus. They had set themselves an extraordinary amount to do in a very short space of time: the truth was they had to get Marrow open as quickly as possible just to earn some money. Salvatore and Marion's contribution had already been spent, and in order for Seamus to find the number of staff he needed he was forced to offer high wages, and pay retainers until he was ready to take them on. Whenever Salvatore or Marion asked him where his capital was, he fobbed them off with some excuse about transaction times and people still owing him money. Marion wasn't worried yet: his cash was going to come in very handy when they were nearer the launch.

Michael, however, was one of the few members of staff not on a retainer. Seamus employed him full-time – mostly because he was cheap – and used him to run errands, of which there were plenty. Although Michael hated this work – he had joined Seamus's team to learn to cook, not deliver invoices and receipts – it allowed him the flexibility to visit his father, which the kitchen hours had not. If Seamus didn't need him, he was pretty much free to do as he liked. He never saw hide nor hair of the French girl again, so finally he assumed she must mean nothing to Seamus, or not any more. Which is why, one afternoon, he decided to try and find her, and set out to check all the cafés that lined Earls Court Road.

He finally arrived at the Happy Egg after having to ask far too many grumpy-faced and unhelpful café managers if they had a beautiful blonde French girl working for them. The question was absurd, and he knew it. The owners would look at him and snort, 'You'll be lucky, mate,' before returning to their tea urns shaking their

heads in amusement. Michael had almost given up hope
when Mave pointed him in the direction of the kitchen,
just as Genevieve was hurrying out laden with plates of
food. When he saw her again he found himself breathing
in quickly; incredibly, her beauty was even more arresting
than he had remembered.

He smiled at her, and was delighted to see that she
recognised him. He apologised for seeking her out, but
Genevieve just laughed and told him to stop being so
English, even though she found it quite charming. She
was pleased he had made the effort to find her again: she
thought they had got on well and she had enjoyed talking
to him. Something had clicked between them, they had felt
comfortable with each other, but apart from anything else
Genevieve felt grateful for any friends she could find in this
city. After Mave and Seamus, she knew very few people.
And she was pleased to see Michael again because she felt
she owed him: he had been instrumental in helping her find
Seamus.

She asked him to wait for her break when they could
have a cup of tea together, so Michael sat down on
one of the Formica benches at the back of the shop
and watched her work. Finally Mave, with a suggestively
raised eyebrow, gave her some time off, and she took
a seat opposite him, setting down two cups of thick,
urn-brewed tea.

'So, Michael, I am so pleased you came to see me! Thank
you. How are you?'

Immediately the two of them noticed how relaxed they
were – and pleased to encounter each other again.

'Oh, I'm OK. Fine, thank you. I came to see how you
were. See how your English was shaping up,' he replied, not
entirely truthfully.

'Not bad, don't you think? How is work? You're still
working for Seamus, yes?'

'Yeah, it's OK at the moment. Quite boring actually. All

the logistics of setting up the new place and stuff.' He paused. 'So you found Seamus, did you?'

Genevieve blushed. 'Yes. Well, actually we are, how do you say it? We are seeing each other again.'

'You're together?!' Michael couldn't contain his astonishment. Shit! So she was the boss's woman after all. In that case he really shouldn't be here, but it was too late now. He looked at her incredulously, wondering if she knew anything about him: he just couldn't imagine this sweet-natured girl with Seamus.

Genevieve looked taken aback. 'Yes, why? You seem surprised?'

'Oh no, that's great,' Michael said quickly, re-ordering his face into an expression of delight. 'It's just – well, Seamus always used to be, well . . . You know.' Genevieve didn't know and looked expectantly at Michael, who realised he was on decidedly shaky ground talking to his boss's girlfriend about his boss, and should really change the subject very quickly.

'Well, his own man I guess,' he said briskly. 'Bit of a loner. But that's great – well done. I'm pleased. What are you doing still working here, then?'

'Oh, I like it.'

'That's pretty strange, seeing Seamus and working here.'

'What? Strange that I am not, how do you say, a kept woman?'

Genevieve was frowning. Michael couldn't believe he'd put his foot in it again. 'No. Well yes, but also . . . I don't know. So what's it like here?' he said quickly.

'It's nice. You see that lady over there, that's Mave and she's really funny. She's my friend now. And all the people that come in here – typical English. I love it. Lots of Australians too. The Australians are noisy, and always in big groups.'

'I bet you get all sorts round here.'

'Definitely, all sorts.' Genevieve raised her eyebrows at

Michael and they began to laugh. She liked Michael. She
looked across at him, carefully now, examining the look
on his face. It was troubled. With their conversation last
time they met still very much in her mind, she asked him:
'So how's your papa?'

Michael was caught suddenly, stumped at what to say. He
realised this was what he had wanted to talk to her about, but
now, he couldn't bring himself to do it. He just looked at
her face, speechless. She could see he wanted to speak and
couldn't. His mouth was open but no sound came. He tried
again, but nothing. Genevieve was overcome with sympathy
for him. 'It's OK,' she said gently. 'You don't have to say
anything.'

Michael still remained unable to respond, paralysed by his
emotions. Genevieve continued to talk, hoping she could
connect with him in some way.

'You know, I do understand. My father, he died a horrible
and slow death. It was awful watching him, not being able
to help him. He really just wanted to die in the end, but the
medicine kept him alive.' Genevieve cast her mind back to
the place she had forbidden it to go. She didn't talk of these
things, ever, certainly never to Seamus, but now she felt she
could, and for this boy, she must.

'You see, it made his pain more bearable, gave him
enough strength to fight just one more day,' she said quietly,
looking down at her tea. 'That,' she paused, remembering,
'that was an awful thing to watch.' Genevieve could picture
him now, his face sallow, lifeless, his skin sagging over his
bones. His eyes were by then sunk deep into their sockets;
every time they flickered open they showed her the deep
pain wracking his body. The attempts to speak, the effort
he had just moving his mouth. Lying there in that soulless
hospital bed, looking on her with eyes that still had not
forgiven. She shuddered at the memory.

'Why did they give him the medicine?' Michael asked,
intrigued by her story.

'I don't know. It was difficult. At the time.' She looked into Michael's face as if seeking sanction, then looked down at her brown tea, and stirred it. 'It was easier when I knew he was at peace.'

The two sat together in silence for a minute. Eventually Michael said, his voice unsteady, 'That is the problem with my father.' The words seemed to come now, so distended from his long silence he could almost see them in front of him in great heavy balloons, falling from his mouth; as though he was watching himself speak. 'He is in a coma. He has been for nine months. I don't know what to do. The doctors say it is best to just . . . you know. But I, I can't say stop. I think I shouldn't in case he can survive, but I don't know when . . .' His voice trailed off.

'Do you think he can recover?' Genevieve asked, concern on her face.

'I think maybe – no, I just hope. I don't know, Genevieve, how can I know?' He looked at her helplessly. But already some of the confusion was draining out of him.

'I don't suppose you will ever know,' she replied. 'But the doctors, they know. You must listen to them. Nine months is a long time,' she thought with a pang.

'But I feel it's tantamount to killing him.'

Genevieve felt uncomfortable; she was sweating now, she wanted this to finish.

'It's brutal,' he said finally.

'*O mon Dieu, oui,*' she agreed softly.

'I'm so sorry,' he said. 'I didn't want to make this so gloomy.'

Genevieve pulled herself together and looked at him. 'No, Michael, it's awful and I know what you must be feeling. Do you go and see your papa much?'

'Yes, every day.'

'And do you have any other family?'

'No, no we don't. My mother left us when I was young.'

'So it's your decision.'

'Yes,' he said, staring into his tea. 'It's all mine.'

Suddenly Genevieve felt very close to Michael. It occurred to her that if there was one good thing she could get out of the horrific experience with her Papa, it was to help Michael now. And somehow, for some reason, she thought it might be good for her too.

'Maybe, if you wanted, I could come to the hospital with you?'

He looked up at her, astonished. He had never thought – but yes, that would be such a relief, to have someone else just to see, to share the load.

'I should like that very much.'

'When do you go? In the evening?'

Michael nodded.

'Then let's go after work – sometime soon.'

'Yes OK, that sounds good.'

'Ring me here at the café and we'll sort out a day.' Then quite spontaneously, without really thinking, she put her hand on his and squeezed it. He was astonished. It felt so comforting, so – just what he needed. Michael looked at her and all the thanks he needed to say were in his eyes. Genevieve felt her heart skip, this was important.

Then Michael suddenly remembered, and looking wary, he asked: 'But Seamus?'

'What about Seamus? I'll tell him tonight.'

Michael was concerned for Genevieve. What would Seamus think?

'I won't tell him if you don't want me to,' she said, laughing at the worry on his face. 'It'll be fine. Don't worry.'

Michael realised then that Genevieve couldn't possibly know what Seamus was really like if she thought he would let a member of his staff go off with her one evening – whatever the reason.

Polenta alla Toscana

100g polenta flour, preferably made in the north-eastern
region of Italy
0.5 litre still Umbrian spring water
Maldon sea salt and freshly ground black peppercorns
4 Sicilian sun-dried tomatoes, chopped
A few fresh leaves Capri rocket
Good, robust extra-extra-virgin Tuscan olive oil
50-year-old Modena Balsamic Vinegar,
aged in ancient brandy oak casks
A few shavings of young parmesan, best would be a
one-year-old Parmigiano Reggiano from Emilia

1. Boil the water with a generous pinch of Maldon salt
in an authentic Florentine copper-bottomed pan. Pour
in the flour.

2. Reduce the heat and stir only with an Umbrian yew
wood spoon, skimming off the scum.

3. After about forty-five minutes, or when all the water
has been soaked up, remove from the heat. Mould into
an abstract cake on a baking tray, brush with oil and
grill for exactly two minutes 38 seconds each side.

4. Serve with the rocket, tomato and parmesan arranged
in a spontaneous artistic fashion. Season and drizzle
with oil and vinegar.

19

Archie Peaks was a man unto whom style flew like a pure white dove, cooing in admiration and settling spontaneously on his shoulders, as if they were the very dovecote of fashion. At fifty-five he still looked remarkably healthy and athletic: his body was trim, and with his close-cropped, silver hair, his perfectly tailored linen suit, one of a selection of Ralph Lauren pastel shirts, a strict no tie rule and, if it was a hot country, no socks and a pair of high quality leather sandals, Archie managed to straddle the boundaries between the impressive gravity of the conservative professional classes and the outré bohemian abandon of the artistic set.

He lived in Islington, north London, in a large, glass, self-designed house that was constantly being photographed for glossy magazines. Not only was its exterior completely see-through, but its interior – cleverly – had no furniture in it whatsoever. A homage to minimalism (all the storage and sitting space was built into the fixtures and fittings, and in a series of miraculous, fold-away-clutter containers), it succeeded in being the country's first genuinely empty house.

His wife, Beatrice, lived with him. Now a wizened ex-Rock Chick, her dark, walnut-lined skin bore testament to the exceedingly good times she'd had as an aristo-hippy in California in the 1960s, and the long afternoons she now spent drinking herbal teas in Venice. These days she got her kicks from her morning pot of green tea and the non-wheat, non-dairy organic-only purée she existed on for nourishment at lunch and dinner – when not entertaining, of course. She spoke with the deep, gravelly voice of a dedicated Gauloise smoker and trembled with the withdrawal symptoms of one who had been forced to give up. Such pollutants were anathema to a lifestyle such as Archie's. She wore the harsh, asymmetrically tailored lines of Jean Muir and the odd Japanese designer, proving there was still dignity and elegance in middle age. Floating about her house and Town in an often extraordinary and occasionally 'challenging' wardrobe, she was a regular on society's charity cocktail circuit and filled her time in Archie's long absences by holding benefits for up-and-coming, but still struggling, artists.

Archie had reached the height of his career. Designing monuments to the new 'millennial modernism' as he called it, he was now personally overseeing projects from Reykjavik to Honolulu. His brand of architectural design, although not always to everyone's taste, certainly got itself noticed. It tended to involve large glass and steel structures fashioned in random shapes and attached to the buildings they were decorating in what appeared to be an entirely random fashion. 'The new distended habitat; a symbol of the post-millennial confusion of our times,' Archie would say. 'A triumph,' the *Architectural Review* pronounced. 'What is this glass turnip?' asked the front page of the *Sun*. But Archie battled on regardless, watching his superstar status grow as further and further-flung corners of the globe requested his municipal touch.

Marion was an old and very dear friend of his wife's, and it was Beattie who had persuaded him to take on the Marrow project as a leg-up to Marion's new business. Archie, for whom patronage and moving in circles of PLU as Marion called it, or 'People like us', came more naturally than passing water, was only too delighted, diary permitting. Although he had assured Marion he wouldn't be able to oversee the execution of his plans on a daily basis, he would leave a man in charge who knew exactly what he was doing, he said, and he would pop in whenever his transatlantic transfers allowed. Marion had been suitably humbled and grateful, and both parties had felt blessed. Archie had smiled the great benevolent smile of one who has so much talent, is so in demand, that he has to choose very carefully where he bestows it, but is always delighted with the effect it has on its recipient.

One Sunday late in October, and a good number of weeks after work had started, Archie's schedule permitted him a couple of hours in London before an important client meeting at the Mercer Hotel in New York. Finding himself at a loose end, and since his wife was on a retreat in the Orkneys, he decided he would pop in and see how the Marrow project was coming along. He was, obviously, proud of his design for the building. Although little could be done to the exterior, by gutting the inside and forming a four-storey atrium in the centre, he had managed to accommodate his trademark glass and steel structure, but this time on the inside. He hailed a taxi at Heathrow, and made his way into the centre of town.

The building Marion had fixed upon to house the new Marrow was a large and daunting space. Once an old warehouse dispensary, its redbrick, industrial facade had a rather imposing effect. Added to its flat roof, wrought-iron window grilles and flat-fronted box-like appearance, it had always struck Seamus as rather a depressing building.

'Nonsense – a blank canvas!' Archie had reassured Marion when she had first voiced her aesthetic concerns about it. These were sentiments she passed directly on to Seamus, reassuring him that Archie would do everything he could to liven it up and make it the landmark of architectural design they desired.

The internal structures of the building, which had been used only for storage for most of the last decade, were distinctly shoddy and would have had to have been completely re-built anyway. Archie Peaks's plan to rip everything out, leaving just the shell of the building, and start again, seemed perfectly reasonable. That is what the builders had been employed in doing up to this point, which now lent the vast interior of the building an eerie, haunted feel as the builders' shouts echoed up through the rafters. Supporting timber beams criss-crossed the dizzy height up to the roof, and the large windows, which stretched from floor to ceiling, felt like gaping holes in what seemed now a very unsteady structure. Every time Seamus visited the site there was less of it, he complained to Marion, who just shushed him and told him to wait and see: Archie was to buildings what Seamus himself was to food: they were in the hands of a master.

The plan was to have the ground floor as an open-plan walk-in exhibition space and café, with the far right-hand set aside for the patisserie counter, which would be supplied by hydraulic lift from the basement where Archie planned to house the ovens. The second floor would consist of a circular mezzanine, set around the protruding steel structure that was the centrepiece of Archie's design. Racked up as if in homage to the pole in the centre, the second floor would entirely constitute thousands of food shelves that would groan with the produce sourced from the country's finest markets. The shelves would be periodically punctuated with curving chrome counters that would service the takeaway, dinner-party and menu-consultancy facilities.

The all-important third floor, which would contain the main restaurant, would be reached by glass elevator from the ground floor. This glass elevator – and Archie had been particularly impressed with himself at this touch – would operate within the shaft of the glass pinnacle, thus affording those both inside and out of it maximum opportunity to show themselves off and spot other people on their journeys up and down. The third floor itself would, in an extraordinary feat of design engineering, come up to and close around the pinnacle – but only in glass. Archie had discovered a brand new toughened clear material being pioneered in the Far East, and had decided it would be perfect for combining the transparent towering effect he required, and the floor space Marrow needed. The glass floor was currently being imported in strips at vast expense from the factory where it was fashioned in Macao. Once it was up, it would give the illusion of space, but the reality was that Marrow would then have a brasserie floor extendable right up to the pinnacle if desired. Flexible furniture arrangements were Archie's speciality. Of course the noise would be deafening, but it would look spectacular.

The fourth 'penthouse' floor, which Archie had already assured Marion wouldn't be ready until well after Christmas, would be its own separate, self-contained design, and incorporate the head of the pinnacle. Marion and Seamus didn't care too much about the niceties of all of this yet: both were just desperate to get the place up and running and making money. Besides, Seamus had looked at the plans and, unable to understand a single pencil stroke, he had handed them back to the building project manager and said, 'Just build the fucker!'

The truth was, Seamus was really missing the energy and excitement of the kitchen, and deprived of such hard physical labour he had become a hyperactive ball of energy committed to wearing himself out before the end of the day and his return to Genevieve. The result was that, when he wasn't surreptitiously meeting other people's staff in dark corners of pubs and attempting to poach them, or arguing with suppliers about bulk purchase discounts, he was wandering around the site hassling people, chivvying builders and questioning the foreman's decisions. As far as the contracted building firm was concerned, he had very quickly established himself as the client from hell.

Archie, who had progress reports from his project

manager twice a week, knew nothing of Seamus's involvement, and indeed had yet to meet the fellow. He was
not particularly interested in Seamus the chef, or indeed
Marrow the restaurant. Names and people came and went.
What endured was the physical evidence they left behind.
Food was disposable. Buildings lasted. Archie had yet to
make his mark in Knightsbridge, and this project, although
admittedly rather small-scale, would give him a showcase
at the heart of the English bourgeoisie. Consequently,
Archie was sitting in the back of the taxi getting quite
excited about seeing the building again. He loved the
power of change, got off on the excitement of radical,
physical refits and, much as a Boy Racer might regard
a ride in a red Ferrari, Archie passionately luxuriated
in the promise of transformation inherent in all bricks
and mortar.

'But it looks like a transparent penis!' shouted Seamus.
'You have to be bloody joking!'

'No, sir, we are not joking. It was clearly depicted on
the plans. Look, here.'

'I never understood those bloody plans, they don't mean
anything to me. What clearly *does* mean something to me
is the outsized plastic dick you are erecting in the middle
of my restaurant! Are you trying to make a fool out of
me? Who the fuck do you take me for? Linford fucking
Christie?'

The foreman was doing his best to weather Seamus's
attack, but it looked like he wasn't going to take no for
an answer. It was at this point that Archie strode into the
building.

'Is there a problem here?' he asked in his quiet, civilised tone.

'Yes!' replied Seamus without turning round. 'This fucking joker is trying to build a fucking cock-shaft all the way
up the centre of my restaurant!'

'I think you may find that that is the central pinnacle which is integral to the design.'

Seamus turned round and inspected the owner of the voice butting into his discussion. Archie, in his black Armani shades, light pink shirt and matching espadrilles, returned his gaze with a calm smile.

'Where the fuck did you spring from? *Miami Vice?*'

Even Archie had to balk at this last. Seamus continued to stare at him.

'It is not a cock-shaft.'

'No? And I'm Ronnie Biggs.'

'It is the central pod of the design.'

'I don't care.'

Archie had often had to deal with difficult clients in his past, but nowadays clients paid him to pronounce. It was a good fifteen years since he had last had to defend one of his designs.

'Perhaps if we could just go over the plans together . . .'

'No, I'm sorry mate, I don't care who you are but the jerk who thought up this ridiculous arrangement is going to have to haul his lazy arse back here and present me with a different design, because this one sucks.'

'Archie!' came a shriek from the far end of the building, followed by the clatter of spike heels over concrete. 'Darling, how *are* you? How wonderful to see you!' Marion's timing was, as ever, immaculate. And before Seamus could inflict any more damage, she had intervened between the two men with a show of flamboyant air kissing.

'Marion, sweetheart, hello. I just thought I'd pop in on my way from Heathrow to Gatwick. See how it was coming along.'

'Oh, just fantastically, we're so excited. I see you have met Seamus. Isn't it exciting, Seamus?'

'You know this character then?'

Giving Seamus a hard stare, Marion replied slowly, to promote better understanding, 'Yes, Seamus, I do.

This is Archie Peaks: the man who is des-ign-ing our build-ing.' Her eyes finished the qualification with a 'So don't fuck it up, please' glare. Then she turned back to Archie and raised her eyebrows in a conspiratorial manner, and taking him by the arm, led him away out of Seamus's earshot. 'You must forgive him, darling,' she hissed. 'He is not the most aesthetically-minded chef, but he'll understand when he sees it all up and running.'

'Er, yes, quite,' returned Archie, relieved he was no longer going to have to bash it out with the menacing-looking thug he had just encountered. Even though he practised his Tai Chi every morning, he wasn't sure if he was quite ready for the fisticuffs Seamus had seemed on the point of initiating. Seamus, meanwhile, had decided he would deal with the penis problem later. With Marion. The foreman he dismissed with a wave of his hand and stormed out of the building.

'So that's the famous Seamus Bull,' said Archie.

''Fraid so, honey, but don't you worry about him, I've got him firmly under control. He's only the bloody cook after all.' Archie and Marion laughed the complicit laugh of the privileged classes, then, striding across the floorspace, Marion insisted Archie take her on a tour of the building, explaining how his genius designs were going to fit together. Archie, who enjoyed nothing more than the sound of his own voice, particularly when it was detailing his own art, was happy to oblige.

When they had finished their tour, Marion tried to tempt him away for lunch: butter him up at Bibendum, she thought. A fine fillet of turbot and a glass of vintage Krug usually worked on men of a certain age.

'Well actually, darling, thank you so much for the offer, but I'm afraid I'm going to have to decline. Unfortunately my old friend Emmanuel Coq got there first, and I promised I'd join him in his new restaurant – it's just across the road you know. Have you ever eaten there? I've heard it's rather good.'

Marion was appalled. 'Emmanuel Coq?' she repeated back to him, driving the disappointment and dread out of her voice.

'Yes. Do you know him? Very refined fellow. Not at all like your Bull man, I must say.'

'No, I expect not,' sighed Marion. Then quickly replacing her PR hat, she continued: 'But Seamus is fiercely talented, you know. His last restaurant was the talk of the town for months and you couldn't get a table there for love nor money.'

'I got one there for £500, I seem to remember. Had some Arab client over, Mr Fazir – absolutely insisted on going to his place. What was it called now? Marrow – that's it. Anyway, of course it was all booked up so Fazir sends his man down there with £500 in cash and we got a table that night. Marvellously ingenious, the Arabs.'

'Oh,' replied Marion.

'It was rather good though,' said Archie consolingly, detecting a deflated aspect to Marion's demeanour, for once.

'Yes, well it should have been,' she replied huffily, not used to being out-talked on these matters. 'So how do you know Emmanuel then?' she tried again, desperate to measure the seriousness of the situation.

'Well, a long time ago he did me the most enormous favour, for which I am and will always be eternally grateful. Dear Beattie was suffering dreadfully from her Irritable Bowel Syndrome while we were holidaying in a friend's villa in Mustique, and we couldn't find anything on the island she could eat without severe stomach cramps. Anyway it just so happened Emmanuel Coq was on his honeymoon – I forget which one it was now – next door, and hearing of Beattie's distress, he offered to cook for her. He practically spent the entire next two weeks at our villa cooking for Beattie, which was absolutely marvellous for us, but probably not so marvellous for his new young wife. Don't think they had much in common conversationally, if you know what I mean. Anyway, I always try and look him up when I'm in town, and funnily enough, this time he called me.'

'Oh,' replied Marion again. It was even worse than she had thought.

'Anyway, my goodness, is that the time? I really must dash or I'll be late.' Marion accompanied him out of the door. 'Wonderful to see you again, Marion. You take care, sweet pea, and don't forget to drop in on Beattie when you can. She does love to see you.'

'Yes, of course, Archie, no problems. Keep in touch, won't you? Bye now.'

'Bye, darling. Be good.'

Marion strode round the corner and, yanking her mobile phone out of her bag, punched in the numbers furiously.

'Seamus? You utter idiot! What were you doing speaking to Archie Peaks like that?'

'I didn't know it was Archie Peaks. Looked more like Don Johnson to me. Anyway, the cunt's trying to erect a penis in my restaurant.'

'It is *not* a penis!' Marion screamed, attracting the attention of more than a few passers by. 'It's a fucking pinnacle!'

'Don't play word games with me, Marion.'

'Anyway it looks like it doesn't matter any more as our Archie has just taken off for lunch with your best friend, Emmanuel Coq. Which means it could all be over by three o'clock. What the hell are we going to do if he pulls out?' Marion wailed, now seriously distressed.

'Why would he pull out?'

'Because Coq will ask him to, of course, and Archie owes the guy a favour. Something to do with his wife on honeymoon or something. Oh God, this is a disaster.'

'Now calm down, Marion, you don't know he is going to pull out. Why don't we just wait and see what happens. Anyway, it won't be any great loss. At least then I won't have to look at a bloody twenty-five foot . . .'

'Oh, do just shut up, Seamus, and try and be a little more . . . sensitive!'

Chilli pasta

4 hot, red, dry chillies, chopped finely
3 cloves garlic, sliced thinly
Olive oil
4 tablespoons tomato paste
A handful of pasta

1. Fry the garlic and chilli in oil until the garlic is sweating and golden and the chillies are shiny and swollen.

2. Scoop out the chillies and garlic and blend with the tomato purée. Stir back into the oil in the pan.

3. Boil the pasta until it is just *al dente*, then drain and tip into the pan.

4. Stir everything together well.

5. Drizzle with chilli oil for extra kick.

20

Salvatore had begun to have 'concerns'. Keen to keep as low a profile as possible, he had so far been very much a silent partner in the Marrow collective, but that hadn't prevented him from keeping an eye on his investment. Knowing that neither Seamus nor Marion were particularly figure-conscious, he had employed his own personal team of accountants to keep track of their expenditure, and was shocked at the results. He was also highly displeased to see that Seamus had yet to deposit his capital in the Marrow account. He had had a bad feeling about this project from the beginning. And it had been little use instructing Marion and Seamus to economise. Marion was still arguing for copper fittings and pearwood furniture; while Seamus would only take on suppliers who charged like Colombians, noted Salvatore ruefully. Both absolutely refused to compromise on quality in either of their fields. The builders' final invoice for the brasserie alone had been more than double the budget.

Salvatore, therefore, had been forced to act like a sort of human dustpan and brush. Every time Seamus or Marion did anything, he had to follow in their wake and sweep up. Thus Marion would order cutlery from Milan, Salvatore would cancel it and place the order with a steel company in Sheffield; Seamus would order a rare Thai fish sauce to be flown in twice a week from Bangkok, Salvatore replaced the supplier with one from a Thai community in South London. It was the only way his accountants could hope to keep Marrow afloat. Every time Salvatore reprimanded either of his partners for their spending, they would tell him debt didn't matter because as soon as Marrow was launched they would be making so much money the banks would be queuing up for their services. This did not convince the Italian.

Still, Salvatore was not overly worried for the safety of his own investment: his share of the money had gone into the building, which had been considerably enhanced in value by Archie Peaks's dramatic designs. Seamus might rant about the 'glass dick', but Salvatore thought it rather fulfilling. Also, as Marion pointed out, with its renovations Marrow would now attract the sizeable band of architecture junkies who, this time, would actually have to go inside the building to appreciate it, rather than gawp from the outside. And once inside, of course, they would be forced to part with some cash. In fact, Marion was wondering if they might get away with charging an entrance fee. After all, there would be Beattie's art exhibitions to justify it too.

Archie was the one member of the Marrow team whom Salvatore had not been able to limit surreptitiously. Marion had been insistent on that. Archie had employed his own foremen and builders – who were of course the most expensive in Europe – and the cost of his exotic materials had amounted to enough to fund a small Third World economy. But this didn't matter, Salvatore reasoned to his accountants; if the worst came to the worst, the building would belong to him – he had had that caveat written into the contract. And he knew an Archie Peaks design never lost its value.

However, the commercial aspect of the Marrow venture was altogether a different story. As Salvatore's accountants presented him with the latest total of expenses, he realised they were reaching crisis point. Not only did Seamus have to come up with his share of the cash *right now*, they were going to have to find a damn sight more, or the place would never be able to open.

Salvatore kept very quiet for several minutes as he perused the sheets of numbers. Placing them carefully back on his huge mahogany desk, he paused in thought. Then, summoning his henchmen, he decided it was time to find out exactly how far Marion and Seamus had got with the project – and to insist on some straight answers. One of his men he dispatched to Seamus, with instructions not to return until he had the money, the other was to go and fetch Marion.

In the beech and cream offices of Marvellous PR, Fuzz had been sweating under a pile of paper since eight o'clock that morning. Marion had made her Account Director of Marrow, which was great as far as the title went, but not so great when she wasn't getting any support. Fuzz knew she had been royally stitched-up by her boss: Marion had flattered her with a directorship of the biggest PR account in town, then starved her of money and resources to run it properly. Guess whose fault it would be if it all went wrong? she thought bitterly. Marion had already said that Fuzz couldn't use any of the other staff, because she 'couldn't afford to let the other accounts slip'. All the preparatory work, the really hard graft, was having to be done by Fuzz and Fuzz alone. And Marion wanted to know why there wasn't more of a buzz about Marrow? Well: she would tell her.

They were meant to have a meeting about it yesterday, but Marion had been 'too busy sourcing cheap pearwood', then she had cancelled again this morning when a scary-looking man in dark glasses had turned up demanding she go and talk with someone called Salvatore. So, once again Fuzz had been left holding the baby when *Caterer & Hotelkeeper* magazine had come in for a briefing. Yes, Fuzz would tell her *exactly* what she thought when she got back from her meeting with this mysterious Salvatore.

*   *   *

Marion jammed her Porsche Boxster into reverse and jolted it rudely into a slot just outside her offices. That parking space was about the best thing that had happened to her all day. Nowadays she spent her whole time running around after other people rather than doing what she wanted to do: creating good PR. If she wasn't rushing from one client to another assuring them she was doing as good a job for them as she was for Marrow, she was trying to clear up after Seamus and Salvatore. All of it was pointless: it was like trying to mend a Dutch dam with Blu-tack. Her other clients were dropping like flies. They were assuming, not totally incorrectly, that there was no way Marvellous could give them its undivided attention when it was handling the biggest launch in town. Plus, Seamus Bull was hardly everyone's first choice of bedfellow: several had dropped out simply because they didn't want to be associated with him.

All of this, of course, would have been completely acceptable, thought Marion, as she slammed the door shut with a touch more force than was probably necessary, if Marrow had been shaping up to expectations. But it was not. Before you even got on to the fact that the place was entirely misunderstood or ignored by press and public alike (what *had* Fuzz been doing?), there was the simple fact that it didn't look as if they were going to be ready to launch on time. What's more, the rather unpleasant meeting she had just had with Salvatore had served to inform her that they might not be able to afford to launch at all – even with Salvatore stupidly cutting all the corners, as it appeared he had been doing behind her back!

How dare he intervene without consulting her? she fumed as she barged through the front door of the building. He didn't know anything about fashionable dining – 'Nothing,' she muttered to herself as she tapped her heel waiting for the lift. Fancy altering their orders after they had put them through! It was tantamount to a Barclays

Bank manager telling Terence Conran he should only use plastic knives and forks. Marion could only comfort spray herself with perfume – much to the consternation of her fellow lift companions.

'Fuzz?' Marion flew into her employee's office in a cloud of No. 19.

'Ah, Marion – at last. We need to talk.'

'Damn right we do!'

Fuzz was disappointed to note Marion was wearing her 1980s Hitler suit with the pointed shoulders, and that the streak of red across her lips was more violent than usual. She obviously meant business.

'OK,' began Marion, throwing herself into a swivel chair opposite Fuzz's desk. Fuzz was the only other member of Marvellous to have her own office apart from Marion. She had been there from the beginning, and was, Marion knew, the backbone of the business. She stayed because of their shared history.

'You know what I'm going to say. The press coverage is shit, the schedule for the opening launch is way behind, and half the journalists still think Marrow is a vegetable. I had lunch with the editor of *Vogue* yesterday and she asked me if Seamus Bull had emigrated. What's going on here?'

Fuzz looked at Marion, who was speaking with the aid of a particularly sharp pencil, jabbing it into the air like a weapon, and drew in a deep breath.

'Marion, you know you need more than one person on this account. I've been at my desk morning, noon and night doing everything I can, but it's too much for me on my own.'

Marion stopped for one moment, pencil in mid-air, and regarded Fuzz. She was shocked to notice her obvious fatigue. Poor Fuzz – she knew she had given her the job of five people.

'Darling, you know I can't afford to give you any more

staff yet. It's really important we don't lose any other clients – as it is we lost Balsamic this morning. Not that I give a toss about that shitty little chain of Italian delis, but it's the principle.'

Four other restaurant accounts had also threatened to drop out, which would leave Marvellous with only the accounts for Porsche, a scarf manufacturer and some D-list TV floozy whose name Marion couldn't even bring herself to remember. She needed her other staff on the restaurant accounts. Marion was seriously worried – it was the first time she had ever had so many eggs in one basket, what with her entire personal fortune and now her business resting on Marrow too.

'Well then, don't complain we don't have enough press coverage.'

Marion sighed and reached for her handbag. Drawing out a Cartier she offered the packet to Fuzz and they both lit up.

'Fuck.' Marion drew deeply on her cigarette. Fuzz was good – really good, and she knew what she was saying was right. She couldn't bollock her for that.

'OK then. We have to work out a different strategy,' she said, thinking hard. 'One that involves least effort, most coverage.' She sucked ponderously on her cigarette for a minute, until a slow smile spread across her face. She looked at Fuzz and said, with a shrug of her shoulders, 'Oh, damn it. Needs must, needs be.'

Fuzz had seen that glint in Marion's eye before. It was dangerous: it meant dirty tactics. But if they had ever needed to fight dirty, it was now.

'Uh-oh. What are you going to do?' Fuzz grinned back. This was why she loved working for Marion: she was not afraid to take risks. Marion turned to her and let a languorous smile spread slowly across her face. Fuzz felt her belly jump.

'Watch me.' Reaching across Fuzz, Marion switched the

conference phone on the desk to loudspeaker. She dialled a number.

'Yes?'

'Seamus, it's Marion.'

'Ah, the bane of my life.'

Marion's eyebrows shot up. 'Huh! Charmed, I'm sure. Now you haven't been out and about recently. What have you been up to?'

'Running around like a blue-arsed fly. Trying to sort this fucking megalomaniac restaurant out, remember – the one you foisted upon me? And avoiding Salvatore's ridiculous henchmen. Every time I so much as move, one pops up from nowhere looking sinister.'

'*I* foisted on *you*? Try again, sweetie. Anyway, we need to do some PR. We haven't had enough column inches this week, and your media profile has dropped dramatically since you took an oath of abstinence.'

Seamus laughed. 'Not abstinence, Marion – no way. I've just been busy.'

'Why don't you come down to Louche tonight?'

'Because I'm knackered.'

'Rubbish, Seamus, don't be soft. You never used that excuse before.'

'OK, I hate that place.'

'Really? That must be why you used to spend so much time there. Anyway we can finish going through those staffing figures.'

'Great, I can't wait,' he said sarcastically. 'No, Marion, it's a no.'

'With some very fine Bolivian I've just got hold of.'

Seamus paused before replying. Now he hadn't had *that* in a while. He thought of Genevieve waiting for him tonight. They were meant to be going to see some arthouse film showing at the French Institute. He couldn't say he was particularly looking forward to it, but he did want to be with her, and she was really keen to see it.

'Well . . . I still don't think so, Marion . . .'

'I'll see you there later then,' she said, and hung up. Seamus raged at the other end of the phone. She always finished her phone conversations like that. He hated it, it was infuriating. Just for that he wasn't going to go.

Fuzz was giggling. 'And you're sure he'll come?'

'Oh, Seamus is addicted to the stuff. He won't be able to resist. I know for a fact Salvatore hasn't been giving him any recently because he is trying to "control his temperament" as he puts it. But the trouble is, Fuzz darling, it's also controlling our PR.'

'And now for my next trick . . .' She was already dialling another number.

'Hello?'

'Henrietta – it's Marion.'

'Hi, sweetie, how are you? I've been looking for you all over. Haven't seen you in weeks. Where've you been?'

'Sardinia, darling – La Costa Smeralda, late season.'

'Oh, Aurora has just got back from there and she said it's wonderful at this time of year. You hardly have to go in the water at all!'

'Quite, darling, it's ideal. Never have to get your hair messed up. Now what are you up to tonight?'

'Oh, hang on, let me see. According to my diary I've got a few launches to go to, then a chat show, but I should be free after that. Why, will you be around at Louche tonight?'

'Oh, I most certainly will, treasure: shall I see you there?'

'Perfect. Marion?'

'Yes?'

'Have you seen Seamus around at all recently?'

Marion grinned at Fuzz. 'No, darling, I've been in Sardinia, remember. But I hear he's been quite sad.'

'What do you mean? Why?'

'Oh, you know. Lonely and stuff. But he did say he might drop in for a drinkie tonight. Why? Anything I can do?'

'Oh no, no, no. Not at all. Nothing. Just wondered, that's all. See you later then!'

'Ta-ta, darling. Big kiss. *Mwah*. See you.'

The Perfect Cup of Tea

One earthenware teapot
One teaspoonful of good quality tea per person,
plus one for the pot
Milk
Sugar

1. Fill the kettle with cold water from the tap.

2. When the water boils, pour a little into the pot and swill it round to warm it. Pour away.

3. Bring the water back to the boil, heap the tea into the pot and pour in the boiling water.

5. Brew. For a 4–5 cup teapot, the brewing time should be around five minutes. Stir.

6. Pour the milk into the bottom of the cup first, then pour in the tea through a strainer. Stir in sugar as required.

21

Genevieve was not enjoying her work today. She felt tired, her customers were grouchy, she had scalded herself on the wretched tea urn and most of all it was cold and rainy outside – again. The Indian summer had been all too brief and it seemed that, now, London was permanently bathed in rain. The only thing that changed from day to day was the drop in temperature. Rain meant dripping-wet customers full of complaints, and Mave was in a foul mood – not an unusual occurrence of late. When Genevieve finally challenged her about it, Mave had claimed it was her arthritis bothering her – came with the cold and the rain, she said. Genevieve, normally one for tea and sympathy, had instead suggested she live somewhere warmer rather than suffer so loudly.

Truth was, Genevieve was less enamoured with her job at the Happy Egg in general. The initial buzz of independence had worn off, and it had ceased to be a new and exciting experience. She thought she had probably grasped the entire dialect of builder-speak by now and knew more than enough words for the female upper anatomy to justify remaining there for her language skills. And even with the pay rise Mave had finally 'generously' allowed her, she still worked over ten hours a day for a pittance, despite what she made in tips.

And she was, she realised, beginning to miss France more and more. Canal Plus, shopping at Printemps, hanging out in cafés, proper meal-times and crunchy biscuits with real coffee instead of all this grease and this – this tea shit everyone drank here. When she complained to Seamus at the end of the day, he pointed out that her time in England would be vastly improved if she didn't spend most of it in a greasy spoon on Earls Court Road and a flea-pit in West Kensington. Although she had pulled a face at him at the time, she knew he was right.

The problem was, she and Seamus were getting on so well together there was no way she could contemplate going back to France now. Their affair had all the magic of before but none of the stress of secrecy – something which allowed it to blossom in a much maturer, more realistic manner. Plus this time both really needed and wanted each other. Genevieve had sought out Seamus for a reason; Seamus saw in Genevieve salvation from the more sordid parts of his life. But for the moment they were irretrievably tied to London: Seamus certainly couldn't leave now he had committed himself to this Marrow project so, as long as Genevieve wanted to be with him, she would have to remain in the city too.

She was beginning to wonder if Seamus wasn't right: maybe she should give up the job and lend him a hand at Marrow. Or at least move in with him – she spent five nights out of seven in his flat now anyway. They were utterly, passionately addicted to one another; they wanted to spend every waking moment of their spare time in each other's company, exclusively. Particularly as their spare time was so hard to come by. They both worked all the hours God gave, sometimes six days a week and from early in the morning until late at night. Their snatched moments together therefore became intense and very precious. Sleeping in each other's arms worked as an antidote to their time apart, and the few hours they spent together in the evening – cooking, watching films, making love – were so pleasurable there seemed little reason to spend them in any other way. After a while, though, the travelling between his flat and her hostel became tedious, and the more she thought about moving in with him, the more attractive the prospect became. It was certainly more appealing than it had been a few weeks ago, now the two of them had a more steady relationship.

Of course Genevieve trusted him: he worked all day and spent every evening with her; every day he asked her to move in with him and join him in the business – she couldn't have further proof of his commitment to her than that. He whispered in her ear that he loved her, he stroked her face in the tenderest of manners, tucking her hair behind her ears, calling her his sweetheart and thanking her profusely for coming back to find him again. All of which made Genevieve glow like a newborn Labrador puppy.

So what could she be missing? What were all these rumours? She did wonder about his past: certainly she knew he had a side to him that could just switch off, alienate all emotions and plunge forward without sensitivity – my God, she bore testament to that, and needed no further proof, but it seemed it was a very remote side. And one, Genevieve hoped, he had learned from. This side, if anything, intrigued her: it was the dark side to his personality, the edge that lent him danger, and it intrigued her rather than put her off. She had witnessed it only once since her return, when he had lost his temper in her hotel. She had seen nothing of it since. They never talked of it, like they never talked of each other's past – he didn't ask her and she didn't ask him, and for the moment that was how they both preferred it. Their conversation was about food, France, England, films, the here and now. Anything else seemed too painful. Their hearts still guarded their secrets.

Of course Mave was delighted to pass on any salacious morsel of gossip that came her way. Drugs, women, binge-drinking and tyrannical behaviour: this was the Seamus Bull the public knew, but as far as Genevieve was concerned they could have him that way. This was the fictional Seamus, the media invention: she had the real one all to

herself. She accepted there might be a grain of truth in
the rumours – otherwise how would they start? But she
was also much happier to believe Seamus's protestations
that none of it was true. After all, what evidence had she
that he took drugs? If he had done, he certainly didn't
any more, and displayed no interest in doing them again.
She had never even seen him drunk. As for the staff –
well, Genevieve was not naïve, she knew what went on
in restaurants, but that was the way kitchens worked. And
now Seamus wasn't doing kitchen service every day; he was
setting up this new restaurant – a very different job.

Then one weekend Seamus had surprised her. Picking
her up from work on a Friday night, he had taken her off
to a place called the Cotswolds, to the quaintest English
country-house hotel. They had slept in a four-poster bed,
gone for long walks in the most exquisite countryside and
had drunk in picture-book country pubs. The autumn
sunshine had smiled on them all weekend and Genevieve
had honestly believed she needed little more to complete
her perfect happiness. In the crook of his arm she had
lain awake on their final night trying to imagine how it
could be more perfect – and failing. She had everything.
What did it matter that he didn't yet know all the secrets
of her heart?

Inevitably, she began to think about her long-term future
as well as the short term. She might miss France, but really,
what did she have to go back for? Both the shop and
the house were now sold – for quite a healthy sum, her
solicitors informed her (something to do with Grèves being
bought up by weekending English), and her aunt was not
enough of a reason to return. Of course she was fond of
her, but the two had never been really close. England might
not be the country she had grown up in, but she had just
as much claim on it as France.

All she did know, above everything, was that she wanted
to be with Seamus. He made her feel different, gave her

a new dimension, pushed her beyond the little village girl she had been before. And Seamus needed her at Marrow. In fact, he was practically begging her to join them. With the money from the sale of the shop and house she could make a real difference. She knew he could do with it; he would never admit that to her, but Genevieve was not stupid, and she had not been able to help overhearing the stressed phone calls he had with bank managers, loan agencies and his business partners. It might well be an excellent investment for her money as well, for if it was half the raging success Seamus said it would be, she would probably end up making quite a healthy profit. Plus it would give her something to do, and it would mean she and Seamus would have something to share, something they could build together.

But, thought Genevieve, as she dumped another pile of egg-smeared plates in the sink, the problem with Seamus's Marrow was that, as much as Genevieve knew about food and serving, waiting, tills, stock checks and management, she knew very little about *dining* – particularly for the fashionable and stylish – and it appeared that this was exactly the sort of restaurant Seamus was opening. Also, she wasn't entirely sure that it was the sort of place she would want to be involved with. She set very little store by style – she was a girl who preferred to concentrate on substance. She was also a countryside lover at heart: when she was little and had dreamed of owning her own place – whether it was a deli, or a café or a restaurant – she had always assumed it would be in a beautiful rural setting. Cities did not inspire her, they suffocated her, and the thought of being tied to this one for the foreseeable future was not enticing.

It was these doubts that had so far prevented Genevieve from discussing her money and her future with Seamus. Anyway, it was clear that he needed her to provide peace away from talk of investment and profits. All in all, it was a tricky decision, pondered Genevieve, as she swept several chips, a dollop of baked beans, a used tea bag and four inches of dirt into her dustpan. Just then one of the less considerate clientèle trod on her toe – and then didn't apologise. It was all Genevieve could do not to cry out. Her French was quite handy in these situations. Whatever she decided to do, she ought to do it soon. Mave's caff was definitely losing its appeal.

When the phone rang, Genevieve ignored it for several rings, hoping Mave would deal with it. Mave, however, was practising one of her frequent bouts of selective deafness, despite the fact she was sitting right next to it, and appeared to be completely engrossed in her *Woman's Weekly*. Eventually Genevieve put down the tray of crockery she was carrying, stalked over to it, snatched up the receiver and asked in a cross voice, 'Yes?'

'Oh hello. May I speak to Genevieve, please?'

'Yes, speaking.'

'Oh, hello. It's Michael here.'

'Michael? Oh, Michael!' Genevieve's spirits lifted immediately. She hadn't seen or heard from him since he had come to visit her in the café and she suddenly realised she had missed him. Missed a friend.

'Michael, hello! How are you?'

He chuckled delightedly at the enthusiasm of her reception. 'I'm fine, how are you?'

'Oh, having a bad day in this bloody café. Every day it's fried eggs, dirty floors, tea that tastes like shit. You English and your fucking diet – it kills me.'

'See you're getting the hang of the language then.'

'Yeah!' she laughed. 'Perhaps I should work somewhere, how do you say, more upmarket?'

'Yes, maybe you should!' Both were giggling, pleased to be speaking to each other again. 'Look, the reason I am ringing was to ask you something quite serious actually, and please, I don't mind if you say no,' Michael went on.

'What is it?' Genevieve was concerned. She could hear the gravity in Michael's voice.

'Well, you remember what we talked about before, about my dad?'

'*Merde!* I completely forgot we were meant to be going to the hospital. Michael, I'm so sorry!'

'Oh, please don't worry about it.' He had wanted to arrange a visit with Genevieve for a while now, but hadn't rung her earlier because he was worried about Seamus's reaction. Also, he thought they might bump into each other at Marrow, but Seamus had obviously been keeping Genevieve away from his work. He knew it was unwise to call her, but in the end she was the only one he could talk to. 'I just wanted to know if your offer still stood.'

'Of course! Let's go whenever you want.' Genevieve couldn't believe she had forgotten. How callous Michael must think her; she had to make it up to him immediately. 'Are you going tonight? Perhaps I could come with you after work?' Genevieve thought quickly: she had arranged to see a film with Seamus tonight, but she was sure he wouldn't mind if she gave it a miss just this once. He hadn't really seemed that keen. But first she would have to shower and change out of her dreadful grease-splattered clothes. 'I shall need to go home first.'

'No problem. You can visit till ten.' Michael was so relieved – he had been counting on talking to Genevieve again. He still had no idea what he was going to do about his father. 'Is nine o'clock OK?'

'Nine is fine. I'll meet you there. Where do I go?'

'It's the Royal Free Hospital, on Haverstock Hill. Go to Belsize Park Tube. Oh Genevieve, I'm so glad you can come.'

'It's no problem – I look forward to it. Belsize Park Tube,' she repeated, writing the name down. 'Shall I meet you at the Tube station?'

'OK, that's probably easier. You know, I really appreciate this, but if you want to change your mind, I quite—'

'Don't be ridiculous, I'm coming. I never change my mind. I'll see you there at nine, Michael. I'm looking forward to meeting your Papa!'

Genevieve had completely forgotten to mention to Seamus that she had bumped into Michael again, and she'd also forgotten to tell him she had offered to go with Michael to the hospital one day. At least, she thought she had forgotten, but she wondered if it wasn't more than that. She had this nasty feeling that Seamus wasn't going to be too pleased about her spending the evening with one of his employees. Then she told herself not to be so ridiculous – it was completely reasonable she would want to help a friend. Anyway, Seamus should be happy she was making friends over here. She rang him on his mobile.

'It's me. How are you?'

'Hey babe. I'm busy. You?'

'Work is very hard today. I want to come home.'

'Give it up, girl, I keep telling you. Then I can too and we can have sex all day long instead . . .'

Genevieve giggled and crossed her legs. 'Listen, darling, I forgot to tell you something.'

'What?'

'You remember I told you that when I came to find you at the restaurant in Notting Hill I met someone who worked for you? A guy called Michael.'

'Yes. Listen, babe, you'll have to hurry – I'm in the middle of a meeting.'

'Well, his father is sick. He is in hospital.'

'Yeah, I know.'

'I said I would go with him to visit his father tonight.'

'What?'

'I said I would go with him to the hospital.'

'What on earth for? Why you?'

'Well, because . . .' Genevieve was stumped. 'Because I

said I would, naturally. Why not? The guy is having a bad
time. It may help him.' Of course, she thought, why else?
Genevieve was not about to explain on the phone in a
crowded café that she sympathised because she had had to
watch her own father die and she thought she might be able
to be of some help. Christ, the only reason Seamus knew
her father was dead was because she was here. He'd never
evinced the slightest curiosity about it. She didn't think he
even knew what he had died from. She had never told him
– but then he had never asked.

'I just said I would.'

'Genevieve, that's ridiculous. That boy works for me,
you can't be seen patronising him!'

'Patronising? What's that?'

'Look, the answer is no. He's a big boy, he can sort it out
himself. It's not appropriate. Leave it alone, will you?'

Genevieve was puzzled. Seamus's voice was getting
louder, and when she had rung him it hadn't been a
question of getting his permission. She had merely been
informing him.

'Seamus, I don't understand. It's no big deal – I'm just
going to the hospital with him.'

'*No*, Genevieve.' A dangerous edge entered Seamus's
voice now, one that Genevieve hadn't heard in a while.
She couldn't understand what his problem was.

'Seamus, I am helping a friend, OK?'

'Oh, so suddenly he's your friend now, is he?'

'Yes, yes, he is my friend!' Genevieve was beginning to
raise her own voice now. What in hell was wrong with that?
Seamus was reacting very bizarrely and she didn't like it one
little bit.

'OK, what's going on?' demanded Seamus.

'Nothing, you idiot!' Genevieve shouted in return – the
first time she had ever raised her voice with him. People
in the café were beginning to stare.

'Don't call me a fucking idiot!' Seamus was really angry

now. 'What's going on here? Is there something I should
know about, Genevieve?' Seamus was bellowing loudly
down the phone and it sounded ugly.

Genevieve lowered her voice and tried to calm him.
'Seamus, you don't understand. You are being jealous, but
there is nothing to worry about. I'll explain it all to you
later, OK? When I get back from the hospital.'

'No, Genevieve, you are not fucking going to the fucking
hospital – do you hear me?'

'Oh yes, I am – you can't tell me what to do. Now please
calm down and don't worry. I have to go now.'

'Genevieve! Hey!' But she had already put the phone
down.

Genevieve was shocked: he had never spoken to her
like that before. What a ridiculous overreaction! Why didn't
he care about Michael and his sick father? Why didn't he
want her doing things on her own? Why did he never ask
her about the past? She was cross now. Seamus certainly
wouldn't tempt her to join him at Marrow if he was going
to treat her like this.

Seamus was also furious. How dare she? What was she
doing, running around town with his fucking kitchen
porter? It was absurd and embarrassing – what would
the rest of his staff say? It was bad enough she was still
working in that bloody shit-hole café! And as for Michael
– well, he had a fucking nerve. Just wait until I see him
again, raged Seamus. In the meantime, if Genevieve was
going to piss off tonight – then so was he.

Drunken Fruits

750g mixed, dried fruits (prunes, apricots, figs etc)
250g sugar
1 litre water
250ml dark rum
Mascarpone to serve

1. Mix the sugar with the water in a saucepan and bring to the boil.

2. Simmer for ten minutes to thicken, then remove from the heat and stir in the rum. And a little bit more.

3. Put the mixed fruits in a bowl and cover them in the syrup. Add a bit more rum. Leave for twenty-four hours, when the the fruits will be plump and swollen with alcohol.

4. Drain the fruits, reserving the syrup. Take out the stones.

5. Serve the fruits with a spoonful of mascarpone and plenty of syrup drizzled over the top.

22

Paul and Nigel were delighted to see Seamus again. It had been ages since they had all got lashed together, and what with them both moonlighting on top of Marrow's retainer, they had some serious money to spend tonight.

'Good to see you again, mate,' Nigel said, whacking Seamus on the back as he came out of the pub toilet.

Holding his nose, Seamus flung his head back and gave a good long snort. He opened and shut his eyes. 'Brrrrrrrooooeeeeee! That feels good. Been a while.' Seamus knew he shouldn't do this stuff – it ruined the palate, but he figured every now and then it couldn't hurt.

'Been a while since we've seen you, mate.'

The truth was, ever since Marion had said 'Bolivian' to him at lunch-time, Seamus hadn't been able to think of anything else. After that phone call with Genevieve – what was that stupid girl playing at? – he had seen no reason not to go out and have some of his own fun. Unable to get hold of Salvatore, he'd called Paul and Nigel. They inevitably knew someone who could. So there the three of them were, in a pool bar on Westbourne Grove in Notting Hill.

'So what you been doing with yourself then, Seamus?' enquired Paul as they arrived at the bar. Then, without waiting for the answer, he asked the barman for three more pints and some table time.

'Got me a woman, Paul,' grinned Seamus, picking up a pool cue and aiming a practice shot over the table.

'Now that makes sense,' Paul grinned back. 'No wonder you've been hiding.'

'I tell you she's sweet. Blonde and cute and . . .' and here Seamus traced his hands around the exaggerated dimensions of Genevieve's curves.

'Nice one,' said Paul, obligatorily.

'Yeah – obviously she has her uses, but the little woman is proving to be a handful.'

'They always are, mate. Best to ignore them when they ask for stuff, I find,' said Paul, whose wife rather enjoyed the fact that she never saw him.

'We going to see her tonight?' asked Nigel, who always thought Seamus's women were rather boring and spoiled their lads' nights out.

'Nah. Not her scene,' said Seamus, cueing the ball up to break. Then, sliding his arm through, he hit just below the centre of the white ball. 'Crack!' as the ball went smashing into the pack, breaking it up. Nothing went in. He handed the cue to Nigel. 'Winner plays Paul. Twenty quid says I win.'

'You're on,' said Paul and Nigel in unison.

Henrietta was wearing Versace tonight. Sparkly, sexy, showy: oh, how she loved Versace. It was 100 per cent reliably effective, reassuringly expensive, fuck-me clothing. Teamed with her high pink strappy mules, her curly hair worn loose and tumbling down her back, Seamus should get no mixed messages this evening, thought Henrietta. She had set her mind on this one. Marion was right: if she wanted excitement she had to stray out of the fold a little. She'd had Sugar Daddy millionaires by the kilo, and she was bored of them. She needed a walk on the wild side. Most definitely. And Seamus was surely the man to take her there. There was no doubt he was sexy as hell, thought Henrietta. Before she left the house, she decided to take off her knickers. Just to 'improve' the line of the dress, of course . . .

*   *   *

Seamus was now £60 down on the pool.

'Not your night tonight, eh boss?' chuckled Nigel, who was £40 up. 'Out of practice, I'd say.'

'All right, Nigel. Your round. And chuck us that wrap while you're at it, will you?'

Seamus set off for the toilets. It was good doing this again. He'd forgotten how much fun it could be. He was trying hard not to worry about what Genevieve was up to – she was only visiting Michael's fucking sick father, hardly the most adulterous thing in the world, but still it was a betrayal. He was furious she was going and even more furious Michael had asked her. Had they been seeing each other behind his back? He'd damn well get it out of her when he saw her, that was for sure. No one made a fool of Seamus Bull. Well, fuck her! He was going to have a good night without her.

He tipped out the rest of the wrap onto the back of his wallet, then hoovered it up through a rolled-up note. Yeah, good fun. Might as well go along to Louche tonight, he thought. Even if it meant giving in to that stupid cow Marion. Seem a shame not to, especially when they had spent the whole afternoon in the pool bar already.

Emmanuel Coq had been promising to introduce Archie Peaks to Rufus for weeks now. Archie was a hard man to pin down, but Emmanuel had finally caught him on a rare night in London, and offered to take him down to Club Louche. Archie wasn't sure if it was his scene, but the moment he arrived he decided it might be fun, and appraising the racks of designer-clad beautiful people, felt instantly at home. Settled in a large leather armchair near the entrance to the club, he was now enjoying a glass of Krug, and was in deep discussion with Rufus about how one expressed the sensation of taste in words. Both men had instantly endeared themselves to each other by offering a panegyric on the other's work.

'Rufus, how wonderful to meet you at last. You know, I have to confess I read your column every week. It's invaluable.'

'My God, don't even think of it, my dear chap. I remember the first time I went to Leeds Airport. I remember it so clearly, it's like a postcard in my mind. That great Perspex tower protruding from the east terminal. Spectacular.'

'Why, thank you. Actually we had great trouble erecting that. Dreadful time with the council . . .' which set Archie off into a terrifically long and boring explanation of local council planning minutiae which Rufus was obliged to listen to for about twenty minutes. This was probably a record amount of time for Rufus to listen to someone else and not talk about himself.

Marion was sitting on her usual perch in the corner of the bar, swathed in body-clinging black chiffon sliced open down her long, brown back. She was peering over at the cosy little trio of Coq, Ruthless and Peaks and thinking that whatever else happened tonight, at the very least they would get some press coverage. The paparazzi knew something was in the air, and there were now three or four of them loitering around Louche's door.

Marion crossed her fingers and whispered conspiratorially into Chris's ear. It was essential to have the barman on your side in these situations, she found. She lit up a long white Cartier and fended off the compliments of those who came to pay court to her. She was too busy watching for Seamus and Henrietta to give her admirers anything more than cursory attention.

'What do you reckon to going down Louche tonight then, eh? Paul? Nigel?' asked Seamus casually, fed up with losing money.

'Sounds good to me,' said Nigel.

'There is that place round the corner from here, though,'

suggested Paul, who lived locally and didn't fancy trekking all the way into town.

'Whatever,' said Nigel. 'Just as long as it serves alcohol.'

'Not that Austrian place, Paul. I am not going in there!' replied Seamus firmly. 'Not after the last time. Schnapps doesn't agree with me – nor you, mate. Anyway, I think I'm banned and you certainly are, Nigel.' All three of them began to laugh at the memory of their last night in the Tyrolean Hut, a surreal Austrian theme bar that had the dubious advantage of a late licence.

'All right, we'll go to Louche,' agreed Paul finally. 'Who's down there tonight then?'

'Charlie. That's who,' replied Seamus, his maniacal grin plastered back on his face.

'God, such a dreadful launch, sweetheart, I can't tell you. Boring, boring, boring,' chanted Henrietta, looking anxiously about her.

Marion smiled, watching her cast around for a glimpse of Seamus. 'Don't worry, he's not here yet,' she told her.

Henrietta blushed, and sat on the stool facing Marion, trying not to look distracted. 'Have you said anything to him about me?' she asked, coyly looking up at Marion.

She was behaving like a schoolgirl, thought Marion, who suddenly felt very tired of playing these pathetic games. Did she really have to play silly buggers with these stupid little people? Or help them play silly buggers with each other? She had been thinking, as she had sat in Louche for the first time in weeks, that this was getting boring. She needed her island in the Bahamas – and soon. She could retire there with Janetta and Fuzz and act her age. Seamus and Henrietta could bloody well sort out their own sex-lives. She was only doing this for the good of the business, but even to her it felt sordid.

'Well, honey, I've done my best, but I'm not a pimp, you know.'

'Funny, I thought that was your profession.'

Marion spun her head round to where the snide inter-jection had come from and found Emmanuel Coq standing there. She wondered how long he had been eavesdropping on them.

'Another bottle of Krug, please, my good man,' he told Chris, finally securing the barman's attention. Then he walked off, without so much as a sideways glance at Marion and Henrietta. He was weird, thought Marion. Weird and rude. She spat out the olive stone from her 'medicinal' vodka martini. Nowadays Marion's no drinking rule was forgotten. She was so exhausted from the launch preparations and holding her business together, she needed something to keep her going.

'Prick!' she called after his retreating back.

'Or not, as the case may be,' responded Henrietta, and both burst into hysterics. Henrietta nearly fell off her stool, and clutching onto Marion she let out a shriek as she recovered her balance. The shriek was (purposefully) loud enough to make Emmanuel turn around and register that they were laughing at his expense. He felt the bile rise in his throat, and stalked off towards his table.

Marion and Henrietta recovered themselves, and were about to take off for the Ladies when a voice from behind Henrietta addressed her.

'Ah! It's the bisexual It girl.'

Henry Hampson, the television producer and one of Henrietta's ex-'squeezes' had appeared. Trouble was, Henry wasn't aware he was an ex. Henrietta had completely forgotten to tell him, and as Henry had been away filming in the Congo, he assumed they were still an item. He slid his hand round her sequinned waist and asked: 'Can I buy you anything at the bar?'

A look of revulsion passed over Henrietta's face. This was exactly the sort of man she was trying to escape from and the last person she wanted hanging round her tonight if she were to stand any chance of making herself available to Seamus. She raised her arm and smacked his hand off. 'Go away, Henry, you're tedious,' she snapped.

Henry looked shocked, and removing his hand, regarded Henrietta with surprise. When she continued pointedly to ignore him, he walked away, wondering why he had been such an idiot to get involved with her in the first place. If he wasn't very much mistaken, the diamond she was wearing round her neck had been a gift from him. But Henry was too much of a gentleman to point it out.

Quite carried away with her new mission, Henrietta fancied she was being sexy and hard, and tossed her head coquettishly. 'Boring as hell, but plenty of money,' she told Marion, when he was only just out of earshot.

Marion was looking at Henrietta curiously. '*Bisexual*, Henrietta?' she asked her.

'Yeah, but only with him.' Henrietta grinned. 'My little joke: if he buys me stuff I'll have sex with him.'

Marion looked disappointed and stubbed out her cigarette. An explosion of noise caused her to glance over to the door. Seamus and company had arrived. She permitted herself a smile, and passed Henrietta the paper wrap she held in her hand.

'Glad to see you are spending my money wisely.' Seamus had fallen right over the lounging figure of Archie Peaks, whose feet were stretched out into the gangway and had, quite accidentally, caught Seamus as he staggered across the room. As he tripped, his eye happened to alight on the magnum of vintage Krug on the table. Archie gave him a polite nod, and moved his feet under his chair.

'Good evening, Mr Bull. I believe you already know my friend Emmanuel Coq, and you must also know Rufus Ransome here, too, I presume.'

'Yeah, we're bosom buddies,' replied Seamus, smirking.

'Well,' said Archie, 'they are sharing this bottle with me. Would you care to join us?'

To his horror, Seamus watched Rufus raise his glass to him, with a big fat slobbering smile on his face.

'I think I'd rather drink arsenic with Colonel Gaddafi, thanks.'

Fixing Seamus with his beady eye, Coq asked snidely, 'Tell me, Bull, how is your supermarket coming along?'

Seamus walked off in disgust. That was the problem with Louche: it was always full of idiots. Paul and Nigel followed him.

'Bunch of cunts, that lot,' said Paul, who had heard from Seamus about his altercation with Peaks and his 'penis experiment' as Seamus called it.

'Yeah,' agreed Nigel, whose greatest fear was having to make conversation. 'If I wanted to talk with arseholes, I'd fart.'

'Seamus!' greeted Marion, as the three men bounded across the bar towards her. 'Fancy seeing you here.'

He bent over her bar stool, kissed her briefly on the cheek she proffered him, and then leaned against the bar facing her. Behind Seamus, Henrietta, looking like a sequinned pink doll, was gesticulating to Marion. Nigel, on the other hand, was once again left dumbstruck at the sight of her. Paul looked at him as if he was deranged. 'Do you want to retrieve your eyeballs from her cleavage, Nige?'

'Got those staffing figures then, Marion?' Seamus asked, his eyes gleaming.

'No, but my friend has,' she said, pointing at Henrietta. Seamus turned round to find Henrietta offering him her best profile.

'Who's your friend then?' asked Seamus, completely failing to recognise her.

Marion was furious. 'Seamus, you must remember Henrietta Gross-Smythe.'

'Oh yeah, Henrietta. All right. How's it going? Sorry, didn't recognise you with—' he was going to say 'that dress on', but knew that wouldn't sound right. Marion rescued him.

'Darling, why don't you show Seamus downstairs?' Then turning to Paul and Nigel and finding herself stuck with them again, Marion said firmly, 'Mine's a vodka martini.'

Once Henrietta and Seamus had reacquainted themselves in the toilet and made their way back to a sofa upstairs, Seamus realised, in spite of his drunkenness, that Henrietta was flirting with him. He was pleased – his ego had been feeling bruised after Genevieve had blown him out for some weedy little kitchen porter, but this girl was reminding him of the effect his power and charisma normally had. Watching her attempts to seduce him was amusing and flattering. He gave her no discouragement.

'So is it really hot? How hot is it in your kitchens?' she asked, squirming in her seat, her head cocked up towards him, her legs crossed away from him, the upper part of her body leaning right into him. She looked at him from behind the escaped tendrils of her hair, and blinked just a little too often, her eyelashes catching in her curls.

'Hotter than you could stand, babe,' Seamus teased. He was enjoying this.

Henrietta burned. Seamus might be responding to her but she wondered how much longer they would have to go on like this before they could leave and get down to the serious task in hand: her orgasm. She didn't want to sleep with Seamus for his conversation, that was for sure.

Henrietta was mortified that she had never had an orgasm at all, and rather like losing her virginity, she felt it was something she ought to get out of the way as quickly as possible. Especially now she was twenty-seven and had been having sexual encounters for over ten years. Admittedly, though, only with posh boys. Seamus, on the other hand, was the kind of man who could probably give you an orgasm just by looking at you. She asked him if he wanted another drink – as he wasn't offering her one –

and taking his order up to the bar, Henrietta decided to hold half-time counsel with Marion.

'How you doing, honey?' Marion asked as Henrietta drifted over.

'OK. But I'm not sure he fancies me. He hasn't even touched me yet,' said Henrietta dejectedly.

'Nonsense. You look devastating in that dress.'

'Try telling him that.'

I don't believe it, thought Marion. Do I have to pay for their fucking taxi fare as well?

'OK then,' she said in short, clipped tones, 'I will.' Leaving Henrietta standing at the bar (and at the mercy of the returning Henry Hampson, who was now certain she was wearing his necklace), Marion turned and marched on Seamus.

'So, Emmanuel, you have a bit of a beef with this character then, I take it?' chuckled Archie, amused by the inner rivalries of a business as egotistical as his own.

'Emmanuel taught Seamus everything he knows,' interjected Rufus, defensively. 'Then he takes off with someone else! Hardly cricket, is it?' Rufus had never watched a game of cricket in his life.

'He is an illusionist. A Great Pretender: he does not have the instinct for cooking that makes a truly great chef. He has the technique – God knows I drummed it into him – but not the true genius,' pronounced Emmanuel. Then coldly, fiercely, he added, 'And he betrayed me.'

'He is a very poor imitator, Archie,' continued Rufus. 'Obsessed with show and appearance, but his cooking has no heart, no soul. It is but a series of ornamental garnishes around the plate.' Rufus was getting carried away now. Really, with these two working against him like this, it was a wonder Seamus Bull had a restaurant at all, thought Archie. But there was one thing he didn't understand.

'Explain to me, Emmanuel. If he is such a monster in the

kitchen, then why are you so worried about his restaurant casting a shadow over yours?'

'Because it's so big!' replied Emmanuel, exasperated. 'It'll make a mockery of Mirage.'

'But Mirage will be something different. It is a small restaurant with high-quality food. Not a fashion-led brasserie like the new Marrow. Hardly in the same league, even.'

'Precisely,' wailed Rufus miserably, who now took Coq's fortunes personally. 'Fashion-led! How I hate those words. Those are the words that have destroyed cooking in this country. Every uneducated customer who comes to Mirage now will spend their whole night staring at the shenanigans going on over the road. That bloody PR woman will make sure there are photographers and scuffles outside every night. It will be the talk of the town – the *only* talk of the town. It will be like this place – only for the public. I know how her sort works – on gossip and fashion. If the editor of *Vogue* eats there, then everyone eats there. If I eat there, then . . .' Rufus stopped. He didn't want to finish that sentence. 'What I mean to say is it will attract the fickle diners, rather than people who take quality and style seriously such as myself – ourselves, should I say.'

Emmanuel took up the baton. 'It will be disgusting. Don't you see the last thing it'll be about is the food? It will all be hype about the venue.'

Archie grinned. 'Well, that suits me just fine.' Rufus and Emmanuel looked at him, confounded.

'Is there really nothing you can do for us, Archie, old boy?' spluttered Rufus, vainly.

'I don't see what. Short of ordering a sign that says *Mirage* rather than *Marrow*.'

'Not a bad idea,' exclaimed Rufus.

'A terrible idea!' growled Coq, who could see Plan A was foundering. Even after weeks of wooing him, the meal at Mirage and the endless vintage champagne, Peaks still hadn't offered to do the decent thing and pull out. It was

worth one last push though, thought Emmanuel, bullish to
the end. He was obviously going to have to spell it out.

'You see, Archie, our problem is that your name attached
to the establishment lends it more weight than it actually
deserves. It makes our task of discrediting Marrow – rather,
should I say, revealing it for what it is – much harder.'

'So what do you want me to do?' asked Archie cautiously.
He wasn't sure where this conversation was going, but he
didn't like it.

'Well,' Emmanuel began, 'I know it's nearly finished
now, but I think it would still have the same effect if, say,
you were to withdraw your support. The adverse publicity
could be enough to start a backlash.'

Coq left the idea hanging in the air. Archie puffed on
his cigar and regarded Emmanuel over the top of his
glass. What Emmanuel hadn't counted on was that Archie,
unusually for the patrons of Louche, had a strong sense of
moral responsibility. And business sense.

'Now that wouldn't be very professional of me,
Emmanuel,' he eventually said, with a slight, but still
detectable, note of reproof in his voice. He glanced at
the stub of grey ash on the end of his cigar and flicked it
into the ashtray, rather as one might swat a bothersome fly.
There was a hint of irritation in Archie's movement. He was
not pleased to be dragged into this singularly ungentlemanly
conversation.

'Tell me, how's your wife?' bulldozed Rufus, fed up
with the double-talking. This was too much for Archie,
and taking umbrage he shot back viciously: 'Leave Beattie
out of it!' his voice shaking with anger.

Rufus quivered. *Ooops,* he thought.

Archie, on the other hand, had been prepared to put up
with these two clowns for a while but he had the measure
of them now. They were on a dirty tricks campaign and he
was being bribed. Well, he wasn't having it. What with the
combined New Age spiritualism of his wife, and his strict

Catholic upbringing, Archie's lifeblood ran rich in morality. He might not particularly like Seamus Bull, but he had no reason to *dis*like him, and he was not about to do him over on the whim of some chap who had once cooked his wife some soup.

Enraged, he put down his glass, stood up, straightened his jacket, and announced: 'Gentlemen, I thank you for entertaining me this evening, it has been most . . . revealing. But I am afraid that our dialogue has taken an unfortunate turn and therefore will have to stop. Goodnight to you both.'

And with that the great architect turned to leave, revealing the disastrous crumpling that so plagued the linen at the back of his jacket.

'So, Seamus? What's the problem with the It girl?' demanded Marion, not happy that the one part of the evening she had taken for granted – Seamus's willingness to shag – was proving difficult to engineer.

'No problem, Marion. I think she's amusing,' drawled Seamus, who was now slumped in his chair, concentrating on not spilling his glass of whisky. The trouble was it had been so long since Seamus had drunk to excess that his body wasn't used to it. The alcohol, therefore, was having a rather more overpowering effect than usual. 'Why?' he enquired.

'She thinks you don't fancy her.'

'So?' he laughed.

'Darling, need I point out the advantages?' Marion asked with her eyebrows raised. Bending down so that her mouth was speaking directly into his ear, she began: 'The girl has an untold number of contacts which could prove rather useful in the coming months. She is photographed wherever she goes – as is the man she is with. She is famously single, and were she to settle down with someone, then the spotlight would be on him as well as her. She has a highly influential national newspaper column that mentions a different restaurant every week: imagine if it was the same one every week. According to marketing men, her brand endorsement level is absolute, which basically means that if we get her behind Marrow then we're made. Add to that the fact that the girl is reputedly loaded, and you may well get your hands on the extra collateral that you seem to find so difficult to locate at the moment, Seamus. The launch is only ten bloody days away – we need to do something drastic! Do you understand what I'm saying? Now, all you have to do is have a few fun and games . . .'

Seamus stared at Marion in amazement. 'Let me get this straight. You want me to shag Henrietta Whatsisname to get Marrow some PR?'

'*And* your collateral. In a nutshell, yes, Seamus, that is exactly what I want.' Then she added as an afterthought, 'Unless, of course, you're not up to the job.'

'What do you mean?'

'Well, perhaps you are no longer man enough.' And Marion raised her eyebrows in the direction of Seamus's crotch. 'I understand a certain habit of yours has the tendency to render one, how shall I put it, disabled?'

'Don't be ridiculous,' he replied, stung.

'Well, it has been known. And we wouldn't want Henrietta putting that about, would we? The poor girl, I suspect, has never been given any pleasure, and it would be a shame if she never experienced a master as a lover . . . Another drink?'

By now Seamus was barely able to focus. Marion could see she was going to have to put the two of them in a taxi anyway. Seamus, however, was not a man to tolerate any slur on his physical prowess, although it was true he was having trouble sitting up.

'Yes, sanother drink sgood,' he replied. Marion duly ordered him a double. By the time Henrietta had reappeared with another double for him, all Seamus could focus on was the flash of her naked thigh, and the sparkle of her dress skimming the very tops of her legs. As she sat down next to him, he reached over and grabbed at the thigh, obeying some basic primal instinct.

'Careful, Seamus,' Henrietta whispered as she leaned over towards him. 'I'm not wearing any knickers.'

By now all thoughts of Genevieve had mysteriously left Seamus's head. He was purely in the here and now. He felt a stirring in his crotch and looked down to see Henrietta's hand resting on him. The voices around him had become a low buzz, and the next thing he knew he was staggering out of the door, being led, hypnotised by the pink sparkly dress. As they left through the front door, the camera flashes blinded him, and instinctively he pulled his arm up over his face. But Henrietta beamed straight into the waiting lenses.

In the back of the cab, the dress was now straddling him. The weight and shape of her body felt different from the one he was used to – her thin lips on his were grinding against his teeth, her tongue slobbering over his chin. He could feel her hands undoing his shirt now, and in reaction he reached up blindly to grab at where her breasts should be. They were smaller, tighter, and the body was bonier and harder than the luxurious curves he expected. Blindly he struggled on until the taxi stopped.

Now they were in a bright, marble lobby. There were men in uniform, a lift, and they were going through a door – and there was a bed. He felt hands now, tracking up his back underneath his shirt, then round his sides and fluttering down his belly to the top of his trousers. The dull desire in him was growing, and turning round he surveyed the sparkling dress standing between him and the flesh that was arousing him. Taking it by its hem, he tore it up over her head, leaving her naked but for her shoes. He was aware of her undoing his belt and fumbling with the buttons of his fly.

As he yanked his shorts down with his trousers, he heard her gasp: despite Seamus's inebriated state, it appeared his erection was still impressive. Henrietta had never seen anything so big before, and just for a moment she wondered if it was really going to fit. But Seamus was on a mission now, one he needed to see through to its conclusion. Standing there in nothing but her pink high heels, gasping at the sight of him gave him the last push he needed.

Flinging her down on the bed, he yanked her legs apart and, kneeling down between them and supporting himself above her head with his arms, he pushed himself straight into her. Henrietta, after a draughty evening wandering around with no knickers and the urgent grappling in the back of the cab, found herself quite ready to receive him: he managed to slide his full length into her with just one push. She cried out, half in pain. This just goaded Seamus further, and heaving himself in and out of her he endeavoured to bring himself to a climax. But as he grunted with the effort, suddenly the drink got the better of him, and to Henrietta's horror, she felt him go limp. Deflated, like a balloon. No longer desperate to fulfil his physical need, Seamus stopped, and pulling out, collapsed on the bed. Within seconds, he was snoring loudly.

Chicken Soup

2 litres well flavoured chicken stock, heated
2 leeks, sliced
2 celery sticks, sliced
2 carrots, peeled and chopped
1 onion, peeled and sliced
350g chicken meat
Salt and pepper
Cream

1. Mix the chicken and vegetables in a pan, then gradually add the stock.

2. Continue to heat, but remove immediately the soup begins to boil.

3. Stir in the cream and serve.

23

Michael left the flat at eight o'clock. It was only a twenty-minute bus ride, but he didn't want to be late, and the bus often took ages to come. The rain had stopped, and the air had an evening freshness. He was wearing a clean shirt he had just ironed, a pair of Chinos and a long dark wool coat. His skin smelled of soap, and his thick, dark hair still glistened from the shower. He felt strangely nervous, but also excited, as he strode purposefully across the estate, head down, hands in pockets so as not to invite attention from the gangs that prowled the territory after dark. He had had to deal with them on a few occasions before, but growing up on an estate meant you knew how to look after yourself. The road was visible now, and he could see a bus thundering towards the stop. Quickening his pace, he reached it just in time. He felt perkier this evening; normally he approached this bus ride with dread.

He settled into a window seat near the back of the bus, and prepared to watch the roll of familiar scenery as far as Chalk Farm. The bus crossed over the busy High Road, then settled into the twisting, climbing route up to Swiss Cottage. A half-way house at the bottom of Belsize Road usually spewed a few drunks onto the bus, and tonight was no exception. Two rag-ridden Scots got on, a man and a woman, clutching bottles and swearing abuse at the driver. Michael stared harder out of the window. A young mother was marching a little boy and his bike along the pavement, screaming at him, but Michael tried not to hear exactly what it was she was saying.

By Swiss Cottage the drunks had got louder, and the driver refused to move the bus out of the stop until they had disembarked. They, in turn, were refusing to co-operate and the situation had developed into a stand-off. The traffic was now held up way back from the Swiss Cottage roundabout. The drunks were swearing and screaming at the driver, who had his chin in his hands and his elbows resting on the wheel and sat staring defiantly at the road ahead. He said, 'Off!' to the Scots periodically, but otherwise refused to pay them any attention. Now, from down the hill, sounded a cacophony of car horns. The noise was unbearable. Michael shut his eyes and tried to pretend he was somewhere else. Outside, away from this city, away from these miserable lives.

The drunks eventually fell out of the bus. The driver closed the doors and pulled out impatiently. The rest of the passengers breathed a sigh of relief. Michael opened his eyes. The drunks had clearly tripped up getting off the bus and the two of them were now rolling around in the gutter. As the lights changed to green, the bus swung up into Swiss Cottage. There was a queue outside the cinema at the roundabout, and Michael watched the men hugging their girlfriends close to them. It was cold in the evenings now, winter was beginning to bite. One of the men reached down and planted a kiss on his girlfriend's forehead. He held his lips on her skin for a few seconds, wrapping his arms around her waist, pulling her into him. She fitted snugly against his body, Michael noticed. Then the bus pulled on and he didn't see any more.

The grey concrete of Swiss Cottage eventually gave way to the tree-lined avenues of Belsize Park and Hampstead, and Michael got off the bus with relief. He had felt claustrophobic all the way. He set off at a pace down England's Lane, heading for the hospital. The wind had got up, and blew leaves into his path. A gust took a handful and threw them at his face. Michael squinted and held his hands up in front of him. Pulling his coat around him, he turned up Haverstock Hill to the Tube station. He sat on a bench outside to wait.

Genevieve surrendered herself gratefully to the steaming flow of water. She leaned back against the shower cubicle and, picking up a sponge, started scrubbing at her skin. It had lost almost all its summer glow, she noted, disappointed. She thought of France now: the shooting season would be well under way. Pheasant casserole for dinner – she could almost smell the aroma coming from the oven in their kitchen. With a shock, she realised it didn't belong to her any more. The kitchen was for sale. Henri, her papa, used to have a good deal going with his friend Alain the butcher. On a Monday morning at eleven o'clock the two would have a rendezvous at a little local café where they would surreptitiously swap big paper bags. The one Henri came home with would be the pick of the weekend's kill (not always legally plundered), while Alain would take home to his wife and children the best of the morning's pastries and several loaves of Monsieur Dupont's regional speciality.

Genevieve shampooed her hair, then wrapping herself in a towel, ran back down the corridor to her bedroom. It was eight o'clock already, and Belsize Park was miles away on the Tube. Patting herself dry as she ran about the room, she dived into drawers and randomly started pulling out clothes, eventually ending up with a black sweater and jeans.

She was curious about this evening. She had to admit she was quite excited to be doing something different tonight, not just following Seamus around. The closer his opening got, the more stressed he was becoming, she had noticed. And she was still annoyed with his tone when he had spoken to her earlier today. When would he learn that he couldn't tell her what to do? She wanted to be with him, but she wanted her own life too. But they still couldn't keep their hands off each other. She smiled to herself. If only she could persuade him to come back to France with her, then she believed they could be truly happy.

She brushed through her wet hair then ran the hairdryer over it for a few minutes. Lightly dabbing cream on her face, she picked up her bag, grabbed the coat Seamus had bought her – she had had no idea England would be so cold, or was it that she had had no idea she was going to be here so long? – and ran down the stairs. She was about to leave, when something occurred to her. Turning back to the payphone in the hostel hall, she pulled a 10p piece out of her pocket, slotted it in and dialled Seamus's number. She didn't like arguing – she wanted to make up, say something nice to him before she went out.

The answerphone picked up. She tried his mobile; it was switched off. She hung up – well, at least he wasn't sitting at home moping, she thought. She would see him when she got back and set it all straight. Finally she would tell him about her dad, and explain everything. It was time she told him about her life since he left her, but he never asked, and she had never quite felt able to tell him. Tonight she would. For now, Belsize Park Tube. She was going to be late.

Michael was pacing up and down on the pavement; it was too cold to sit on the bench, and he was beginning to experience the rising nausea of disappointment. It was almost as if he had expected it though, he thought. Why would someone like her want to spend time with someone like him? He'd give her ten more minutes.

'Oh my God, Michael, I am so sorry!' Genevieve ran up to him, still panting from the climb up the stairs in one of the deepest Tube stations in London. Delight shot through Michael's body and he spun round to find Genevieve's angelic face searching his, her long blonde hair tied loosely back at the nape of her neck. She put her hand up to her chest as she caught her breath, then reached up and kissed him on either cheek.

Michael was astonished at the gentleness of her touch. Genevieve felt embarrassed at his look of shock. 'I'm sorry. We French – we kiss everybody,' she smiled.

'Fine by me,' he grinned. Then, instinctively he guided her up the hill with his palm resting lightly on the small of her back. When he noticed it was there, he pulled away.

'So have you been to see your Papa already today?'

'No, not today. You know, Genevieve, he is in a coma.'

'Yes, you told me. But sometimes people who are in comas can hear everything around them.'

'Yeah, I know. Actually, I talk to him all the time,' Michael confided.

'Do you?' asked Genevieve, looking back at him.

'Yes,' he replied, a little shyly. 'I ask him stuff. Like I used to before the accident.'

'What was the accident?'

Michael looked down at the pavement. 'I'll tell you.' The words hung in the air. Genevieve understood 'later'. Somehow she knew this was a significant moment for him.

'Have you taken anyone to meet your Papa in hospital before?' she asked quietly.

'No. No, I haven't.' Michael was embarrassed now.

The great big concrete slabs of the hospital came into view. Now it was Genevieve's turn to feel nauseous. Hospitals were nasty, grim, miserable places. She started breathing more quickly, then determined to bring herself under control. Michael noticed – the building had a similar effect on him – and his hand went up to her back again.

'Was your father in hospital too, Genevieve?'

'Yes, he was,' she replied, but didn't say any more. Somehow she knew this was a significant moment for her too. She hadn't been into a hospital since Papa's death. She looked at the rising grey mass before her, attended as

it was by a wreath of ambulances, a patchy and confusing
network of yellow lines and signs everywhere pointing
to departments with incomprehensible names. Urology.
Pathology. Radiology. Accident and Emergency. It was
chilling, thought Genevieve. In the evening gloom the
hospital looked macabre, particularly with the huge, dark
church crumbling in front of it. Genevieve steeled herself
as they went through the doors and entered the bright
antiseptic purgatory.

Later, Genevieve and Michael held hands as they walked
out of the hospital doors. Both were silent. They each
squeezed the other's hand for reassurance. It lightened
the moment, and then they could look at each other.
Michael's heart was pounding, Genevieve felt unsettled.
She had a burning desire to talk about it.

'Do you have time to go for a drink?' she asked him.

Michael was all too pleased. 'Yeah, sure. There's a pub
just over there.'

The landlord of the pub was quite used to shaken
customers coming from the hospital. Being opposite it
meant he either served people champagne for births,
releases and reprieves, or stiff double spirits for deaths,
terminal illnesses and emergency procedures. He made it
his business to guess exactly what each of his punters
wanted the moment they came in the door. These two
would be spirits, he could see that. Mind you, he'd had
that chap in before and he'd had a pint then. The drink
for those still waiting to hear.

'Pint of lager and what would you like?'

Genevieve scanned the row of bottles inverted behind
the bar. She settled on the cognac.

'I think I'll have a brandy, please,' she said and, looking
round the interior, bathed comfortably in the warm, orange
glow you can only find in English public houses, she spied
an empty table in the corner. She made her way over while

Michael got the drinks, and as she sat down, she let out a long-held breath.

That had been awful. The tiny, claustrophobic room, the relentless panting of the artificial lung, the lifeless face contorted with tubes. And then the way Michael had gently picked up his father's – John's – hand and stroked it the whole way through. She had been transfixed by it. The way he had smoothed the sheets over his frail body, talking constantly to him in a low, comforting tone, forcibly driving the fear and the pain from his voice. The way he had talked about what he was doing now, about his new friend Genevieve, and then he had introduced her to him. Genevieve had sat on the other side, holding his other hand, trying to talk to John too, guided by Michael. Yes, it had truly been awful.

She looked over at Michael, slumped at the bar. He went there every day. She recognised how trapped he was and she remembered how it felt. No way out. Torn between the guilt of hating it and the misery of enduring it and the hope that it might all return to normal. Miracle recoveries, those words that invade your mind like double agents, twisting the truth, postponing decisions, prolonging the suffering. So much of it was resonant of a time that was still so recent for her.

'Here you go.' Michael put the brandy glass down in front of her. 'You all right?'

'Yes. I think so. Are you?'

'Thanks for coming, Genevieve. Suddenly it makes it all seem like less of a dream. Less of a nightmare.'

'What are you going to do, Michael?'

He studied his pint. Eventually he said, 'I can't do anything. Just talk to him. Visit him every day. Let him know I'm still here for him.' Michael really wanted to tell Genevieve all about it. Everything seemed more real now that he had shared it with her. Without prompting, he began to explain what had happened.

It was so stupid, so pointless. He had taken him to the cinema, to a Clint Eastwood film – he loved them, Michael told Genevieve. It was difficult getting him out of the flat as he had severely damaged his back in an accident at work. He had always worked as a waiter and one day he slipped with a pile of plates and that was it – he could never work again; he couldn't lift anything after that. As he got older the disability became worse and he really needed Michael. The Council would send over a nurse every now and then, but it wasn't enough. John had wanted him to leave – 'go and seek his fortune' – but his ambition was to become a chef and he thought he could easily train in London and look after him at the same time.

That night, they had been slowly walking back through the estate when a car had screeched round the corner, lost control and smashed into Michael's father. He had been thrown six feet in the air and had landed on his back on the bonnet of the car, then rolled over and bounced off into the road. They had only just crossed over, and his father was walking nearest the kerb. Normally Michael walked on the outside. He had been about to move over: it should have been him.

The car had driven off and Michael had never even caught the make, let alone the number-plate. He was too busy trying to help his dad. To start off with he had thought he was dead, he told Genevieve, and he just knelt beside him, horrified, in shock, perhaps praying – he wasn't sure. A neighbour had seen it happen and called an ambulance, and when the paramedics arrived they had found a small pulse. It had been like a gift from God, he said. He had never been religious, never gone to church, never really thought about any of that stuff, but at that moment praying was the only thing he felt he could do to help his father: and it had worked. His life had been saved.

Genevieve waited. He was still looking into his pint. Then she asked him again, softly, 'But how long will the hospital let it go on for? The machine. How long can they wait for him to wake up?'

Michael flinched. Almost inaudibly, he replied, 'They want me to agree to have it turned off.' He finally faced Genevieve. His face showed utter despair. 'I just don't know what to do!'

Very gently, she tried to help him. 'You know, Michael, it's not just him suffering. It's not just how long your papa can stay like that. It's how long *you* can bear it.'

Michael looked again at her, desperate for something to cling onto. She continued. 'Tell me – be truthful. Do you ever wish he would die?'

Michael stared at the table.

'I thought that about *my* father,' she told him, tears standing in her eyes. 'Every day I would wake up and I would crucify myself because the first thing I would wonder was if he had died in the night. And part of me thought how much easier it would be if he had.'

'Sometimes I do think that,' Michael said quietly.

'Well, that's normal, so you mustn't feel bad about it.' Genevieve's words seemed to be coming from deep inside her somewhere. She hadn't talked to anyone about Papa, not even Seamus, and here, quite spontaneously, all the things that had been eating her about it were working themselves out into the open. Understanding Michael was understanding herself. She felt strangely triumphant.

'What about if he did have a chance, and I let him die. What then?'

'Michael, did your father love you?'

'Yes. Absolutely.'

'So what would he want for you now? Would he want you to go on proving how brave and how strong you are like this? Or would he want you to go out and live life – 'seek your fortune' or whatever? He loved you, and all that he ever wanted for you was to be happy. And to be happy you may have to do something terrible. But maybe it is what he would tell you to do.'

Michael stared at Genevieve. She was glowing, there was something about her, about the look on her face. He couldn't help but be infected by her certainty, touched by her strength. It was as if she saw everything very clearly.

'Grim places, hospitals, anyway,' he said, and drank some lager.

'I hate them,' said Genevieve with force.

'I once had to go into hospital when I was little,' continued Michael. 'I broke my wrist, falling off a climbing frame. I loathed it. The smell, that's what I used to have nightmares about.'

Genevieve nodded. 'English hospitals smell the same as French ones.'

'It's always when you're a child, isn't it? Appendix or a broken leg or broken arm – the kind of stuff you do to yourself when you're a kid. Then it's old age – when you go back to die,' Michael reflected. Genevieve was distracted, looking at the floor. 'Don't you think?' he prompted. 'You must have broken something when you were a kid?'

Something passed across Genevieve's face and she looked away. She couldn't answer.

'Genevieve?' She didn't respond, it was like she hadn't heard him. Michael began to worry. What had he done to upset her?

'Genevieve!' he tried again. 'You OK?' She was frozen, unable to speak. He reached out and touched her hand. It was lying palm up on her lap, and at the squeeze of his fingers she glanced down.

'You OK?' he asked again.

'Yes, fine,' she replied. 'Excuse me, I have to go to the bathroom.'

In the toilets the light above the sink reflected on the small beads of sweat forming across her skin. She felt terrible all of a sudden, like she was going to faint or be sick. Maybe it was because she had had such a long day, she thought – or perhaps she had caught some bug. But deep down she knew this was coming from somewhere else. The colour was draining from her cheeks; her skin was glistening clammily under the light. Genevieve felt dizzy, and she stumbled into one of the toilet cubicles. She was breathing too quickly, she realised, she was going to be sick. She was being forced back to that place, to those images, to the smell, the people who had surrounded her, forced her, to the searing pain she had carried around with her as testimony for weeks to the glaring light that had shone on her, waking her, telling her what had been ripped out of her . . .

Genevieve vomited down the toilet, her guts in spasm, spewing, spewing, until everything inside her was gone. She crouched there, slumped against the cold porcelain, reeling, her nausea slowly subsiding. Eventually she managed to stand up, and leaned her head against the side of the cubicle. She was drained, no strength left.

She had been a long time in the Ladies and Michael had started to get worried. When he saw her returning, so pale, he was even more anxious. 'Something's wrong, what is it? You look ill.'

She sat down next to him, and he took her hand again. It was clammy. Michael was beside himself. Why was it that anything good that came near him was instantly defiled? Anything of any beauty, it seemed, was ruined by his touch.

'I'm so sorry,' he croaked. 'What can I do?'

Genevieve turned slowly to him and produced a weak smile. 'It's not *your* fault,' she managed, her voice shaking.

'What is it? What's happened? Have I said something?'

She looked at him, and saw his face cracked with fresh worry.

'Michael,' she said slowly, 'I have been in hospital before. It was *affreux* – terrible.'

He squeezed her hand – it was ice-cold, but sweating. Gently he stroked it with his thumb. 'It's OK. You can say it,' he said calmly. His voice sounded strong and safe. She looked up at him, at his kind eyes, at his understanding. 'You should say it, you know.'

'It was a long time ago. I was young.' His eyes continued to hold hers, his hand gripped hers securely. Her mouth opened and the words fell out. 'It was for an abortion.'

Michael nodded, but the images began to play in the front of her mind again; her vision blurred, and as her head fell forward, Michael caught her in his arms.

'Oh my God, Genevieve, you poor thing.' With her head against his chest she began to sob: great, heaving waves that went through her, but in a strange way seemed to be exorcising the pain. He stroked her hair as she shook on his chest with the physical and mental upheaval the admission was causing her. She gripped onto him tightly, using him like a buoy as the pain ripped through her, the cries wracked her body.

Eventually, the tears began to subside. He held her very close, and bent down to kiss the crown of her head. When she was so calm that she could have been asleep, he gently moved her.

'I'm taking you home,' he said.

'No!' struggled Genevieve. 'Not just yet.' Her voice was hoarse. She pulled herself from him and opened her sore eyes. Spying her brandy on the table, she was about to pick up the glass, but Michael reached for it instead and, still cradling her in his other arm, he raised it to her lips. The smell swam through her brain, potent and reviving. Gently he poured some liquid between her lips, and the wet film she let dribble onto her tongue stung her senses into action. Michael released her.

'It's, it's a . . . a bad memory,' Genevieve said, her voice still trembling.

'It's OK, don't say any more. I'm going to get you a glass of water and then I shall take you home.'

He got up and made for the bar, leaving Genevieve to collect herself. She was stunned by what had happened to her, the part of her Michael had dislodged, quite by accident. It was a sordid, filthy part of her and she hadn't wanted to acknowledge it – ever. But it was out now. And yet it wasn't over, she realised with dread: the whole episode was irrevocably bound up with Seamus.

When Michael returned with a glass of iced water, Genevieve thanked him and sipped it. It worked – she felt better as the cool stream slipped down inside her. It was strange, she thought. She had just humiliated herself so completely in front of Michael, someone who was practically a stranger, and shared with him her most intimate secret – and yet she still felt comfortable with him. No, more than that. She felt safe.

Michael watched the colour slowly return to her cheeks. 'Come on, Genevieve, let's find a taxi and get you to bed.'

Bloody Mary

1 part vodka
3 parts tomato juice
A generous dash of Worcestershire sauce
Squeeze of fresh lemon juice
Pinch of celery salt
Dash of Tabasco sauce
Freshly ground black pepper

1. Pour the tomato and lemon juices over ice in a tall glass.

2. Add the vodka, Worcestershire sauce, celery salt and Tabasco. Stir.

3. Twist black pepper over the top.

4. Garnish with a wedge of lime, a celery stick, and a stirrer.

Best mixed by Salvatore Calabrese, Head Barman at The Lanesborough Hotel.

24

A dull, low tone, gradually crescendoing in volume and intensity, eventually jolted Seamus into consciousness. Unable yet to open his eyes, his mind tried to make some sense of it. What was it, and where was it coming from? As he lay there, prostrate, a heart palpitation sent a seismic tremor through his body. The tone, he realised, was coming from his head. It's a hangover, he thought. A big one.

He peeled back one eyelid. The scratch of the material against his skin was like sandpaper as he shifted his head to free the other eye. The shock of light – and the vertigo – were enough to warn him to attempt no further movement for a while.

The low tone was now becoming a pounding. Seamus shivered: another palpitation. Involuntarily, he groaned, and the noise brought the pain in his temples into a concentrated point. He attempted to dislodge some large object in his mouth – he thought it might be his tongue. Then it set upon him, like a trained assassin moving in for the kill – a raging thirst. Liquid, he needed liquid. Painfully, he moved his head so his eyes could make out the side table, and there, like an oasis, stood a small green bottle of mineral water. But oh! So far away!

Heaving himself up from the horizontal, he knew he had about a two-second respite before the pain kicked in. He reached out for the bottle and twisted off the top, at which point his two seconds were up and the pain descended on him like a thick, all-encompassing fog. To his amazement, he noted his trousers were round his ankles, along with his shorts. He poured the water down his throat, realising too late that it was fizzy. He couldn't swallow it quickly enough and the bubbles landed in his stomach like cluster bombs, precipitating the muscular spasms that precede retching.

He tried to stand, but the stretch to reach down and pull up his trousers sent his head into a spin. As he staggered across the room, the floor was rocking: was he on a boat? Torn between the need to vomit and the need to quench his thirst, he knew he wanted a bathroom. Catching sight of a door handle on his right, he grasped it as his knees began to give way. He fell through the door – into a corridor. He was in a hotel. With the desperate effort of a man who needs to vomit more than anything else, he crawled back into his room on all fours. Another door, this time on his left, swam into his line of vision, and scuttling through it, he just made it to the bidet in time.

The retching lasted for ever. And then when he thought he had finished, he retched some more. Finally, it seemed the nausea was subsiding. He opened his eyes again. A deep yellow, bilious liquid was splattered like a spin painting across the white porcelain. The smell told him there was whisky in there somewhere. The worst of hangovers.

As he lay slumped on the marble floor, exhausted from the vomiting, the second stage took hold. Anxiety ran through his body like an angry ferret, seeking out information and memory. *Where was he? How did he get here? What had happened to get him here?* Random images began to flash through his brain: a pool table with Paul and Nigel; Marion's brown back exposed through the slit in her dress; a large tumbler tinkling with ice and amber liquid.

Genevieve – *where was Genevieve?* Panic took hold of his heart. My God, that was right, he had argued with her, they hadn't been together. Why? She was going off with Michael, his fucking kitchen porter. Despite his physical state, Seamus felt his blood pressure rise at the memory of it, but he couldn't dwell on this. His memory was coming back faster now, images were pouring into his brain. A cab somewhere else – Louche! Archie Peaks's foot, the evil smirk on Coq's face, a pink sparkly skirt, a pair of naked legs in the back of a black cab, a bony body, too small, too small ... Oh my fucking Christ! That girl – Henrietta. Where was she now? Not here, thank God. What had they done?

Adrenaline coursed through his body. Sweat was now beading over his skin, another hot flush, the pain was unbearable – he had to lie down. Gauchely trying to co-ordinate his limbs, he stumbled back into the room where he had woken and fell onto the bed. Still. He had to keep very still.

But his brain would not stop working. The worry was forcing him to piece together the where and the when and the how. The room seemed familiar, but he couldn't place it. What hotel was he in? Was he still in London? His eyes alighted on a pad of paper on the bedside table. There was writing on the top of it – it swam in and out of focus. His head flinched in agony at the effort of reading it. *The Lanesborough Hotel.* For one sweet moment he thought of Genevieve and their night here, his heart leaping at the memory, dissolving his pain for only a phantom second: and then the crashing realisation hit him. He hadn't been here last night with her.

'Good morning. Marvellous PR.'

'Hello. May I speak to Marion, please?'

'I'm afraid she's not in yet. It's Fuzz here, can I help you at all?'

'Yes, I'm sure you can. I'm ringing in relation to the chef Seamus Bull. It's Harry Stabbe here from the *Evening Standard*. We're running a picture in this morning's edition of Bull leaving Louche last night with Henrietta Gross-Smythe, and we have reports that the two proceeded to spend the night together. I wonder, is there anything you can confirm or deny about this?'

'Hello, Harry – well spotted, you've got a scoop. I'm afraid I am in a position to deny nothing at this stage: you have the picture.' Fuzz was thinking on her feet. She had to give them something to get it on the front page but she had to get Marrow in there too. 'All I know, I'm afraid – and this is completely off the record, obviously Harry . . .'

'Obviously, Fuzz.'

'. . . is that relations between Henrietta and Seamus have been growing ever more intimate over the last few weeks. There are no plans as yet, but put it this way, the It girl is no longer quite so lonely as before, and the Chef, whilst waiting for the opening of his huge gastro-venture Marrow next week, has had a little more time on his hands. I gather that they met professionally – Henrietta has been advising Marrow on guest-lists and exclusive memberships – but the two have grown close on a more personal level. Marrow, you could say, has brought them together.'

'Can we infer then that the two are an item?'

'Darling Harry, you can infer what you like – you are the press!'

'Marvellous!'

'Isn't it?' Fuzz didn't want to lose this yet. 'Promise them more,' she could hear Marion saying. 'Always keep them hungry.' 'Now I'll tell you what I can do for you, Harry – that is, if you are prepared to run with this story in a fairly prominent position.'

'The photo is front-page, but the story is just the lead diary item at the moment.'

'Well, meet me in one hour in Wiltons in Knightsbridge, and I'll give you an exclusive. But I need to make some calls first.'

'That's perfect, Fuzz, but can you give me any more for the second edition in the meantime?'

'Well, I did overhear Seamus saying last night that he

was thrilled to his very marrow . . . I suppose you could quote him directly on that. I definitely heard him say it.'

'Lovely, thanks Fuzz. See you in Wiltons at eleven.'

'See you there, Harry.'

Fuzz put the phone down and leapt up off her chair. Front page! At last, some publicity. It was easy when you knew how – Marion was so clever. The phone started ringing again. Where the hell was her secretary? As if on cue, her office door opened and the hapless Darren poked his head timidly round to apologise for being late. But before he could open his mouth to speak he was cut off by Fuzz in her best Marion tones.

'Darren, you're fucking late. I've been answering the phones all morning. What do you think I am, the bloody receptionist?'

'No, Fuzz' he replied tirelessly. 'That's me. I'll get it.'

'Too late!' shouted Fuzz as she snatched up the phone, but already Line 2 was ringing. 'Good morning. Marvellous PR.'

'Oh, hello there, this is Charles Darling from the *Peterborough* diary on the *Telegraph*. I wonder if I could talk to someone about the chef Seamus Bull?'

'Yes, of course. Can you hold the line one moment, please, Charles.' Darren had his head back round Fuzz's door and was mouthing frantically at her. 'What *is* it, Darren?'

'I've got the showbiz editor of the *Sun* on the line! Says he wants to talk to you about Seamus Bull.'

'Shit! Say that I'll call him straight back – and get Marion in this office right now! Tell her we've struck gold at last.'

Seamus pulled his head out from under the pillow. This was bad, really bad. The evening was now coming flooding back. He'd left Louche with Henrietta, he remembered now, then they had come back here. He tried hard to remember what had happened next and could only assume by the state of his attire when he woke up that sex had been attempted. But just how far they had gone was something probably only Henrietta could answer. That part of his memory was so far staying resolutely blank – but by the current state of affairs he'd be surprised if he'd been able to raise more than an eyebrow. Christ only knows where she was now, but that was not his problem. His problem was Genevieve.

Every time he thought of her, guilt seared through his body, branding him like a criminal. Still, he thought, marshalling his arguments, he might just get away with it. She wouldn't have to know – how could she, anyway? His dear, sweet, gorgeous Genevieve, oh what had he done? She was right – he was an idiot. All he wanted now was to be with her, enveloping her sweet-smelling body with his, nestled up against the cushioned silkiness of her skin, her hair lying tangled over his chest as she stroked his aching head with her soft, cool hand. Why, oh why had he got so drunk? He'd thought he was over all that stupid carousing now.

He had to get out of this place, it was making him feel worse. A shower – that might help. He just about felt ready to handle that now, but first: room service. He picked up the receiver, and asked for stomach settlers, still water and their strongest selection of painkillers. And a Bloody Mary. To his dismay he noted he was still slurring his speech. He ran his hands through his hair in despair.

He had to get back to Genevieve, something told him it was urgent. She might have been trying to call him in his flat and he hadn't been there. Well never mind, he would put last night behind him – just pretend it had never happened. It was an aberration, that's all it was. He'd even try to forgive her about the fucking porter. He would go straight to the Happy Egg, take her in his arms and tell her he loved her – because he did, yes he did, he loved his Genevieve! Christ, he realised that now. How could he have not known before? Why was he such a fool to argue with her? He needed her, needed her to take him away from all this crap, from Louche, the drugs, the drink – she could do it, he didn't want any of that when he was with her. It was only when he wasn't with her he got into trouble.

Under the jet of steaming water in the shower he felt better. The water was washing off the sordidness of the night before and his head was finally clearing. He would marry her and they would go and find some gorgeous little restaurant in the countryside, rear their own cattle, keep their own chickens, grow their own vegetables, and people would flock to eat his food – served by her. He would even call the restaurant *GENEVIEVE'S*. Whatever she wanted. He would tell her all this now, because suddenly their future seemed so perfect. No more worrying about phallic glass structures, no more recruiting thousands of staff, no fretting about suppliers and launches and 'fashion factors' and 'target clientèle'. Marion could stuff it. He would pull out, gather up his sweet Genevieve and run away to make them the happiest couple in Europe.

By the time Seamus had finished in the shower he was practically whistling. But as he emerged he had to face the reality of his surroundings: the same hotel where he had brought Genevieve for their first night together. Sometimes he even sickened himself.

He looked outside the window – unbelievable! Salvatore's ridiculous henchman was still following him. With dread he suddenly realised that he couldn't just run away from Marrow. Not if he wanted to keep all his fingers. Still, if he wished to know what had happened last night, the one person he could probably ask was his tail.

He turned back into the room. His surroundings revolted him; he had to get out of here as quickly as possible, wipe the whole thing from his memory. A nasty incident, and one that would never happen again, he told himself. Never. He pulled on his clothes – they smelt of booze and smoke, he would have to go home and change first. He saw the painkillers on a little silver tray beside his bed and swallowed them with as much water as he could manage. Then he picked up the Bloody Mary, chucked the celery and the swizzle stick on the floor, and downed it in one. And waited. His stomach accepted it, thank Christ. In his experience, hangovers were best defeated when they were ignored. And if that didn't work, then three pints at lunchtime usually did the trick.

He picked up his jacket – thankfully it still had his wallet in it – and was just about to leave when the trill of a mobile phone interrupted him. He checked his pockets – it wasn't his; he didn't think he would have taken it out yesterday evening and he would never have programmed his to ring with that naff tune. However, anything could have happened last night, and changing the ring on his mobile was well within the bounds of possibility. He followed the sound, and eventually found a small leopardskin phone kicked under the bed. With horror, he realised it must be Henrietta's. He looked at the display screen. Jesus Christ, it was Marion calling – that was all he needed. She was there last night, of course, so she probably knew: he had to tell her to keep this to herself.

'Marion?'

'Hello? Who's this?'

'It's Seamus.'

'Ah, good morning to you, Lover Boy. Now what exactly are you doing answering Henrietta's telephone at ten-thirty in the morning, I wonder? Had a good night, did we?'

'Marion, shut the fuck up and listen, will you!'

'Shut up yourself, Seamus. I want to speak to Henrietta. Is she there?'

'No, of course she's not. At least, I can't see her anywhere. Look, Marion—'

'What do you mean "of course"? You've got her phone, haven't you? Where are you? I've tried your flat and your mobile and there was no answer.'

'I'm in the fucking Lanesborough of all places, but I'm leaving now. Fuck knows where Henrietta is, but she's left her phone. Now look, Marion, I'm being serious now. Not a word about this to anyone, do you hear me? I don't want anyone knowing. I mean it, OK?'

'My lips are sealed. Now, can you make lunch? I thought you, me and Henrietta could all do lunch together so I've booked a table at Daphne's for one o'clock. You won't believe how much we've got to discuss. Can you make it?'

Seamus stared at the phone in disbelief. The woman was hardly credible. 'Marion! No! No, no, no, no, no! D'you hear me? NO!'

'Oh come on. It's only lunch.'

Seamus was desperate – she didn't understand. 'Look, this is the situation. Last night was a terrible mistake, and I want to forget the whole thing as quickly as possible, OK? Don't fucking tell anyone and you can fucking cancel lunch, all right?'

'Oh come, come Seamus, it's not that bad,' laughed Marion. 'You have no idea what we are going to get out of this.'

He couldn't believe the way Marion was talking; it was making his headache even worse. He realised there was no reasoning with such a madwoman.

'Look, I'm going to leave this phone at the reception for Henrietta to pick up – you can tell her that. And you, Marion, just keep your mouth shut about this, OK? Not a word! Or I'll—'

'You're being ridiculous. At least come to lunch so we can—'

But Seamus had hung up, correctly assuming there was nothing he could say that would have any impact on Marion whatsoever. He fled the room. Avoiding the lift – just the thought of the motion would be enough to send him back to the bathroom – he walked gingerly down the stairs into the lobby. He was acutely conscious of the smell of his clothes and the possible witnesses amongst the staff to the events of last night. It was a long way from the stairs to the reception, and it felt like a gangplank with everyone watching him. They probably knew exactly what had happened – which was more than he did.

He chucked his credit card on the reception desk, not able even to look the clerk in the face. After what seemed hours, someone returned with a slip for him to sign – £650!

How much booze had they drunk? Two bottles of vintage Dom Perignon? He hadn't noticed the bottles in the bedroom. But as he lifted his head to complain, he knew it was hopeless. He would look even more of a fool if he had drunk them and not remembered. He deserved it – it was his own fault. He had to go and find Genevieve – after he'd changed his clothes, of course – but quickly.

Spotted Dick

75g raisins and sultanas
125g butter
125g caster sugar
175g self-raising flour
2 eggs, beaten
Milk to mix

1. Cream the butter and sugar together in a bowl.

2. Add the vanilla essence, then beat in the eggs a little at a time.

3. Fold in half the flour, then fold in the rest with enough milk to keep it sloppy. Stir in the fruits.

4. Pour into a greased, greaseproof-paper-lined pudding basin, cover in greaseproof paper and secure with string.

5. Place in a half-full pan of boiling water and steam for one and half hours.

6. Serve with custard.

25

'You know, you're lookin' decidedly peaky, young lady. If I didn't need you here I'd send you home sick. What you been up to then? I don't want you giving me anything nasty.'

Genevieve smiled feebly at Mave. She felt terrible, and would have given her eye-teeth not to be working today. But days off sick just weren't in Mave's vocabulary. And what would she have done if she had stayed away? Where would she go? What she could really do with was a big hug and lots of tender loving care, but her boyfriend wasn't taking her calls. She had phoned Seamus when she got in last night and again this morning, but there was no answer. He couldn't still be cross with her, could he?

'Oh, I'm all right, Mave,' she replied. 'I was sick last night and I think it's just left over from that. I went to visit Michael's father, John, in hospital and I had an allergic reaction.'

'Oooh, I don't blame you. Those places always make me feel right funny. I remember when our Derek was taken ill – must be ten years ago now – and once they got him inside they wouldn't let him out. Next place he saw was the mortuary, Lord rest his soul. I won't go in them any more after that – you never know what's going to happen to you. 'Ere, you have a nice cuppa tea and a sit-down for five minutes, while I just pop out and get us the paper.'

'Thanks, Mave,' said Genevieve gratefully, taking the cup from her and collapsing into one of the caff's many uncomfortable chairs. It wasn't even the lunch-time rush yet and she was exhausted; she didn't know how she was going to make it through to the end of the day. She had barely slept last night after she had got home, her mind struggling to cope with her admission to Michael and her extreme reaction – what had happened and what it meant.

Maybe she would try Seamus one more time. She really needed to talk to him, about so many things. About her job, about moving in with him, about her money, but most of all about last night. She had to tell him about the abortion. She was appalled and confused that it was Michael who she had told – a relative stranger, instead of Seamus, the man she loved. She almost felt as if she had been unfaithful. She had never talked to anyone about it before. The only people who had known were her father, who was now dead, and her aunt, who had only ever obliquely referred to it. And now Michael. Why had it been so easy to tell him? Seamus was the person who really needed to know – she needed him to share the pain with her. Just thinking about it made her feel sick again. She dialled his home and mobile numbers – *still* no answer. Oh God, where was he when she needed him?

At that moment, four bus drivers from the nearby depot came in demanding the Full English. Mave was already hurrying out the door for the newsagents, leaving her to cope on her own. Genevieve swallowed down her nausea and returned to the kitchen.

Seamus had missed Genevieve's call to his flat by only a matter of minutes. He had just left – re-showered (he was still sweating out the alcohol from last night), and changed, and was heading for the mini-cab rank at the end of his road, on his way to the café, when he passed the newspaper-seller. He stopped dead in his tracks: the billboard that decorated the front of the stand had his name on it.

Gripped by a cold panic, Seamus reached over and picked up a paper from the pile. There was a picture of him and Henrietta on the front page. Despair flooded through him. It was definitely him, even though he had his arm over his face, and anyway, there was no mistaking him as the picture, he noted, was captioned with his name. How was he ever going to explain this to Genevieve? In the foreground was the grinning face of that woman. Beside the picture the headline read *BULL GOES GROSS*. The words swam in front of him.

'Oh! Jenny, Jenny!' screamed Mave, as she bustled in the door. 'I think you'd better come and take a look at this, my poppet. You're not going to like it one little bit, I'm afraid!' Mave, however, clearly did, if the relish in her voice was anything to go by.

'One second!' Genevieve shouted back. She was busy trying to juggle two fried eggs and four bits of bacon for the last of the bus drivers, and the timing was critical. The eggs had to be runny, otherwise he would complain and demand another serving. Mave, however, could not wait that long to impart her news, and had shuffled into the kitchen before Genevieve could even finish her sentence.

''Ere, Jenny. Have a gander at this – your bit on the side looks like he's got his own bit on the side.' And she thrust a copy of the *Evening Standard* in her face.

Genevieve was used to Mave's comments to this effect, and only glanced over to her casually while she shovelled the eggs onto a plate. However, when her eyes alighted on the front-page photograph Mave was holding out to her, she managed to drop both on the floor. It was Seamus all right, hiding behind his hand; his other was around some girl in the shortest dress Genevieve had ever seen, grinning ecstatically into the camera and looking stupidly pleased with herself. Dropping her spatula on the floor now too, she took the paper, numb with shock. Beneath the headline *BULL GOES GROSS* she read the following words:

Celebrity Chef Seamus Bull, whose absence from the London scene has been sadly noted for the last few weeks, last night made a dramatic re-entrance to the society fray. The reason for his brief retirement may now be explained by the latest development in the handsome Chef's notoriously varied love-life. The country's most famous single girl, Henrietta Gross-Smythe, It Girl extraordinaire and a regular patron of the most fashionable and stylish events, appears to have altered her status. The couple were pictured leaving the celebrity drinking club Louche in the early hours of this morning, before going on to spend a romantic night together in London's only five-star hotel, The Lanesborough. A source close to the couple confirmed that they have been romantically involved for several weeks now. The two met whilst Gross-Smythe was working as a consultant to Bull's forthcoming gastro-venture, Marrow, an ambitious new four-floor food emporium in Knightsbridge, due to open next week. Bull was said to be 'thrilled to his marrow' with his latest conquest, and friends are already suggesting there could be wedding bells soon.

Genevieve had no idea what to say or think. Already debilitated by the events of yesterday evening, this was more than she could handle. Walking out of the kitchen, she undid her pinny and, deaf to the protestations of Mave, was opening the door of the caff to walk out when Seamus himself, somewhat breathless, rushed in. Genevieve stared at him as if he were a ghost. One look at her face and Seamus knew she had seen the paper. One look at Seamus's face and Genevieve knew he knew she knew.

Seamus crumpled. He almost fell upon the stricken Genevieve, taking her in his arms, and urgently launching into his defence.

'Oh my darling, sweet Genevieve! I am so sorry you have had to read that pack of lies. I hoped to reach you first to warn you, save you the distress! Here, come with me, come home. I'll explain everything.'

Genevieve was trying to pull away from him, too tired and confused to know what to believe, but he held her in his grasp. Pinioning her by her shoulders Seamus looked her straight in the eye. Her face was a blank.

'My darling, you must believe me: none of this is true. When you work in the spotlight like I do, it gives these, these . . .' Seamus was searching for a word to express his disgust with journalists, 'hounds – these vultures, a licence to print whatever they like. Yes, I was in Louche last night, and so was that girl. But I tell you, until last night I had never met her before. She asked me if I would drop her at her flat on my way home, and I agreed. It was nothing more than that. You have to believe me. They took a photograph of us as we were leaving, and that story is all total bullshit. I swear to God,' Seamus was practically shaking her now, 'I swear on the truth of my love for you that that is all there is to this story.'

Seamus stopped and looked at her. Her face was still blank. He continued, desperate to make her believe him: 'I haven't done it yet because I wanted to come straight here and find you first, but the next thing I am going to do is put out a press release denying the whole story. You, Genevieve, are the only one true love of my life. You're all I care about. Listen to me.' Seamus was desperate. 'I want you to marry me so I can prove it to you. I love you, Genevieve. Only you. It has only ever been you.'

The fascinated bus drivers and one or two other customers who had drifted in had quite forgotten their food as they watched this romantic interlude being played out before them, and now burst into spontaneous applause. Seamus sheepishly grinned at this unexpected audience, glowing with excitement at the words that had popped so naturally into his head. He peered again into Genevieve's face. He noticed, suddenly, that she was pale and drawn, her eyes were drooping, and even her lips had gone pale. At that moment, Genevieve's eyes closed, her legs gave way, and she fainted into his arms.

When she came round, Genevieve found herself cradled on Seamus's lap in the back of a taxi. He looked more concerned than she had ever seen him. Her head was still hazy, but here was the person she had been aching to see for hours, holding her in his arms. She smiled up at him. 'Seamus!' she sighed happily, feeling safe now, feeling better.

'Oh, Genevieve, I'm so glad you're all right. You poor thing: you have to take it easy. What on earth happened to you last night? Mave said you had been sick. What did Michael do to you? You must tell me! What happened? What did he do?'

'Oh, *he* didn't do anything. It's a long story,' she mumbled.

But Seamus was not going to be fobbed off like this. He was too angry to wait – he needed to know now. All the guilt that he felt about his behaviour last night was now displaced by anger directed at that little fuck, Michael. After witnessing Genevieve's obvious distress, he needed to blame someone, and if it was someone other than himself then all the better. Particularly as this meant he had a target on whom he could exorcise the emotions that had gripped him so fiercely. And Michael was, after all, his habitual target.

'What happened at the hospital? Did you go there?'

Genevieve felt too weak to talk about it now. She just wanted to be caressed and held, and looked after. She needed to order her thoughts before she could work out what it was she wanted to say.

'Seamus, it's nothing to do with Michael. Please, let's talk later.'

'No, tell me now. So I can help you.'

Genevieve had no strength to fight him. But her thoughts were becoming clearer, and as she lifted herself up from his lap, and rested her cheek against his shoulder, she tried again to calm him. 'It was nothing. Just some bad memories, that's all.'

Seamus pushed her back so he could see her face. 'Tell me! It must have been more than that. Did he hurt you?'

'Of course he didn't. Now please stop it!' she begged. Then slowly she remembered: the photographer, the newspaper. But it didn't seem real; it seemed like a cheap fantasy, this world of Louche and paparazzi snaps. What was real was this man, the sexiest man Genevieve had known, the tenderest lover, holding her now in his arms, his concern for her as plain as day in the expression on his face. She looked at him again, this time curiously, recalling words she thought she had dreamed.

'Seamus, what did you say to me in the café?'

He smiled at her. 'I asked you to marry me.'

She swallowed hard. '*O mon Dieu!*' she eventually exclaimed. 'It wasn't a dream then?'

'No, it wasn't. Listen: I love you and I want to be with you. I want you in my life – permanently. Will you be my wife?'

'Seamus, I don't know. It's so quick . . .'

'No, it's not. It's been six years.'

'Yes, but since I came back – only a few months.'

'Sssh, baby, you come here and rest for a while. I'm going to look after you now.'

'Seamus, I had something to say to you as well, you know. Something good. I have some money – not much, but perhaps it will make a difference. I'm fed up with working in Mave's caff. If I put my money into Marrow, can I help with it too?'

'Of course, sweetheart, you know I would like nothing more. That's what I have always wanted.'

If she wished to work with him in London, then that was fine by Seamus. The dream of the restaurant in the country faded as quickly as he had conjured it. Seamus then paused for what he judged to be a decent amount of time, before asking: 'How much money do you have?'

'I have about £500,000.'

Seamus went white. 'How much?'

'£500,000.'

He stared at her, speechless.

'Is it enough?'

'Oh yes, my darling, it's enough.'

Today was turning out better than Seamus could possibly have imagined. Much, much better.

Virgin Mary

Tomato juice
A generous dash of Worcestershire sauce
Squeeze of fresh lemon juice
Pinch of celery salt
Dash of Tabasco sauce
Freshly ground black pepper

1. Pour the tomato and lemon juices over the ice in the glass.

2. Add the Worcestershire sauce, celery salt and Tabasco. Stir.

3. Twist the black pepper over the top.

4. Garnish with a wedge of lime, a celery stick, and a stirrer.

26

Salvatore had had quite enough of Seamus Bull by now. As his business partner he expected to see slightly more of him in person than he did on the front pages of newspapers, and for a man who was holding back on a serious amount of cash, he certainly didn't seem to be shunning the high life.

Salvatore threw the paper down on his desk in disgust and rang the henchman he had sent to trail Seamus. He confirmed the story: Seamus had indeed been in Louche yesterday evening and had then spent the night at the Lanesborough – where he had drunk vintage Dom Perignon. He was now on his way back to his flat in another cab – with *another* woman.

Enough, thought Salvatore, is enough. If Seamus didn't voluntarily come up with the money, then it would have to be extracted, his way. And if Seamus couldn't be trusted to run Salvatore's investment, well, then he would just have to be disciplined. Salvatore was used to things going his way. But before giving his henchman the order, he hesitated. Perhaps he should just check the details with Marion. Besides, he needed to know whose side she was on. He dialled her mobile number.

'Marion? It's me. We need to talk.'

'Salvatore! Hello darling, how *are* you?' she shrieked, with more affection than was usual. Marion was exuberant, for had she not, after all, just had one of – if not *the* – best lunches of her entire career.

But he ignored her, and continued in a tone dangerous enough to check even Marion's mood: 'We have a money problem and I have tried hard to solve it, but your Seamus keeps running away from me. If Bull does not come up with the money, then it will be your failure too, Marion. *You* gave me your word he could be relied upon. I foresee that I am going to have to . . . take action, shall we say.'

'No need!' replied Marion, relieved that their salvation appeared to have arrived just in the nick of time. 'All our problems our solved! This morning I had a phone call offering us £1 million. Yes, Salvatore, I'm not joking. ONE MILLION POUNDS STRAIGHT UP!'

The Italian paused. This he hadn't expected. 'I think you had better come and explain,' he said stiffly.

'Yes, of course. It would be my pleasure. I've come up with a plan, a wonderful plan, and Seamus is going to have more money than he needs to pay you off – and what's more, he'll have it by the end of the week!' Marion was exultant. 'But first I need to get back to my office and find Seamus. Do you know where he is?'

'Yes.'

'He needs to hear this too. Can you tell Seamus to meet us at your trattoria this afternoon?'

'Don't be a fool! I've only just had that media magnet slung off my street. I don't want him bringing his merry band of photographers back through my front door. Forget it! Every little paparazzi in the world wants a picture of Seamus today.'

'I know, isn't it marvellous?' exclaimed Marion, delighted.

'You come and explain yourself first, Marion. I need to know what's going on, as I am feeling a little anxious,' Salvatore said, in a manner that left no room for dispute.

'OK, then,' she sighed resignedly. Damn, she thought, she wouldn't be able to go and find Seamus this afternoon and tie the deal up. Nothing, however, could dent her joy for long – not after her fabulous lunch with the editor of *Hiya!* magazine.

*   *   *

When Seamus arrived back at his flat the building was crawling with photographers. Fortunately, none of them knew about the back entrance (Seamus's one pre-requisite to his estate agent when he had bought it), and he successfully managed to get Genevieve upstairs without either her noticing the photographers or them noticing her. He wasn't sure Genevieve was ready yet to witness the way he dealt with the press.

Genevieve, for her part, was overwhelmed. She thought Seamus was being rash, but it wasn't every day a girl received a marriage proposal. Besides, so many emotions were running through her already. Guilt about Michael, horror about Seamus's press story, elation at Seamus's proposal, and the anxiety-inducing decision she had come to last night to offer Seamus her money. She hardly knew if she was coming or going. As for the press story – well, she reasoned, there was no way Seamus would have asked her something so important if even the tiniest bit of that story in the papers had been true, and all the horror she had felt when she had seen it had now been expunged.

In Seamus's bed she was already a million miles away from all the fears that had been stalking her – from newspapers, from gossip, from her grotty little bedroom and her grotty little job and, more importantly, she was a long way from any hospitals. She lay there, sipping the hot toddy Seamus had brought her, the infusion of ginger running like a cleanser through her mind, the whisky warming her and bringing strength back to her bones.

Seamus too was exultant: buoyed up by the high of the decision he had made about Genevieve, the power at being back in control of events again, and the elation of a rosy future that now seemed to be within his grasp. But more than that, there was this money Genevieve had quite suddenly sprung on him. What

an incredible stroke of luck! But, with the arrogance
of one who expects success, Seamus realised he had
always somehow expected the money to appear. He
had never really doubted it. It was confirmation that
Marrow was the right place for him and now was the
right time. OK, so fleetingly he had had his doubts but,
having been victim of fate a few times in his life, he
had learned to believe that everything happened for
a reason. If Marrow wasn't meant to be, then this
gift of money would never have appeared. And now
the thought of taking on such a daunting task with
Genevieve by his side was much more attractive than
it had been previously.

'But Seamus, we don't have to do it for very long,
do we?'

'What, my darling?'

'Run Marrow? I don't want to live in the city all my
life. We could do it for just a year, say, and then we
can go somewhere beautiful and open a small restaurant
together . . .'

'And have hundreds of children running round!'

'Yeah,' said Genevieve a little less enthusiastically, her
heart sinking. Everything was not quite perfect. There
was this last thing that she needed to deal with.

'Seamus, there is something else.' She paused, gathering herself to go through with this conversation at long
last. 'You know when you left France that summer?'

'Yes, my love,' he said, holding her close to him tight,
in case someone took her away; in case something tried
to confiscate his happiness.

'Well . . .'

At that moment the phone rang. Genevieve paused.

'Ignore it, darling. There is no one I want to talk to
right now other than you.'

'Well . . .' but it was too late, her courage had gone,
cruelly dislodged by the ringing of the phone. Maybe

she didn't really have to say it. She could just leave it. Apart from anything else, she didn't want to spoil this perfect moment, this happiness they were sharing. Maybe another time.

'Oh, it's OK,' she said quietly. 'It's nothing.'

'Fuzz, Fuzz! This is too fantastic for words! Oh, how brilliantly it's all worked out!'

Fuzz let out a sigh of relief. Neither she nor Marion had dared hope for a *Hiya!* deal, but as soon as the photograph had appeared in the morning paper, Richard Raker, the editor, had been straight on the phone to Marion, desperate to meet her for lunch. So Marion, whose diary was fuller than Rufus's stomach, had simply downsized her table at Daphne's to two, and three hours later had emerged back in the offices of Marvellous quite pink in the cheeks with excitement.

'Are you ready for this, Fuzz? Sit down, because you're going to need to.'

Fuzz took the chair opposite Marion's desk.

'He wants to pay us a million!'

'A million?!' Fuzz nearly fell off her chair.

'Yes, a million! But of course he needs the wedding to be a spectacle for that sort of money, but God, with you and me organising it, that's hardly going to be a problem.'

'I don't believe it – a million?! That's a record, isn't it?'

'Not quite, but it just shows what the combined guest-lists of Seamus and Henrietta are worth. This is brilliant news for Marrow, not to mention the fact that Seamus will finally have some cash to put into it. God, I can hardly believe it myself, I'm still shaking!'

Fuzz had never seen Marion so excited by her own success, but then she had never seen Marion pull off such a coup before. She should never have doubted her:

she truly was a PR master. When Raker had rung them, both women knew it could only mean one thing: he wanted to be the first to bid for rights to the Bull-Gross wedding, but neither had realised he would be willing to pay so much money. It was apparent that the circulation war between *Hiya!* and its rivals was tougher than they thought. There was only one tiny hitch in the plan, as far as Fuzz could see: Bull and Gross weren't even engaged.

'Oh God, that's not a problem!' screamed Marion. 'That's the least of our worries. Even if they're not remotely interested in each other, it would be so good for their profiles – and their wallets – they'd have to do it. It's not every day you get offered that sort of money. No, our problem, Fuzz, is how to make it worth one million. Now let's see – it'll have to be near London so we can get all the guests to turn up – unless we have it somewhere exotic and charter a plane. We'll have to decide on that one quickly. Naturally we'll book Elton for the music and Donatella for the wardrobe. The bride and groom'll need at least three changes – Raker wants to make this the cover story over three issues. We'll have to have the most enormous feast to emphasise the food theme. Marrow will cater it, of course, and perhaps we can give the magazine a few of the more exclusive recipes, but it's the detail we need. The extravagance of these events is always in the detail.

'Now, I remember Henrietta once telling me how much she loved elephants. You know she went to Africa on some charity Save the Elephant thing, and ripped her new Berardi dress, but she said she didn't mind at all because the elephants were so cute? Well, perhaps we could have the bride and groom arriving on elephants. Ring London Zoo and book two now.'

Marion was stalking the room now, in full 'creative'

flow, the pitch of her voice getting higher as the urgency of everything they had to organise dawned on her.

'I've given Raker the provisional date of 15 January, which means we've got absolutely no time: we'll have to start this afternoon. God, if only I didn't have to see bloody Salvatore.' Marion glanced at her watch. She still had a couple of hours before she had to leave, and she was on a roll now – her creative juices were really flowing, and she wasn't going to squander it.

'Now, how much can we exploit Henrietta's society contacts? Well, we can certainly get Lord Linley to make the thrones, and perhaps we could borrow some doves from Highgrove to set free when the vows are read? The Prime Minister, I hear, is a big fan, and Chelsea FC have just made her their mascot, so that guarantees some Italian glamour. And the cake simply must be a centrepiece. We could get Sabatier commissioned to make a solid silver sword to cut it with – now that would be a lovely detail. What do you think?'

But Marion wasn't asking, and continued before Fuzz could so much as look up from her notebook. 'Now what about the entertainment? Cirque du Soleil is a must. Maybe that bloody TV floozie on our books could compère it, we desperately need to get her some publicity, her father's paying us a fortune. Jewels by Asprey and Garrard, naturally, but we need a theme, a dress theme . . .'

Marion was interrupted by Darren. 'Phone call for you, Marion.'

'Not now – can't you see I'm being creative?'

'It's Henrietta Gross-Smythe. She says it's urgent.'

'Ohmigod – patch it through immediately!' Marion shrilled, then, without missing a beat, she picked up the phone and effortlessly switched pace. 'Henrietta, darling!' she cooed. 'Congratulations – how was it? Did the earth move?'

'As a matter of fact it didn't, Marion.'

'Oh. Well, don't worry, darling, these things often take a little practise.'

'Marion, it was horrid. I don't want to talk about it.' Which was clearly why Henrietta had rung.

'Whatever can you mean? I've had Seamus on the phone already today telling me how thrilled he is. What's going on?'

At this point Henrietta burst into floods of tears. 'Oh God, it was awful. As soon as we got to the hotel you'd booked, Seamus couldn't ... He couldn't ... Well, he just couldn't! We got so far and then he sort of ... collapsed. Completely passed out on the bed and nothing I did could rouse him – in any way. So I tried sleeping next to him but he was snoring so loudly I couldn't. So in the end I ordered two bottles of champagne and took them home in a limousine. And I left my mobile phone behind! It's a complete and utter nightmare!'

'Oh, come, come, Henrietta. Don't be silly. Seamus was just tired, that's all. Anyway, I've got much more exciting things to talk to you about. I've just had lunch with the editor of *Hiya!* magazine, and guess what?'

'What?' Henrietta, all of a sudden, had stopped crying. *Hiya!* magazine was to Henrietta what three Michelin stars were to Bull and Coq.

'He wants to have dinner with you and Seamus on Monday of next week and make you an offer you can't refuse.'

'What sort of offer?'

'Henrietta – he wants to cover your wedding!'

'My wedding?! What wedding? Who am I getting married to?'

Marion drew in a deep breath and did her best to remain patient. The inbreeding in the aristocracy was sometimes horribly apparent, she thought, and never more so than in the case of Henrietta.

'To Seamus, darling.'

'Really? Am I really? How awfully exciting! Oh goodness, Mummy *will* be pleased. I've finally done it: I've bagged a husband! That means I can stop going to all these dreadful parties – oh, and at last I can buy a Range Rover and a spaniel. I'm going to go down to Battersea Dogs Home this very afternoon. He must have liked me much better than I thought. What fun!'

Grilled Sea Bass

One fillet of line-caught sea bass
1 tablespoon olive oil
Herbs for studding
Salt and pepper
A wedge of lemon

The sea bass can be the king of fish. Handled with skill, dressed only very lightly, it can have the succulence of steak.

1. To prepare, stud the skin with seasonal herbs – summer ones work best. Lightly brush the fillet with olive oil and season.

2. Place under a hot grill and judge the timing depending on the thickness of the fillet; roughly three minutes each side.

3. Serve with the lemon.

27

Launch night was now less than a week away, and the preparations were beginning for Marrow's 'show dinner': the meal it was customary to prepare for the great and the good of the food world to demonstrate exactly what it was the restaurant could do. The penthouse suite, Archie Peaks had assured them, *would* be ready by launch night, with the kitchen installed, and this was where the dinner would take place. Everyone else was to be entertained downstairs in the brasserie. To this party Marion had invited every habitué of Louche she could think of: every cast member of every soap opera, every pop star, every Brit actor and fashionable actress, every TV presenter, every DJ, every author, every poet, every politician, every chef, every gardener, every journalist – everyone, in short, who had ever appeared, or was likely one day to appear, in *Hiya!* magazine, that great directory of the most esteemed in Britain today.

As a riposte to rumours that the quality and the pre-eminence of Bull cooking could not survive in such circumstances, Marion had advised Seamus that his plans for the show dinner should be the peak of culinary ambition. It was, therefore, to be a seven-course gastronomic feast, to which had been invited a few select Michelin-starred chefs, five or six of the most influential restaurant critics, the editors of four national newspapers and three of the most influential glossy magazines, the Prime Minister and his wife, one or two minor royals and a smattering of other VIPs. So while the launch party in the brasserie below was to establish Marrow's fashion status, it was upstairs at the dinner where the restaurant's real reputation would be won or lost.

The pace of the preparations increased as the opening night approached, and all staff were now needed on the premises all of the time. Marion and Fuzz were frantically breakfast-ing, lunch-ing and dinner-ing as many style journalists they could get to answer the phone, ensuring a steady flow of 'trend'-based articles on the impending opening. Adèle was in charge of overseeing the progress of the staff training and the prompt delivery of the restaurant's equipment, Paul and Nigel were in charge of the cooking trials. Even Archie Peaks had turned up to supervise the last few days of construction.

Seamus was trying to control his nerves. He was elated Genevieve had finally moved into his flat, and to finally show her his new restaurant – *their* new restaurant – except that, what with all the launch preparations, they saw less of each other now than before. When he was at Marrow, he was so busy he didn't even have time to think about her, and when they were at home he was so preoccupied with what Coq might be doing to sabotage his restaurant and how Salvatore was planning to collect his debts that he barely noticed she was there.

Added to this, Seamus was also having to deal with something much more serious – his terror of going back into the kitchen. It had been so long since he had cooked professionally; the fear that he might have lost his touch was keeping him from so much as slicing a tomato. His role in the kitchen had become solely supervisory. He had even stopped cooking for Genevieve, and they either ate out, took out or she cooked. Often they skipped dinner altogether. When you worked around food all day you became much less interested in eating it.

It had been almost three years since he had opened the first Marrow, and in the intervening period he had increasingly relied on his staff for the cooking. At Marrow he had been surrounded by a band of dedicated employees, a tried and tested team who worked together exactly to his instructions. All of a sudden Seamus now had a Budget Manager, a Marketing Manager, his bloody all-seeing and all-doing PR, two other Head Chefs, legions of young chefs whose names he couldn't even remember, let alone oversee what they were doing, and a team of completely unestablished unknowns lined up to work directly under him in the penthouse restaurant. All the staff he had worked with before, he had had to move over to the brasserie: that restaurant was so huge he needed people down there he could trust. Paul he had made Head Chef, and he had sent Nigel down to be his deputy. The two of them had their work cut out – between full service at lunch and dinner they were going to have to churn out up to six thousand dishes a day. But if anything went wrong it wasn't on their heads – it was on Seamus's. Seamus had also promoted Sarah to deputy in the ground-floor patisserie, working under a top pastry chef whom he had poached from the Savoy – surprisingly easy pickings after a bottle of '86 Cristal at Louche.

The rest of his stalwarts had been lured away by Coq – an exodus he had not been able to stem with offers of more money from Marrow's seemingly 'bottomless budget'. Coq had offered them huge promotions – two were to take the helm each of two of his restaurants, one was to become his own personal Head Chef at Mirage, and Albert Bresson too had been tempted out of retirement and given the plum job of maitre d' at Mirage. Albert was of the old school approach to the restaurant business – nothing could persuade him to work in a fashion-driven 'food warehouse'. Others had been lured not just by power and money: a spell of absence from Seamus's ritual bullying had quickly served as a reminder that life need not be a screaming hell on earth. Coq often found that seducing the Marrow staff was simply a matter of a few kind words;

flattery was enough to dispel any misguided feelings of
loyalty they had.

Still, the body count had not been unbearable; the
casualties Seamus had suffered had been sustainable –
just. Apart from Albert, he had kept the real talent:
Adèle, Paul, Nigel, and of course Michael. But then Coq
had no idea about Michael. No one knew about Michael
– not even Michael himself. He was the trump card up
Seamus's sleeve.

For his part, Michael had been doing some serious
thinking. Far from being lured away by Coq, Seamus had
kept him so busy that he barely noticed anything else existed
apart from Marrow. But being busy again did not make him
happy: Michael realised he had to do something different
with his life. He needed to get off the estate; he needed
to get out from under the tyranny of Seamus, and most
of all he needed to break the dreadful circle of misery that
had been his life since the accident. He had had enough.

Indeed, the only attraction London held for Michael now
was Genevieve. She spoke to him with an intimacy no one
else did, she was the only person he could really feel close
to, who tried to understand him. But she was involved with
his monstrous boss, and Michael was not sure if he could
bear to watch. Of course it was her decision, and as long
as that was what she wanted, Michael wouldn't dream of
saying anything. But it almost meant he couldn't be her
friend: they would never be equals.

Oddly, it was Archie Peaks who offered Michael a way
out. Dropping into the brasserie one day, Archie had
asked Seamus if he might throw him together some lunch.
Gripped by icy panic at the thought of preparing food –
even something as basic as a salad – Seamus said he was
far too busy, and grabbing the nearest member of staff, who
happened to be Michael, he had muttered something about
meat orders and fled the kitchen. With a store cupboard
full of sample provisions from suppliers anxious to win

the largest account in town, Michael had undertaken the request with relish. Instead of a quick risotto, or even a sandwich, he decided to enjoy himself. It had been so long since he had actually cooked a proper meal, he was desperate for the opportunity to do something creative.

First, he made a consommé using fish stock he had been making that morning for the restaurant's stores, adding some lemongrass, chilli and a touch of Vietnamese fish sauce. To this he added a handful of steamed mussels. He accompanied it with one of the lightest, sweetest bread rolls Peaks had ever tasted – the product of Michael's tests on the bread ovens downstairs. He then grilled a fillet of sea bass, which he served on a colourful bed of succulent diced, roasted peppers and courgettes, surrounded with tiny jewelled heaps of tomato concasse and dressed lightly in a saffron vinaigrette he had blended with the fish stock. For dessert, Michael treated Archie to some of Marrow's almond ice cream, (made by himself), scooped out in a pretty pear shape, and balanced between two almond *tuiles*.

By the time Archie had licked the last drop of ice cream from his spoon, he knew he had just eaten one of the best meals of his life. Not because it was particularly original or indeed dramatic, but simply because, in Michael's hands, the flavours had been released in a way Archie had never before tasted. The boy's enthusiasm and talent was obvious in every part of the meal. Now Archie was not someone to turn a blind eye to genius. Pausing over his single espresso, he considered what he might do. Taking out his palm top computer, he looked up a number, then reached for his mobile. After a brief conversation, he drew out a leather-bound pad and pencil from his top pocket, scribbled down a name and address, and went in search of Michael. He found him scrubbing baking trays in the back of the brasserie kitchen.

'Michael, my dear chap!' he cried.

'Hello, Mr Peaks,' said Michael shyly, hastily wiping his hand to accept Archie's outstretched one.

'What a truly exceptional meal!'

'Well, thank you, I'm glad you enjoyed it,' said Michael, beaming from ear to ear. Archie pumped his hand, slapped him on the back, then he allowed a very grave expression to settle on his face.

'Now listen to me, Michael, I have something important to say to you. It takes an artist to know an artist. You have talent, real talent, and a sensitivity for your materials that is rare. I don't say this lightly: I may know little about gastronomy, but I do know about artistry. Let me give you some advice, in return for the meal. I don't know what you're doing in this Godforsaken place – but you're wasted here. If you have a talent, young man, you should nurture it. You should be training with a master, and not mucking around in this oversized cafeteria.'

Michael tried to point out that this was what he had previously been doing but that it had all gone wrong somewhere. Archie just looked at him and shook his head.

'You should go and train in France, where cuisine was born and where people still practise it for its own sake rather than to be the biggest, or the best, or the most fashionable. Now here is a name and address,' and Archie passed Michael the folded slip of paper he had written on, 'of a dear friend of mine in the Loire Valley. His restaurant has been awarded three Michelin stars every year for the last ten years. I have just telephoned him to tell him about you. He is intrigued, and not least because he needs a new apprentice at the moment.'

Dumbstruck, Michael accepted the piece of paper. Opening it, he read the name: Davide Duchamps. *Davide Duchamps!* Michael nearly collapsed. This man had gone down in the record books for being the first owner of no less than six Michelin stars. His Parisian restaurant and his Loire Château had both, incredibly, received three stars each one year, but he had moved out of Paris soon afterwards, claiming that he did not like spreading his attention over two places. His restaurant in the Loire was world-famous. And Archie had given him, Michael, an introduction.

'You think about that, Michael, and you make your own decision. But my advice is, if you can find the right way to exercise your talent, you will be a happier man.'

And with that, the great architect was gone.

Michael did indeed think about it – in fact, he could think of nothing else. He knew it made sense, but what about Marrow? He had given Seamus his word he would stay, especially after Seamus had promised he would promote him. And, much more to the point, what about his father?

The place was awesome, thought Genevieve. It wasn't pretty, it wasn't beautiful – it wasn't even particularly unusual. But it was big, and its size was what made it impressive. Not only was the floorspace of Marrow huge, it was also high, and as Genevieve looked up through the layers of transparent flooring, she realised she couldn't make out where it stopped. It was almost as if the building had no roof.

The vast space echoed to the sound of drills, saws and hammering – not to mention Seamus's loud vocal contributions. Builders not engaged in plying their instruments hummed and haa-ed, giving their opinion on various constructions, their toolbags slung importantly over their shoulders; delivery men in blue overalls were heaving endless boxes in from outside. A rather stern-looking woman, immaculately made-up and dressed sharply in a black trouser suit, stood over them with a clipboard, checking their contents. Genevieve watched her as she pulled out glasses, plates, cups and cutlery. Seamus had introduced her as Adèle, and she had smiled at Genevieve politely, but as soon as Seamus had retreated into his office, she had continued to ignore her.

Genevieve tried to take in the building, but imagined the difficulty she was having with it was architecturally deliberate. The ground she stood on looked like white marble, and the huge warehouse windows that traced the outline of the building had been extended to ground level to let in maximum light, which bounced off the floor in a blinding silver sheen. The windows were so big they looked as if they could be doors, but Genevieve had noticed when she was outside that you couldn't actually see through them – they were tinted to stop people peering in. The huge floorspace was focused on a massive structure that rose out of the middle of it: a huge glass and steel column, which incorporated a hydraulic glass lift. She followed the column up through the building, almost to the very top. Halogen lighting hung in great strings around the space, entwining metal rods that pointed randomly off the ceiling. And everywhere was the Marrow logo – green, bulbous lettering that branded every window, every light, every wall.

Someone was shouting at her, and she turned round to see a builder, with the badge *Foreman – Ground* on his chest, hurrying towards her. He was excitedly brandishing a hard hat.

'You got permission to be in here, love?' he asked.

'Um,' began Genevieve hesitantly, 'yes, I think so. I'm with Seamus Bull.'

Seamus had brought her here for the first time yesterday, but the moment they had walked in the doors he had disappeared off to his office, leaving her stranded with nothing to occupy her. She had been embarrassed – she wasn't used to being a spare part, and in the end she had left. Last night she had asked Seamus to find her something to do, but all he had done so far that morning was briefly introduce her to Adèle before taking off somewhere. Adèle had looked at her with distaste, and the last thing Genevieve wanted was to be babysat. Now this man was questioning her very presence – even though she was a part-owner. The situation was ridiculous.

'All right then, love,' said the foreman, 'but you should be wearing one of these. And tell Mr Bull to put one on too, can you? Can't count the number of times I've told him already,' he added wearily.

Genevieve took the hat and put it on quickly, just as a pile of rubble emptied itself five feet from where she was standing.

'Oi! Watch it up there!' shouted the foreman.

'Sorry mate!' came an echoing response.

'This floor chips far too easily, I tell you,' the builder continued to Genevieve. 'Won't stand a chance with the high heels them girls wear nowadays.'

Genevieve thought this was probably rather important, and was about to say so when over the other side of the room she saw Michael carrying a large cardboard box. She thought she would feel shy at seeing him again, but instead it was elation coursing through her body that caused her to cry out his name.

The shout echoed around her. He turned to see who had called him, and saw her standing in the middle of the floorspace. His face broke into a smile, and he put down his box and walked over to her.

'Genevieve! Good to see you! How are you? You OK now?' he asked, then blushed as she reached up to kiss him on both cheeks.

'Yes, I'm fine, thank you, Michael.'

'I'm so sorry I didn't ring immediately, but I thought you would probably want some time on your own. Actually I tried to get hold of you at the café this morning.' Michael's words were tumbling out, his eagerness a measure of his concern.

'Oh, I don't work there any more.'

'Yeah, Mave said.'

'I've come to work here, with Seamus,' she said shyly,

painfully aware that 'working' was the last thing she was doing.

'Must be more fun than chips and beans.'

'I hope so,' Genevieve replied, then, before they could explore the implications of her move any further, she quickly added: 'Thanks so much for the other night, Michael.'

'Well, I'm glad you found Seamus in the end. I was worried about you,' he said, desperate to keep any emotion out of his voice.

'Oh, yes,' she said. Then left the silence hanging between them. He obviously assumes I talked it out with Seamus, she thought, knowing that she had done no such thing. Both looked away.

Eventually, seeing that Genevieve was at a loose end, Michael offered to show her around. She accepted gratefully and followed him over to the lift shaft. She was already beginning to relax a little.

Seamus, meanwhile, was supervising a tasting of the canapés Paul and Nigel would be preparing for Marion's party. With over 600 guests coming, they had their work cut out. Seamus was impressed with what they were planning: tiny umbrella leaves of raddiccio filled with goat's cheese, grilled then dressed in a tomato vinaigrette; wild mushrooms individually encased in minute pastry boxes; deep crimson Parma ham wrapped around tiny pieces of pink calves' liver; fat scallops seared and skewered with a tiny piece of green mango; sashimi minced onto tiny porcelain spoons and dressed in a sweet, hot pepper sauce, and many more bite-sized concoctions of similarly ambitious inventiveness.

Paul and Nigel had clearly learned more from him than he thought, Seamus acknowledged wryly, but something worried him: he didn't seem able to taste as well as he used to: when the delicate slivers of Parma ham landed on his tongue, they weren't quite as salty as everyone else pronounced them to be; the green mango not quite so sweet, the sashimi not quite so fresh. Seamus brushed the thought to the back of his mind. Just then he saw Genevieve walk past with Michael.

'Why, that little fuck!' he cried, leaping up and sending crostini spinning across the table. 'I don't believe it! The fucking cheek!' he spluttered as he bounded after them. 'Oi! Michael! What are you doing?'

The two spun round.

'Didn't I tell you to shift those boxes up from the ground floor? Get back down there now. I need it all done by lunch-time.'

Michael sighed, and turning to Genevieve he gave her an apologetic smile before going back to the lift. Genevieve was shocked. The venom in Seamus's voice was ugly. More than shocked, she was angry: Seamus had brought her in here, abandoned her with nothing to do, then confiscated the one person who was trying to make her feel at home.

'Michael was only showing me round,' she said crossly.

'I don't care – he's got a job to do. How come whenever I turn my back you're always with Michael, eh? Is there something I should know about?'

'Don't be ridiculous. It's just I haven't got anything to do – I feel useless here.'

'Well, go and ask Adèle to look after you. I'm too busy.' And with that Seamus marched back to Paul and Nigel, leaving Genevieve alone – again.

Michael knew it wasn't going to work. There was no way he could even speak to Genevieve while Seamus was around, and if that was the case, he thought, then why was he staying here? Michael heaved the final box of olive oil bottles up onto his shoulder, and winced with the effort. He had hoped to try and discuss the Duchamps offer with Seamus, even ask his advice, but it hardly looked as if he was going to get a reasonable response now. He staggered over to the lift, and was just about to press the button to call it down to the ground floor when the doors opened and Seamus himself stepped out.

'Michael – I want a word with you,' he said savagely. 'You fucking leave my future wife alone, do you hear me?'

Future wife?! thought Michael, appalled.

'I don't want you anywhere near her, all right?' and he pushed Michael back, just hard enough for him to lose his balance and drop the box, which crashed to the floor. Olive oil began to leak out in a thick, viscous puddle. 'You clean that up, you clumsy idiot!' shouted Seamus triumphantly. 'And I shall be docking the cost of those from your wages.'

This time Michael did not apologise. He looked at Seamus with obvious resentment. He didn't have to take this any more.

Seamus waited for Michael to say something. 'Apologise!' he barked.

'Chef – I need to talk to you.'

'What about? I don't want to talk to *you* – now get out of my sight!'

Michael looked Seamus right in the eye, then realised it was useless, and silently walked off in search of a mop. Seamus smiled to himself, puffing his chest out. Well, that was *that* little problem sorted.

Above him, Genevieve moved back from the balcony, out of sight.

Bitter Herbs

These are used particularly in Jewish cuisine, particularly during the feast of Pesach, the Passover, as a symbol of the bitter times the Jews suffered.

A plate of these herbs is served at the feast, and can include Romaine or endive lettuce, cress, horseradish or chicory. Collectively they are known as *maror*.

28

Michael smiled as he opened the blind. The early December skies had given way to glorious sunshine; the light was white through the frost-ridden glass. As if he needed a sign. He dragged over a chair, and stood on it to look out through the window. He huffed on the window pane and peered down across the estate. The ground was silver and hoary, the estate blocks rising out of their silver sheets like tall, grey monuments to his oppression. The image imprinted itself on his mind, for the last time, on the last day in thousands.

He turned back to the room, and his eyes settled on the rucksack stashed on top of his wardrobe. He felt a jolt go through him: that rucksack, those things in his wardrobe, would soon be all that was left. His life would be unburdened, ready for new challenges. He felt no sadness though, only excitement: the conviction that he had made the right decisions last night had stayed with him through till morning. In fact, if anything, sleep had confirmed them. There was no doubt, no room for prevarication; above all, he knew it was what his father wanted. He felt as sure of this as if his dad had just walked into his room and told him so himself. He would have been smiling, smiling proudly. How he used to be. Funny, loving, wise, fun. Not silent, motionless, unfeeling. Brain dead.

The decision to finally let his father rest in peace was obvious as soon as he had made it. He had sat in that armchair – his dad's armchair – in a trance, the options whirring round his head. He had no idea how long he had been there, staring at the grey TV screen. It could have been ten minutes or ten hours. But as the logic fell into place, so did his emotions. Once he had accepted that hope was remote, that the longer he waited, the longer he prolonged both their agony, then there was only one answer. And it felt as right in the light of day as it did in the cold dark of last night. With the decision made, Michael felt nothing but relief and growing conviction about his plans for a new life.

He pulled his clothes out from the cupboard, and pushed them into his rucksack. All except his one suit, and a shirt. He knew Dad would like him to wear a suit for this occasion. He wasn't having a funeral – he couldn't afford it, but there would be a priest and a service in the hospital room before he was to be cremated. Even the details seemed less shocking to him now.

He put the suit and shirt on and looked at himself in the mirror. He looked different, but he couldn't work out what it was. That he suddenly wasn't so miserable? That he had something to look forward to? That he wasn't so tortured by indecision? That he was stronger? Michael felt all of these things. They showed in the glint of his eye, and the flush on his cheek. Not only was he about to do exactly the right thing – the best thing even – but it was also going to release him, to set him free from the cage of his life.

He knew he wouldn't stay a moment afterwards. There was no reason to. The thought of leaving the slavery to which Bull had condemned him delighted him. But in truth, Michael doubted the future success of Bull's Marrow. He had suspicions that Seamus might have over-reached himself this time. The new Marrow was on such a large scale that it left too much margin for error, and even in big restaurants people noticed errors. Plus, Michael thought, fashion was a notoriously fickle monster.

He couldn't wait to leave the flat. It was stale, full of memories of times now past. It was his father's home, their home together, and with one of them gone now it was different. Haunted by its silence, overshadowed by the creaking of its memories, it was torture just to be there. And if he was saying goodbye to his father, then he was certainly saying goodbye to this place.

No, the only reason to stay was Genevieve. And that was what had confused him last night. He had known for a while that it was time to do something about his life, but it was only last night he had found the courage to make that change. Once he had decided to follow the doctors' advice, to release his father, everything had fallen into place. Everything, except the ache he felt at leaving Genevieve. He could leave the flat, leave London and start a new job in a new country with a new life. It was in his power to do that. But Genevieve was another matter. He couldn't control his feelings, he couldn't ignore them, he couldn't change them. Thinking of her was compulsive. He wanted to be near her all the time. Every time he shut his eyes she was there. And all of this was new to him, although he knew what it meant. That he was in love with her. And Michael had learned that love was not always a happy thing.

Painfully, last night he had finally come to the conclusion that he couldn't be near someone with whom he was in love but who he couldn't have. The only thing he could do to limit the pain, he resolved, was to remove himself from her presence. And if he couldn't have her, he certainly couldn't sit by and watch while she was destroyed by someone who was incapable of loving her enough. He would never be able to explain this to her. If he saw her to say goodbye, he knew he wouldn't be able to trust himself not to voice his fears. No, he could not interfere, that much he knew, therefore he had to take himself away. Quickly and quietly. He would have to learn to live without her.

He closed and locked the door of the flat behind him, and began his final journey to the hospital. His

feet crunched on the frost, his shoes leaving the track
of his path across the estate to the bus stop. The freezing
wait, the welcome sight of the Number 31 as it finally
appeared round the corner. A ninety-pence ticket, a seat
by the window at the back, the bright lights and warm air.
Belsize Lane, the hill, Swiss Cottage, Adelaide Road and
off, now walking in the bright sunshine down Englands
Lane. Each stride was portentous, a step closer to the next
stage of his life. He had made this journey so many times
now, but this was the first time he had made it and felt he
was going somewhere.

The hospital loomed in great concrete slabs as it emerged
from behind the hill. The sight of it always sickened him,
but this time Michael kept his nerve. He walked through
the electric doors, and followed the chipped cream walls
along to the lifts, up, up, up to the fifth floor. He turned
right along the corridor and his shoes squeaked noisily on
the lino. He nodded to the Sister who sat at the desk at the
top of the ward, and she beamed back at him. But today
Michael did not stop to talk to her like he usually did.

He could see the curtains were already drawn around
John Shaw's bed. Today they looked like a shroud. He
heard him before he could see him, the heave and hiss
of the ventilator as it sucked and blew the air out of his
useless lungs.

Michael pulled back the curtains for the last time. His
dad was exactly as he had left him last time – inanimate,
lifeless, frail. A woman in a dark gown and dog collar –
the priest – sat at his side and began to say something
to Michael, but he wasn't listening. He was looking at his
father, and was amazed to feel that somehow he was no
longer there in front of him. But he could feel his presence
at his shoulder, willing him on. The doctors were gathering
in their white coats behind him, and as he sat down and
took his dad's hand, he became even more convinced that
this was nothing but a lifeless body and that his dad was

elsewhere already. The priest was reading something from the Bible, and Michael shut his eyes. He could see only his father's face. It was unscarred, as it had been before the accident had disfigured it. He was grinning at him, the grin he always wore, offering him encouragement. He was still with him, and always would be.

He opened his eyes and saw a doctor bending over him, holding out a clipboard and a pen. Michael took it, knowing what it was. He looked at the dotted line at the bottom of the page and slowly signed his name. He turned back to his father and squeezed his hand between his, murmuring gently to him under his breath. He closed his eyes again and heard his dad's voice, telling him everything was going to be all right. He knew he would always be able to hear him saying it.

And then – silence. He snapped open his eyes and looked up. Everything was the same as before, but suddenly there was no noise. The peace he felt in the room seemed to lift everything from his shoulders. Michael felt like he was floating. The pink plastic lung had stopped moving in its glass dome. Tension now was beginning to seep out of his body, certainty and freedom running in in its place.

A doctor removed the mask from his father's face – it was the first time he had seen him unobscured for months. He ran his hand over his head and hair, but his skin already felt cold and rubbery and he knew that his dad was not in that lifeless body.

'Bye, Dad,' he said, then he stood up and quietly made for the fresh air, and his future.

Stuffed Marrow

1 large ripe, perfectly good marrow
1 onion, peeled and diced
1 fat clove of garlic, crushed
125g large swelling rice
450ml animal stock
75g toasted nuts
125g fungi, sliced
Salt and pepper
Olive oil

1. Slice open the marrow, spoon out the soft, untampered flesh. Sprinkle a third of the flesh with salt and drain off the juice by sandwiching it in between two sheets of kitchen towel and compressing heavily. Discard the rest.

2. When the flesh has drained, fry the onion and garlic in oil in a pan until soft. Add the marrow flesh, then the rice and the fungi.

3. Add the stock and stir continuously. Cook until all the stock has been absorbed into the rice, making each grain fat and swollen, with a slight crunch to the bite.

4. Stir in the nuts and season. Stuff the marrow with the rice mixture, dribble with oil and cover with foil. Bake in a hot oven for about thirty minutes.

29

The sun was not shining quite so brightly on Seamus that morning. Parked right outside the front entrance of Marrow – with only a day left until opening night – was a large white lorry. Its contents were clearly emblazoned on the side: *McCain Oven Chips* it read, in huge lettering, with a picture of a fluorescent yellow chip underneath, just in case you had missed the idea. And directly above the lorry hung the newly installed sign: MARROW. Six enormous green letters suspended on wire from the top of the building, specially designed to glow luminescent in the dark.

On the opposite side of the road, several bodies were crawling over each other like maggots in a fisherman's bait-box, wielding cumbersome cameras at various angles in order to take photographs of the lorry – and the sign above it.

Coming from behind the lorry was the most almighty racket, and every now and then a large, burly figure would dart out from behind it and shake its fists at the photographers. It was, of course, Seamus, and it was his bellowing that was filling the Knightsbridge thoroughfare with a din loud enough to compete with the traffic. The recipients of his temper, a small wiry man accompanied by a large, rotund one, seemed not in the least bit daunted by his outburst – rather, they appeared to be hugely amused.

'Get this fucking lorry out of the way of my restaurant, you bastards!'

'Absolutely nothing to do with me, Bull, I'm afraid. I certainly don't use produce like that. Prefer to make my own *frites*. I'm afraid you'll have to arrange for it to be removed yourself.'

'Nothing to do with you! Like hell – if you think I'm swallowing that then you seriously underestimate me, Coq! This is your stupid little gimmick, and frankly, if this is the best you can do then you might as well just give up now. Oi! You! Stop taking pictures!' This last was directed at one of the photographers who had broken away from the pack into the road to get a close-up of the two chefs together.

'Have you got permission to photograph my building? Come here – give me that camera now. *Oi!*'

At the sight of Seamus steaming across the road towards him, the cars screeching to a halt and a bus almost mounting the pavement, the photographer took the wise decision to terminate his project and beat a hasty retreat. Despite the fact that he was burdened by his cameras, a portly belly and a wheezing cough, after years on the Diana beat he knew how to scarper, and it didn't look like Seamus was going to catch him. No one could run faster than a paparazzo.

'I don't fucking believe it! You're scum, you are!' shouted Seamus after the retreating figure. 'Your mother will pay for this, you cheap little dirt-digger!'

Just behind the lorry, a stretch limousine with tinted windows had slipped quietly in by the kerb. Inside, Salvatore had been watching the full horror of the scene unobserved. He noticed that there was also a fifth member of the party by the lorry and that she, unlike the others, was strangely quiet. She was the most extraordinary-looking girl, Salvatore thought: beautiful clear skin, a near-perfect figure, her angelic face topped with a crown of astonishing white-blonde hair. Every Italian's dream, really. She was looking at Seamus in the strangest manner, as people generally did when they first came across him, except now Seamus had returned to the group, and passed his arm protectively round her waist – and she didn't step away.

Salvatore's attention was distracted again by the movements of the fat man, who on closer inspection he determined must be Rufus Ransome, the restaurant critic – often
pictured in news stories with Seamus, and most recently on
a stretcher, he seemed to recall. Rufus was now waddling
up to Seamus and the girl, and was emitting the most alien
of noises. It wasn't until Salvatore had stared at him for
a few seconds that he realised the succession of guttural
hiccups issuing from his wobbling lips were in fact Rufus's
version of laughter.

'Oh Bull, just to think – oven-cooked chips! And you
were going to serve all the food "to the exacting standards
of your last establishment", I do believe. Looks like you
weren't quite telling the truth, eh, doesn't it? Dear, dear,
you wait till the features desks hear about this one. "Top
Chef in Fast Food Con", or perhaps "Marrow is a load of
Bull" – oh yes, I rather like that: makes quite a snappy
headline, don't you think?'

Seamus's rage had been checked by the presence of
Genevieve – that is to say, he hadn't actually physically
attacked anyone yet, but the sight of this nasty little
queen coming over all snidey with him was more than
he could handle. He raised his fists, and was about to
pounce when Rufus jumped behind Coq before Seamus
could reach him. Of course the photographers, on whom
Seamus had turned his back for one moment, were loving
this and their cameras were clicking hungrily at the scene.
Whirling round, Seamus caught them creeping up on him,
and charged at the pack with a roar. Knowing now the
game was up, the snappers gathered up their cameras and
ran, scampering in different directions. In the distance, a
police siren began to wail.

Rufus continued his taunting and his paroxysms of
hiccuping giggles from safety, behind the other chef. Coq,
meanwhile, stood perfectly still, watching the irritation
of Seamus as a scientist might observe a cell change

under the microscope. Seamus had by now noticed the limousine. A shiver of fear went through him: here was Salvatore to collect his money and Seamus didn't have it. Getting Genevieve's money out of probate and over to this country was proving a long process. He was also less than pleased that Salvatore had encountered him whilst he was right in the middle of a fight. He let his fists drop and, grabbing Genevieve roughly by the hand, he stalked back into Marrow.

Inside the limousine Salvatore sighed. What had started out as merely an irritation was now growing into a full-blown headache. Lifting his jacket, he pulled out his mobile phone and dialled.

'Marion? It's me . . . We have problems. We have a press problem, a police problem and a chef problem . . . Yes. I need you down here now.' And with that Salvatore stepped out of the car, gathered his henchmen around him and walked into Marrow.

Inside, Seamus was shouting at random members of staff. Adèle was standing petrified on the phone as Seamus gesticulated wildly towards the lorry – as if it was her fault. Genevieve was disappearing upstairs, casting around as if she was searching for someone. She looked distressed.

'I want you to get the police round here right now!' ordered Seamus. 'You can't park a lorry in the middle of Knightsbridge.'

'I'm afraid you can,' countered Salvatore. He appeared like a vampire from the shadows, the two large sinister shadows at his shoulders standing guard like Egyptian Sphinxes. 'I organised special permission for that, if you recall, at your specific request. My contact on the Council was most obliging, pushing through that special permission. I suggest you *don't* call the police.'

Seamus growled in frustration, and turned back to Adèle. 'Get that bloody lorry removed, will you, and find some fucking bollards or something so no one else can park there.'

Salvatore had come to the conclusion that if it wasn't for Seamus owing him money, he would rather enjoy having him disposed of. The idea that this maniac was being entrusted with the best part of Salvatore's business was terrifying. He had convinced himself it would be all right up till now, but he was no longer sure. Quite apart from extracting his money from this one million pound marriage (to the girl with the white-blonde hair? He had never seen her before, and she certainly didn't look like a 'society girl'), there was also the small practicality that the restaurant was opening tomorrow and he needed a chef. He kept the henchmen back.

'Adèle, get Marion on the phone for me,' continued Seamus, shouting. 'This is a fucking PR disaster. That woman can do her job for once, instead of spending all my money on useless socialising!' Adèle passed him the phone, which was already ringing Marion's number.

'Marion?'

'Yes, Seamus?'

'We've got a disaster on our hands. Some jerk – namely Coq – has arranged for a frozen chip lorry to be parked outside my restaurant, and bloody photographers have been taking pictures of it all morning. If we don't watch it, it's going to be front-page news tomorrow that Marrow's serving fucking fast food. You've got to do something about it!'

'Please.'

'What?'

'Do something about it, *please.*'

'Oh, for fuck's sake, Marion, when did manners ever come into anything?'

'I'll put Fuzz onto it, we'll issue a statement. Anyway, where have you been, Seamus? I've been trying to get hold of you since yesterday. I needed your approval on a very important press release. I had to put it out without showing you in the end because every time I called I was told you were unavailable. Are you at Marrow? I'm on my way over.'

'Yes, I am – but just sort this fucking lorry out first, will you.' Seamus handed the phone back to Adèle, then looked around for Genevieve. He couldn't see her, but at that moment Paul and Nigel found him.

'Congratulations, mate,' said Paul unenthusiastically, clapping him on the back.

'Yeah, well done, mate, smart move,' managed Nigel, enviously.

Seamus looked puzzled. 'Congratulations for what?'

'On your engagement.'

'How the fuck do you know?' Seamus was astonished: how did Paul and Nigel know about him marrying Genevieve?

'It's in all the papers this morning, boss. Haven't you seen?'

Seamus began to feel alarmed. 'What papers?'

'All of them, boss. Here, this one's got it in too,' said Nigel, passing him a tabloid he had tucked under his arm, folded open on the relevant page.

There was the picture of Seamus and Henrietta leaving Louche, and underneath it ran the headline *CHEF FINALLY TO GET H-IT-CHED*! Seamus didn't even read the details. His vision had gone red as his blood began to boil behind his eyes. All he could think of were the words 'important press release'.

'Adèle!' he said, with such a menacing calm that even Paul and Nigel looked alarmed.

Adèle jumped. 'Yes, boss?'

'Get Marion back on the phone, will you!' Somehow, even though he was speaking in low tones, Seamus's voice seemed to echo right round the building.

'I'm here, Seamus, what on earth can be the matter

now?' announced Marion shrilly, as she clattered in person across the floor. Unfortunately, her Manolos were leaving a trail of stab-marks in her wake, much to the consternation of the foreman, who was running after her, frantically waving a hard hat in one hand, and gesticulating at the floor with the other.

Seamus turned on her, and let loose the full force of his temper. Marion tried not to look startled at the blast, but not even she had witnessed anything quite so terrifying from Seamus before. It wasn't so much what he said, or how he said it, as the thunderous expression on his face. He looked as if he might pick her up, fling her about a bit, then shake her into a thousand tiny little pieces.

'What the FUCK is this?' he demanded, waving the paper at her. 'These – these lies! There's only one place this could have come from, Marion, and don't think I'm stupid enough not to realise that! Who EVER gave you permission to speak for me about—'

'Seamus, if you'd just let me explain . . .'

'EXPLAIN?! I should think you've got some serious explaining to do, you . . . you witch! What the fuck do you think you're doing? Let me tell you, lady, you've got to put a stop to this right now. I want retractions in all the papers tonight, or I shall phone up all the sodding editors and do it myself. Which will make you and your stupid fucking PR outfit look like pieces of shit!'

'Now, Seamus, just calm down for one moment.' Marion had realised that this was going to be tricky, but she had never imagined Seamus would react quite so badly.

'*Calm down?* How can I calm down when you are trying to marry me off to some stupid ugly cow whose name I can't even pronounce? I had no idea even you could be such a stupid bitch. Surely, Marion,' he continued, the sarcasm heavy in his voice, 'in matters such as these, it's customary to ask the groom first?'

'I tried to reach you all of yesterday, Seamus, but . . .'

'So you went ahead and made it all up anyway?'

'Look – just listen to me for one moment.' Marion was desperate to make Seamus understand. No way could she let his temper jeopardise this deal. 'Let me explain why I did it. *Hiya!* want in on the deal. They rang up after they saw the story about you and Henrietta in the *Standard* and offered us a million pounds if we would sell them the exclusive wedding rights. We couldn't say no to money like that and we needed to act immediately, so I thought it best to keep your options open for you, and say yes for now.'

'I don't fucking care if they offered the governement's gold reserve!'

'Well, how was I to know you would feel like this yesterday? After all, I was under the impression that you were finding it hard to locate any money at all at the moment.'

'That's none of your fucking business!'

'Of course it's my business, Seamus.' Marion sighed despairingly. 'In fact it's damn near a third of my business!'

Seamus ignored her. 'Phone the editors now – issue a statement. Right now!'

'Please, Seamus, just calm down and think about this. You have to do it. We need the money and we need the publicity. There *is* no other way. Please!'

But Seamus had no intention of changing his mind. On the contrary, he was amazed Marion was still trying to persuade him into it. Was she mad? Marrying someone for publicity? It was the most ridiculous thing he had ever heard.

'Fucking ring them!' he shouted, at such volume that a crowd was beginning to gather at Marrow's door. But

Marion refused to be frightened. She had not got where she was today through cowardice, or indeed, as she said to herself now, through pandering to the male ego.

'Look, Seamus, you know any marriage that appears in *Hiya!* is over in a year anyway. You could be divorced within six months and the whole thing would be over and you'd be £500,000 richer. It's not as if it's exactly hard work. You just have to pose for a few shots, and turn up on the wedding day. We'll organise the rest, and we can start divorce proceedings as soon as—'

But Seamus had decided on desperate measures to silence Marion once and for all.

'There's one very simple reason why I can't do it,' he told her icily. 'I'm already engaged.'

Now it was Marion's turn to be silent. In fact, she was struck dumb. Seamus was gleeful in his moment of triumph, as he watched her try to digest this information.

'What do you mean, already engaged?' she spluttered.

'I'm going to marry my girlfriend and she is going to become a partner in the business. From today.'

This was all too much for Marion. 'Your *girlfriend*? What *girlfriend*?' and she collapsed into a pearwood chair conveniently positioned nearby. As she sat on it, its feet buried themselves a quarter of an inch into the marble.

'No one you know, Marion, thank God.'

'You mean you're marrying a nobody?' she spat in disgust. This was too much.

Seamus was now desperately casting round for Genevieve, whom he couldn't see anywhere. Not quite wishing to call out her name, since it would seem a bit absent-minded to have mislaid her already, he eventually spied her descending in the lift.

Marion meanwhile, who never took no for an answer and wasn't about to make this the first time, had rapidly marshalled her persuasive skills, and prepared to re-enter the battle.

'You know, Seamus, you could always just do the betrothal shoot. We needn't announce that you're not actually going to get married. We can just let it drift away. People will forget anyway. You know what they say – tomorrow's fish and chip paper.'

But Seamus was too transfixed by the sight of Genevieve to pay any more attention to Marion. She wore the most extraordinary look on her face, one of bitter disappointment, and something inside him dislodged, painfully.

Then Genevieve caught Seamus's eye, and she smiled at him nervously. She had been frightened and dismayed by his temper, of which she had seen more and more over the last few days. Not to mention what she had seen happen between him and Michael, but there he was looking at her with such longing. It was obvious he loved her, and she wanted to love him – she really did. She just didn't quite know what to do.

Pointing to the lift, Seamus said calmly, and with such certainty that not even Marion could contradict him: 'That is who I'm marrying. Her name is Genevieve and, as you can see, she is quite a different person from the one in that photograph. She is also going to invest £500,000 of her own money in the business, so you can stop worrying about celebrity fees.'

By this time Genevieve had made her way over to Seamus.

'Darling, meet Marion, the woman who has been spreading lies about me and some other female. She's our business partner.'

Genevieve could see Seamus was furious, and was glaring at Marion, but she decided to cool things down while she tried to understand exactly what was going on. So she stretched her arm towards Marion and said pleasantly, 'Hello, Marion. How nice to meet you.'

Marion couldn't refuse the hand extended to her and was forced to unravel hers. Fixing Genevieve with the most evil look the French girl had ever received, she limply took the hand – barely touching it – and replied, 'Genevieve. Well, I can't say we've heard much about *you*. Tell me, are you a fairly recent addition to Seamus's life?'

'Marion . . .' began Seamus furiously, but Genevieve was there before him. She didn't need Seamus to fight her battles for her, and after months of conversation with Mave, she was no longer thrown by comments like these.

Looking Marion straight in the eye, she said, 'No, actually. I have known Seamus since he was twenty-two. Which, I imagine, is longer than you have.'

'Oh, you know him well, do you?' replied Marion, a smile spreading across her face as something occurred to her. Suddenly Seamus didn't want this exchange to continue . . .

'Right, leave her alone.'

His tone was menacing, but Marion was too furious that her plan had been scuppered to care. She hadn't lost yet, and throwing Seamus a vengeful look she continued: 'So you'll know all about the night he spent in the Lanesborough with Henrietta Gross-Smythe then? Barely a week ago. Oh, here I have Henrietta's mobile phone. I believe she left it behind in the hotel room. She asked me to pick it up for her. No doubt you will be seeing her before I will, so you'd better keep it. Or maybe not. Henrietta, by all accounts, wasn't too happy with your performance,' and here Marion turned to Genevieve and smirked. 'Apparently he's hopeless in bed these days. Still, he wasn't much cop when I had him either.'

Marion's words had exactly the desired effect. Genevieve stood aghast, and turned to Seamus. One look at his face was enough to tell her it was all true. Her mind a blank, all she could think was to run away, and focusing only on the front doors of the restaurant, she fled before Seamus could catch her.

The Digestif

A digestif is an after-dinner drink that aids digestion.

King of the digestifs is brandy, with cognac the highest majesty of all. Other digestifs include ports, sherries, grappas and crème liqueurs. A few of the more bitter digestifs help settle an upset stomach.

Digestifs are enjoyed in small amounts and savoured for their potent aroma. They are to be enjoyed like a good conversation, not gulped in quantities.

As to be expected, there is a fine line in the amount drunk between decorum and debauchery.

30

Salvatore shook his head. *Incredibile*. What had he got himself into? Feeling wearied by the whole situation, he took a seat on one of the chairs scattered over the floor of the restaurant. Distractedly he noted they were pearwood – an order he thought he had cancelled. In the ensuing chaos both Seamus and Marion had taken themselves outside after the retreating Genevieve, leaving Salvatore with his henchmen to work out whether this meant Seamus had £1.5 million, £500,000 or, indeed, no money at all to put into the Marrow coffers. Salvatore suspected it was probably the latter. God damn that lunatic! Losing one woman worth £1 million was careless. Losing a second worth half a million was plain stupid.

'The restaurant's backer, I presume?'

Salvatore looked up. The thin man he had seen arguing with Seamus outside Marrow earlier was walking across the restaurant floor towards him. Behind him the fat man was struggling to keep up. Salvatore didn't say a word. He folded his arms across his chest and faced his approaching interlocutor. His Sphinxes clenched their ham-like fists.

'You appear to be having a few problems with your chef,' Coq persisted, unfazed by Salvatore's silence. 'Do please excuse the intrusion, but I was outside, and I'm afraid I couldn't help overhearing.'

Salvatore flinched.

'Allow me to introduce myself: I am Emmanuel Coq, proprietor of Mirage, the premises across the road.'

Suddenly, Salvatore looked interested.

'I was wondering, actually, whether you were looking for some assistance?'

'Some assistance?' repeated Salvatore, raising one eyebrow. He had heard of this Coq. He knew who he was – the most decorated chef in town.

'Yes, indeed. For this place. You see, I would be very interested in investing.'

'Would you?' replied Salvatore, raising the other eyebrow. 'How interesting. I am indeed the restaurant's backer – and majority owner. You are talking to the right person. I am Salvatore. That is all you need to know.'

'Pleased to make your acquaintance, signor. Forgive me, but your reputation precedes you. I must assure you that I hold nothing other than respect for you and your business.'

The two men nodded to each other, a tacit understanding reached: Coq knew about Salvatore, and he didn't mind. Salvatore knew Coq knew, but his knowledge was not a threat.

Coq continued: 'There is one problem though. As I am sure you can understand, were I to invest in Marrow, I would need sole creative control over the food.'

'You're saying you wouldn't want to share the premises with Bull?'

'I'm afraid that would be completely out of the question.'

'Yes, I understand. But you see, Bull's share of the premises is worth one million pounds, and if I were to remove him, I would need a replacement with that kind of money as well.' Salvatore eyed Coq beadily. He saw reflected in Coq's gaunt face the same malevolence and corruption he knew existed in his own. Suddenly he felt rather attracted to him.

'The money is not a problem,' Coq told him gruffly. 'I have several successful businesses of which I am sole owner already. But there is one other condition as well. I simply cannot work alongside that woman Marion either. She revolts me, you see.'

'Really?' This news did not unduly upset Salvatore. Indeed, he found Marion's methods rather tiresome too, and really all the work he needed her for had been done already: the pre-publicity, the party. If it was necessary, they could easily hire another PR firm. There was, however, the problem of her money. Coq read his mind.

'Perhaps her investment could remain, but her involvement should cease. I believe the phrase is "silent partner"?'

Salvatore nodded. 'And when could you get me this money to replace Bull's?'

'Boff!' Coq tossed his head. 'A few weeks, nothing more. It shouldn't take me too long to sell Mirage.'

This didn't pose a problem to Salvatore: a rather lucrative ship had come in that morning, and he was anticipating a sizeable amount of revenue in the next week or so. That should cover the running costs until Coq's capital arrived.

'Well, I can't foresee that being a problem,' he said eventually. 'I shall inform Marion that her services are no longer required. You have made me a very interesting proposition, Monsieur Coq. Let us explore it further over dinner tonight.'

A broad grin broke out across each man's face. The deal was sealed.

'I shall send a car to pick you up from here at seven-thirty,' Salvatore said smoothly. 'In the meantime, I suggest you look to your kitchens: you have a party for a thousand and a seven-course dinner for twenty-five to prepare for tomorrow night. Do please feel free to start immediately.' And with that Salvatore gathered his henchmen around him and made for his limousine.

Unfortunately, just before he was out of earshot, Rufus, who had been skulking behind Coq during their conversation, exploded in a fountain of spittle. 'Emmanuel! What on earth are you doing? You can't possibly be investing in Marrow! After all we have said about this place! Are you mad?'

Coq turned to him, and regarded his squat figure. 'I'm afraid not, Ransome. On reconsideration, I find taking it over by far the better option.'

'But what about everything I have said and written so publicly about it? I couldn't possibly retract and support you in this!'

'Tough,' Coq replied.

Rufus was incredulous. 'But Emmanuel, after all we have been through together! My dear chap, do please reconsider!'

Salvatore, who knew how powerful Rufus was in the industry, and who was also, by this stage, fed up with obstacles blocking the path to his biggest money-laundering venture yet, had now retraced his steps back to Coq. Tugging his arm, he whispered quietly in the master chef's ear: 'He is an unnecessary problem. Get rid of him.'

Coq grinned in complicity. 'No problem, Signor Salvatore. His editor is dining in my restaurant as we speak. I'll have him sacked.'

Genevieve knew exactly where she was heading. It was the certainty of her destination – right now the only certainty in her life – that was keeping her sane. She had to talk to someone about her predicament, and that someone was Michael. He was the only person she could be honest with. He had not been at Marrow that morning, and although she had no idea where Michael lived, Genevieve knew where she would find him: at some time he would return to the hospital. That was where she was headed.

Genevieve had so much she needed to say, so much bubbling up inside her, and she knew that with Michael she could let it all out. He was the one person she could trust, whose thoughts and judgements she would value. And she knew that he would know the truth about Seamus.

The Tube finally stopped at Belsize Park. Genevieve had been going spare on the train: it hadn't gone fast enough, her mind had been racing too quickly. She practically ran up the stairs of the station and kept on running up Haverstock Hill until she reached the turning for the hospital. Her skin was beaded in sweat, glistening in the cold, midday sun. If he wasn't there she would wait for him until he arrived. She went through the doors and, ignoring the queasiness in her stomach as the familiarity of the hospital smell hit her, she marched purposefully towards the lifts. She needed the fifth floor: she could remember exactly where his father was. To her relief a lift was already there: she didn't want to have to wait, didn't want to have to think. She couldn't stand to be alone with her pain.

A hospital porter, clad in outsized blue overalls, got in the lift with her and looked at her strangely. 'You all right, love?' he asked.

'Yes,' she replied, puzzled. Suddenly a paranoia overtook her that he would try to admit her, and in her hysteria she imagined she would be kept in hospital against her will once again. Panicking, she punched the button for the next floor and fled the lift as soon as it stopped, taking the stairs to the fifth floor instead. She needed the Jeanne Barnham Ward. Casting around, she eventually saw a sign, and hurried down the corridor towards the ward. Please let him be there, she thought. Please let him be there.

She saw the Sister through the glass in the swing doors to the ward, but couldn't quite see through to where his bed was. As she burst through the doors, she started to announce who she had come to see and then stopped: he was gone. John Shaw's bed was empty. Genevieve walked over in a trance. 'Where is he? Where have you taken him?'

She felt the nurse's hand on her shoulder.

'I think you'd better come and sit down,' she said gently.

Genevieve sipped the hot sweet tea, grateful to the Sister. So Michael had finally done it: he had said goodbye. She felt pride and awe mingled with bitter disappointment at not seeing him. She hoped he was all right, but despair took over as she realised she wouldn't know where to find him now. The only place she could contact him was at Marrow, and that was the last place on earth that she wanted to be. She felt sad, very sad, but the tea was doing her good. She was calmer now, more rational. She considered her options. She needed to talk to someone, but she couldn't find Michael. She didn't have anywhere to go: she couldn't go back to the flat, Seamus would surely be waiting for her there. The only place she could go was Mave's. Yes, that is where she would go.

'You feeling a bit better now, dear?' asked the nurse, noticing the colour had returned to the girl's cheeks.

'Yes, I am, thank you. And thank you for the tea as well,' said Genevieve shyly.

'Oh, no problem, dear. These things are always a bit of a shock.'

Genevieve got up to leave, but she couldn't resist asking one more time. 'You are sure, absolutely sure, he didn't leave a note or anything?' She had no idea why she thought Michael would have left a note, but she was so desperate to see him she imagined all sorts of possibilities.

'No dear, I'm afraid not.'

Genevieve sighed. She felt in her pocket and pulled out her change. £2.70. Just enough to get her to Mave's.

'Well dear,' said Mave, drawing heavily on her sixth consecutive Rothmans since she had sat down. 'If I were your mother I know exactly what I would say to you.'

She regarded Genevieve over the top of her teacup.

The girl was a sorry sight indeed, her eyes blotchy and red, her screwed-up tissue held scrunched up against her nose, shame and pain wracking her face. She had landed herself in a very sorry state of affairs, and as much as Mave didn't like to involve herself in these things, she had felt it necessary to flip the CLOSED sign on the door while she heard the whole story from start to finish. Other people's business was always interesting, but this was definitely worth listening to uninterrupted. Frankly, she couldn't help admitting she had a soft spot for this girl. She had had it all coming to her from day one, of course – and Mave had told her so at the time. And had she listened? Of course not. These young people never did. But she could see what needed to be said, and she would say it once again, now there was a chance her advice might be heeded.

'He's bad news, my girl, and he always will be. He's not your type, you know. You don't suit. You're a little country girl, all sweetness and light, and he's a ruthless city boy with no thought for anyone but himself. What's more, you both come from different countries. You've got all your life ahead of you: don't ruin it by tying yourself to someone who is going to make it a misery.'

'But what if it's not true, Mave? What if he doesn't see other women, and it is how he says it is, all made-up lies in a newspaper?'

'How much more of your life are you prepared to ignore it for, eh? How many headlines do you want to read? And to be frank, my girl, how much more evidence of his real character do you need? After what you told me today I would have thought it was obvious what that man was like.'

'But Mave, I swear to God he loves me!'

'But do *you* love *him*?'

Genevieve paused. The thought of him no longer excited her. In fact, it repelled her.

'You know,' she said after a while, 'I think I love the memory of him. I love the man who was in France – the man who he can be. The man he was. But no, Mave, you are right. I don't love the man he is.'

'Good. Well, I'm glad that's settled then. Now, young lady, you've found out what you needed to know from your little jaunt across the Channel, I suggest you pack your bags and go back home. You're not from round here, Jenny. You've had your little visit, you've had your fun, and now it's time to go home.'

At that moment the door opened and a large, broad-shouldered girl came in. 'Hello Mave,' she said mechanically, before making for the kitchen.

'Who's that?' asked Genevieve when she was out of earshot.

'That is your replacement. Hilda, the German student. Great little worker she is too.'

Genevieve felt her tummy vault. She had been replaced. There was no room for her here now. She looked out at the street: the newspaper-seller, the backpackers, the yellow lines, the Tube station, the dustcart. All of it, somehow, seemed so English; so foreign. Mave was right. This wasn't where she belonged. She had to go back to France and start her life over again. She had found out all she needed to know about Seamus, about this country. Her mother might have been born here, but Genevieve didn't feel English. She was French, and that was the country where she belonged. She would pack her bags and go back straight away. Her money still hadn't come through from France, and all it would take would be a phone call to halt the transfer.

But first she had to say goodbye. And she had to tell Seamus what she now realised she had come all this way to say.

Melting Moments

100g butter
6 tablespoons caster sugar
½ teaspoon vanilla essence
1 tablespoon cornflour
75g plain flour, sifted
Pinch salt.

1. Cream the butter and sugar together, then stir in the sifted dry ingredients.

2. Roll the mixture into small balls of about 5 centimetres, place on a greased baking tray and flatten.

3. Bake for 15 minutes in an oven pre-heated to 180°C.

4. Place on a wire rack to cool, but eat whilst still hot. The biscuits will pop and melt on your tongue.

31

Marion was pacing the pavement outside Louche, her mobile phone clamped firmly to her ear, her long dark ponytail and the tails of her ankle-length coat flowing out behind her. The street-lamps were just beginning to come on, and the light was at that tricky point of dusk, where everything was half-visible and yet also half-invisible. Marion, dressed all in black, looked like a shadow. She had been forced outside into the cold by the only club rule Louche imposed upon its members: no mobile phone calls were allowed inside its portals. Thus, in the reverse to an office building where employees are frequently seen perched outside on the pavement gasping on their cigarettes before going to work inside, at Louche one worked outside, and smoked inside.

Five paces to the right she stalked. 'Damn!' she uttered, then, repunching a number on her handset, she spun on her stilettos and stalked five paces to the left. Then she repeated the manoeuvre.

'Bloody hell, Salvatore, for God's sake, answer the phone!' she swore. Then she paused, mid-stride. 'Hello? Is that Salvatore? Well, for God's sake put me on to him, you monkey! Salvatore? *Is that you?*'

'Yes, Marion.'

'Oh, thank *God* for that – at last! Now listen, all hell has broken loose. Rufus Ransome has just turned up at Louche in tears saying you've sacked Bull from Marrow and replaced him with Coq! God alone knows where he got this lunatic idea from, but I need to put out a release denying it immediately. Bloody story is all round Louche already.'

'In that case, you won't need to put out a release.'

'What?' Marion responded suspiciously. 'What exactly do you mean, Salvatore?'

'Well, if they know already then there's no need to issue a press release, is there?'

'Jesus Christ, are you saying this is true?'

'Yes, it is true.'

'What the hell is going on here?' Marion started to pace again, furiously stabbing at the pavement with her heels. 'Now listen to me, Salvatore, I'm a bloody partner in this business too, you know, and you can't go round making drastic changes like this without even consulting me! Who the hell do you think you are?'

'I'm the controlling partner, Marion. And NOBODY argues with me. Now I've put up with your stupid little frivolities – from sinking marble to Amazonian chair timber, and I've had enough. I want this restaurant to work. From now on your involvement has been reduced to that of silent partner. And your PR services are no longer required either.'

'SILENT PARTNER?!'

'Yes, Marion. Now I have to go. Any problems, please speak to my assistants – or Emmanuel Coq. I will no longer take your calls. Goodbye.'

'Salvatore – wait! Are you sacking Marvellous? You can't do that! Salvatore! Please!'

But it was too late, he had disconnected. Marion stared at her phone in disbelief. After everything she had done! She couldn't believe it, it simply couldn't be true. But there was Rufus bawling his eyes out at the bar, proof positive she hadn't just dreamt the last conversation. Salvatore and Coq must have been in cahoots all along – it was the only explanation she could think of for such a vicious stab in the back. Marion stared at her mobile with incredulity. Then suddenly, it rang. Thank God for that! It had to be Salvatore calling back to say it was all a huge misunderstanding. Or a sick joke. Or a dream. Anything!

'Hello, Marion speaking.'

'Marion? It's Richard Raker from *Hiya!* magazine.'

'Richard!' Marion's heart somersaulted out of her chest and up into her mouth. 'Hello, how are you?' she asked nervously, suddenly thrown terrifyingly off-balance.

'Not well, I regret, Marion. *Thanks to you.* I have just heard that Bull is no longer Head Chef of the biggest restaurant in town, and more pertinent to my situation, he is not engaged to Henrietta Gross-Smythe at all, but to someone entirely different and of absolutely no interest to our readers. All of which is incredibly embarrassing as the latest issue of the magazine has just gone to press announcing our exclusive coverage of Bull and Smythe's forthcoming wedding. *And* promising an exclusive behind-the-scenes look at Marrow – "In the kitchen with Seamus Bull". I think, Marion, that you will therefore accept that you have not only led me up the garden path, but have endangered the entire reputation of my august magazine. I am phoning to let you know that I shall never be doing any business with you or any of your clients ever again. And I shall also be using my influence to dissuade others from contracting your services in the future. You are finished. Goodbye.'

Marion slowly folded away her mobile phone. She was ruined; Marvellous was destroyed. With Raker against her she would never survive. And since she had taken on the Marrow account she had lost all the others. Even her Porsche had gone. Slowly her long, elegant legs folded beneath her, and she found herself collapsed on the pavement in a pool of black wool. The tramp who sat outside Louche morning, noon and night, and at whom Marion had once or twice imperiously flicked a fifty-pence piece, now offered her the stub of his roll-up cigarette. She almost took it.

Inside Louche, Rufus's mood was no better. In fact, he was several steps ahead of Marion, having graduated from his initial shock to a violent distress. Chris, the barman, was sympathetically mixing him brandy cocktails to numb the pain, but the litany of self-pity that was issuing from his fat lips was unstoppable.

Henrietta, meanwhile, had decided to celebrate her forth-coming nuptials with an early evening glass of champagne. Spotting Rufus in his obvious state of upset, she was very quickly informed of the details. But the little she could make out from Rufus's blubbing left her rather unclear about her own situation. Was she engaged or single? Employed or unemployed? Then she spotted Marion outside, hunched against a wall and smoking a cigarette. Now this really *was* serious. No one dented Marion's cool. Still clutching her champagne, Henrietta teetered outside, and prodded the shaking black figure in the shoulder. Marion looked up and groaned – that was all she needed, someone else to spread the good news.

'Darling, whatever can the matter be?' Henrietta asked, her voice resonating with what appeared to be genuine concern. When she got no response, she tried offering Marion her champagne. 'Here, have some of this, sweetie. Bubbles always make things better.'

Marion eyed the glass and Henrietta warily, as if both might be poisoned. Frankly, nothing would surprise her about today. In the end she decided to go in out of the cold and sit on a proper seat. Inside, back in Louche, she collapsed in a red velvet armchair, traces of mascara-tinted tears still visible on her cheeks. Henrietta perched on the arm beside her and began gently to stroke her hair.

'There, there,' she said consolingly, 'it can't be that bad. From what I can gather from Rufus, Seamus already has a girlfriend, so it looks like I've lost a husband. You're not the only one with some bad news to bear.' Henrietta had taken the news of the collapse of her marriage with considerable stoicism. After all, she had never quite been able to believe her good fortune. She had been looking for a husband for nine years and one had never materialised, so she didn't see why it should suddenly happen now.

'Marion, darling, do tell me what on earth has happened to you. How can I help you feel better if you won't tell me what's wrong? Has Marrow really gone pop?'

'Oh, more than that, honey,' hiccupped Marion, feeling a little less distraught with Henrietta stroking her hair and feeding her champagne. 'I'm finished, over. I'll never work in PR again. I've lost my business and all my money is tied up in a place I have no control over. That bastard Salvatore has gone and made me a silent partner.'

'Oh dear. Here – have some more champagne.'

'Thank you, darling – you really are being very sweet. Basically, today has been a total waste of make-up.'

'Talking of which, sweetie, I hate to say it, but it's mostly halfway down your cheeks.'

'What?'

'Your make-up.'

'Oh God! Is it really?' exclaimed Marion, revived now in a way the champagne had so far been unable to do.

Henrietta smiled at her, then tenderly wiped a black dribble from the corner of her eye. Marion stared at Henrietta, transfixed. Without thinking, Henrietta lifted the teardrop of mascara up to her lips and licked it off her finger. Steadily, she returned Marion's enraptured gaze. Slowly, Marion slipped her hand in Henrietta's and caressed the inside of her palm. Still holding Henrietta's gaze, she said: 'I think I'd better go to the Ladies and fix myself up. Will you come with me?'

Henrietta's body had begun to tingle in a way it had never really tingled before. 'Yes, oh yes,' she replied.

Seamus could think of only one thing to do in this situation. Drink. And there was only one place he could think of to drink in – or at least, where he could drink without being besieged by the bloody press. Everywhere he went they were falling over each other, clamouring at him to comment on his marriage to that damned posh girl. Louche then was where his cab was taking him. Christ only knew where Genevieve had got to. That bitch Marion, he couldn't believe she'd stitched him up like that. I'll throttle her, he thought, but even as he did so Seamus knew deep down that Genevieve would have found out anyway sooner or later. It was hardly easy conducting a private life when you had a team of crack photographers up your arse the whole time, he noted ruefully. Well, she would just have to accept it. It had been a mistake, he hadn't meant it and anyway he had been blind drunk. He didn't even remember doing it, for fuck's sake. Hadn't he already told her he loved her? Christ, he'd even asked her to marry him – what more did she want?

Seamus took another slug from the bottle he'd picked up from an off-licence on the way. He had waited for ages for Genevieve to come back to the flat but she hadn't appeared. He couldn't imagine where she was, but one thing was for sure: she'd have to come back eventually – she didn't have anywhere else to go. And with that realisation, and after he had finished the bottle of whisky and half bottle of vintage port that remained in the flat, he'd got bored of waiting. And he needed another drink.

'There you go, sir, that'll be ten pounds.'

'Ten pounds! Are you joking?'

'No sir, it's on the meter. And you might tip me for all those bloody paparazzi types I had to dodge. Not to mention waiting while you practically held up the off-licence.'

'Well, I'm not fucking employing you again.'

'No need, sir, we pick up our own fares.'

Cassandra was on duty at Louche's reception and she knew a hurricane when she saw it. Chris, too, was instantly

aware that trouble was headed his way, and even before
Seamus had reached the bar, he had poured him a large
double brandy on the house. It wasn't until Seamus had
downed it that he realised he was sitting right next to Rufus.
The fat man had gone strangely quiet when Seamus had
arrived, hoping he wouldn't notice his presence, allowing
him to slip from his bar stool and make a quick escape.
But the truth was he was so paralysed with fear he was
unable to move at all. Seamus looked him up and down,
slowly appraising him from head to toe. He couldn't help
but notice Rufus's swollen red eyes, even more puffy than
they usually were.

'What's the matter with you, then?' Seamus asked
gruffly.

'I-I-I-I've been sssssssssacked,' stammered Rufus.

'Oh?' said Seamus, raising his eyebrows – best news he'd
had all day. 'What for?'

'B-b-b-because I didn't like Mmmmarrow.'

Seamus started to laugh. A deep, throaty, sadistic laugh.
'And who managed that then? Was that our wonder girl
Marion? Done something right at last!'

'Nnn-n-n-no. N-n-not Marion.' Rufus began to shake
even more. It suddenly occurred to him that perhaps
Seamus didn't know.

'Well, who was it then?' Seamus was suddenly curious. Rufus was petrified, but like a rabbit caught in the
headlights, there was nothing he could do to avoid the
oncoming crash.

'C-c-c-c . . .' Rufus was finding it hard to get the word
out.

'Who, God damn it? Spit it out, man!'

'C-c-coq!'

'*Coq?* What do you mean, Coq?' Now Seamus was
confused.

Rufus could see no way out. He decided to make a run
for it, but as he slipped off his stool, Seamus caught him

by the back of his jacket and spun him back round. 'Now don't you run off, Ruthless. I haven't finished talking to you. What do you mean, Coq?'

'C-c-c-coq is c-c-c-cooking at M-m-m-marrow now.'

Rufus screwed up his eyes, ready for the explosion. Seamus was still confused though, Rufus sounded as if he was talking utter nonsense, but there was something about the fear on his face that made Seamus think twice about dismissing it completely. It couldn't be true, could it? He needed to know more, urgently, but seeing that suspending Rufus by the neck of his jacket was not encouraging his fluency, he dropped him heavily back on his stool, and summoned another double brandy from Chris.

'Now, Rufus,' he said slowly, reining in his rising temper as best he could. 'Tell me again – slowly. *Who* is cooking at Marrow?'

'C-c-c-coq.'

'And who employed Coq?'

'S-sss-Salvatore.'

'Salvatore?'

'Yes, Salvatore. He said he was having a few problems with his chef.' Rufus was warming up now. At last he had someone who would listen to him, and he too had another double brandy on the bar. 'Emmanuel asked him if he wanted a replacement for you and gave him your share of the money.'

Seamus took deep breaths. It didn't help. Clenching and unclenching his fists, all he could see around him was a red mist. Focusing at last on the brandy bottle that Chris now regretted putting in front of them, Seamus picked it up, and letting out the most almighty roar, brought it slamming down on the bar, shattering the bottle, and showering all those nearby in brandy and shards of glass.

'The fucking *baaaaaaaaastaaaaard*!' he roared, at the top of his voice. 'The double-crossing, thieving, manipulative BASTARD!' he bellowed again, this time flinging the neck of the bottle across the bar. It missed a pop star's throat by inches.

Seamus didn't dare stop shouting. If for one moment he was to stop ranting he would have to recognise the enormity of what this meant for him. That now, professionally, he had nothing. His terror kept his voice at full volume, and every glass in the house began to fall victim to his fury, as he swept like a raging bull through the bar, hurling drinks and customers alike against the walls, his temper irretrievably unleashed, like an evil genie. Cassandra was dialling the police – not for the first time this year over Seamus Bull, she noted, while Chris and most of the people in the bar did their best to shelter underneath the tables.

In the middle of all this, in walked Genevieve. She surveyed the scene and the dervish at the centre of it. Seamus had his back to the door at this point, and couldn't see that she had walked in. She watched while he upset tables, kicked over glasses and bottles and shouted unintelligibly, ranting at 'fucking Coq' at the top of his voice. She placed the bag she was carrying with her at her feet. Very quietly, she said his name. He stopped immediately, and the bar fell silent. He turned around. His face was red, his clothes and hair dishevelled and he was panting. But she had stopped him.

'Genevieve!' he said incredulously, his voice full of shame, but also with love and wonder. A thought occurred to him: had she come again to rescue him from his misery? Slowly, the bar guests began to poke their heads out from under the tables and behind chairs.

'Seamus, I've come to say goodbye.'

'What? No! Genevieve, please – don't!' Seamus stammered.

'It's too late – I've made up my mind. I don't belong here, and I don't belong to you. And you – you don't belong to me. I'm going home.' Genevieve was more sure of what she was saying than of anything since she had arrived in this country. But it didn't stop her from feeling her guts twist at every word.

'Genevieve, I beg you, please don't leave me. I need you now!'

'No, you don't, Seamus. You need things for yourself. You need fame and you need celebrity and you need recognition, and you need to be the best. And you will find none of that in me.'

'No, I don't – you've got it all wrong. Look – I've given it all up – the restaurant and everything!'

Genevieve was shaking her head, but Seamus continued, desperately: 'Where are you going? Tell me – are you going to France? I'll come with you. I love you, Genevieve, and I want to marry you. We'll live together in France, I promise. Please, please don't leave me!'

Seamus was now on his knees amongst the shards of glass and broken furniture, and the sight of him, so humiliated, so distressed, was pitiful. But Genevieve had made up her mind to say it, and say it she would.

'I'm sorry, Seamus, but we can never be together. You see, there is one thing I can never forgive you for. When you left me in France all those years ago I was pregnant. All my letters and phone calls you never returned – they were begging you to come and help me. In the end my father made me have an abortion, and I regret it now even more than I did then. I needed you so much, Seamus. But you weren't there. I came back to find you, but I see that you are still not here. It's over. I'm sorry. I'm not sure it ever began. Goodbye.'

And with that she picked up her bag and walked out of Louche.

Cassandra put the phone down. She guessed they wouldn't be needing the police after all. The guests slowly returned to their seats, a low, embarrassed muttering showing their contempt for Seamus, the looks they threw him demonstrating their total derision. Chris and his staff began cleaning up the bar as best they could. Rufus pulled his head out from under his jacket. Seamus was still on his knees, his eyes fixed on the spot Genevieve had last been standing.

Straightening his tie, Rufus ventured over and patted him consolingly on the back. 'There, there, old boy,' he said. 'Plenty more fish in the sea. Here, let me buy you a drink.'

Seamus turned slowly, and looked at him. Rufus tugged at his arm, trying to lift him off his knees. It was embarrassing for a chap to be caught in this position. Eventually, Seamus relented and allowed Rufus to pull him to his feet and across to the bar, as if in a trance. He had lost his business, his woman and a child he had never even known he had had, all in the last twenty minutes. Rufus led him like a lamb. Really, Seamus seemed rather adorable, all quiet and miserable like this.

'There, there, old chap. Now what we both need is some good news. I say! I've got a jolly good idea. Why don't you and I write a book together, eh? With your cooking skills and my writing ability I bet we'd be a hit. I've got all this wonderful research I inherited from my father, you see. It's about creating a food map of the world, tracing civilisation through diet, and it draws the most wonderful conclusions from anthropology, psychology, sociology and what have you – all through food. It could be a real smash hit, you know, and it could set you and me up for life – make us real stars. How about it? Nothing to lose, eh? What do you say?'

Seamus looked at Rufus. This was what he was left with. How perverse that Rufus would be the only one who was there for him in the end.

Maybe it was the high drama that had just unfolded before

his eyes, or the shock to the brain of having to duck flying glass and other missiles, but Henry Hampson, the TV producer, had been sitting nearby, and as he emerged from behind his bar stool he had an idea. This larger-than-life duo could make fabulous television . . .

At that point Marion and Henrietta reappeared from the Ladies, quite oblivious to all that had happened in their absence. Both were quite flushed in the face, and grinning from ear to ear.

'Well, hello, you two,' said Marion to Rufus and Seamus. 'How are you? I say, Henrietta and I have just come up with the most wonderful plan. Seeing as I'm now the most hated PR in London, I've decided to become an agent. And Henrietta is going to be my first client. I'm going to manage Henrietta, and make her into a superstar. Not just a star, you understand – this girl is going to be a legend!'

Rufus and Seamus turned to look at Henrietta. She continued to grin, then looking adoringly at Marion, she spoke with new confidence and certainty: 'I've just had my first orgasm!'

Epilogue

In the taxi, Genevieve tried hard to stem the flow of tears that were erupting from deep inside, shaking her body uncontrollably. She had felt so cruel saying it to him, but in a small way she also felt relief. The pain that she had carried around with her for so long could start to heal; the words were spoken, the story had been told. Seeing Seamus like that had been, even now, a shock, but she realised more than ever that Mave was right: she and he were two very different people. They didn't belong together. And saying what she had said to him had been hard, but there were no more secrets. Her life could really begin again. Now she had made the decision that her life no longer lay here in London, all she really wanted was to be home, back in her own country, for a fresh start.

She looked at her watch. It had just gone half-past six, and the last train to Paris that evening was the 18:53. The taxi was going to have to go faster than this. Her sobs were subsiding as panic at missing the train took over. Distractedly, she looked out of the window. Inevitably it had begun to rain and in the dark of the London streets, water pelted down and then splashed up from the puddles.

She couldn't remove the image of Seamus from her head – it helped to deal with the pain of parting from him. He had looked so pitiful, so out of control, not like the man she had thought she knew. Relief flooded through her at her narrow escape. She had just stopped herself from making a terrible mistake. She looked at her watch again. It was now twenty

to seven and they were stuck in a traffic jam on the Strand.
She knocked on the partition window of the cab.

'Please, as quickly as you can. My train leaves in ten
minutes!'

'All right, all right, love,' grumbled the taxi driver. 'Keep
your flippin' hair on.'

As they crossed Waterloo Bridge, Genevieve felt her pain
dissipating as fear took over – fear of missing her train and
being stuck in London. She absolutely couldn't spend one
more night here. It would be torture now.

Michael handed in his ticket to the guard, who punched
it and waved him through onto the platform. It was the
last train this evening for Paris; he had meant to catch an
earlier one, but it had taken him longer to pack than he
had anticipated. He had given most of the stuff in the flat
to a charity shop; all he owned now was in the rucksack
on his back.

He heaved his bag onto the rack above his head, and
settled down in a seat by the window. He had never been
to France before – in fact, he had never been abroad,
and he was looking forward to it. Looking forward to
something different, something far from the monotony
that had governed his life so strictly for so long. He
swallowed hard: he was trying not to think of what he
was leaving behind. The thought of abandoning her was
tearing at his heart. Her face rose before him, and he tried
hard to shut it out. He mustn't think about her now!

He pulled his guidebook out from his coat pocket and
determinedly started flicking through. There were several
B&Bs round the Gare du Nord in Paris, apparently. He
would pick one to stay in and then catch a train for the
Loire the next day. He had phoned Davide Duchamps
earlier to warn him of his arrival, and had quickly realised
he was going to need to learn more French. He turned
to the mini-dictionary at the back of the book, and tried

to concentrate on the words. Michael's mastery of the language was limited to school lessons and the odd gastronomic phrase used around the kitchens. But the words on the page in front of him had no meaning. Outside the rain drummed against the roof of the station, deafening everything.

The taxi dropped her right outside the Eurostar terminal, just as the clock clicked to 18.50. Genevieve raced for the counter.

'Single to Paris, please.'

'You'll have to hurry, madam. The last train leaves in two minutes.'

'Yes, yes I know!'

'That'll be sixty-five pounds, please.'

The ticketing clerk was moving painfully slowly, chatting to his next-door neighbour, pausing before he punched out the ticket on the machine. Genevieve practically snatched it off him when he passed it to her, and ran for the platform. Just as she arrived, the guard was shutting the gate.

'Sorry, love, platform's closed now. You'll have to wait for tomorrow.'

'No, please, you don't understand – I have to get on this train. I can't stay in London any longer. Please let me on! *Please!*'

The guard looked at her. Her hair was wild around her face, her eyes desperate. There was something very ethereal about her beauty, he thought, fragile almost. He took pity on her.

'All right then, hurry up. Still some seats in the front carriage. You'd better run.'

Relief flooded through Genevieve. She rushed through the gate and onto the platform. It was empty, the long concourse stretching out before her. Suddenly, she felt acutely alone. She started to run up the platform, but it was a long way to the front carriage. She was so afraid of missing the train now, she made for the nearest door and leapt on.

The doors swished open and she heaved her bag in behind her. She turned round and squeezed through the partition doors into the end carriage, any carriage, it didn't matter. Then she stopped. Shock, then relief, then finally elation took hold of Genevieve. Michael looked up and saw her. The train slowly drew out of the station and his own face mirrored the smile breaking over hers.